summer
stage

ALSO BY MEG MITCHELL MOORE

summer

---

stage

A NOVEL

MEG MITCHELL MOORE

wm

WILLIAM MORROW

An Imprint of HarperCollins*Publishers*

This is a work of fiction. Names, characters, places, and incidents are products of the author's imagination or are used fictitiously and are not to be construed as real. Any resemblance to actual events, locales, organizations, or persons, living or dead, is entirely coincidental.

HarperCollins books may be purchased for educational, business, or sales promotional use. For information, please email the Special Markets Department at SPsales@harpercollins.com.

FIRST EDITION

Designed by Bonni Leon-Berman

Library of Congress Cataloging-in-Publication Data has been applied for.

ISBN 978-0-06-302616-2

23 24 25 26 27 LBC 5 4 3 2 1

To My Family

AUTHOR'S NOTE

READERS OF MY 2019 novel, *The Islanders*, will recognize the setting and a few of the main characters from that book who become minor characters in this book. Some readers may note that while four years have passed in the real world since the publication of *The Islanders*, these characters are only two years older. To avoid setting the story in the middle of a summer when life (and summer theater) in many tourist destinations had not returned to normal due to the Covid pandemic, I chose to move the calendar forward and massage time a bit. I hope you will join me in this suspension of disbelief, or, as my character Sam might say, don't @ me.

summer
stage

April

Timothy

It was Timothy Fleming's landscaper, Kyle, who suggested the koi pond. At first Timothy resisted.

"You should do it," Kyle persisted. "People find a lot of peace in koi ponds. Some people really get to know their koi."

"They get to know their koi?"

"They do." Kyle flashed his teeth, almost blinding Timothy. "You've made it, Mr. Fleming. You made it a long time ago. What do you have, two Oscars?"

"Yes," admitted Timothy. In his head: Plus a Tony.

"So why not enjoy it? Spend the money!"

It wasn't the money. It was more that sometimes the boy who grew up in a small ranch house on Block Island, nearly as far away from Benedict Canyon as one could get while staying in the same country, came to whisper at Timothy like a spirit in a haunting. "Who do you think you are?" murmured the ghost of the boy. "Hooo. Do you thiiiiiink. You aaaaaare."

Kyle was what, twenty-eight? Skin fresh, cheeks full, body muscled. He was waiting for his big break, like everyone in Hollywood: the guy who drove your bus on the Universal Studios tour, the girl who foamed the milk for your cappuccino. So much collagen! "Okay," he said finally. "Okay, Kyle. What the hell. Bring on the koi."

"Yeessssss, Mr. Fleming!" Kyle's smile was so wide and so genuine, and his fist pumped the air so willingly, that it nearly warmed Timothy's cold, cold heart.

"But give my assistant, Alexa, the instructions on feeding. Left to my care, they'll die."

"Of course."

That was back in February. Now it's April, which means in New England it's mud season, and in Los Angeles it's—April. On Block Island there will be ruts in the dirt, potholes in the road, a chill in the air. Timothy doesn't miss it, except when he does, and then he misses it a lot.

Sitting and watching the koi, surrounded by blue elderberry and bush sunflower and figwort and whatever else Kyle had decided to plant, Timothy readily admits that Kyle was right. All seven koi have survived—nay, thrived. Timothy named them after the Seven Dwarfs, and the difference in their markings has always made it easy for him to tell them apart. A parent is not supposed to have favorites, he knows this, despite not being a parent himself, but secretly he favors Grumpy, whose orange and white stripes are more or less even in size. Doc has a splotch of black on his head that closely resembles a beret, Bashful a bovine design of black and white, and so on, all the way to the completely orange Dopey. Timothy *has* found a lot of peace in watching them, the C-curves their bodies make, the swish of their translucent tails as they pass over and under one another, even their trusting, gaping mouths at feeding time.

He peers more closely at the koi. Is everything all right? Grumpy seems, well, grumpy. Sneezy and Sleepy, normally quite close, appear to be in an argument, origins unknown. Along with the koi, Kyle convinced Timothy to acquiesce to a multilevel waterfall, and sometimes Timothy wonders if his yard calls to mind the New England miniature golf courses of his youth (you had to leave the island to play mini golf, of course, as you had to leave the island to do most things back then), where a ball hit too hard from the seventh hole might land at the bottom of an over- or under-chlorinated water feature.

California: the land of milk, honey, and koi. Sneezy and Sleepy are probably okay. Right? He supposes that koi relationships, like any others, have their ebbs and flows.

His phone buzzes, shattering both his reverie and his concerns. It's Gertie, his ex-wife. Speaking of ebbs and flows; speaking of relationships.

"Timothy! Are you busy?"

"A little," he says, untruthfully but convincingly. He came by the Oscars and the Tony honestly.

"Do you want me to call back another time?"

"No. No, that's okay," he says magnanimously. "I have a few minutes." Timothy hasn't been truly busy for a long time.

Timothy Fleming is old, by Hollywood terms, but not so old he's ready to be put out to pasture, by himself or anyone else. Talented—yes. The talent is indisputable, well-documented, even inevitable. He's wealthy. If not wealthy beyond his wildest dreams, certainly wealthy within their boundaries, because in fact his dreams have always been oversize. And yet, and yet. Like every-one else on this green Earth save the fictional Benjamin Button (a role, by the way, Timothy Fleming turned down, *that's* how many offers he had in the mid-aughts) he isn't getting any younger. He's been waiting for the right new project to come along for twenty-seven months now, and in those twenty-seven months he turned sixty, sixty-one, then sixty-two. There had been Covid, of course, and Covid hit the entertainment industry hard. But work is well underway again; Hollywood is abuzz with activity; he has many friends and acquaintances and also people who, truth be told, he doesn't care for who are back at work, busier than ever. Or at the very least claiming to be.

"Okay, good," says Gertie. "I need a favor."

"Shoot," he says.

"I need a theater," she says.

"Okay," he says. "You know I don't have a theater, right?"

"For the summer. I'm doing Shakespeare! I'm doing summer theater, finally! Before I go to shoot in Portugal. I've always wanted to do summer theater."

"You have?"

"Well, sure. You know I've always hoped I'd be able to get back to my roots." Gertie is a Juilliard graduate, classically trained. "And I'm forty-two now. The camera isn't going to love me forever. I need to think about my next steps. I'm going to be Beatrice in *Much Ado.*"

Once upon a time Timothy had been deeply in love with Gertie. The problem was that he was also in love (lust) with half of Hollywood, and it wasn't until Gertie had tired of his wandering eye (followed closely by his wandering hands) and divorced him that he realized what he'd once had, and given up. The issue was not that his and Gertie's sex life had not been phenomenal—it was. The issue was that all of Timothy's sex lives were phenomenal. Back then.

How he had loved being married to Gertie though! God, he'd loved it.

"You have a role, and a play, but no theater?"

"Right. We had a venue in Connecticut, but it *just* fell through. Pipes burst and it flooded, and there was major damage. They pretty much have to tear it down to the studs and rebuild. It won't be ready for summer."

"Who's *we?*"

"A guy I have. Blake. A producer."

"Uh-huh," says Timothy, suddenly and irrationally jealous.

"So my question is, don't you have a friend from high school I met that one time at the opening of *The Devil in Here?* The one who owns that theater on Block Island? Gary Something?"

"Vinny. Vinny St. James." (No saint, by the way; Vinny was the one who'd introduced Timothy to beer, then vodka, then pot, then for a brief and terrifying time, LSD.) "And yes, he owns a theater on Block Island. But it's a *movie* theater, sweetheart, not a *theater* theater. I'm not even sure it's operational as a movie theater right now."

"It used to be a *theater* theater, I thought."

"Well, yes. A long time ago. It's not set up that way *now*."

"But it could be again."

"It would cost a lot."

"Money isn't the issue, Timothy. This guy I have, his pockets are *deep*. Really deep. Silicon Valley deep. The issue is that we need a venue, and every summer theater planned their seasons months ago, so no functioning spaces are available. Will you talk to him, please, Timothy? Will you at least ask if he'd consider letting us use the theater?"

In his mind, Timothy gives a cartoonlike sputter—Gertie's favor requests can be outlandish!—but in actuality, his voice remains calm and measured. "Summer Shakespeare people don't go to Block Island, Gerts. Its whole vibe is down-to-earth. It's an island of the people, for the people, it's not really a Shakespeare summer theater kind of place."

"If we build it," says Gertie, "they will come."

"Too soon," says Timothy, although it's been thirty-five years since he auditioned for Costner's role in *Field of Dreams* and was deemed too young for it. Imagine being too young for something!

"Sorry, sorry. But trust me. This production will be so good people will line up to get to that island."

Timothy doesn't point out that people already *do* line up to get to that island—every day in the summer, whole oceans of people board the ferries from Point Judith and New London and Newport. They just aren't Shakespeare people. For the most part.

He sighs. "I'll talk to him. But there's one condition."

"There's always a condition with you, Timothy."

"Not always."

"Okay, *fine,* what is it? A quarter of the box office? A third? You can't have a third, that's way too much. Do you really need the money?"

He lets that question sit without a reply—they both know the answer is no, neither of them needs the money, the movies have been more than kind to them both—and gazes at the koi. Grumpy seems to have cheered up; Bashful and Dopey are hanging together; Happy looks, if not exactly happy, at least content. And Timothy now knows what he wants.

"It isn't the box office. I don't care about the box office. I want to direct."

"Sigh," says Gertie, and Timothy tenses, because this is one of Gertie's habits he has definitely not missed.

"You aren't supposed to say the word *sigh,* Gertie. We've been over this. You're just supposed to sigh." He waits. Nothing. He relents. "Okay, why are you sighing?"

"Because I love your directing work, but I already have somebody signed up to direct."

"Who?"

"Never mind that, Mr. Nosy."

"Well, whoever it is, I'm sure he'll get over it, especially if the venue changes."

"Maybe it's a *she,* Timothy. Why do male actors always think that women can't direct Shakespeare?"

"Because they can't." He waits for her intake of breath before he says, "*I'm kidding,* Gertie, obviously. Of course I'm kidding. Is it a she?"

"No," says Gertie bleakly, and Timothy, sensing that if he waits long enough his wish will appear, says not a word; tries, in fact, to move not a muscle, though he can feel one of his famously expressive eyebrows rise in anticipation. "Argh," says Gertie. "Okay, fine. Okay, you win. You secure the venue, you can direct."

May

Sam

Don't cry, Sam tells herself. Do not cry. You are nineteen years of age, technically an adult, and you are fine. You were in a bad situation, and you weren't really harmed, although you feel like you were. Well, yes, you were harmed. You need to acknowledge that, because acknowledgment is the first step toward healing. But now you're out of the situation. Don't cry, don't cry, don't cry.

She bites the inside of her cheek, which is already raw, because she's been biting it all week.

Don't cry.

It's the Sunday of Memorial Day weekend, unseasonably warm, and Scarborough North beach in Narragansett, Rhode Island, is mid-July packed. Sam Trevino eases her rental car into one of the last two remaining parking spaces. The car is due at 4 P.M. at the Enterprise in North Kingston, and it is two o'clock now. She's not dressed for the beach, but whatever. She's missed the ocean this past nine months. She's going to see it, even if it means a late charge, the wrong clothes. The car isn't in her name anyway.

She locks the car door—all of her possessions are in the back, right where she threw them when she left the city—and removes her shoes. Between the pavilion and the water's edge she has to wind herself around children building sandcastles and older people reading paperbacks and sunbathing girls and a group of teens playing volleyball with a beach ball and no net, but eventually she gets there. She squats down and rolls the legs of her jeans up as far as they will go, which is not very far, because the jeans are straight-legged. She wades in.

"You're going to get wet," says a potbellied little girl with a bucket hat and a stripe of zinc across her nose. Shovel and pail in her hand. She squats down and digs industriously in the sand, looking up at Sam as she does.

"Probably," Sam acknowledges.

"What's that?" The girl points at Sam's ankle.

"It's a turtle tattoo."

"Why?"

"I went through a phase where I really liked turtles."

She nods, accepting this. "Where's your bathing suit?"

"Forgot it." The girl purses her lips skeptically and begins to fill the bucket with sand. The shovel is slightly too small for the task. "I mean, I didn't *forget* it." Why does Sam feel the need to set the record straight with this girl who's, what? Four or five? She just can't shake the habit of caring what everybody thinks about her all the time. (But she must! She must shake it!) "I didn't know I was coming to the beach. It's sort of a surprise."

"Why didn't you know? I knew *I* was coming to the beach. My mommy told me."

Sam squints toward the horizon. "Well," she says after a time. "I thought I was going to stay where I was for a long time. But as it turned out I was wrong. So now I'm here, unexpectedly. And my mommy didn't tell me."

"Where were you?"

"Xanadu," says Sam. Because that's the name Tink, their manager, gave to the place where they all lived, on the Upper West Side: that beautiful, beautiful apartment with the ugly, ugly soul.

"That sounds pretty," says the girl.

"Sure, it *sounds* nice," says Sam. "But it really wasn't."

"Okay," says the girl. She hauls herself up from the sand and lifts her pail. She emits a small noise of effort or dismay.

"You got that?" asks Sam. "You all good?"

"Got it," says the girl. She looks back toward the crowded beach. A thin woman in a black one-piece is half standing from her chair, waving at the girl. The girl points herself toward the woman. "Bye," she says over her shoulder to Sam.

"Bye," says Sam. "I hope you have a good beach day." I hope you have a good life, little girl. I hope you stay off social media.

The tide is low. The beach is long and flat. A lifeguard blows a whistle; a gull squawks; someone's radio plays an ancient song that Sam's dad likes: "You Can't Always Get What You Want."

You can say that again, Rolling Stones, thinks Sam. You can definitely say that again.

She checks her phone. She has seventy-two unanswered texts, most of them from members of her former household. Her de facto family. Her *ex*–de facto family. Nothing from Evil Alice, of course, but messages from Scooter, from Nathan, from Cece and Kylie and Boom Boom. She deletes all of them without reading them. Every single one. Even Boom Boom's, and Boom Boom is always good for a laugh.

But she's still holding the phone, and the hand holding it itches—or maybe it actually hurts. Isn't there some Bible saying about cutting off the hand that offends you? Truly, she doesn't know much about the Bible. She was raised a devout atheist. She's not going to cut off her *hand*. Obviously. But she might just . . .

She might just toss her phone into the ocean. Like Lorde, in that "Solar Power" song! Before she can reconsider, this is exactly what she's doing. The instant she lets it go she realizes this is a terrible decision environmentally, and she thinks about the seals or piping plovers or other sea life that might be ruined by her rashness and her ignorance, so she wades out and retrieves the phone, soaking her jeans up to the knees in the process. Maybe she'll just throw it in the trash. No, she can't do that. That's also bad for the environment. She inspects the phone. It's sufficiently ruined. No amount of time sitting in rice is going to get this thing working again. Okay, maybe that's fine. Goodbye, TikTok. Goodbye to the past nine months of her life. Goodbye, Tucker, and especially, goodbye, Evil Alice. Goodbye, everything.

She wipes the phone on her thigh and sticks it in her back pocket. Before she leaves she scans the beach for her young friend and sees her sitting in a miniature version of her mother's beach chair, legs crossed at the ankles. She's eating a sandwich. Lucky girl. Sam is hungry.

"Returning?" chirps the young woman, a few years older than Sam, who works at the counter of the rental place. *Darcy*, her name tag says. She's got a face full of makeup and her hair is done up in a twist and secured with a massive claw clip. She's wearing business casual clothes, the kind you'd get at Marshalls or T.J. Maxx, a white button-up blouse and high-waisted trousers. Darcy probably went to college, or maybe she didn't, but either way, look, now she has a perfectly respectable job where she comes in at nine and leaves at five and nobody scrutinizes her content or tells her she's too famous or not famous enough or her numbers are terrible and she might want to consider a new collab but could she please take care of that yesterday because it's already sort of late.

(Maybe Sam's mother was right—maybe Sam should have gone to college, like her brother, Henry, who is studying philosophy at Middlebury.)

"Returning," says Sam. "Under the name Tink Macalester." Tink rented the car for her. Tink had been happy to see Sam go; Tink wasn't liking the "energy in the house."

"All right, Ms. Macalester!" Darcy taps away on her keyboard, glancing up at Sam every few strokes. Sam wonders if Darcy recognizes her. "Let me just enter your return into the system, and then you can be on your way. Have you removed all your possessions from the vehicle?"

"Yup." Her luggage is outside: one super-oversize duffel, three smaller bags, a backpack. If Sam left anything else in the apartment Tink promised to ship it to Narragansett, but Sam's faith in that promise is slim.

Darcy prints off a bunch of paperwork, taps the edges to line up the pages, staples the corner, and hands it to Sam with a smile. "Have a *great* day, Ms. Macalester. Thank you for driving with us, and we hope to see you again in the future." Sam looks behind Darcy and to both sides, but there's nobody else in the place. She supposes Darcy is employing the royal *we*.

It occurs to Sam as she exits the office and studies her luggage that without her phone she doesn't have a way to contact an Uber or a Lyft to get home. You can't exactly hail a cab in this part of Rhode Island, the way you can in New York City. She can't call Henry, who is staying in Vermont this summer and living off campus with his girlfriend, Ava. (*"Why?"* Sam asked him once. "Why'd you pick *philosophy* to study? So you can sit around and *think?"* "Why not?" Henry had answered. And that, Sam imagines, is an example of a philosophical conversation. No, thank you to that.)

She doesn't know the phone numbers of any of her high school friends. Nobody memorizes phone numbers! And even if she did she's not in touch with them right now. They used to drop her DMs but she didn't always have time to answer them—she'd been inundated for a while there, and the pressure to keep up was monumental. At some point her high school friends had given up, resentful.

She sighs and pushes the glass door of the shop back open. Darcy looks up from her computer, more surprised than delighted.

"Hi," says Sam. "I'm back again! I—uh. I lost my phone." Darcy looks skeptically at Sam; she probably saw the outline of the phone in her back pocket when she exited. "I mean, I didn't lose it. I have it right here. Obviously. But it got wet, and it's not working, so I can't call for a ride. I was wondering if I could use your phone? Just real quick."

Darcy narrows her eyes and glances behind her, where three desks sit in a neat triangle, each with a phone on top. "We're not supposed to let people back here . . ."

"Please? I'll be so quick. It will just be a sec. You can watch me the whole time, I'm not going to do anything shady."

"Okay." Darcy sighs. "But be *super* quick. If my manager comes in and you're back here, I'm totally screwed." She points to one of the desks. "That one's mine."

"Thanks," says Sam. She ducks behind the counter and hurries to the phone. She tries to turn her back to Darcy as she picks up the receiver and dials, because she's worried that the call will blow her cover and she doesn't want Darcy to listen in.

She knows only one phone number by heart, because she's known it her whole life. The phone rings once, then twice, a third time. She can picture the room where it's ringing: a kitchen in a three-bedroom Cape not far from here, the stove with the back-right burner that doesn't work, the freezer that doesn't make its own ice, the canisters of flour and sugar on the counter. The round table with four chairs where Sam ate every meal of her childhood, except for the two separate times she was gone as a kid. Then for the past nine months, gone again.

On the fourth ring, an answer.

"It's me," whispers Sam, curving her back away from Darcy. "I need a ride. I'm at the Enterprise in North Kingston. Can you come pick me up?"

Ten minutes later Sam's mom's Subaru pulls up to the curb,

and Amy Trevino lowers the window. Her face is like a crossword of emotions: down, five letters, *H-A-P-P-Y.* Across, nine letters, *P-E-R-P-L-E-X-E-D.* Down again, using the *D, W-O-R-R-I-E-D.*

Don't cry, Sam reminds herself. Do. Not. Cry. You're fine! You're so, so fine. This is your mom, and here she is in her car, and you're going to get in and go home and regroup and everything is going to be *fine,* because everything is okay, and nobody died.

(Is this the new barometer of success? Nobody died?)

"Honey!" says Sam's mom. "Why didn't you tell us you were coming home? I would have prepared things for you! Your dad's going to be so happy to see you."

Sam gets in the passenger seat; her mom reaches across the emergency brake and opens her arms to her, and Sam leans into the arms, and she cries, and she cries, and she cries.

June

Sam

SAM MAKES IT two and a half more days without her cell phone. She has her laptop, and she can use that to check her texts, an activity she tries to limit to a few zillion times per day. There's nothing from Tucker. Not. One. Single. Message. Maybe he's tried calling her. Not that she wants him to. In fact, she expressly asked him *not* to call her, and she's hoping he actually listened to her. *Is she hoping?* Of course. A little. Not really.

On Wednesday she asks to borrow her mom's Subaru after her mom's back from teaching school to take herself to the AT&T store in South Kingston.

"Do you have insurance on your phone?" Amy wants to know.

Do I have insurance on my mental well-being? Sam thinks. "No," she says. "I'm sad to say I think I opted out."

"A new phone is going to cost you a fortune," worries Amy. "Do you need money?"

"No, I have money, Mom. I was earning money all last year."

"I still don't understand that."

"It's complicated," says Sam, even though it is, in fact, not all that complicated. She made money for doing a job; pretty straightforward. "But it's fine. I have enough for a new phone. Promise."

"You sure you don't want to keep the same number?" asks the guy at the store, Shawn—nose ring, eyebrow ring, lip ring. "Most people keep the same number."

"Different number," says Sam. "I'm sure."

Shawn unboxes the new phone with the precision and reverence of an art restorer unpacking an aged canvas. He tells Sam that her contacts will transfer automatically from the cloud. "Your photos too, if you had them backed up." Sam shudders. She doesn't want to think about photos. She says, "What about my apps? Tik-Tok, Instagram, et cetera?"

"You may have to re-download them onto this baby." He taps the new phone. "And in some cases they'll ask for your username and password again."

"And if I don't want them?" Obviously Sam knows her way around a phone, but she just wants to make sure.

Shawn shrugs. "Then don't download them. Nobody's going to force you to be on social media if you don't want to." He grins.

Sam makes a noise halfway between the harrumph a grumpy old man would make when faced with a universal remote control and the hmmm of a pensive research librarian. Shawn is right. She doesn't have to download anything she doesn't want. It's exactly that easy, and it's also exactly that hard.

When she's paying, and they're both waiting for the printer to spit out the pages of the contract, she notices that Shawn is looking at her funny.

"What?" she says.

"You look familiar to me," he says. He squints, and the piercing in his eyebrow wiggles. "Do I know you from somewhere?"

She snatches the pages, grabs the phone. "I just have one of those faces people think they know," she says. "This happens to me like ten times a day."

The first thing she does when her contacts finish downloading from the cloud is call Henry. Ava answers. (Why is Ava answering Henry's cell?)

"Sam?" Ava's voice is deep and measured and very, very calm. "Henry's in the shower. But I knew he wouldn't want to miss a call from you so I thought I'd grab it."

"Perfect," says Sam insincerely. She doesn't think people should answer each other's cell phones except in cases of emergency, e.g., if the person is waiting to hear about an organ transplant or is on the wait list for an audience with the pope.

"He's out of the shower!" says Ava. "Here he is."

Henry comes on the line. "Sam? What's up?"

"I need backup," says Sam. "I'm home. And I need backup."

"What kind of backup?"

"Just . . . I don't feel equipped to be an only child right now. I need you, Henry."

She can almost feel Henry smiling. "I can't come home. I'm just beginning an eight-week immersive language program."

"You're *what*?"

"I'm learning Greek."

"*Henry!* Why?"

"I'm learning Greek so I can read Socrates in the OG." Of course he is. Of *course* Henry is learning Greek so he can read Socrates in the OG.

"But I need you," she says. She allows a little wheedle into her voice.

"You don't need me. You'll be fine. Mom and Dad must be happy to have you home."

"They're grudgingly happy," she says. "Reluctantly happy."

Henry says something to Ava Sam can't hear, then he returns to the conversation and says, "Nah. I'm sure they're legitimately very happy. You're the Prodigal Daughter, returned. The Golden Child."

If she were drinking anything she would have spit it out. *"I'm the Golden Child? Uh-uh. No way, Henry. You're the Golden Child."*

"Ah, no. Samuel." He used to call her that to annoy her, and in fact it used to annoy her, but now she's old and mature, so she lets it go, maybe even likes it. "Definitely, definitely, *most definitely,* you are the Golden Child."

There's something in Henry's voice—what? It's as close as Henry ever gets to bitterness, and coming from anyone else it would probably roll right off Sam's skin like water off wax, but it's Henry, and so it stings.

It's two or three days later that Sam wakes in her childhood bedroom to a gentle tapping at the door. She opens one eye, then the other. A voracious June sunlight is blasting through the curtains, and she can tell by the way it's hitting the foot of her bed that it's at least midmorning.

She doesn't answer.

Again comes the tapping. Taptaptap. Taptaptap. Obviously it's her mom—who else would it be?

Sam covers her face with her pillow and asks the pillow, "What?"

"Honey? Are you okay in there?"

"I'm sleeping!"

"Okay." A pause. "I was just wondering about breakfast."

"What about it?"

"Well, if it's happening. For you. It's almost eleven. I had a yogurt but I could make waffles . . . ?"

Sam hears a scratching and snuffling too. These are the sounds, she's sure, of the rescue dog her mom is currently fostering. Kona. He came with the name, but he's not from Hawaii, so who knows. Amy fosters rescue dogs in the summers, caring for them until they find their "furever home" (her mom's phrase; her mom loves a pun).

"Hello? Sammy? You in there?"

After nearly a year of no parenting whatsoever, Sam feels her mom's attention focused on her like a laser. Yes, it has been wonderful to see her parents. Yes, her mom made Sam's favorite dinner last night, eggplant parmesan, pappardelle noodles on the side and marinara sauce from Arturo Joe's, and that had been wonderful too, superbly satisfying. In the TikTok house nobody ate real, nourishing food, unless they were trying to make something for content. They subsisted on Twizzlers, or vodka and Red Bull and Cheez-Its, or nothing at all. Waffles actually sound good, now that she thinks about it. She can't believe how hungry she is, even after all that pasta.

"Why aren't you at school?" she asks her pillow.

"It's Saturday, silly!"

"It's Saturday?" This means Sam has been here for almost a week. How is that possible? Where has a whole week gone?

"It is. Next week I have four full days, a half day on Friday, then, boom. Another school year done."

Sam lifts the pillow from her face so that she can say, "That's great."

"I know. I'm so ready for this school year to be over. You can't see me through the door, but I'm doing a happy dance."

Please don't *actually* be doing a happy dance, thinks Sam. She watches the knob turning, and the door opens. In comes Kona. He sits expectantly, even politely, next to Sam's bed, maybe waiting for an invitation. She goes back under the pillow.

Her mom follows right behind Kona; she can feel this, even though she can't see the entrance. At one time—truly, it's nearly impossible for Sam to believe this—her mom had roamed the streets around New York University, writing plays, presumably wearing clothing that was more interesting than her current Loft teaching wardrobe, which she accessorizes with dramatically unmatching pieces from the local farmers market. Amy's Saturday outfit, she sees, when she once again removes the pillow, is even worse than her teaching outfits: gray sweatpants with a Middle-bury seal on the hip, an Old Navy T-shirt. Sam's mom is pretty, with curly hair that's reddish brown, and a decent body for an old person, but gosh, it's like she's trying her hardest not to let anyone know.

Kona whines. He's not getting on the bed. Sam and Kona have no relationship, and she's not about to get attached to a dog that could be leaving any minute.

"So, waffles?" Amy asks. "Yes or no?"

"Yes, please."

"Give me fifteen minutes, okay?"

"Okay."

Sam has slept twelve hours at a stretch for the past several nights and is beginning to feel the energy returning to her body, the elasticity to her skin. She has started drinking water again, and stopped drinking alcohol. In New York she had sort of forgotten about water as a beverage option. (Turns out, water is delicious!) Her parents have been welcoming and hospitable and delighted to have her; they asked only one question, on the first day: What happened?

"I don't really want to talk about it," Sam said. "I'm just happy to be home."

Her parents are hopelessly uninformed about and uninterested in social media, which, in Sam's current situation, is a blessing. They must know that simply googling her name would bring a wealth of information, that if they cared to join Twitter and searched for mentions of Sam they'd find entire bathtubs' full of vitriol directed against her and, yes, some support too, but an un-balanced amount of vitriol. Her mother has long resisted social media because she never liked the idea of students following her (or, in some cases, as other teachers have reported, asking to be followed!) and her father hardly ever knows where his phone is when he doesn't need it for work, never mind how to use it for more than calls and email. So when Sam said she didn't want to talk about it, they took her at her word.

Today, she eats her waffles while her mom sits across from her at the kitchen table, offering her syrup and sliced strawberries and whipped cream and orange juice and a lot of lovely things but sort of *too many lovely things*, if that makes sense—and presenting, along with the food, more questions.

Has Sam thought about her plans? Has Sam considered reaching out to the guidance counselor from the high school—Amy can facilitate the conversation, if that would make things easier!—to talk about reinvigorating some of the applications she'd started senior year? Does Sam know there is no shame whatsoever in collecting a few credits at a community college while she gets the rest of her plan together? Community College of Rhode Island in Warwick, not so far away at all, has some viable options! Sam could use some time there as a springboard to a more prestigious four-year liberal arts college, like the one Henry attends! Has Sam thought about getting a job, and if so, what kind of job, and how does she expect to get there—they don't have an extra car? (Her parents don't know how much money Sam brought in at the collab house, and she's not about to share numbers. They'd find it suspicious, even though it was all quite aboveboard. Replacing the waterlogged phone was merely a drop in the bucket. So to speak.)

Sam eats her waffles faster and faster, not just because they are delicious (they are; her mom makes them from scratch, with actual buttermilk) but because as long as her mouth is full and she's chewing she can point unapologetically in the direction of her jaw without answering.

Amy brings out the college catalogs next, a thick stack of bright colors, fall foliage, happy, engaged young people.

Sam swallows. "How'd you get so many of these so quickly?"

"I've had these right along. You got oodles of them your junior and senior years. I just put them aside in case we needed them. And look! Good thing I did."

"Good thing," says Sam. "Where's Dad?"

"He had to run out and take care of an emergency at the Backman house."

Sam wishes her dad were here to provide reinforcement: he might be on her side. Greg didn't go to college—and see, he's doing just fine! He loves his work as the owner of a small HVAC company; he's a well-respected member of the community; he makes a fine living, if not quite enough to enjoy all the luxuries that someone like Uncle Timmy enjoys. Her dad never even complains about going to work.

"Thank you for the waffles," says Sam. "They were good, really."

"Do you want more?" Her mom is so eager that it sort of breaks Sam's heart. "I made a lot of batter. Probably too much!"

"No. Thanks, Mom. I'm stuffed."

Like a ghost, Kona is there fixing Sam with his big sad brown eyes. He puts his head in Sam's lap and sniffs around a little bit.

"Um . . ." says Sam.

"He's just showing his affection for you," her mother says. "He and his littermates had a really rough start. They were found on the side of a highway in rural Tennessee."

"I feel like he's trying to date me," says Sam. She moves Kona's head out of the way and rises from her seat to rinse her plate and put it in the dishwasher, but before she gets a chance her mother says, "I've got this, sweetie," and takes the plate from her.

This kindness starts to feel like a trap, as Amy continues, "Do you want to go for a swim later? Your friends must be home from college; have you been in touch with any of them? I think I saw Catie Connolley getting out of her car at the Coast Guard House last week. Like she was going to work. Maybe you could get a job there! Wouldn't it be fun to see more of Catie?"

Sam feels like she might suffocate under the focus. It's like walking around with a weighted blanket on her shoulders—a weighted blanket that is made only for deep sleeping. It would not be fun to see more of Catie. Catie Connolley is studying biology at the University of Virginia, and she and Sam have about as much in common as a unicorn and a Maine coon cat. Their friendship pretty much ran its course senior year—maybe even before that.

And then, like it's an afterthought, Amy delivers the most relevant piece of information of the day—in fact, the most relevant piece of information of the week, and, as it comes to be, the entire summer: "Did I tell you about Uncle Timmy?"

Hearing her uncle's name causes a little blip in Sam's heart. She used to love her uncle so much. She still loves him, of course. But she doesn't know him anymore. Just his name makes her think of the dressing room at the Golden Theatre on Forty-fifth, the smell of backstage, the fading light outside the stage door after a matinee.

"No," she says. "Did he get married again?"

"No! I mean, I don't think so. He's spending the summer on Block Island! Directing a Shakespeare play. *Much Ado About Nothing.*"

"They do summer theater on Block Island?"

"Not typically. But this summer, yes. And you'll never believe who's starring in the play."

"Who?"

"Gertie."

"Wait, *what? Gertie* Gertie?" Sam had been heartbroken when her uncle split with Gertie Sanger. Gertie was a de facto mother to Sam during her time in Los Angeles, a time that had been exhilarating and chaotic and bewildering. Sam wouldn't have survived it without Gertie: her calmness, the feel of her scarves against Sam's neck when she hugged her, her long cool fingers braiding Sam's hair.

"Yup."

"He's living on Block Island? Right now?"

"Not yet. He's coming on—let's see." Amy consults her wall calendar, a complimentary gift from the dog rescue organization. "He arrives a week from today."

"Where's he staying? In a hotel?"

Amy rolls her eyes. "Some fancy house his high school friend owns and barely uses, I guess. Some mansion. You know Timmy. He's not going to live in a single hotel room when he can have a whole house."

"A whole house," repeats Sam, sort of in a whisper, as an idea takes shape. "Is he really living there by himself?"

She hasn't talked to Uncle Timmy since she went to live in the collab house. She sees him online, occasionally on TV, if an old movie of his is playing, and he sends her a birthday card every year with a ridiculously large check in it, but they haven't *talked*.

"I suppose so. I mean, I guess so. It's not like I'm up-to-date on his personal life." Her mom sniffs.

"What?" says Sam.

"What nothing," says Amy. She closes the dishwasher just a little too hard, and the counter seems to quiver.

"You sniffed."

"I have seasonal allergies."

"*Summer* seasonal allergies?"

"Yes."

"I've never known you to have allergies."

"Late onset."

Sam gives her mother a skeptical look that Amy doesn't see; Amy and Kona depart the kitchen together, side by side, like members of a wedding party leaving the church. Sam reaches for her phone, making sure, in the transfer of her contacts to the new version, her uncle's number made it through unscathed. She's not going to use it yet. She'll wait out the next week, see what the vibe is at home. But she wants to know that it's there if she needs it.

Timothy

How CRANKY HE IS! Timothy Fleming, in line for the Block Island Ferry, Red Sox cap pulled as low as it goes, which is not so low that he's not recognizable. He longs briefly for the days of the pandemic, when a strategically sized face mask coupled with the cap could obscure his identity almost entirely. Don't be a jerk, Timothy, he tells himself sternly. You can't *long* for a *pandemic*.

What is he *doing* in this line? He should be on a plane.

The night before, he'd flown from L.A. to Boston, then stayed in a deluxe king at The Langham on Franklin Street. His assistant, Alexa Thornhill, had assured him that The Langham was now more desirable than The Ritz-Carlton or the Mandarin Oriental, where he'd usually stay, not that he had reason to travel to Boston all that often. The Langham was hipper, she'd said, which he didn't much care about. More private, she'd said too, which he *did* care about. A car had picked him up that morning and delivered him to Point Judith, where he now stands in line with everybody else waiting to board the 12 P.M. high-speed ferry. He's jet-lagged, yes, and he's under-rested; the mattress at The Langham was too soft for his aging back, and he feels a twinge each time he moves at the wrong angle.

I should have flown, he thinks again, as the line moves forward onto the boat and he holds out his ticket for the kid to scan. But that was easier said than done; the only way to fly direct from Boston was to charter a private plane, and, honestly, he would have felt ashamed if word got out on his home island that he'd paid three grand for such a short and unnecessary flight. Anyway, he thought he might like the experience of the ferry.

Alexa had said she could send the ferry ticket right to his phone so he wouldn't have to worry about the paper, but he's too much of a dinosaur to trust a ticket on his phone. He wants to *hold* the ticket in his wrinkled old hand. Actually, his hands are still quite nice: his fingers long and slender, piano fingers. He's always gotten compliments on his hands. Never played the piano though.

The top deck is not an option for Timothy—he sees that immediately as people start to board. It's going to be packed up there; it's Saturday, so families are arriving for the week ahead and couples and groups of college kids are coming for the weekend, and, of course—of course!—there are the inevitable bachelorette parties, with their thermoses of Bloody Marys and their short shorts and their heads of long, long hair that they'll toss around with increasing vigor and lack of spatial awareness the faster the Bloodys go down. It's inside seating for him.

The ferry sets off from Point Judith into a bank of fog, obscuring the fishing boats filling the port, the circling gulls. No sooner has Timothy chosen a seat, tipped his head back for optimal sleeping, and pulled his Sox cap even lower than he can feel someone staring at him. He squeezes his eyes together more tightly, but he can't shake the need to peek. Finally he opens his eyes a crack.

A woman is sitting directly across from him. Next to her, on the floor, is a dog: a mix of some sort, the best kind, whitish with uneven ears and a marking above one eye that looks like an actual human eyebrow. The dog is staring at him too, and because of the marking the dog appears to have the single eyebrow cocked.

"You're Timothy Fleming," says the woman, smiling.

"Guilty," he says charmingly, half raising his hand. He tips the brim of his hat and closes his eyes again.

The woman says, in a library whisper, "I loved you in *You Can Go Home Again*. Oh, and *Wonderful*. And *Days of Old*. Really, in everything."

Timothy shifts. His palms are itchy and his toes are beginning to sweat and he really, really wants to go to sleep. Nevertheless, he smiles at the woman. He hates when famous people complain about being bothered in public. It's the price you pay, he always tells actors just starting out. You give up some of your basic rights to privacy, but in return you get to be part of the most exciting, most soul-sucking, and simultaneously most soul-feeding, most *interesting* profession in the world. You probably get a lot of money too. You get a charmed life, so please don't complain if someone you don't know wants to talk to you.

Now he stacks up all of this wisdom and advice, shuffles it, and deals it right back to himself. Without the public, he tells himself, you wouldn't even exist, Timothy Fleming.

"Thank you so much," he says. "That means a lot, truly." (It still does, actually, every time.)

The woman is in her late-ish thirties, with big dark eyes and curly hair that stops just this side of wild. "I'm Joy Sousa," she says.

"A pleasure."

Four seats away from the woman are two teenage girls. Timothy wouldn't have known that the girls and the woman were together except that every now and then one of the girls smiles at the dog.

"What are you doing on Block Island?" asks Joy

There's no going to sleep now. Well, the high-speed ferry takes only thirty minutes. He can sleep when he gets to the house. Why not sell a ticket as long as he's awake? "I'm headed there for the summer. Directing a summer production at the Empire Theatre."

"Oooh! The Empire! I didn't know they did live theater. I thought it was only movies."

"They usually don't. It's just this summer."

"How exciting. You grew up here, right?" At his nod, she continues, "I knew somebody famous had come from Block Island. I'm new to it myself. And by *new* I mean I've lived here thirteen years! But sometimes I feel like a newcomer, because, you know, I don't go back like seven generations. My friend Holly mentioned something about a play. She's a Realtor, and she was looking for housing for some of the actors. She didn't say what play though, and I don't think she mentioned the Empire. And she *definitely* didn't say your name! I would have remembered if she'd said Timothy Fleming was coming to town!"

"She may not have known. I'm in charge of my own housing."

"Sure. Got it. I'm sure you have . . . a staff or whatever. You probably don't need *Holly*. What's the play?"

"*Much Ado About Nothing*. We open the second week of August." He tries not to notice how Joy's face falls a bit. She was probably hoping for *Mean Girls* or *Wicked* or *Hamilton*, something with rousing musical numbers that launch themselves into your consciousness, sticking there with the strength of caramel to a molar. People either like Shakespeare, or . . . they just feel very nonexcited about him. The nonexcited people may have read too much Shakespeare in school and don't want to read another word of his again, or they've never read him and they're intimidated by the thought of it. But the language is beautiful! And timeless! And so very wise. And spoken by the right actors, not intimidating at all.

"This play is very accessible," he says. "Really and truly. It's no *Lear*; it's no *Henry VIII*. It's a comedy, with lots of plot twists and mistaken identities and so forth. You should come see it. It's a hoot."

"Sold!" says Joy. "If Timothy Fleming tells me to do something, I'm going to do it! Are you *in* it too? Or just directing?"

"Just directing. Not *just* directing. I mean, I'm directing."

She looks disappointed.

"Gertie Sanger is going to play Beatrice," he offers.

Joy squeals. "*Really?*"

"Cross my heart."

"Gertie Sanger is spending the summer on Block Island! Wow. Take that, Vineyard. You may have the Obamas, but look at us! Gertie *Sanger*. I can't believe it. Weren't you two . . . a thing?"

"We were married. Got divorced." He doesn't say, *Biggest mistake of my life.* But possibly he thinks it.

"Wow," Joy says again, sitting back. "This is shaping up to be one exciting summer. You have to come by my shop, tell all your actors to come too! I own a little bakery in town. We specialize in mini whoopie pies, all different flavors. Raspberry, key lime. Chocolate, of course. A bunch of other flavors. When I first started making the whoopie pies my brother said they tasted like little Joy Bombs so that's what I named my shop! Joy Bombs. We ship all over. We just got into Whole Foods. It's almost impossible to get a baked good into the freezer section of Whole Foods, you know."

Timothy didn't know.

"We have lots of other great stuff. We have a full espresso bar. We have mocktails that we serve in mason jars. Seasonal. But we can make anything. Cappuccino, mocha, dirty chai."

Timothy is intrigued. "What makes it dirty?"

"Ha! It's not actually dirty. It's chai, you know the tea? With steamed milk and an espresso shot. It's the espresso shot that makes it dirty. Quote unquote. But my shop is very clean, I promise. And innovative, if I do say so myself." She taps the cooler at her feet. "I was just on the mainland meeting with a supplier for this high-end, super-creamy, locally produced almond milk. You have to try it. The ferry guys wanted me to stack this with the other luggage, but I was like, no way. With what this costs per ounce I'm not letting it out of my sight!" She looks sidelong at

Timothy, assessing. "I'm sorry. I'm jabbering. I'm just not used to being in the presence of a celebrity, so I got nervous, and when I get nervous I can't stop talking. It's the Portuguese side of the family. We're talkers. Actually, the other side is Irish, and *we're* talkers too. So there's really no hope for me."

I could have flown, thinks Timothy. Why didn't I fly? There's a good chance nobody would have found out about the chartered flight.

He's so very tired.

"Wait until I tell Anthony I met you!" Joy says. "Anthony is my boyfriend. I feel silly saying that, I think I'm too old to have a *boyfriend*, but I don't know what else to call him."

"Some people say *partner*," Timothy ventures, because she's looking at him so expectantly.

"They do! Yes, they do, Timothy Fleming. When I hear someone say *partner* I always assume they're talking about a same-sex couple. Not that there's anything wrong with that! But I feel like I'm misrepresenting my relationship." She taps the cooler again, as if she's letting it know she's still there, and then points to the teenagers. "That's Maggie, my daughter, and her friend Riley. They're obsessed with TikTok." Involuntarily Timothy winces. TikTok took his niece, Sammy, away from him. "And this is Pickles," Joy says, pointing to the dog, who settles her chin between her two front paws and closes her eyes. "The girls actually do know how to make eye contact, I promise, but they don't like to show off about it, in case the other teenagers get jealous."

Despite his best efforts to detach himself, Timothy chortles and Joy, obviously pleased with herself, beams.

"Where are you staying? I'm sorry, I shouldn't ask you that, that's a very personal question. For a famous person. Maybe for any person."

"A friend's house," he says. "An old friend." He decides to leave it at that. Block Island is a *very small* island. No need to advertise to the paparazzi. (Does Block Island have paparazzi? He imagines the photographer for the weekly *Block Island Times* hiding in the bushes, waiting for Timothy to emerge.)

"Ahhhh," Joy says. She nods sagely. "Smart. Away from the riff-raff. How long has it been since you've been home?"

"It's been a while. About four years." Those had been dark days for Timothy for a number of reasons. His mother had just died, and they were on the island to scatter her ashes. He'd lost a role to Colin Firth, and his marriage was over. Amy was barely speaking to him.

"Well, I'm sure the whole island will be abuzz when they hear we have a celebrity in our midst. Once you get yourself settled, you'll have to come by the shop so you can try a Joy Bomb or two. On the house." She winks. "I should let you get back to what you were doing."

Timothy nods. Over the years he has perfected his celebrity nod. It's polite and perfunctory without being dismissive; the nod, he hopes, says, *Thank you for turning your attention elsewhere* while also saying, *Please remember me fondly when it's time to choose your next viewing experience.* He has also perfected the fan handshake (fandshake), wherein he puts his left palm over the other person's hand, like a priest or a politician, indicating warmth and caring while signifying an appropriate amount of personal remove. During the pandemic he set the fandshake aside, so he's out of practice.

Joy rummages in her bag and pulls out a paperback. A thriller, by Leonard Puckett. *No Time Like the Present.* On the cover a slender black-gloved hand holds a gun. Long ago Timothy was up for a part in an adaptation of a different Leonard Puckett book. The part had gone to Tom Cruise. Timothy never saw the film; he'd heard the book was better. The book was almost always better. He never read the book either.

With Joy immersed in her paperback, Pickles the dog now snoring, and the teenagers paying him no mind, which he tries not to take personally but sort of does, Timothy deems it safe to duck outside onto the lower deck of the ferry. Crowded, but not as crowded as the upper deck must be. Timothy sidles up to an empty spot at the railing, pulling his cap down even lower so that he has to peer up under it to see properly. Here come the announcements about disembarking and where to pick up luggage and bikes. And here, as the fog seems to part, revealing what would be the proscenium arch if this were a theater, come the familiar shops lining the main street, the awning of the National Hotel, the bikes and people and dogs and mopeds, and it seems to Timothy Fleming that all the world really is, as the great Bard wrote, a stage, and all the men and women merely players.

The scent of the air tugs at his nostalgia, bringing him back to long-ago summer days, girls in bikinis, the salt water in his hair, on his bare skin, in his heart. When he first moved to California he didn't understand how to navigate that foreign place. But he's been there far longer now than he hasn't, and it's all familiar to him: the scrubby vegetation; the endless, twisting drives up to the canyons; the wide flat path along the ocean in Santa Monica, where everyone is perpetually twenty-three; the heart-stopping promise of driving into Malibu—always a promise, even if you've been there a thousand times.

Now *this* landscape seems, for an instant, alien. And yet it's not. "Home," he whispers. This goddamn island. How far he's strayed in his life, such highs and lows he's lived, and yet it gets him, every time.

His phone buzzes, breaking his reverie. He doesn't recognize the number, but it's a Rhode Island area code, so, what the heck, he answers.

"Fleming," he says quietly, lest someone at the railing recognize his voice or his name and turn around.

"Uncle Timmy!" cries a voice—familiar, yet not exactly. "It's me. It's Sammy. I'm home!"

"Sammy. You're home? What about New York?"

"New York is over."

He smiles into the phone. He's so happy to hear Sam's voice again. It's been a long time, nearly a year, since he's talked to her. It's hard to believe that years ago there were months at a time when he saw her more than he saw pretty much anyone else. "I hadn't heard."

"It's over for *me*," she clarifies. "For now."

"Fair enough. Anyway, nobody wants to spend summer in New York." The passengers are all moving toward the exit now. He'll join the end of the line.

"Exactly." A pause. "That's why I'm calling. I heard you might have extra space where you're staying. Your friend's house?"

"Floyd," he says. "Yes, I'm using my friend Floyd's house." Floyd, he understands from the photos of the house he saw online, has come a long way since their high school days, almost as far as Timothy has. "It's a big house."

"I'm sort of, well, not sort of, I'm definitely looking for a change of scenery." A pause, an audible inhalation. "I'll just come right out with it. I've been here for almost two weeks, and I don't know how much longer I can stand it. Could I spend the summer with you?"

"With me?"

"I could help with whatever you need, or pay rent, or both . . ."

Timothy hesitates. It's not about rent, obviously. It's also not about Sam—he'd love to have Sam! He's delighted that she's left New York, left all that silliness behind, possibly come to her senses. It's about Amy. "Does your mom know you're asking me?"

"Not yet." Sam clears her throat and laughs uncertainly. "But she'll be fine with it."

Metaphorical warning bells are sounding all over the place, but Timothy can almost ignore them over the chatter of the passengers. One of the extremely young ferry workers (do they hire actual children now?) is motioning him on toward the luggage pickup.

"I mean, if you're sure about that. If you're *absolutely sure* about that, I'd love to have you for the summer." His niece: the light in the darkness; the Scout to his Atticus; the daughter he never had. His heart lifts and he moves with the other passengers, a new, hopeful spring in his step.

Amy

SUNDAY. AMY COMES in from the grocery store, the straps of her reusable grocery bags digging into her wrists. She kicks open the door, no arm free to open it gracefully.

"Hello!" she calls. "Hell-oooo! Sam? Kona?" Greg left early for the Backman house—even though it's Sunday, he has items on his to-do list he's itching to get to.

No answer from Sam, she must be sleeping still, but Kona comes skidding around the corner, delirious with joy. If he could talk surely he would say, *Ohmygod you're back you're back I thought you were never coming back.* "Hey boy," she says. "Let me put these down and I'll give you a good scratch, okay?" Kona, seeming to understand, accompanies her to the kitchen, allowing her space. She hefts the bags onto the counter and squats in front of Kona. Has anyone in the history of the world ever been as happy to see a person as Kona is to see Amy? "I know," she tells him, scratching and rubbing. "I know, I know, I *know*."

When Kona is sated, or at least partially so, Amy begins to unload the groceries. She bought all of Sam's favorites: black cherry kombucha, Doritos (an unlikely combination, to be sure, but sometimes there's no accounting for the taste and metabolism of a teenager), strawberry Greek yogurt, a pomegranate, even though the pomegranate looks well traveled and cranky. Amy tries to buy summer fruit in summer, but for Sam she has made an exception.

She's got her head in the refrigerator, trying to make room for all of the different varieties of milk—now that Sam is home she has to keep oat milk *and* almond milk on hand, plus cream for Greg's coffee, and her own 2 percent—when she hears a sound behind her. Her heart jumps and she turns from the fridge and says, "Holy geez!"

"Sorry, Mom. I didn't mean to scare you." Sam, who has come in stealthy as a cat, is up earlier than usual, and dressed: high-waisted cutoffs, some sort of wraparound halter top whose beginnings and endings Amy can't discern. High ponytail, lip gloss.

"I bought your favorites!" Amy opens her arms wide to introduce the bounty. "I didn't get dinner food, though. Dad has tickets to the Paw Sox, so I thought maybe we could go for clam rolls at Monahan's. What do you think? I bet you haven't had a clam roll in a while!" Amy is surprised to find that she feels nervous suggesting this, like she and Sam had one date that went okay, not great, and she's not sure if a second one is in the cards. To distract herself while she waits for Sam to answer, she starts the next grocery list—she hadn't realized how low they are on butter, and also on granola. Sam loves granola.

"Mom . . ." says Sam.

"We can go anytime," says Amy. "No more papers to grade, I'm flexible."

"*Mom.*"

"Yup?" Amy looks up.

Sam gestures at the foyer, where, Amy now sees, is . . . a duffel? Was that there when she came in? "Thank you for buying all of this. But I . . . I'm taking off."

"What?" Amy is genuinely bewildered. "Where?"

"Block Island." Sam may as well have said Timbuktu, or Myanmar, or the Solomon Islands, so much do the words *Block* and *Is-*

land fail to register as having anything to do with a place Amy might know. "After you told me about Uncle Timmy's play . . . I've been thinking . . . and yesterday I called him, and it turns out he has a *lot* of extra space in the house he's staying in. So I thought—" She clears her throat, looks to the ceiling, blinks rapidly. "So I thought I might go stay there for a while."

"But you just got here!" cries Amy.

"I've been here for two weeks, Mom." Amy's eyes fill; she feels as neglected and hurt as a schoolgirl excluded from birthday party plans, her hand not holding a crisp pink invitation when every other girl has one. Don't bring up Christmas, says a little voice inside her head.

"It's great being here," Sam goes on, driving the knife farther into Amy's heart. "It really is. I just feel like I need to . . . figure some things out. And I can't do that at home."

"Why not?" To her own ears Amy's voice sounds a little like a strangled cat.

Sam sighs and touches her hand briefly to her high, perfect ponytail. "Because I get major childhood vibes when I'm here."

"What's so wrong with that?" protests Amy. "You had a perfect childhood!"

"I know. I had a good childhood." (Amy tries not to notice the substitution of *good* for *perfect*.) "But I don't know how long I can spend in that bedroom, with the decorations from like five years ago. It's nothing personal."

"Four years," says Amy. "The room redecoration was for your fifteenth birthday." The hours they'd spent poring over the Pottery Barn Teen catalog! The thought they'd put into exactly where to hang the bulletin board, the fairy lights, the fake ivy climbing the back wall!

"Four years," concedes Sam. "But you know what I'm saying." She doesn't look at Amy to confirm that Amy does, in fact, know what she's saying. Instead she's intently inspecting a cuticle on her ring finger, right hand. "Uncle Timmy has ocean views, and all this space." She widens both her arms and her eyes to indicate the space Uncle Timmy has.

Amy chews her lip and thinks. These are the rules of being the mother of a teenage girl in the first quarter of the twenty-first century: Be present, but half in shadow. Do, but don't ask to be done for you. Don't cry, even if you're disappointed. And, if you happen to be Amy Trevino, whatever you do, don't bring up Christmas.

"You can't leave already. You didn't even come home for Christmas." You did *not* just say that, says Amy's inner voice. Please tell me you didn't.

Sam rolls her eyes. "*Mom.* I told you so many times. I wanted to come home for Christmas! We weren't allowed to leave. We had to be there for stuff. There wasn't enough time."

Henry and Ava had come from Middlebury for Christmas; Ava's parents were traveling internationally. Ava had stayed in Sam's bedroom. Amy was happy to have her. But of course it wasn't the same as having Sam.

There ensues a long pause, during which Amy looks at Sam and Sam looks back at Amy, and neither of them seems to blink, even to breathe, and then Sam says, "Soooo . . . I'm trying to get the next ferry. Do you think you could drop me? If not I'll get an Uber."

"Of course I'll drop you," says Amy. Her voice cracks, but she and Sam both pretend they didn't hear it. Amy's unnecessarily full refrigerator, her meager new shopping list, the cramped kitchen: all of these must seem small to Sam, just as Amy fears her life must seem, especially when compared with a famous uncle, an island mansion. How is Amy supposed to compete with *that*?

Kona lets out a low, gentle whine, and Amy tells him, "You can come for the car ride. After all, you're all I have left."

"Don't be dram*a*tic, Mom. It's not like I'm going to L.A. I'll be right across the water."

"And you'll visit, right?"

Sam hesitates, drops oversize sunglasses onto her face. "Um, maybe? Or maybe not. But *you* can visit *me* whenever you want. Life's more fun on an island anyway."

"I guess it is," says Amy, because she doesn't want to be argumentative, and also because it's true. One more rule Amy forgot: Be grateful for what you get, even if it's but a crumb.

Timothy

TIMOTHY SINKS INTO a lounger, stretches his feet in front of him, his arms over his head, and just—relaxes. For a long, delicious moment, he relaxes. He watches the wind turbines turn in the great distance. Seeing their great arms move round and round increases Timothy's sense of well-being and calm.

"Thank you, Floyd," he whispers. "Thank you for this."

The lounger sits on a second-story wraparound deck, and the deck is attached to the house belonging to Timothy's high school buddy, Floyd Barringer. Floyd, Timothy now understands in a way he hadn't before, has come a very, *very* long way from the punk he was in high school. You'd think skipping school to smoke weed at Mohegan Bluffs would be damn near impossible with only thirty-two students in the high school, total, but Floyd managed to find a way, and usually he coerced Timothy to join him, and Vinny St. James too. (It was the seventies, after all—Floyd and Timothy were trying as hard as they could to develop their very own island counterculture. Never really took.) After Timothy went west, Floyd cleaned up his act, went to college, got an MBA, married his college sweetheart, and acquired a fleet of furniture delivery trucks in Attleboro, Massachusetts. To that he added five investment vacation condos in Mazatlán, Mexico, an off-island building supply store in Kingston, Rhode Island, a wealthy man's paunch, and, of course, this, his second home (the first is near the building supply store): a breathtaking, Nantucket-style, five-bedroom, four-bathroom *palace* on Mohegan Trail, overlooking the blue-gray Atlantic, whose color today, with the sun shining voraciously, giving the whole island a bright, scrubbed-clean look, is actually hewing pretty close to electric blue.

"No AC," Floyd had said unapologetically over the phone when he first offered the use of the house to Timothy—Vinny had told Floyd that Timothy would be spending the summer on the island. Floyd and his wife are traveling in Scandinavia this summer.

"No problem," said Timothy, wondering if it was.

"It wasn't a money thing. Suzie just didn't want to have a reason to cut off the ocean breezes. There'll be like two days all summer that you're going to wish you had it. If there's a real heat wave, I usually get off the island. Nice hotel in Newport, something like that."

"Got it," said Timothy. Thinking about that conversation now he can't believe Floyd has become someone who escapes to a "nice hotel in Newport" when it's too hot in his multimillion-dollar island home. He remembers buying Floyd burgers at Ballard's because Floyd couldn't afford his own.

He rises and walks to the deck railing, and looks all the way out to the horizon. The ocean goes and goes and goes. You could see, from here, why people used to believe the world was flat. "Floyd, you wily bastard," he says to nobody.

Timothy, in the years and years he's spent in Los Angeles, has of course been in houses five times as big as this, or even ten—houses right on the beach in Malibu, or in the hills above; houses so big you might wander into the east wing during a party, never to be seen again; houses where the purebred Alaskan malamutes have their own house nearly as big as Floyd's on the property of the actual house—but *this* house on *this* island, owned by *his* stoner friend, well. Everything about it makes Timothy happier than anything has made him in a long time. (His ex-wife, Gertie, used to become *irate* seeing those Alaskan malamutes living in Los Angeles, so far in spirit, climate, and geography from their native habitat! Oh, Gertie could go on about that.)

You enter Floyd's house on the bedroom level, then go up a flight of stairs to the open-concept kitchen and family room. This means the wraparound deck on which Timothy now reposes is accessible from the main story, and sits far above ground level. Besides the three loungers, arranged in a row, there's a set of wicker furniture, appropriately, even *artistically* weathered, with off-white, pristine cushions. To the right of the kitchen a panorama of windows surrounds a sturdy oak table to create a breakfast nook. The table is *reclaimed,* Timothy supposes, although honestly he's never understood what people mean when they say that. Reclaimed from what? Makes it sound like somebody stole something.

Timothy isn't always a breakfast person, not in California, but here, in Floyd Barringer's house, with the turbines beckoning him, the great clay cliffs dropping down to the ocean, he wonders if he might just become one: it would be nice to make regular use of that nook. Maybe, he thinks, as he closes his eyes and begins to drift off, Floyd had things figured out from the beginning. Stay close to home, close to your roots, fight the temptation to go looking for more and more and more. Eat more meals in a nook.

The chime of the doorbell startles him; there must be a speaker somewhere on the deck, to allow him to hear it. It wouldn't be Sam already—she said she would text once she'd boarded the ferry. He pads into the house and down to the entry level, peering through the window at the side of the door to see . . .

"Gertie!" He opens the door.

"The one and only!" She leans toward him, lips glossed and puckered, and he turns each cheek to accept the kisses. It's like they've done this a thousand times, because they have, in fact, done this a thousand times.

"I thought we were meeting at the theater tomorrow. Wasn't that the plan?"

Without preamble or invitation, without truly giving Timothy time or space to step aside, Gertie ushers herself past him and up the stairs, and there's nothing for Timothy to do but follow. "That was the plan, yes," she says. "But, oh, Timothy. We've got some problems to deal with, and I wasn't sure they could wait until tomorrow."

"What kind of problems?" Timothy is panting gently, while Gertie, who is always in phenomenal shape, could probably recite Ophelia's monologue from act 3 with no effort.

"Let's just say, Timothy, that Blake is producer in name only. In reality, he's got no idea how to put on a play." She pauses and looks around. "*This* place," she says. "Holy hell, Timothy, this place is *incredible.*" Her eyes have a familiar gleam—nay, a dangerous gleam. A whiff of her perfume remains behind as she passes through to the back of the house, out the slider, and onto the wraparound deck. It's the same perfume she's worn since Timothy first met her, nearly two decades ago, on the set of *Committed People.* He's read that smell is the most nostalgic of all the senses, something about the olfactory and the amygdala, and, yes, now the memory of his early days with Gertie hits him with the force of a brick. God, she was beautiful. Still is.

No, he tells himself sternly. No, no, no. You messed that up, okay? You messed that up like you mess up everything. You can't go back.

He's not privy to Gertie's current cosmetic secrets—nor does he want to be—but to the naked eye Gertie Sanger appears not to have aged so much as a minute in the last decade. The golden undertones of her fair skin, the wavy reddish-blond hair, the green eyes, the famously high cheekbones ("the cheekbones that launched a thousand ships," a *Vanity Fair* writer had penned in 2005, after Gertie's stunning turn in the film *Helen After Paris*) all look as they always have.

Gertie comes back in from the deck, pauses in the breakfast nook, and makes a little noise of delight. "Oooh, this is nice. Bet you eat breakfast here every day. Or you would if you ate breakfast. There's just something about the Atlantic Ocean, isn't there? It's like in California the ocean is saying, *Hey, come right down here, put your feet in the sand, come to my level.* But out here the ocean is like, *Whoa, buddy! Admire me from afar. I'll let you know when I'm ready for you.*" She laughs. "I love that, about out here. Who'd you say owns this place?"

"My friend Floyd." Timothy points at the wall, where a photo of Floyd and his two kids hangs—but Gertie has already passed by and doesn't see it. She's not actually trailing scarves and bits of lace and gauze behind her, but something about the way she flows from room to room gives the definite impression that she is.

"Look at this fireplace!" she cries. "It's so *New England.* I do love a stone fireplace, in a climate where you can imagine needing it to stay warm in the winter. And, oh, these windows here—tasteful and not ostentatious. It's Luxury Lite." Timothy rolls his eyes, but he's smiling. It's a very good description. "Do I know this Floyd?" Gertie's back on the deck now, calling to him from there.

By the time Timothy and Gertie wed, Timothy's life had become far more Hollywood and much less Rhode Island, and the only people from his past in attendance at their nuptials had been Amy, Greg, Sam, and Henry, and Amy and Timothy's mother.

Gertie pops her head back in, eyebrows raised. "Do I? Know Floyd?"

"Nope," says Timothy. "You've never had the pleasure. We weren't married long enough."

"Trust me," says Gertie. "We were married long enough."

Timothy ignores this. "Speaking of pleasure, Gertie, to what, specifically, do I owe *this* pleasure? The pleasure of your arrival here, today?" He follows her out to the deck.

"You always told me you couldn't wait to get off this island," says Gertie, as though he hasn't asked a question about an entirely different topic. "But now that I'm here, I have to ask . . . *why?*" She leans her elbows on the railing and puts her chin in her hands and gazes out. *Gertie Sanger enjoys a reprieve from her busy life,* might read the caption in a magazine article about Gertie's Shakespeare summer. "To me this looks like paradise."

Timothy sighs. "Do I have to spell it out?"

"Please do," Gertie says dreamily. "Please spell it right out."

Timothy joins her at the railing, keeping a careful distance from his elbow to hers. Elbows can be so fraught. "For one thing, we didn't live in a house like *this.* We lived in a ranch in the dead center of the island. I know it's an island, and it's not that big, but from our house you actually had to work to see the ocean. The airport, we could see with no problem. But there were days when you could just as easily have been in Ohio. For another—can you imagine the winters here? You're seeing the island right now on its very best behavior. But let me set you a different scene, if you please. It's early March. It's been raining for a solid week. Ferries were canceled three days in a row. You haven't left the island since you went Christmas shopping in early December, except for the time you made a day trip to get a tooth pulled in Point Judith." Gertie winces, which Timothy thinks is very kind of her. Gertie was born with perfect teeth; she's never had one pulled in her life. "So you're standing in this cold, driving rain, and you know there's a world out there where people live in California, where people are *surfing* in January and *drinking cocktails outside,* and the sun is always shining—"

"There's June Gloom," says Gertie. "The sun isn't always shining in California! People always forget about June Gloom."

"Well, I know that *now*. But back then I didn't. Back then I just wanted out."

"Also, California is either burning or quaking, or it's melting. It's going to be the first to go when climate change takes hold."

"I'm pretty sure climate change has already taken hold," says Timothy.

"That's true." For a moment Gertie looks sad. Now that they're outside, in the unforgiving natural light, he can see that the delicate skin underneath her eyes is webbed through with very, *very* fine lines. Nothing the right lighting won't hide for a few more years. But. Not forever. Gertie's idea of going back to her theater roots is wise and also brave. She hasn't done theater since her Juilliard days, when she was plucked from a lineup of talented (but less talented than Gertie) and beautiful (but less beautiful than Gertie) acting majors to audition for a supporting role playing Pacino's daughter in a heist film set on the Turkish coast. She got the part, and she never looked back.

"So, Blake," says Timothy. "Is he coming? Will he be here this summer?"

"Oh, no," says Gertie. "Nope. Not until the opening. That's why I'm trying to figure out these problems that have cropped up."

"What problems?" Timothy fixes his gaze on the wind farm while Gertie talks. Issues with housing for the actors. The costume designer's first check bounced. No rehearsal space yet secured. Shoddy communication with the casting director. "And we probably need to hire a part-time dramaturg," says Gertie. "But Blake's never even heard of a dramaturg."

"Why isn't Blake here, dealing with any of this?"

Gertie frowns. "It's not a good idea. For us to be in the same place, Blake and me. That's why he's where he is, and I'm here."

"Geez, Gerts," he says. "Where'd you *get* this guy?"

"I got him . . ." Her voice trails off uncertainly. "Does it matter?" Timothy doesn't answer. *Does* it matter? Is Gertie sleeping with Blake? Well, she's an adult. She's allowed to bed whomever she wants to bed. If it weren't for Timothy's wandering eye, they might still be together, after all! Gertie is monogamous by nature; she never wanted to look for a different partner. She wanted to grow old on a porch with him somewhere, she'd always said.

(Look at them now, though! They're on a porch! Well, it's a deck. But close enough.)

"He was fine when we were working with the theater in Connecticut, because most of this stuff was established there, you know? But the pivot to the island sort of threw him. He's not really a details guy. He's not super familiar with how theater works."

"And now we need a details guy."

"Exactly. Or gal. We need a production manager."

"Hmm," says Timothy. "What's the budget?"

"That's the thing. Blake is tricky." She catches her lower lip with her teeth. "He was reluctant to give Block Island a shot. So I sort of told him . . . well, I sort of told him that the theater came with a production manager. And now I can't really go back and ask him for another position. He'll get weird about it. He's funny about things sometimes."

"Gertie!"

"I know," she says. "I know. I think I'm just going to hire someone and pay them on my own."

"Who are you going to hire? We're not in Manhattan anymore, Dorothy. We don't *have* a production manager."

Gertie waits. Save for the calls of a few gulls that have materialized, and the faraway roar of the ocean, it's quiet.

"What?" he says, reading something in her gaze. "What?"

"It's just that we actually do know someone. We know the perfect person for the job."

"Who?"

She reaches over and punches him on the arm, playfully, mostly, but it sort of hurts. Gertie is stronger than she looks.

"*Amy.*" Timothy regards her blankly; he feels almost as though he's never heard the name before. "Your sister, Amy. Sam's mom? She's right across the water!"

"Oh, no. No. I can't ask *Amy.*" Not after the stuff with their mother; definitely not after telling Sam she could live here.

"Are you kidding? She's perfect! She worked for that off-Broadway theater when she was an undergrad . . ."

"She did?"

"Timothy! *Yes.* She and I used to talk about theater all the time when you and I were together. That's how we bonded at holidays."

"That was thirty years ago!"

"We were together thirty years ago? When I was twelve?"

"No, I mean Amy's undergrad theater experience was thirty years ago."

"But some of that stuff is evergreen. And doesn't she direct plays at the high school now? Didn't she do some community theater stuff?"

"I think so." He doesn't want to admit that Gertie seems to know more about Amy's background than he does.

"She's plenty qualified. And she's super organized. She's *very* hardworking. She has summers off!"

All of these things are true. "But we haven't been on good terms . . . I don't know."

"Timothy," she says. "Please?" He sighs. "*Please?*" she repeats. She fixes him with her famous green eyes. He never could resist Gertie, back in the day, and as it turns out he can't resist her now either.

"Fine," he says. "Okay, I'll ask her. But if she says yes, *I'm* paying her, not you. And we're *not* telling her that. She'd see it as charity, and the last thing she wants from me is charity. As far as Amy is concerned, her salary comes from the same pot as everyone else's. That Hugh Jackman thing . . . oh, she still carries that around with her."

"What Hugh Jackman thing?"

"I don't want to talk about it," he says.

"You sure?"

"Positive."

"Thank you, Timothy."

"Don't thank me yet. She hasn't said yes."

"She will," says Gertie. "She has to. I can't have this show fail." Gertie lifts her elbows off the railing and stretches her arms above her head. "You know how it goes in our business. *Who's Gertie Sanger, get me Gertie Sanger, get me a Gertie Sanger type, get me a young Gertie Sanger, who's Gertie Sanger?*"

"Oh, I know," says Timothy. "Believe me, I *know*. I was *who's Timothy Fleming* about forty years ago. But you're twenty years younger than I am. You have so much time left!"

She shakes her head. "Not really. Right now I'm hovering between *get me a Gertie Sanger type* and *get me a young Gertie Sanger*, and I want to get all my ducks in a row before we get to *who's Gertie Sanger?* I've got the chops for Shakespeare, Timothy. I've got the pedigree. You know I do. I've just got to show the world."

"First you need to show the island," says Timothy.

"The island," says Gertie. "And then the world." She pauses. "So you'll ask? You'll definitely ask Amy?"

"I'll ask. But it's not going to be easy," he warns. "Not with Sam living here."

"*What?*" Gertie does an actor-y version of delighted surprise, a palm to each cheek. "*Sam's* living here? Here in this house? I thought she was in New York, doing that TikTok thing! I've watched some of her videos! She's delightful. They had this dog in the house, Murphy, and they used to do this thing where Murphy, well, everyone called him Murph, but anyway, where *Murph—*"

Timothy cuts off the rest of the sentence; he doesn't want to hear it. "Yeah. TikTok didn't work out, I guess." Timothy can feel his face pull into a sour position with the word *TikTok*. Sam was such a talented young actress. His work in *To Kill a Mockingbird* with Sam playing Scout to his Atticus is still the performance he's most proud of in his career. Not because of the Tony! (But that didn't hurt.) If Amy had let her stick it out after *My Three Daughters* was canceled, he knows Sam would have made it. Really made it. Instead she spends her time crafting silly videos of who knows what, a dog named Murphy apparently, nickname *Murph*, or puckering at the camera, talking about her *clothes* or her *nails* or her *nightclubbing activities*. Not using even an ounce of her God-given talent.

"Why didn't it work out?" asks Gertie, with real interest. Gertie and Sam had become quite close during Sam's year in California. Gertie managed to occupy a space somewhere between de facto mother and very cool aunt. After the Disney show got canceled, Sam had cried on Gertie's shoulder, and Gertie had smoothed Sam's hair off her face and told her all of her own terrible rejection stories, like the time she lost the lead in *Legally Blonde* to Reese Witherspoon. She'd had callback after callback after callback, all for naught. "Hollywood can suck your soul one day and nourish it the next," Gertie had told Sam.

That probably pissed Amy off too, that Gertie had known how to comfort Sam in exactly the right way, and Amy hadn't. (So many things pissed Amy off, especially when their mother, Rose, was sick.) Timothy knows that when he and Gertie divorced, Gertie was nearly as sad to have Sam out of her life as she was to have Timothy gone. Probably a bit sadder, if he's being honest with himself.

"I don't know what happened. She didn't say, she just said she'd decided to come back home, she needed a break, but then home felt sort of suffocating after just two weeks—"

"Shocker," says Gertie. "Nobody wants to live with their parents at that age!" She pinches the bridge of her nose between her fingers and says, "Well, maybe it would make Amy feel closer to Sam if—"

Gertie's cell rings, and as she answers it she mouths *Sorry* to Timothy and walks back into the house. Timothy follows her down the stairs to the bedroom level. "Hi, Holly. Yes. No, I get it. I do. It's not your fault—sure, sure. I understand. Okay. Yes. Please do. I'll let my manager know. No, you don't need to call her. I'll take care of it. My assistant is on vacation . . . yup, sure. I appreciate that." She hangs up and fixes Timothy with her megawatt smile. "That was Holly the Realtor. My first local contact! She was like, 'I can't believe I'm talking to Gertie Sanger!'"

"She said that?"

"Well, no," admits Gertie. "But she might have thought it. Do you think you know her? Holly the Realtor?"

"No, I don't know Holly the Realtor, Gertie. I lived here hundreds of years ago. There are many, many people I don't know on Block Island."

"They all know *you* though!"

"Maybe," he says modestly. Probably, he thinks.

"Would you mind bringing my suitcase in, sweetheart? It's just out on the front steps. It didn't quite make it in." She's now opening the doors to the bedrooms one by one. "Which one are you sleeping in? Oh, wait, I can tell of course. This is the primary. En suite bathroom. You still haven't learned how to make your bed, have you?"

Suitcase? Timothy thinks.

"I went to see this woman Holly this morning about my housing because Blake said the production was going through a local Realtor," explains Gertie. "Blake said I was all set. But Holly didn't have a house for me! Some sort of oversight. Like I said, Blake isn't really a details guy. She was going to make some more calls while I came over here. Unfortunately, none of her calls panned out.

Apparently everything on this island books up by November, if not before. There are literally *no available houses*."

"So what are you going to do?" asks Timothy. He knows, of course, what Gertie is going to do. He heard it in the word *suitcase*.

"That woman, Holly, was very sweet. She asked me if I'd consider sharing a house with another cast member, if something came through. I had to tell her no. I mean, I'm not going to *share a house*." She smiles again. "Unless it's with you, of course, Timothy."

There it is, thinks Timothy. He supposes this is as close to a polite request as he's going to get. He has a sudden memory of Gertie's beautiful face, swollen from crying, outraged and bewildered, the day she moved out for good. *You're the very worst person in the world, Timothy,* she'd said. *Because when you break someone's heart you do it so gently. I wish you'd straight up be an asshole about it, like every other man.*

"And Sam," he reminds her now.

"And Sam!" Gertie cries. "Of course. Which room do you think Sam will want? Do you think she'll mind the two twins? *I* can't sleep in a twin, that's for sure. You know how I whip myself into a frenzy in the night. I'd fall right off."

"I remember." Oh, how he remembers! His heart hurts with the remembering.

Gertie opens the door to the next bedroom. "Ooooh, wait, nobody has to sleep in a twin, this one's also got a queen. So that's three queens, the twins, your king. Look, Timothy, with the windows way up high that look like portholes? It's just like being on a ship! Remember that cruise we took through the Greek Isles on Scorsese's yacht? And there was that awful storm . . . ?"

Yes, Timothy remembers the Greek Isles; he remembers Scorsese's yacht; he remembers the storm; he remembers (there is a heat that rises to his face now, thinking about it) how he and Gertie, absolutely smashed on excellent Metaxa, whiled away the hours of the storm in their stateroom.

"Did you get a chance to grab that suitcase?"

"Getting it now." Timothy opens the front door. *Suitcase*, it could be noted, is an inadequate, almost quaint word for this thing, which looks more like a steamer trunk from the first-class cabins of the *Titanic*—heavy, and fit for a long, long ocean voyage. As he lifts the top part of the suitcase (thank goodness, the thing has wheels on the bottom), he can feel himself giving in: to Gertie's needs, to her charms, to her feigned helplessness, perfected from two solid decades of bending the world to her whims. Trying to hold your ground against Gertie, he knows, is like a piece of tissue paper trying to hold its ground against a wall of water. He delivers the case to her bedroom—already it's her bedroom!—and she sits on the edge of the bed, bouncing once or twice, half excited little kid, half sober furniture tester.

"Ohhh, I can't *wait* to see Sammy. We're going to have so much fun together! It's been so long, for all of us. We're going to be like a small dysfunctional family on an extended vacation. Is she old enough to drink yet?"

"Not legally," says Timothy. "But I can't remember the last time that stopped a nineteen-year-old."

"Right!" says Gertie. "Didn't stop *me* at nineteen. At nineteen I was in my second year at Juilliard, going to that bar on Seventy-second . . . what was that bar called? I can't remember. There was always ice in the bathroom sinks for some reason. First place I ever drank tequila. When will Sammy be here?"

"Later today. She's going to text me when she gets on the ferry."

"Perfect!" Gertie is off the bed now, kneeling beside her steamer trunk/suitcase. She rummages for a while, flinging pieces of clothing out and onto the floor, until she pulls out a sleek black box. "Speaking of drinking," she says. She rests the box on the bed, as carefully as you'd rest a sleeping child, and opens it to reveal a slender clear bottle filled with amber liquid and wound round with thin cords that evoke a string bikini. "Look what I have!" she says. "It was a good luck gift from Blake."

Timothy does a double take. "Rhum Clément 1952?" No *way* there's nothing between Blake and Gertie. That particular year, he knows, sells for over one thousand dollars a bottle. You wouldn't give it to just anyone.

Not that he cares if there's something between Blake and Gertie. He and Gertie haven't been an item for years. He doesn't care, right? Of course not.

He turns the bottle over with reverence, looking for the number. Each bottle of Clément 1952 is individually numbered. Timothy has tried this rum only once in his life, on a trip to Martinique with Gertie a decade ago. Dry, woody, hints of spice and fruit. Really exceptional.

"I think he was going with some sort of an island theme," says Gertie.

"Martinique is in the Caribbean," mutters Timothy. "We're in New England."

"And he's getting into the rum business," Gertie adds.

Timothy would like to meet this Blake, so he can take his measure. But Blake told Gertie that he won't be coming to the island until opening night. Too busy, who knows with what. Probably playing with his money!

"Why's this Holly person calling you about this?" asks Timothy. "Where's Janelle?"

"Janelle is on her honeymoon," says Gertie. "I promised myself I wouldn't bother her. Where's *your* assistant? Taylor, right?"

Timothy doesn't want to admit how quickly he's gone through assistants. "Taylor got a better offer."

"Aw, come on. A better offer than working for *you*?"

"Ha. Believe it or not, yes. Better offer than working with me. She wants to do stand-up so she got a job at a comedy club. They'll let her go on twice a month but she has to bartend full-time to do it." This isn't exactly true. Taylor does want to do stand-up, but she left because she found Timothy's "energy" to be "negative more often than it was positive" and she wanted a "warmer working environment."

In his head, he suggested that she get a job stoking the fire in a pizza oven—will that be warm enough for you, Taylor? But only in his head. Out loud he wished her luck and bought her a *very generous* Starbucks gift card. She was constantly sucking some kind of caffeinated concoction through a reusable metal straw and reminding him to reduce his dependence on Amazon. Then he'd hired Alexa, who'd moved out from Massachusetts practically alone, only a previously estranged father to help her, and who brought in any delivery packages without a word of admonition, quietly breaking down the boxes for recycling.

Gertie looks longingly at the bottle of rum. "I'll tuck this away, and we'll bring it out on a special occasion! Maybe after opening night. If all goes well." She chews her thumbnail and sits back down on the bed, looking up at Timothy. "Do you think all will go well?"

"Of course it will," says Timothy. He shoves his doubts where nobody can see them, but he has to wonder: A big Hollywood star shows up without housing? What else is going to go wrong?

"Timothy. I really think you should call Amy sooner rather than later. I think you should lock it down."

"I'll call her tomorrow," he finds himself saying. Gertie squeals. "But just to reiterate, she can't find out the money is coming from me. Promise?"

"I *promise*," says Gertie. "I double and triple promise." Gertie claps her hands together in that childlike way she has; it's a habit that has always made her seem much younger than her age, a habit both enduring and endearing. "Now that that's settled—"

"I wouldn't call it *settled* yet. I still have to ask her."

"I consider it settled. I have faith in you, and in Amy. So, now that that's settled, what do you want to show me? What's the next jewel in Floyd's crown?"

In for a penny, thinks Timothy, in for at least ten pounds. "Well," he says. "I guess you should see the stairs that lead down the cliff and to the beach."

Gertie snaps her fingers suddenly, a little close for comfort to Timothy's startled ears. "Malachy's! *That's* the bar we used to go to at Juilliard."

She wraps her arms around Timothy and squeezes him hard, and he tries not to breathe in her very particular scent, and he definitely tries not to smell her hair, and if anyone asks it wasn't on purpose that both of those things happened.

Amy

ON MONDAY AMY is sitting at her kitchen table, her laptop open in front of her, making her to-do list for the summer. Not so much *at* her feet as *on* her feet is Kona, one paw wrapped possessively around Amy's ankle, snout between her insteps. Every now and then Kona sighs and shifts and rearranges his snout, which is warm and dry and surprisingly pleasant on the foot.

Amy's Summer List:
1. Plant heirloom tomatoes (do not let them die this year)
2. Teach Kona how to roll over
3. Host neighborhood block party
4. Read *Anna Karenina*
5. Learn to knit a baby hat so that when you are retired you can knit baby hats for newborns at South County Hospital

She studies the list, then renumbers the last item with a six and creates a new line with number five,

5. Learn to knit

Her cell phone rings, and Kona lifts his head, offended.
"Sorry," Amy tells Kona.

"Amy? It's Bianca!" Bianca is Amy's contact at Friends Forever Rescue Organization. "I have wonderful news to share. Kona has found his furever home."

Instantly a panicky feeling rises in Amy. "How can he have found his furever home? Nobody has come to meet him!"

"Right. I should say it's pending approval by the family. But they're repeat adopters, and they've read his file, and they've watched that lovely little video you took of him at the beach. I've spoken with them on the phone, and I don't anticipate any issues. They're coming down from Maine, so they'll be in the area tomorrow. I'll collect him from you around noon."

Amy never should have made that damn video. In the video Kona had chased a tennis ball and brought it willingly back; he'd sat on command; gone into an enthusiastic down/wait; and shaken a paw, his left. They were still working on the right. Amy knew that would come in time. It always did.

"But—but," she says. "What if *we* wanted to keep him?" It was never in the plans to keep Kona. Greg is allergic, and he's willing to take allergy medication for the brief foster periods, but they've agreed he shouldn't have to spend his life medicated so Amy can have a dog.

Bianca becomes brisk, businesslike. "If you truly wanted to keep him, Amy, you should have spoken up within the first seven days of Kona's arrival at your home. You know the rules."

"I never even taught him to roll over!" says Amy. She highlights number two on her list and presses *delete*.

Bianca titters. "Oh, Amy. You're such a hoot."

"I wasn't being funny."

"I'll be by to collect Kona and his things tomorrow. And if you're open to another foster experience I think we can probably find you a new friend fairly quickly."

"Maybe the family from Maine won't like him," says Amy.

"Maybe I misrepresented him in the video. Maybe he'll have to stay here for the rest of the summer."

"Maybe!" says Bianca brightly. "But probably not."

The next person who calls is her brother, Timothy.

"Is Sam okay?" is how Amy answers the phone.

"What? Amy. Of course Sam is okay. Why wouldn't Sam be okay?"

"No reason," says Amy. She and Timothy, as close as they once were despite the difference in their ages, have scarcely talked in the four years since their mother died. Amy knows this is mostly on her; she still resents the way everything went down at the end. (If Amy's being honest, it's mostly because of the Hugh Jackman thing—but Timothy doesn't know how heavily that weighs on Amy's mind.)

"I didn't call about Sam. I called to offer you a job! With car privileges!"

"A job? I have a job."

A beat of silence. "Don't teachers still have summers off?"

"How do you know I'm not teaching summer school?"

"*Are* you teaching summer school?"

"Well. No. Not this summer."

Timothy starts talking, and Amy listens. He tells her about his conversation with Gertie, and about the play's producer, Blake Allard, who doesn't know anything about theater, and about all of the things that might slip through the cracks if they don't find somebody who knows what they're doing to take on the role of production manager. He tells her the salary, which is a very, very good salary.

"I don't know . . ." says Amy, when Timothy stops. But she feels like inside her a small flower bud is beginning to open itself up to the sun. She looks again at her summer list. Without Kona on there it seems malnourished, maybe even pathetic. Let's face it, she's not going to read *Anna Karenina*. Every summer she intends to do it, and every summer she fails. She likes to read beach books at the beach, not Tolstoy! And she has a long time left to learn to knit. To get her full pension she needs to teach until she is sixty, a full seven years away. Babies will still be being born in seven years, and those babies will need hats, just as the babies of today do. That leaves only the tomatoes, and the block party. She doesn't even like hosting parties. Does it make any sense to turn down Timothy's offer for a few tomatoes?

"Think about it, okay? There's nobody else I'd rather have."

"You're not going to get me with flattery," she says untruthfully, because the fact is flattery helps a lot, and she's leaning toward taking it—she's leaning so far she could potentially fall over.

She looks into Kona's eyes. Kona's eyes are such a deep brown, and the sclera so unobtrusive, that his eyes seem to blend into the dark fur of his face. Amy can't read Kona's expression.

"Call me later, once you decide. Okay?"

"Okay," says Amy. "And Timothy?"

"Yup?"

"Tell Sam I said hi. But tell her like I said it very casually, like it's not a big deal."

"Not a big deal," says Timothy. "Got it."

After she ends the call Amy sits, staring at the phone, thinking. The side door opens and in comes Greg. Kona's tail thumps once, twice, and Greg bends down to pat him on top of the head.

"I thought you were at the Backman house," says Amy.

"I was. I came home for lunch, and to give you a kiss." She points her face toward his, and he kisses her, but he must see something in her expression, because he says, "What's wrong?"

"Kona's leaving," she says. "Tomorrow. I'm bereft."

"Oh, no, sweetheart. I'm sorry." He puts his forefinger under her chin and tips it up. "We knew this would happen eventually, right? But I'm sorry."

"And *Timothy*," she goes on, "had the nerve to offer me a job! As production manager for *Much Ado* at the Empire!"

"That's great," says Greg. "I'm going to wash up. We have some of that pizza left from last night?" Amy nods. Greg washes his hands like a surgeon does, with extreme attention to each digit, every nail.

"Is it great?" Amy asks.

"Isn't it?"

"He already took Sam," mutters Amy. "Now he wants to take my summer?"

"He didn't take Sam," Greg says reasonably.

"He took her before."

"Timothy *housed* her when Sam went to LA. He didn't *take* her."

"Took," insists Amy. "He took her back then, and he took her again this summer."

"Sam chose to live on Block Island for the summer. Who wouldn't prefer Block Island without parents over Narragansett with parents?"

Amy feels like she might start crying. "You'd rather be on Block Island?" First Sam, then Kona, and now Greg. Everyone wants to leave her for something better.

"Of course not! Baby. No. That's not what I meant. I just meant, she's nineteen! It's nothing personal that she wants to separate a little bit. That's what kids do."

"I know that," Amy relents. "I do understand the concept of separation. But does she always have to separate so . . . dramatically?" Sometimes it feels as though Sam's life has been nothing but a series of separations broken up by brief periods of reunification. She sighs and turns back to her list. "Anyway. I'm not even sure if I want to do the job with Timothy! I was planning on relaxing this summer. I made a list of things I want to do." She points the computer toward Greg so he can see the list. "I'd have to take the ferry over every day."

"Oh, well, sure, that could be a pain," admits Greg.

"But Timothy's friend, the one whose house he's living in, has a car I can use while I'm there."

"That sounds good! You couldn't bring a car over every day, obviously." The car ferries book up weeks or months in advance.

"Also, there's a salary."

"Yeah? Is it a good salary?" Greg rummages in the fridge and pulls out last night's pizza. He points at it questioningly, and Amy nods to let him know he can eat it.

Amy names the number Timothy gave her.

Greg whistles. "I mean, that's decent money." He removes the plastic wrap from the pizza. "We could use it. Do you *want* to do it?"

Amy studies him. There's a space between his two front teeth, because when Greg was growing up his parents couldn't afford braces. His stubble is coming in a little gray, but his eyes are the same vibrant blue they've always been, and his dark hair is still fingers-through-it thick. He still, on certain occasions, makes her heart go pitter-patter. Right now, though, her heart is clenched tight as a fist, and the air in the room feels chaotic. Timothy sometimes has that effect on her.

"Sort of," she says at last. "It might be nice to work with real actors, on a real production. With financial backing, and an actual costume designer, and a dramaturg if we need one—"

"What the heck is a dramaturg?"

"It's like an editor, basically. For a play. In the case of Shakespeare, they do historical research . . . that kind of thing."

Greg nods enthusiastically, which she appreciates—she knows that he does not in fact care what a dramaturg does. But that's Greg for you! A good egg. Good egg Greg. She tries to imagine herself showing interest, even feigned, in the intricacies of an environmentally friendly heating system for the Backman house.

"And while of *course* I love working with teenagers, it might be nice to work with adults." She loves her high schoolers. She does.

But teenagers are so . . . well! High school students are walking, talking balls of hormones wrapped in contradictions, rolled in drama, and covered with a thin coating of turmoil. And she hasn't had a hand in a real production, with real actors, since leaving New York all those years ago.

"Plus you love Gertie."

"Darn it, I *do* love Gertie. Despite my best efforts." For a while, when Gertie was Sam's de facto mother, Amy had tried not to like her. But she couldn't help it. Gertie is impossibly likable. That's one of the reasons she's such a star.

"So you'll do it?" Greg smiles. "I think it would be good for you, to have a project. Plus you'll get to see more of Sam this way."

"I haven't decided yet." She opens the refrigerator herself now and stares at the contents. She's not hungry. She's—unsettled. "Greg? Do you think we should just do it?"

"Do what? Take the job?" Amy watches Greg take down one piece of pizza, then two. Is he going to go for three? It's almost mesmerizing, waiting to find out. Yes. Yes, he is going for three. Now he's gathering his keys and his cell phone, preparing to get back to the Backman house. Filling his water bottle.

"Should we google Sam, to find out what's going on with her?"

"Nope. We have a deal, remember?"

They *do* have a deal; they made it the first day Sam was back under their roof. "I know," she says. "We have a no-googling deal."

"She'll talk to us when she's ready."

"Or not," says Amy.

"Or not! And that's okay too."

"Not really," says Amy, but Greg is already gone, so she's saying it to Kona.

The thing is, she meant what she said to Greg. This is not the first time Amy has lost her daughter to Timothy. Timothy is technically Amy's half brother, though she never thinks about the fraction. They had the same mother, different fathers. Timothy's dad had disappeared when Timothy was only two; David and Rose met when Timothy was five; David adopted Timothy, and Amy, born four years later, never saw her father treat him like anything but a son. The four of them lived in the ranch house in the center of the island until Timothy left at age eighteen, returning, it seemed, only for funerals.

The first mistake—okay, not *mistake* per se, but the first *step*—was Amy's, seven years ago. Amy sent Timothy a video of Sam, age eleven, performing in a middle school production of *Anne of Green Gables*. Sam had brought the house down. She'd blown away all the other six, seventh, and eighth graders; watching her was like you'd imagine it would be to watch Venus and Serena on the Compton courts where they got their start. Incredible potential, not yet completely realized.

Later that same year, Timothy accepted the role of Atticus Finch in *To Kill a Mockingbird* on Broadway. By this point he was well established as a box office star, and he'd also directed both film and theater. He called Amy and gave her the name of the casting director. Sam, Timothy thought, would make a perfect Scout! Amy should bring her down for the audition.

"Absolutely not," said Amy. She'd only sent the *Green Gables* video because she was proud and because she thought Timothy would enjoy it, not because she was looking for any next steps.

"Why not?"

"I really don't want to start down this road."

"What road?"

Of course he knew perfectly well what road! "Timothy. We're happy here. Everything is good."

Amy Trevino—Amy Fleming then—had earned a B.F.A. in dramatic writing from New York University, then dipped a toe briefly in the playwriting waters before withdrawing it. (The water, it turned out, was inhospitable, her skin thinner and more prone to goose bumps than she'd known.) She'd left New York all

those years ago with her sanity intact; she'd bowed out of the theater world and decided to live in Narragansett and marry a small-
business owner she'd dated two summers in a row and have two
un-famous children with normal lives and normal friends because
that was the kind of life she wanted. In truth, that was the kind of
life she thought most people should have.

And if a small part of her ever second-guessed that, ever bought
tickets for a show at the Providence Performing Arts Center and
read through the program and looked longingly at the playwright's
name and perhaps read his or her or their bio and wondered what
might have happened if . . .

Well, that part was very, very small, even minuscule, and it
was easy to tamp it down, because she loved her husband and her
children and her job at the high school, and directing high school
theater was every bit as rewarding as . . .

Okay, maybe not *every bit*. That was a bridge too far. But it was
almost always very rewarding. On the good days, of which there
were many.

Some.

Enough.

Usually.

"It's not a road! It's just a . . ." Timothy paused, and she realized
he couldn't complete the metaphor.

"Come on, Timothy. You're talking about having her compete
with kids who've been acting since the cradle. Why would we set
her up for disappointment like that? She's not a child actor! I'm not
a stage mom!"

"Just bring her down, Ame, I'll talk her through it, let her know
it's a good experience to have under her belt no matter what. But
honestly, I have a really good feeling about this."

"*Argh,*" said Amy.

Once Sam got wind of the idea, there was no stopping her.
Sam would have walked from Narragansett to Manhattan, on ice

or over coals or through a tunnel full of crocodiles. She wanted to try.

Amy drove Sam down to the city for the audition, maneuvering her Honda Pilot carefully through Midtown, paying an exorbitant amount of money to park in a teeny tiny parking garage, leaving the keys reluctantly with a guy in a blue polo shirt who scarcely looked up from his phone when he took them. During the audition she sat in the hallway with the other moms. (Were they moms? Or were some of them professional child-audition handlers? She wasn't sure; they all looked so intense, so thin and well-groomed, so *shiny*.) She checked in via email with the substitute teacher who was covering her English classes at the high school. The freshmen were taking their test on *The Odyssey*, and anxiety was high.

Amy hated to miss *Odyssey* day.

There was a minute—okay, perhaps a ten-minute stretch—when being in the hallway outside the audition studio, feeling the nervous energy coursing through the place as each potential Scout disappeared into the room and returned, listening to the music and tap-dancing sounds from another audition in a different studio, caused Amy's Manhattan juices to flow again. For those few minutes she was no longer Amy Trevino of Narragansett, owner of a reusable coffee cup stamped with the words ENGLISH TEACHERS GET LIT, but Amy Fleming, New York University undergrad, wandering Bleecker Street in her boot-cut jeans and her platform clogs. She was remembering pieces of her former life—the carrot-ginger dressing at Dojo on West Fourth, the play she'd written sophomore year for her Fundamentals of Playwriting class—when Sam emerged from the audition room, flushed, biting her lip the way she had when she'd won the third-grade spelling bee. (Her nemesis, Miley Finnegan, put two *S*'s in *disappear*, rendering Sam victorious.)

That's when Amy knew everything was about to change.

There were two callbacks, the second with the great Timothy Fleming himself, to test the chemistry, which of course was spot-on, and then a call from the casting director to Amy, offering Sam the part.

Timothy's own agent, Barry "the Bastard" Goldman, wanted to sign Sam to his list—and he hardly ever signed children.

"She doesn't need an agent," Amy told Timothy. "This is a one-off. This is just an experience she's going to have, and then she's going to return to her regular life, and if she wants to pick up the theater thing in college, well, then she can be my guest."

"There's no obligation," said Timothy. "But Barry is a hot ticket. If he wants Sam, you guys would be fools to turn him down. There are people who would literally give away an organ to sign their children with Barry."

"Surely that's not true," said Amy dubiously. "An organ?"

"Maybe a lesser organ," said Timothy. "A spleen or a spare kidney, one of the organs you can technically live without. But you catch my drift."

Amy wanted Greg to feel the same concerns she felt, but Greg had stars in his eyes too. He was an HVAC guy, the son of a plumber, who was, in turn, also the son of a plumber. A kid of his on Broadway!

"Let's just do it," said Greg. "The play, the agent, the whole deal. Why not, right?"

"Why not indeed," murmured Amy.

"It would be silly to turn it down," said Timothy. "You've got nothing to lose."

Just my daughter's soul, Amy thought grimly.

Mockingbird ran for three months, from April to June. Amy's school arranged for a long-term sub through the end of the year so that she could relocate to the city and see Sam to and from the theater for each performance. The reviews were stellar; in the *Times* review, the critic called Sam's Scout "luminous" and "soulful."

Two weeks after the show ended Barry the Bastard got Sam an audition for the part of the youngest sister in *My Three Daughters*, a remake of the 1960s hit *My Three Sons*, with a feminist twist.

Even starry-eyed Greg hesitated at this one.

"Let her audition," said Timothy. "The chances are so small that she'll get an offer. It's just more good experience."

She got an offer.

"*No*," said Amy. "Absolutely not, sweetheart. I'm sorry. But we're not moving to Los Angeles."

"Why not?" asked Sam.

"Because I have a job! And your father has a job. And Henry made the varsity soccer team. Our lives are here. We can't just pick up and go to California!"

"Uncle Timmy says I can live with him and Gertie."

"Negative."

Then Timothy called her. "Listen, Ame. I know this feels scary to you. But she's got real talent. I think turning this down would be a mistake."

Amy helped Sam pack; she flew with her to LAX; she delivered her into the arms of Timothy and Gertie. Amy and Greg and Henry visited at Christmas and again during the school vacation in April. Each time Amy saw Sam she felt as though she'd grown ten months for every one she'd been gone. "What are we going to do?" she asked Greg bleakly. "How will we get her back?"

"It'll work itself out."

"In what world do things work themselves out with no help from outside forces?" muttered Amy. Greg was so much more optimistic than Amy.

As it turned out, things did work themselves out. The show ended the following June, when Barry the Bastard informed Amy and Greg that *My Three Daughters* had not been picked up for another season. He'd already told Sam, but he was giving them a "courtesy call."

"That's the bad news," said Barry.

"What's the good news?"

"I've got a stack of auditions sitting right here," said Barry. "She can start going out on them as early as tomorrow."

Greg and Amy discussed it. They wanted Sam home. Amy called Timothy.

Timothy said, "Are you sure? I think she's got something here."

"We're sure," said Amy. "But Timmy, please don't tell her this is coming from me, okay? I don't need a strike in my column before she even gets off the plane. You have to tell her you're going on location or something. *You* have to give her a reason to come home. I don't want that to be on me. Promise me?"

"I promise," said Timothy. "You might regret it someday, but I promise."

By now Amy has lost track of how much time she's spent on Memory Lane. She pulls herself back to the present. Kona is still at her feet; Sam is still on Block Island; the world, however slowly, is still turning. But she knows now what she wants to do.

She texts Greg.

I'M TAKING THE JOB.

Despite her efforts to keep cool, a frisson of excitement pops up in the general area of her belly. The smell of the greasepaint, the roar of the crowd. Why the hell not; *Anna Karenina* can wait another year.

Sam

DIFFERENT DOOR THIS time, but again Sam wakes to a gentle tapping. She pulls herself out of sleep.

"Sammy?" Her uncle, sotto voce.

She considers ignoring him; perhaps he has less endurance in the sport of door knocking than her mother. But her uncle did let her move into this beautiful house—he hadn't even hesitated; she'd started packing up her things in Narragansett the day she talked to him, and taken the ferry from Point Judith the very next day. The least she can do is answer.

Although now she can't help wondering: Has she replaced one familial authority figure knocking on her door with another? Is what seemed like a promotion actually a lateral move? After all, she'd barely found a spot for her toothbrush when Uncle Timmy told her that Sam's mother agreed to take on the job of production manager for the play. Sam has left home for the summer, but in a way home has left home too.

"Yes?" she croaks, her voice scratchy with sleep.

"Going into town," he says. "I thought you could come with me. We'll leave in ten minutes."

This doesn't sound like an offer: it sounds like a directive. Sam tries not to mind. She gets dressed: cutoff shorts, a tank, a Middlebury baseball hat that Henry gave her for Christmas his freshman year. What a relief it is not to worry about what she looks like all the time. What a relief also not to have to worry about *content*.

"Where are we going?" she ventures, when they are in Floyd's borrowed navy jeep, pulling out of the long driveway from the borrowed house, and then driving the rolling hills with the spar-kling (borrowed) morning water to the right of them. They pass the giant white hotel with the red roof and the strip of Adirondack chairs in front of it; they go around the tiny traffic circle with shops to either side of it; they pass the theater. Her uncle showed her on her first day that this is where the play will take place. She glances sidelong at Uncle Timmy. He's wearing a Red Sox hat and a white T-shirt and a pair of knee-length gray shorts with faint black stripes on them. He's so familiar, and yet he's also a stranger.

"We're going for coffee," he says. "And summer atmosphere. One thing about this place you have to give it credit for is how summer feels like summer." He maneuvers into a parking space on a street just off the main road. It's a tight fit, and a car pulling up behind him honks. He turns to Sam and says, "Goddamn tour-ists." Then he gives her a wicked smile and says, "Just kidding. I don't care about the tourists. I just wanted to feel like a local again."

"Is *goddamn tourists* what locals say?" She's lived close to here for much of her life, but she isn't a local.

"I suppose so. I don't know, really. It's been a long time since I was a local on Block Island."

Sam looks around. She sees a place that rents bikes and mo-peds, and a clothing store, and an ice cream shop. She's sees a guy who she would absolutely swear, from the back, is Tucker, but then he turns around and she sees that he has a longer, thinner nose and a completely different hairline.

"This does not seem like a place you would have come from, Uncle Timmy," she says, once her heart has quieted from the shock and then the un-shock of the not-Tucker.

"Why not?"

"I don't know—it just doesn't. You're so *California*."

"Really? I think I'm exactly half there and half here. I just hide the here part most of the time when I'm out there. Come on, I want to show you this place."

They get out of the jeep and she follows him into a little café with a sign out front that reads JOY BOMBS. Timothy says, "I discovered on my first day here that this shop has the best coffee in town outside of Floyd Barringer's espresso machine. And they make these mini whoopie pies that are out of this world. You ever have a mini whoopie pie, Sam?"

"I don't think so. No."

"You ever been to this café?"

"Nope." Even though Block Island is just a short drive plus a ferry ride from her childhood home, Sam's family didn't come here much, or really at all, once her grandmother, Rose, sold her house and moved off the island. They have beaches close enough to them, and Sam spent those months in New York City for *Mockingbird* when she was twelve, then the year in L.A., and then, by the time she was back, until she left again for the collab house, she just wanted to live a regular life with her friends. It didn't occur to any of the Trevinos to catch a ferry to Block Island, in the same way it doesn't often occur to New Yorkers to take in the view from the top of the Empire State Building.

Joy Bombs is small and homey, with several little tables, half of them occupied, and a glass case holding the mini whoopie pies her uncle mentioned as well as an assortment of other baked goods. The whoopie pies come in several flavors: chocolate, key lime, raspberry cream, espresso, lavender. Sam orders a cappuccino and a key lime whoopie pie, and Timothy orders an Americano and a cinnamon scone. When Sam holds out her debit card he waves it away and says, "Don't be silly. It's on me." Sam pulls her baseball cap lower on her face, but even so, she thinks the teenager ringing in their order might be making a connection. She turns quickly to find a table.

The waving away of the debit card reminds Sam of the conversation she needs to have with her uncle, so when he brings over the two coffees (Sam has carried the glass plate with the scone and the whoopie pie) she says, "Uncle Timmy. How much do you want for rent?"

"I don't want rent, Sam. But thank you for offering."

"I can pay you. I made money this year." In addition to her TikTok money Sam has a significant chunk from her acting work—which, she knows, her mother is hoping she'll use to go to college. Uncle Timmy gives Sam a look that might be—what? Disdainful, that's what. But he hides it quickly. "I did," she insists. "I made money. At the collab house, in New York." She eats the whoopie pie in two bites. It's delicious: the perfect size, the perfect flavor.

Uncle Timmy pulls apart the scone and looks at it. "You made money at the collab house?" He says *collab house* the way some people might say *sandwich made out of rotten garbage*. "No, thank you, Sam. I don't want money from you. Especially from there."

Especially from there? she wonders. What is that supposed to mean?

"Okay," she says. "Thank you?" (It's sort of a relief, actually. She might need her money, for what's coming next. Whatever that is.) "If you change your mind though . . ."

"I won't." (Is it bad that she's relieved?) "But I do want something."

"What is it?"

"I want you to audition for *Much Ado*."

Sam is horrified. The thought of getting up on a stage! Absolutely not.

"Absolutely not," she says. Then, seeing her uncle's expression, she softens her voice. "I mean, no, thank you. I can't do that."

Uncle Timmy takes a long pull of his coffee. "Why not? We haven't found our Hero yet."

"Your hero?" She twists her mouth.

"Capital *H*. Hero. Second female lead behind Beatrice."

"Oh, right." She remembers now, from the movie. She's never read the play.

Uncle Timmy leans forward and looks at her beseechingly. "You'd make a fabulous Hero. You're exactly the right age, and I know you have the range. It's right up your alley!"

"I don't act anymore."

Now her uncle takes a bite of the scone and considers her while he chews and swallows. At last he says, "You *haven't* acted lately; that doesn't mean you *don't* act, or can't act."

"I feel anxious just thinking about it. No, I can't do it. I'm not a Shakespeare person, and—no."

"The best *Shakespeare people*, as you put it, Sam, are those who understand humanity. The way to say the words can be learned and practiced. And we all know from the way you played Scout that you understand humanity."

Well, that's almost enough to get her to consider it. But, no. No no no.

"I'd love to help you out in some capacity, but I think I'd be better behind the scenes. Whatever you need me to do, I'll do it. Take notes during rehearsals, or, I don't know, program design." She actually would not be a good program designer, but that's an issue she can deal with if he takes her up on it. "Sell tickets. Concessions!"

"Concessions?"

"Sure. I can sell M&M's, Sour Patch Kids . . ."

He gives her a searching look. "Samantha. I really want you to think about this. Someone with your talent . . . at a time like this, when you're *right here* . . . with no plans—this could be the perfect vehicle for you."

"Who says I don't have plans?"

He tosses a skeptical look her way, which she tries to ignore by focusing on her coffee. She lets her eyes roam toward the bakery case, considering another whoopie pie. Perhaps the lavender?

"*Do* you have plans?"

"Not specifically. But I've sworn off acting. I know that *that's* one of my plans." Sam has sworn off acting, and sex, and social media—is it possible that soon there will be nothing left? The thought bats its wings at her like a hummingbird.

It's at about this time that Sam notices the girl behind the counter *really* staring at her. *Oh, boy*, thinks Sam. *Here we go. May as well get this over with.* She goes back up to the counter and reaches for a coffee stirrer. The girl is wearing a name tag that says *Maggie*. She's pretty, with wild curly hair pulled back into a ponytail. No makeup. She doesn't need it.

"Hey," says Sam.

"Ohmygod, you're Sam Trevino." The girl is practically vibrating with something—nerves, or pleasure, or a combination.

"Yup," says Sam.

"Do you think you could take a selfie with me?"

"Sorry, I can't," says Sam, and the girl's face falls.

"Okay."

"It's not you. It's just that I'm not doing anything online right now. If people take pictures of me I can't control that. But I'm not voluntarily going to be in any photos or videos or anything for a while. I hope that's okay." Sam takes a deep breath and lets it out. She's practiced this line but this is the first time she's had to say it out loud.

"Sure, yeah, I get it, I totally get it. Once you left the collab house—"

"Right." Sam cuts her off. She really doesn't want to talk about it. But of course this girl knows. Everyone her age knows.

"My mom is *freaking out* about that guy you're with," the girl continues. She met him on the ferry."

Sam glances back at the table. Uncle Timmy is scrolling through his phone. The scone is gone. "That's my uncle. Timothy Fleming. He's an actor. He's way more famous than me." Sort of, she adds, in her head.

The girl's eyes flick to Timothy, then back. "Well, *I* don't know him. But my mom is like, ohmygod he's in my shop! She's freaking out so much she won't come out of the office. She's pretending she's working on payroll but trust me she's *not* working on payroll. She does payroll on Thursdays, and it's Wednesday."

"Bring your mom out."

"What? Really?"

"Yeah. Bring her out." Sam motions to Timothy to come up to the counter, which he does, carrying the empty plate with him and placing it neatly in the dish bin near the garbage.

Maggie goes into the back, and she comes out with a woman who looks so much like her—same wild hair, same pretty face, same anxious, delighted expression. "This is my mom, Joy."

"Ah," says Uncle Timmy. "Joy Bombs Joy. From the ferry!"

"Joy Bombs Joy from the ferry!" the woman repeats, enchanted. Everybody wants to play it cool in the midst of fame, thinks Sam, but almost nobody can. "I can't believe you actually came in. I can't believe it!"

"It's not even my first time. I've become fond of the coffee."

"It's *not*?" says Joy. And, "You *have*?" To her daughter she says, "Maggie! Get him another. What are you drinking? It's on the house."

"It's an Americano." Timothy holds up a hand. "But please, no need. I'm at my limit." He smiles his charming smile, and Sam thinks about how ridiculous it is that people want to give free stuff to celebrities all the time when really it's the celebrities who can afford it and the unknown, regular people who could probably use the free stuff. *The world is topsy-turvy*, as her mom used to say.

The conversation with Joy Bombs Joy goes on for about ninety seconds, and Sam knows that ninety seconds is the right amount of time for a person like her uncle to talk to a civilian, so when time is up she says, "Don't we have to go meet with that guy now?" and her uncle looks at her gratefully, and they say their goodbyes and scoop up their coffees from the table. Sam has her hand on the door handle, about to pull it open, when Maggie comes up behind her and says, "Sam?"

Oh, no, thinks Sam. You seemed pretty cool, Maggie. Don't make me regret anything about our conversation. I said *no selfies*. She turns, ready to squiggle away with a gesture of apology or even one of annoyance, but Maggie isn't holding her phone. She's just standing there, looking wholesome and sweet and very, very young, and she says, "Just so you know. I think it's awful, what Evil Alice did."

Unexpectedly tears spring to Sam's eyes. She glances at her uncle; he's looking at his phone and doesn't appear to have heard. "Thanks," Sam says. "Thanks a lot." Then she swings open the door, and her uncle holds it for her like the old-fashioned gentleman that he is, and together they venture off into the bright summer morning.

Timothy

THE ONLY MAIN role not yet cast is Hero, so one morning, just after eleven, Timothy, Sam, and Gertie sit in the living room.

Timothy's laptop is open on the low coffee table so they can all watch together the tape from the three leading contenders, culled from auditions held at the New York City casting office. The morning started off overcast, but now the sun is starting to push its way through the clouds, and they can see a little slice of ocean through the wraparound windows.

"Should Mom be here?" asks Sam. "Or should we Zoom her in?"

"I asked her," says Timothy. "Casting isn't in her purview for this job, but I asked her anyway. She said to go ahead. She's tying up some loose ends at home, and she'll be on the island tomorrow. Are we ready to do this?"

Sam and Gertie nod. Timothy leans forward and presses the *play* button, and the first Hero appears. She's standing in front of a dark screen, wearing all black. Her long dark hair, stick straight, is pulled back from her face in a half-up, half-down style. Timothy glances at the audition log. Twenty-two, a recent graduate of Yale Drama School. Each actor is reading the same section: Act 3, scene 1, Hero, Margaret, and Ursula in Leonato's garden. A person off camera reads the lines of Margaret and Ursula—and Beatrice, when she enters the scene.

"If it prove so," concludes Hero, "then loving goes by haps; some Cupid kills with arrows, some with traps."

"What do we think?" Timothy asks, pressing the *pause* button.

"Hmm," says Sam.

"Well . . ." says Gertie.

"There's something about her that's not quite right," says Timothy. "But I can't put my finger on it."

"It's a hint of masculinity in her voice," says Sam. "Her voice isn't light enough for Hero."

Timothy turns to her: his niece is a wonder! "That's exactly it, Sam. Thank you."

"Well done, Sam," says Gertie merrily. "Next!" Timothy presses a key to play the next audition, and they all watch the candidate carefully.

"Body language," says Timothy.

"Hesitation in the delivery," says Gertie.

"Light vocal fry," says Sam. "Pass."

There's something not quite right about the third one too. When she finishes reading, Timothy closes his laptop and sighs.

"They all sound too old," says Sam. "I'm not saying they *are* too old—mid-twenties should be fine for Hero. I'm just saying that whatever their ages they don't *seem* youthful enough. None of these three seems carefree and trusting, the way Hero needs to be." (Timothy had caught Sam perusing the script the other day.) "These three deliver the lines, sure, but they seem sort of . . . imperturbable."

"I think your inner casting director is trying to claw her way out of your midsection, Sammy," says Gertie. "You're exactly right."

Sam smiles wryly and looks down at her hands—but she does seem pleased. She looks up again and adds, "I think Hero needs to have the innocence of a teenager. Not that teenagers are innocent, but you know what I mean. Someone who hasn't been knocked down a lot yet."

"*You're* still a teenager," Timothy points out. "You've got the chops. And if I do say so myself, you've got the pedigree. You're here! Why don't you read for it? I know we talked about this, but I have to bring it up again. I just have to."

"Absolutely not," says Sam instantly. Her face reddens. "No way." There are times when Sam doesn't look a bit like her mother, and times when she looks *exactly* like her mother. Genetics are so funny that way. When her face goes red she looks exactly like Amy, but Timothy senses this isn't the right time to point that out.

"Sam—" he begins. Sam is such a talented actor! And here's a perfect part for her! How can she not even consider reading for it? But he can tell by the change in her body language—shoulders tucked in, chin pointed slightly away from him—that he can't push it. He can't even push it very, very gently.

"Nope," she says. "There's no way I'm going onstage this summer. For me to go onstage hell would have to freeze over, and *then* pigs would have to fly right through the frozen hell."

"So . . . it's a no?"

"It's a rock-hard no," says Sam. Now she looks even more like Amy. When Amy was, oh, seven or eight, and Timothy was a teenager, she had some world-famous fits of stubbornness, over something she wanted and couldn't have, or had to do and didn't want to. Their mom used to call her Un-Amiable Amy, which of course made Un-Amiable even angrier. Those were the times Timothy would pop her in the car and drive her past Painted Rock in the dark, sometimes turning off the headlights so she'd squeal with joy and terror.

Gertie snaps her fingers. "There's one I haven't looked at yet. I forgot all about it until now. My agent wanted me to take a look at it—it's a client she just signed, and I thought she might be too young, but now that we're talking like this I wonder if she's worth a look."

"How young?" asks Timothy.

"I have to check. I can't remember."

Sam is tapping on the screen of her phone. "Kate Beckinsale was a teenager when she was cast in the movie version. I can't figure out if she was eighteen or nineteen . . ."

"Let me run and grab my laptop. We'll at least take a look." Gertie rises gracefully from the couch—it's lower than Timothy's at home, and he knows when it's his turn to get up he's going to be hard-pressed to rise without a grunt and a twinge—and disappears down the stairs that lead to the bedrooms. Timothy moves his computer out of the way, and when Gertie returns she sets hers up in the place where his had been. She retrieves the tape from her inbox and says, "This is Amelia Rees." She checks the notes that came through with the tape. "She's an infant. Seventeen."

Sam says, "Still in high school?"

"She's—let's see. She graduated from high school a few weeks ago. She's about to start her freshman year at Northwestern, for performing arts."

"Underachiever," says Sam, rolling her eyes.

"Let's give her a look," says Gertie.

They all sit back and watch Amelia Rees do her thing. When she concludes—"Of this matter is little Cupid's crafty arrow made, that only wounds by heresay"—they let out a collective sigh.

"She's perfect," whispers Sam.

"Stunning," says Timothy.

"She's got the young-old thing going on," adds Sam. "Fresh and invigorating, but her voice is mature enough to handle the Shakespeare."

Gertie smiles and claps her hands. "You guys. We need to get Amelia Rees on the island *yesterday*. I think we've found our Hero!"

Amy

ON THE FERRY, Amy sees someone waving at her, trying to get her attention. Before she discerns who it is she waves back, then immediately wishes she could rescind the wave. It's Charlene Daniels, mother of one of Henry's former classmates. Long ago, during Amy's all-too-brief maternity leave, they had been part of the same playgroup. Charlene is fine in bite-size doses, but she practices the sport of competitive mothering, and there are fifteen minutes left in the ferry ride, and Amy doesn't want to make conversation with Charlene for more than two of them.

Amy looks quickly back down at her phone, but Charlene is already threading her way through the seats toward Amy, then she's taking a seat next to her.

"Hey, stranger!" she says. "What are you doing going out to the Block?"

Amy says, "My brother's in town." She hopes that Charlene will take the hint.

Charlene foists upon Amy one of her knowing grins. "Oooohhh. *The* brother?"

"I only have one."

"Maybe I'll have to follow you off the ferry, wink wink!" When Amy doesn't respond, Charlene says, "I heard that Henry is *killing* it at Middlebury! He just got some big award? You and Greg must be so proud."

"We are," says Amy brightly. "Of course we are." In fact Henry did just receive one of the philosophy department's major grants. How does Charlene know this? This is the place where Amy is supposed to ask how Charlene's son, Logan, is doing, but she finds herself muzzled by an uncharitable refusal to give Charlene what she wants.

No matter; Charlene is going to get to it anyway. "Logan is a year behind Henry, at Boston College. He took that gap year, remember? Did Habitat for Humanity?"

"I remember," says Amy. How could anyone forget? No sooner had Logan climbed aboard the bus to West Virginia than Charlene was plastering a HABITAT FOR HUMANITY bumper sticker on her car and outfitting herself, Logan's dad, and Logan's two younger sisters in matching Habitat T-shirts.

"And Sam . . . ?"

"She's home," says Amy. "For the summer." She doesn't feel like getting into the details about how Sam is not actually, technically at home.

"Oh, *good!*" says Charlene. "It must have broken your heart when she didn't come home for Christmas!" (How *does* Charlene know everything? It's like she has an internship with the town crier.) "And then what happened in the spring."

Amy swallows and looks away.

Charlene peers at her. "Wait a second," she says. "You know about all of that, right?"

Amy feels her cheeks start to flame. "Of course I know," she says. She hopes her voice sounds steadier than it feels. Damn it! After all these years Charlene can somehow still put her on her back foot.

"I figured," says Charlene. "Ohmygod, you had me wondering for a minute. Your *face*! I wish you could see your own face."

Amy does not wish she could see her own face. "I'm sorry," she tells Charlene, "I have to take this." She indicates her phone, which is not ringing or buzzing, and picks it up as though it's doing both.

"Hey!" she says, convincingly, she thinks. "I was just about to call you!" She waves at Charlene, who looks slightly annoyed as she gets up to go. "I know!" Amy tells the lovely imaginary person on the other end.

Once Charlene is at a safe distance, she ends the fake call and stares at her phone. She hates that Charlene knows something about Sam that Amy doesn't know.

That's it, she tells herself. That's enough. I can't do this any longer. I'm googling. Her finger hovers over the phone screen. She's about to do it! But there's no time; the announcer comes on the intercom to dispense instructions on disembarking; the opportunity passes, and so too does the desire. Sam has asked her not to google, and she wants that trust to remain unbroken.

Focus, Amy, she tells herself. Focus on the play. You have a job to do.

When Amy gets off the ferry, she calls Timothy, as instructed, and he directs her to where he is in the parking lot. She makes her way down the gangplank and through the throng of day-trippers, finding Timothy leaning against a brick-red Wagoneer. His arms are crossed, he's got sunglasses on, jeans, expensive-looking loafers without socks. When he sees her, he tips his sunglasses forward and smiles, looking for all the world like the movie star he is. He hasn't lost his charm. He steps up to her and opens his arms and they hug. It's been a long time since she's hugged Timothy. Not since their mother died.

"You look good," she says. "You look like you made it through the pandemic mostly unscathed."

"That's not what my cholesterol numbers tell me," he says,

flashing another smile, bigger this time, if possible. "But thank you. You look good too." He gestures to the Wagoneer. "Your chariot, madame."

"Yeah? Really? All for me?"

"All for you."

"Where's *your* chariot?"

"Oh, well. I keep the actual jeep, the sides-off jeep. Not because it's better . . ." (It's better, thinks Amy. Of course it's better.) "But because I thought you might have, you know, things to lug around. In your capacity as PM."

"Sure," she says. "I might lug some things."

"Key's inside. Full tank of gas. I've arranged with the parking guys here for you to leave it in their lot overnight, so it will always be here. Key to the theater is on the same ring."

"Perfect," says Amy. She will not ask Timothy where Sam is. She's promised herself that she'll let Sam live her own Block Island life, while Amy lives *her* own Block Island life. If she happens to run into Sam, that's one thing. If she happens to check her location on Life360 and then "run into her," that's also one thing, just a different one thing. "I have a meeting at eleven with a Realtor about a barn that I'm hoping will work for rehearsals. Do you want to come?"

Timothy checks his watch. "Gertie and I have a casting meeting with New York at eleven-thirty. I'd better not. I leave it in your capable hands."

Amy looks at her hands. They look careworn, that's for sure, but are they capable? Well. She hopes so. "Got it," she says. "We're bumping up against the beginning of rehearsals, so unless it's flooded or on fire I'm assuming it will work."

Timothy grants her another one of his megawatt smiles. "That's my girl," he says. "I knew I hired you for a reason."

Amy tries to bristle at this, but her heart isn't in it. She's no more immune to the famous Timothy Fleming charm than anyone else. "I knew I said yes for a reason." She taps the Wagoneer, then climbs into the driver's seat and starts the engine.

When Timothy first moved to L.A. he came home every Christmas, first with a ticket that Rose and David paid for and then, once he started making real money, with one he paid for himself. Then he was flying himself first-class, and before too long he couldn't come at all. He was too busy, or he was on location, or he'd rather fly them all out to him, because wouldn't it, after all, be nice to spend Christmas in L.A. for a change?

By the time Amy got to college Timothy was here, there, everywhere. Splashed across the cover of *People* magazine. Walking the red carpet of this or that awards show or premiere; associated with this actress or that one. Her junior year Timothy took Amy and her roommates to see *Miss Saigon,* front row, then out to the just-opened Lespinasse in the St. Regis. Her roommates *couldn't believe* they were out with Timothy Fleming.

She's thinking about all of this as she drives the Wagoneer carefully along Water Street, hooking a left on Dodge and then a right to get to Corn Neck. It's so crowded! So much more crowded than when she and Timothy lived here all those years ago, yet despite the changes the nostalgia tugs hard at her. A tear forms in each of her eyes. Four of them then, two of them left now. She blinks hard; she can't afford to cry, she doesn't want to hit a moped.

To make herself smile she recalls a conversation she and Timothy had after David's funeral, some twenty-five years ago. (A massive heart attack in his sleep; it could have been worse, but of course, it could have been better too. He could have lived longer.)

"For all intensive purposes he was my dad too," Timothy said at one point, as they stood near the bar at the post-funeral gathering, pouring out generous servings of whiskey.

"I'm sorry, *what?*" she'd said. "What did you just say?"

He mistook her reaction for being offended. "He was, Ame! He was in my life from when I was five. He's the only father I knew. He gave me his name!"

"No, that's not what I'm reacting to. Did you just say *for all intensive purposes*?"

"What's wrong with that?"

Amy was actively grieving, but she could scarcely stifle a laugh. "The phrase is *for all intents. And. Purposes.* Not *all intensive purposes.*"

"No, it's not," said Timothy. Amy grabbed a cocktail napkin from the hors d'oeuvre table, scribbled the two phrases down, and he squinted at the napkin, then laughed. "Okay," he said. "Okay, okay." But she sensed something behind the laugh: deep down, he was smarting from the correction. She sometimes forgot that he'd been a mediocre high school student, and that he'd gone to college for only a year. His voice was so commanding, his very presence was so commanding, even back then, that he presented like someone with advanced degrees in at least five different subjects.

Amy was working on her master's in education, teaching. And here was Timothy, buying a house in Laurel Canyon. Selling that one; buying one in Beverly Crest, then the one where he still lives today, in Benedict Canyon. Vacationing in French Polynesia, Tuscany, Norway.

He was everywhere, and yet farther from Amy's grasp. More movies. *Wonderful. You Can Go Home Again. We Were So Young.* Dating Gertie Sanger, then marrying her. *Committed People.* He was as familiar, and also as untouchable, as the Big Dipper.

"Intensive purposes," she says aloud, giggling. She keeps her eyes peeled for the barn. She watches for pedestrians; she brakes for a clot of moped drivers who have stopped *right in the middle of the street to chat.* She takes a mental voyage through all the summer jobs she held here in the past. Desk clerk at the Narragansett Inn. Beach chair girl at Ballard's. Ice cream scooper at The Ice Cream Place. The two weeks she spent as a chambermaid—she hadn't lasted long at that job. She'd been a terrible chambermaid, constantly undone by the thought of what had gone on in the sheets she was changing.

Before she knows it she's arrived at the barn, on the west side of Corn Neck Road. She's beat the Realtor there, so she parks and wanders around and tries to peek in the windows, which are impenetrable, owing either to the lack of light inside the barn or good old-fashioned dirt. So busy is Amy with her spying that she's spooked when someone comes up behind her and says, "Hello there! So you're looking to buy?"

Amy jumps and whips around to see a tiny woman in unnecessarily high heels. "You must be Joanne." Joanne nods and holds out a hand; they shake. "Sorry, I hope I didn't give the wrong impression. I'm looking to rent, just through July."

Joanne purses pink lips. "Just through July?"

"Yes. For rehearsal space for a production in August at the Empire Theatre."

Joanne sighs. "I can show it to you, but I don't know if that'll work. I'd have to take it off the market—and the owner is set on selling . . ."

"Let's take a look," says Amy. There's no time to find another rehearsal space, and she's certainly not above name-dropping if it comes to it.

Inside, though there are no stalls, no hay, the unmistakable odor of horses gone by lingers in the air. A fly buzzes around Joanne's head and she swats at it, and off the fly goes, charting courses unknown. Who can say what sort of critters are hiding elsewhere? Nevertheless, the lights Joanne flicks on are strong and far-reaching, the concrete floor is level and looks as if it could be easily taped to delineate the stage and the actors' marks.

"Nothing a good airing out can't fix," Amy says brightly. "A few big fans in the corner, a good scrubbing." (Can Amy hire Sam to scrub the barn?) "What's the fee for a month?"

Joanne swats again at the same (or a different?) fly. "That's what I'm saying, see. It's not for rent."

Amy draws in a breath, and when she lets it out she says, "I'm sure you're familiar with Gertie Sanger."

Joanne's eyes grow wide, then wider. She nods. "Of course."

"And probably also Timothy Fleming." Another nod. "That's who's here, working on this play. It's big-time, Joanne. It's going to bring the island a lot of attention. A lot of tourist dollars. Heck, maybe even more people looking to buy homes here." Joanne's eyebrows go up. "And we really, really need a place to rehearse. I mean, I can't imagine telling Gertie Sanger I wasn't able to find her the space she wanted." Amy shakes her head regretfully, as though playing out Gertie's reaction. "And I can't imagine you're going to sell it before the end of June, which means nobody would be closing on it before July is over, right? I'm not a Realtor, but I know these things take a while." She fixes Joanne with a stern and expectant look, the one she uses on students late with an assignment.

It's almost visible, almost audible, the act of Joanne relenting. "I'll have to talk to the owner," she says. "But you know what, Amy? I bet we can work something out. I'll let you know for sure this afternoon."

When Amy pulls back onto Corn Neck Road she's feeling pleased with herself and her negotiating skills. She decides to check out the theater. She parks in the ferry parking and crosses Water Street, turning left toward the Empire. She uses the key Timothy gave her and opens the door, cautiously at first, then with the strength and authority she supposes she should feel.

She takes a gander at the stage. The curtain is missing. She pulls her notebook out of her bag and writes: 1. **Curtain.** Next she walks up and down the aisles, looking at the seats. She counts four that are visibly broken, but there may be more, once she makes a closer inspection. She writes: 2. **Seats.**

In the concession area she spies a popcorn machine that looks like it hasn't been used since Kurt Cobain was alive. She writes: 3. Concession area.

What else? Bathrooms, probably. But before she can investigate her phone rings: Joanne. Yes. Yes, Amy can meet her back at the barn to go over a few details. Yes, she's ready to sign a lease and pull together the rental fee. Yes yes yes.

She'll be back tomorrow. She'll make a more comprehensive list, and she'll get started. Okay! Shoulders back, chin up. Okay, Amy. Let's do this.

Sam

IT GOES DOWN *like this.*

In May Sam enrolls in her mother's alma mater, New York University; in early June she graduates from high school. She wants to be in New York City, but when she digs deep into her psyche she knows that that's the only thing drawing her to NYU. She doesn't want to spend the money she made from the Disney show and Mockingbird *on tuition for classes she isn't interested in taking. But she doesn't know what else to do, and her mother is so excited for her. Her dad is excited for her. Henry is excited for her, although he hoped she'd apply to Middlebury, or at least the University of Vermont, so they'd be closer to each other.*

In June, she worries. But she also gets a job waiting tables at PJ's Pub, and she goes to the beach during the day, and she makes and posts a lot of videos on TikTok. She picks up a bunch of followers. Then more, and more, and more. It doesn't matter how silly or inane the videos are, or even what they're about. People are eager to know what the third daughter from the once-popular My Three Daughters *is up to! More videos, more followers.*

In July, she gets a DM from Tink Macalester. Sam has heard of Tink, the mastermind behind one of the biggest collab houses in L.A., Rainbow House. Tink wants to start a collab house in Manhattan: the first of its kind on the east coast. She's got six people signed on already, and she needs a seventh and an eighth. Tink was a fan of My Three Daughters back in the day, and she's been watching Sam's videos. (She loved the video where Sam put makeup on one of her mother's rescue dogs to the sound of "Let's Get It On.") Really, Tink could watch Sam's videos all day long. Tink thinks Sam has the It Factor.

"Like anyone really knows if that's a thing! The It Factor!" Tink says, laughing, when they connect by phone. (People in Tink's world are always "connecting" or "circling back" or "putting a pin in" discussions.) "But if it is, you have it, girl. You have it."

Is Sam interested in joining them in Manhattan's first-ever collab house?

Hell yes, Sam is interested in joining them! The first payment for NYU is due in a little under a week. Tink got to her just in time: She'll lose just the initial deposit. That's a loss she can absorb.

Her mother is devastated; her father is confused. Henry is disapproving. But Sam turned eighteen in March. They all agree she's old enough to make her own decisions, even if nobody agrees with them.

The TikTokers move in in September. Seven of them at first, all young, all beautiful. Xanadu, Tink decides to call the house. "It's a metaphor for an idyllic place," she explains, though Sam, daughter of an English teacher, already knows this.

Tink is thirty-four years old but looks twenty-five. She dresses like she's sixteen, or, when the occasion calls for it, forty. She's part den mother, part therapist, part party planner, part party attendee, part accountant. She doesn't live at Xanadu; she "splits her time" between New York and L.A., and pops in both expectedly and unexpectedly. She has her own key.

The boys: Scooter, Nathan, Boom Boom, Tucker. The girls: Cece, Kylie, Sam. Everything would have been fine if they'd stopped there, but Tink wants an equal number of boys and girls, so the last person to move in is Alice. Alice and Sam have the same skin tone, similar hair color. They're nearly the same size, so they can share clothes. In the beginning, this feels like a blessing—Alice is the sister Sam never had! By the end, it's a curse.

Sam is riding her bike up Corn Neck Road on the way to the

beach. Strictly speaking, it's not her bike—it belongs to her uncle's friend Floyd, but both Uncle Timmy and Gertie have assured her that she can use it as much as she wants to. Floyd, they're willing to bet, is not much of a cyclist.

The island is only seven miles in circumference, so it's maybe three miles from Mohegan Trail to Corn Neck, but oh, the hills! The hills. Feels like twenty miles. Sam's sweating; she's panting; her heart rate is skyrocketing. She stops to rest for a moment, and to sip from her water bottle, when an unfamiliar car pulls up alongside her, and a very familiar voice says, "*Sammy?*"

Sam peers through the lowered passenger window. "Mom? Whose car is that?"

"It's Floyd Barringer's," says Amy. "It was part of my deal with Timmy. Obviously I couldn't bring a car over on the ferry every day, so he said I could use this while I'm here."

"There was an extra car?" pants Sam. "All this time? And I've been *biking*?"

Amy shrugs and says, "Looks like it!" a bit too merrily. "I think I found a rehearsal space! It's a barn just up the road from here. It's technically for sale, but they're willing to take it off the market for the month of July. I guess the money we're offering, plus the cachet of having Gertie Sanger rehearse there, is worth it. This barn is perfect, Sam. I feel like I'm earning my keep!"

Sam knows she should say something kind and supportive, like, *Good job, Mom!* Or, *I'd love to see the barn!* But she's feeling neither kind nor supportive; she's feeling sweaty and thirsty. So what she says instead is, "Are you going to be here every day?"

"Every weekday, for now. Until we get closer to tech. Then, probably some weekends. Maybe I can stay over at the house with you guys! Save myself the trip. Kidding, I'm *kidding*, Sam, don't look so disheartened. I won't cramp your style. I promise."

"Don't worry about it," says Sam. "I don't have much style right now anyway."

Her mother laughs and says, "Oh, come on, now. You'll always have style." She waves at a car to go around her and says, "Do you have *any idea*, Sam, how much this place has changed since I was growing up here?"

Sam rolls her eyes and thinks, Oh, great. Just what I was hoping to get out of the afternoon: a trip down Memory Lane. "How would I know that, Mom? I'm not like some island historian."

Her mother laughs again: her good mood seems to be impenetrable. "Did you know there weren't even mopeds here in the seventies?" As if on cue, a moped rushes past them, a girl's hair flying out from underneath the helmet. "Did you know you couldn't just hop on a ferry on a whim? The ferries didn't run that often! You had to *plan*."

"You have to plan now, Mom."

"So!" Amy says brightly, ignoring this last comment. "How's everything going at Timmy's?"

"Fine. Good."

"Sam—are you okay? Are you really okay?"

No. I don't know. Maybe. Probably not. "Yes," says Sam finally, whether because it's true or because she thinks it's what her mother wants to hear, she's not sure. "I'm really okay."

"Do you want to talk about what happened in New York?"

Sam blanches. "Right now? Through a car window?"

"Well, no. But you can park your bike and hop in. We could get an ice cream or something."

Sam softens a bit at that—but just a bit. She does love ice cream, and she recognizes the peace offering. But she does *not* want to talk about what happened in New York, not with her mother, not with anybody. She shakes her head and purses her lips and says, "I don't want to talk about it. I just want to go to the beach and fall asleep for like a year and a half."

"Okay," says her mom. She puts the Wagoneer in gear, checks her mirrors. "Okay. But wear sunscreen, okay?"

Sam rolls her eyes again, harder this time. But she says, "Okay." Cece did a lot of skin-care videos; Sam actually learned a lot about good sunscreen from her.

Once her mom is gone Sam pedals that last hundred meters to the parking lot, parks and locks her bike, and walks through the pavilion and onto the beach. She surveys the beach—it's crowded, but not awfully so—and picks an empty spot in the sand to lay out her towel. She stretches out on the towel, then, remembering her mother's advice and Cece's videos, sits up and reaches into her backpack for a bottle of sunscreen. She's looking down, squeezing out the sunscreen, when two feet with darkly painted toenails appear in her line of vision. She looks up, shielding her eyes from the sun with her hand. It's Maggie, from Joy Bombs. A distraction from her own thoughts—hooray!

"Hi. Sorry to bother you. Am I bothering you? I just wanted to say hi." Maggie shifts her feet on the hot sand. She's wearing a bikini top and tiny shorts. Sunglasses. Messy bun.

"You're not bothering me. And hi back." Sam gestures to the end of her towel. "Sit, if you want. Don't burn your feet. Are you by yourself? Not working at the café today?"

Maggie sits carefully on the edge of the towel as though worried about taking up too much of it. She crosses her feet underneath her. "My mom gave me today off."

"Nice."

"Sort of. But she has an ulterior motive." Maggie stretches out her legs and flexes her toes. "Her boyfriend's son is coming for two weeks on Friday, and they'll want me to babysit. Max. He's six."

"Is it a good or bad thing that the boyfriend's son is coming?"

"A little bit of both, I guess. He's cute. But it gets crowded. I mean, it already got a little crowded, when Anthony moved in with us. Sometimes I miss when it was just me and my mom. I want her to be happy, of course I do, and she loves Anthony, but sometimes I miss us, the way we used to be, when it was just her and me and that's it." Maggie makes a little embarrassed face and shrugs. "That probably sounds weird."

"Not at all," says Sam. "I think it makes sense." She watches a boogie boarder ride a wave. "Moms," she says. "Even the good ones are complicated."

Maggie snort-laughs and says, "Yeah."

"I was just really grumpy with my own mom."

"Why?"

"No reason. Just in a bad mood."

"I don't think of someone famous like you having a mom. Or like bad moods."

Sam laughs. "Are you kidding me? I have both. The whole month of May was an endless bad mood for me. Endless. I feel like I just pulled myself out of it."

Maggie nods. "Because of Evil Alice. Sure. I get that. It's just that even with all of that, I don't know anyone who wouldn't trade places with you in a second."

"*I'd* trade with *you*, Maggie."

"Shut up. Don't tease me."

It's true, though. Maggie is so young and unspoiled by the world, so full of optimism and goodwill. "I'm not teasing. I mean it. You've got killer hair. You live on this gorgeous island, you probably don't have people constantly saying awful stuff about you online, you work at an iconic café—"

"I don't have a *choice* about where I work," says Maggie, stopping short of petulant, but not that short. "And I'm not sure it's iconic."

"Trust me. It's iconic. Also, you're cooler than everyone around you, and you don't know it yet. Believe me, Maggie. I know what I'm talking about."

Maggie twists her mouth and says, "Thanks. Even if you're just saying that to be nice."

"I'm not. I'm not that nice actually."

Now Maggie laughs and says, "Yes, you are." She turns away from the water and waves at a figure moving down the sand. "There's Riley," she says. Then, "Ugh. She brought Jacob."

"Boyfriend?"

"Yup."

"Not a fan?"

"Not really. I guess he's okay. They're just, I don't know, annoying together."

"They look annoying," says Sam loyally, even though of course she can't really tell from here. All she sees is a tall girl and a slightly taller boy in a baseball cap.

"What's that say about me?" asks Maggie. She picks up a fistful of sand and lets it out slowly, as though through an hourglass. Then she stands and brushes the sand from the backs of her legs. "That I want everyone to be alone, so I don't have to share them?"

"It says you're human," says Sam, and the grateful smile Maggie gives her is enough to put her in a better mood.

Amy

WHEN AMY WAS growing up on Block Island you'd be more likely to come across the rare grasshopper sparrow than an espresso drink. Now there are at least three coffee shops to choose from! The Friday after securing the rehearsal barn she's going into Joy Bombs, which Timothy has raved about, when a woman on her way out stops, stares, and says, "Amy! Amy Fleming! Ohmygod, Amy. I'd recognize you anywhere. It's me! It's Holly Anderson!"

"Holly?" Amy doesn't know anyone named Holly. Does she? She peers at the woman. She's short and curvy, with wavy blond hair and big blue eyes. Those fake eyelashes that look like spider legs on some people but actually look pretty good here. "Hi . . . ?" she says uncertainly, raking through her memory.

The woman shakes her head. "Silly me. You don't know me as Holly Anderson. You know me as Holly Lewis. Amy! You used to babysit me!"

Holly steps back into the shop and Amy follows her. "Holy moly," says Amy. "Holly. Of course." She babysat Holly when she was sixteen and Holly was, what? Eight or nine? So that means the woman in front of her, little Holly Lewis, with the pigtails and the crooked front teeth, is now . . . she does some quick math (not her forte) . . . is now forty-five years old. With beautifully straightened teeth. "That seems impossible. That so many years have gone by."

"I *know!*" Holly bobs her head enthusiastically. "I heard you were here for the play."

"I am," says Amy. "I am here for the play."

"I have a daughter who's almost as old as you were when you were my babysitter, if you can believe that!"

"I can't," admits Amy. She's remembering now. She was sixteen in 1986. Holly's parents attended a regular Wednesday-night card game on the other side of the island. Holly's little sister (what was her name?) went to bed at eight o'clock, and Amy allowed Holly to stay up and illegally watch *Facts of Life* at nine-thirty, provided she scooted into bed immediately after and feigned sleep when her parents returned from the card game at ten-fifteen. Her parents thought Holly was too young to watch *Facts of Life*, and looking back from the vantage of adulthood Amy realizes that she *was* too young. She feels a little guilty now.

"Look, here's my Riley!" says Holly. A teenage girl—tall, gorgeous, in small shorts and a cropped tank top—is walking toward them, holding a coffee cup in one hand and a cell phone in the other. "Her best friend's mom owns this place so she spends ninety-six percent of her time here," explains Holly. "And most of her money."

"I got this one on the house," says Riley.

Holly links her arm through her daughter's and says, "Honey, this is Amy Fleming! She used to be my babysitter! One hundred years ago!"

"Hi," Riley's disinterested eyes flick over Amy, and she grants her mother a half smile and says, "Can we go? I'm supposed to meet Jacob."

No *nice to meet you*. Amy's teacher radar senses trouble. She can always pick them out: something hooded in the glance, the dangerous combination of insecurity and overconfidence, the merger of discomfort in the new body with knowledge of what it's capable of. It's always something the moms can't see. Poor Holly.

"Trevino," she tells Holly. "My married name is Trevino. I'm not a Fleming any longer."

Riley perks up immediately. "Trevino? As in Sam Trevino?"

Amy nods. "Yup. She's my daughter." She thinks, Here we go. If people here know Sam, people with no ties to Narragansett, does everyone know Sam?

Riley turns to her mother and says excitedly, "Maggie told me Sam Trevino is here!" Her face lights up like a Christmas tree, and she suddenly looks younger, and more vulnerable, and sweeter. In fact, she reminds Amy of little Holly Lewis laughing at the TV, a bowl of popcorn on her lap. "Sam Trevino. From TikTok. She got like really famous. Then she left TikTok, and everybody was like, where did she go? But she's here! She's here on this island!"

"She's here," confirms Amy. Her stomach clenches in that familiar worried way it does when she thinks about Sam and New York. Every time Amy successfully forgets about Sam's fame—every time Sam becomes simply Amy's daughter again, not a TikTok star—something pops back up to remind her. Would it have been this way had Sam led a private life after *Mockingbird*, after the Disney Channel? Will it be this way for Sam if Sam ever goes to college? Maybe, but famous people go to college all the time. Look at Natalie Portman. Look at the Obama daughters.

Riley glances at her phone and says, "I'm going to go now, okay, Mom?" To Amy she says, "It was really nice to meet you." So she does have manners, thinks Amy. She takes them out when she needs them. "Please tell Sam . . ." She takes a deep breath and blinks rapidly. "Never mind. I just hope I get to meet her sometime."

"I hope so too," says Amy, though she's not sure she does.

"Bye, Mom."

"Bye, sweetie." Then, "Get your drink," Holly tells Amy. "We can sit for a minute, if you have time."

Amy looks at her watch. "I have a little bit of time. I have to be at the theater soon. I've got a to-do list a mile long." She orders a mocha, with whipped cream, thank you very much, and joins Holly at one of the small tables.

"That's what I wanted to talk to you about," Holly says. "The play. I'm a Realtor now!" She pulls a business card out of her bag and pushes it across the table toward Amy. The card names a realty agency in town, and in the corner is a photo of Holly, looking serious and businesslike in a white blouse. "I worked for the Chamber of Commerce forever, but I thought I was ready for the next step in my life's journey, so I got my license last year. The market is exploding. You know, I handled the housing for some of the cast."

More like *mishandled,* Amy silently corrects her, thinking of Gertie shacking up with Timothy and Sam because her housing fell through, but of course she doesn't say that. Instead she says, "That's great. I wish I knew about you the other day; I was trying to find a barn to rent for rehearsals. It's all sorted out now though."

"Did you go through Joanne? I bet you went through Joanne."

Amy nods. "I did, I went through Joanne."

Holly sighs. "Everyone calls Joanne first." She shrugs as if to shake off that reality. "That's okay though. It is what it is. Joanne's been doing it longer. Is there anything else you need? Local people for jobs? I don't know the first thing about how a play works. But I do know pretty much everyone on this island, due to my former capacity with the chamber, and, of course, my present work in the real estate market." Amy has to keep herself from laughing at the realization that little Holly Lewis, who once laughed so hard at something Tootie said on the *Facts of Life* that soda shot out of her nose, is now using phrases like *my former capacity with the chamber.* (In 1986 soda was an acceptable evening beverage for a nine-year-old: oh, those were different times indeed!)

Is there anything else she needs? There's a *lot* she needs. An electrician and a plumber to look over the theater. A curtain builder! (Is that a thing?) Potentially an exterminator. Someone to print the programs, and, later, ushers to distribute them and seat the audience members. But the most important thing, of course, is to make sure that there are audience members to seat, and even with a name like Gertie Sanger that's not a guarantee. It's hard to get people's attention these days. "I don't suppose you're hiding an experienced Broadway publicist in one of your properties," she says. "That's a stretch, I bet, right?"

"Hmm," says Holly. "Broadway publicist . . . huh, yeah, that might be a stretch—" She taps her nails on the table and looks to the ceiling, closing her eyes and granting Amy a good view of the stunning eyelashes. Then she opens her eyes and snaps her fingers. "But wait. Hold on. Does it have to be a *theater* publicist?"

"Well. I mean. We are putting on a play, so . . . preferably, yes."

"I think you should meet this woman I found a summer rental for on Corn Neck Road. Her name is Shelly Salazar. She definitely came from New York. And yes, she *was* a publicist, for books. The reason I know that is because she kept dropping names of authors I'd never heard of, because I don't read." She says this proudly, in the way that English teachers, and, Amy guesses, book publicists, don't care for. "I'm so busy, you know," Holly adds, indicating her realty card. We're all busy, thinks Amy. "The only name she dropped that I knew was Anthony Puckett, because he lives with my best friend, Joy, who owns this place! Since he's known Joy he's literally been working on the same unfinished book about his dad, while Joy runs herself ragged *here*." She rolls her eyes in solidarity with the unseen Joy, and Amy appreciates this. Score one for the Sisterhood. "But my point is, I bet she's worth meeting. Maybe she knows someone."

"Can you send me her info?" asks Amy. She pulls out her phone and she and little Holly Lewis exchange numbers, then

Holly shares the contact with her. It arrives on Amy's phone's screen with a satisfying zing.

"She's definitely a big fish on a small island," says Holly. "You'll know what I mean, if you meet her."

Amy leaves Shelly Salazar a voice mail right away, and by noon she's received a call back. At three o'clock they meet, at Shelly's request, for a drink at Poor People's Pub. Shelly is there first, and there's no mistaking who she is: among the sunburned tourists and the families eating a late lunch or early dinner before the ferry back to the mainland, she is wearing a spaghetti strap dress that Amy is sure comes from a designer she herself is not aware of, unless they sell it at the T.J. Maxx in North Kingston. Shelly's face is fully made-up, her nails are painted, her hair is long and blown-out, with a subtle blue streak in the back. Big fish, small island is right, thinks Amy. All this, for Poor People's Pub. What does this woman look like when she goes out in the evening in New York City?

Shelly orders a tequila on the rocks with soda water and a lime, then looks at Amy expectantly. Oh, what the hell, thinks Amy. She's getting on the ferry after this. She'll have plenty of time to sober up before driving home. She orders the same.

When they have their drinks Amy goes over her conversation with Holly, her need for a publicist for the play, the duties the job would require. She asks about Shelly's background.

"Oh, I know lots of people," says Shelly. "Lots. I worked in books, yes, but I dated this older man who donated a lot of money to the Public." Shelly's face grows sober. "I went through the biggest heartbreak of my life because of that man this past winter," she says. "I thought I was in it for the sex and the dinners out at the expensive restaurants, but when he left me it turned out I was in it for him."

"I'm sorry," says Amy.

"He started dating a twenty-three-year-old," says Shelly.

"Ew."

"Right?" Shelly smiles appreciatively. "He was addicted to younger women. And I was addicted to him. And then I turned thirty . . ." The sentence trails off briefly and then Shelly's eyes flick to Amy's, and she says, "Well. Anyway. I had made really good money as a publicist. My dad helped me figure out how to go out on my own when I was twenty-four, and I did well. I worked really hard. I saved a lot. The man I was with always picked up the check, and maybe that's not very feminist or enlightened of me, but it was fiscally fortunate. So I put a blue streak in my hair and I decided to take the summer off."

"Sounds lovely," says Amy.

"It was," says Shelly. "I mean, it *is*. Obviously. It's beautiful and relaxing. But I'm *so* bored. I'm. So. Bored. I've been working since I was fourteen years old. My first job was bagging groceries at Roundy's in Wisconsin. This is the longest I've gone without working or going to school—or both—since then. Please give me something to do, Amy Trevino." She puts her hands flat on the bar of Poor People's Pub and casts a pleading look in Amy's direction. "I signed a lease through Labor Day, and I'm subletting my apartment in New York so I can't go back. I've been over this island with a fine-tooth comb, and there's nothing else for me to do here. Please. *Please*."

"It does sound like you have the right kind of connections—" Amy begins.

"I'll do it," says Shelly. "I need a couple of days to get myself together, and I could start . . . next Tuesday?" She offers her hand, and Amy shakes, and it's only after she's back on the ferry that she realizes she never officially offered Shelly the job before Shelly accepted it. But you know what? It's one more thing off the list.

Timothy

THE FIRST OFFICIAL production meeting takes place in the barn that Amy has procured on the last Wednesday in June. When Timothy gets there Amy is taking a Shop-Vac to the far corners, dragging around behind her an industrial-size black trash bag into which she is depositing random pieces of trash too big for the Shop-Vac to inhale.

"I like what you've done with the place," says Timothy, when she turns off the Shop-Vac. Amy snorts. She winds up the cord and sits at a small card table with three folding chairs around it.

"We're going to need something bigger than this for the read-through," says Timothy, indicating the table.

"It's on the list," Amy tells him. "I'm on it."

There's a comical dark smudge along the side of Amy's face, and with her hair tied back she looks a little like Lucille Ball in the "Men are Messy" episode. Timothy weighs his options and decides Amy will be more irked if he mentions the smudge than if he doesn't. If she notices it later in the mirror, he won't be there.

"And what are we doing about bathrooms?"

"Bathroom trailer coming tomorrow," says Amy.

"Wow! You really have thought of everything."

"That's my job," says Amy. (Does she say this shortly? He can't tell. This might just be how she talks after years and years of wrangling high school students.)

"I didn't expect you to do the actual hands-on cleaning yourself."

"Didn't you?" (Is Amy in a mood?)

"You could have hired someone."

"Who am I going to hire, Timothy? A barn cleaner? I don't know how to find a barn cleaner on an island! Easier to do it myself. Make sure it gets done right." (Yup. Mood. Amy must never, ever find out that Timothy is paying her salary out of his own pocket.)

Just then a woman pokes her head through the door and says, "Am I in the right place?" She sees Timothy and says, "Ah! I see that I am. Jane Wyndham."

"Jane Wyndham, our illustrious stage manager!"

"Obviously you're Timothy. I'd know that face anywhere." Timothy does his modest chuckle, the one he reserves for people in the business, which is different from the chuckle for civilians. Jane Wyndham looks *very* New York–stagey—not very islandy at all. Brisk and no-nonsense. She's got short, jet-black hair, lots of earrings up and down each ear, dark lipstick. Black clothing. She's, what? Maybe forty? She could be a year or two older or younger.

"Indeed I am," says Timothy. "And this is my sister-slash–production manager, Amy Trevino, and you've found our rehearsal barn."

"It was hell getting an Uber," says Jane, and Timothy sees Amy roll her eyes. Amy stands, shakes Jane's hand, and gestures to the table. They all sit.

"Okay," says Amy. "Production meeting number one. I'll take notes." Timothy can practically see Amy thinking that she will try to out-brisk Jane, maybe even out-no-nonsense her.

"First item of business. We need fans in here," says Jane.

"On order," says Amy frostily.

"How many?"

"Three. Three giant ones."

Jane sucks in her lower lip and says, "We might need four."

"They only had three."

"Well, there it is, then," says Jane. She rises from the table. "So, we'll mark out the stage here?"

"I was thinking the opposite direction," says Amy. "Get the width."

They both look at Timothy. He feels like he could step one of two ways: in one direction there is a ditch full of crocodiles and in the other a bucketful of snakes.

"I'll take a look," he says. "When we're done here."

"Okay, next item—" begins Amy.

"When's your hard out for people to be off book?" Jane asks Timothy.

"Aren't we getting ahead of ourselves?" suggests Amy. "We haven't even started rehearsals yet."

"Not at all," says Jane. "These are the things I like to know from the beginning." She shrugs unapologetically. "It's how I work."

Timothy clears his throat. "I'm going to see how the actors respond the first couple of days," he says. "Then I'll let you know."

"That should be fine," says Jane, and Timothy can almost hear Amy saying, *should?*

Jane has the Notes app in her iPhone open and is tapping away on the screen. "Another question. Will the cast be allowed to have a plus-one at opening night?"

"Geez, I don't think we've thought that far ahead," says Timothy. "Have we, Ame?"

"Definitely not."

"Okay, well, let me know. It'll be here before we know it," says Jane. She holds out her hand and says, "Tape?"

"Excuse me?" says Amy.

"Tape. For the floor."

Amy rolls her eyes at Timothy, *hard*, but she has the tape in the bag next to her chair. Of course she does! She's a teacher, and a mom, and a planner. She always has the tape.

"Before we tape up this floor," says Jane, "I wonder if it could be a little cleaner?"

Timothy thinks, *Uh-oh*, and looks at Amy.

"That floor is as clean as it gets," says Amy. "Trust me."

"Trust her," agrees Timothy. Things feel precarious; Amy must never, he reminds himself again, *ever* find out that Timothy is paying her salary.

"Okay," says Jane. "We'll work with what we've got. Honestly, I've seen a lot worse than this for rehearsal space. I think it's going to be great! We're, what, six weeks out from opening?"

"Yup," says Amy. "Six weeks on the nose, but we've got the July Fourth holiday coming up so it's going to be more like five weeks."

Jane claps her hands together. "Great. I love a challenge like this, especially when the talent is there. And I know the talent is there." She leans toward Amy and taps the side of her own face suggestively. "Dirt," she says. "Right there." Amy lifts her hand to her own face, alarmed, and mimics Jane's motions. "A little to the left," says Jane. "That's it. You've got it."

Amy shoots eye daggers at Timothy.

Once Jane has taped the floor, they wrap up the meeting, and Timothy offers to help Amy get the Shop-Vac into the Wagoneer.

"I've got it," she says.

What, he wonders, has he done to make Amy so irritated with him?

July

Timothy

GERTIE COMES UPSTAIRS when Timothy is bent over his script, making notes for the table read the next day. She stands near him for a moment. He can feel her, and he can smell her—that subtle but distinctive perfume—but he's determined not to look up. He's concentrating. Gertie doesn't move; her presence grows and take shape, and finally he lifts his eyes and says, "May I help you?" Then he says, "What are you wearing, Gerts?" She's fully decked out in red, white, and blue. White shorts, pristine white sneakers, red sparkly tank top, and, on her head, a blue cowboy hat. "Are you going to a rodeo?"

She laughs. "No. Fourth of July parade. I came to invite you."

"To a parade? No, thank you."

"Come on, Timothy! Doesn't it sound so old-fashioned and small town and *American*? I love it. People in L.A. are too cool for parades. Sam's coming too, if that helps."

"It doesn't. I need to work."

"Timothy! Don't be a party pooper. It's a holiday."

He puts down his script and his notes, takes off his reading glasses and regards Gertie. "Did you forget, maybe, that I grew up here? I've seen all the Fourth of July parades I need to see, thank you very much."

"But there might be a fife and a drum!"

"I have no doubt there will be."

"Or we can go to Ballard's," she says. "I heard Ballard's is the place to be on the Fourth."

He howls with laughter at that. "Ballard's on the Fourth of July is like spring break in Daytona on *steroids*, Gertie. Trust me, that's not the scene for you. You would get mobbed. Literally."

She sits next to him on the couch, a little too close. "Wait a second. I see what's happening here. You're nervous about the beginning of rehearsals!"

"No, I'm not," he says immediately.

She's almost gleeful. "I can't believe it. Timothy Fleming is nervous. I didn't think you *got* nervous."

"Of course I get nervous. Especially when I'm directing. Don't you get nervous?"

"Certainly. Terrified, every single time I have to do anything, step on a new set, meet a new acting partner, *anything*. Most people do. But I thought you were immune." She smells very, very good. He tries to inch away but accidentally inches closer.

"Well, Gertrude, I guess I'm not immune."

"*Don't* call me Gertrude. Don't you dare." She punches him lightly on the arm. He doesn't want to admit it, but she looks darn good in the cowboy hat.

"Gertrude," he says again, releasing a smile.

After a bunch of seconds, during which Gertie appears to be deciding how to react, she smiles back. "One of my Juilliard professors used to quote Jack Lemmon: 'The day you stop being nervous is the day you should leave the business.'"

"Hmm," he says noncommittally. It always irks him just a little when Gertie references her Juilliard years. It reminds him of the wide gulf that exists between her résumé and his, of the fact that she is classically trained while he's always made it up as he goes along.

After high school Timothy attended the University of Rhode

Island for a year, rooming in Fayerweather with a kid from Warwick named Alan, wearing his hair long, smoking too much. He
studied for that one year in the theater department under the
illustrious James Flannery, landing the part of Emil in Mamet's
The Duck Variations. Unheard-of for a freshman! One of the two
leads. Flannery took a lot of heat for that. Timothy took a lot of
heat too—so much heat that he knew a role like that wasn't going
to come his way again until at least junior year. By then he'd be
twenty, practically over the hill. So before the first boats of the
season appeared in Great Salt Pond that May, he'd made his decision. No more hierarchy bullshit. No more waiting. No more college. He was taking the twelve hundred dollars he'd saved from
his various bellhop gigs, he was buying an old Datsun from a guy
in Pawtucket, and he was heading west to seek his fortune. Or at
least to find an agent.

He found Barry! Back then Barry the Bastard was Barry the
New Kid on the Block, cutting his hyper-ambitious teeth on the
marrow bone that was Hollywood in the early eighties, signing
everyone he thought might have a shot, releasing them once it
became clear that they didn't. Barry was only four years older than
Timothy, but the difference felt like a decade or more. He was so
polished—so sure of himself. He had so many pairs of loafers.

"I'll work hard for you, sir," Timothy heard himself saying, the
day they made their partnership official.

"Christ on a hamburger bun," said Barry. "Don't call me *sir.*
We're pretty much the same age." He consulted his notes. "You're
going out tomorrow on an audition for a commercial for cold
tablets. I'll have Shirley write down the address for you. Be there
at ten-thirty."

"Cold tablets?"

"Don't screw it up, kid. I'm taking a chance on you."

Why, Timothy wondered, did Barry balk at Timothy's use of *sir*
and yet felt no compunction about calling Timothy *kid*? Timothy

didn't point out this inconsistency; he simply said, "I won't screw it up."

And he hadn't. He booked the commercial. Then he booked two more commercials, a walk-on part in a long-forgotten TV pilot, never picked up, and then the career-making role in *The Devil in Here,* where he mixed (so the papers told him) Pacino's bravado with Christopher Reeve's approachability and the resonance of a young Donald Sutherland. Eighteen months later, Timothy Fleming was a star.

By the time Gertie Sanger was taking her Scene Study 1 class at Juilliard, Timothy had amassed a lengthy filmography, done two separate stints on Broadway, and had just taken on his first film directing role, in *Days of Old.* The rest, of course, was history. Is history. He's been very, very lucky. There is no denying the fact of it.

And yet! And yet. After all these years, that long string of credits, the Oscars and the Tony, there's still, when he's around Gertie, a voice that pokes at him, prods at him, says, Pssst. Hey you. You're a fraud. A huckster. Gertie studied from the masters, but you didn't. She's the real deal. You're not.

"Last chance!" says the real deal, rising from the couch. "If you come with me I'll buy you a Popsicle."

"I don't eat Popsicles," he says.

She tips her hat at him and glides away. "Everybody eats Popsicles on the Fourth of July. To say you don't is practically anti-American."

"Haul me up before the committee," he grumbles. But it's too late; she's already gone, and his clever retort is wasted.

Sam

THE HOUSE RULES *are on a whiteboard in the improbably high-ceilinged kitchen. (Tink explains that the owners, art collectors from China, bought the apartment above this one and demolished it so they could have the ceiling space.) Rise by 10 A.M., no matter what. Keep a running list of potential video ideas on the right side of the whiteboard at all times. No drinking Sunday through Wednesday. Content, content, content, all the time. When you're in public, remember who you represent. You represent yourselves, Tink writes on the whiteboard.* <u>But you also represent me. Don't forget it</u>*. She underlines the last two sentences.*

By October they've settled into a rhythm. They rise as close to ten as possible. Breakfast at home. Kylie and Nathan both know how to cook. Hangover cures on Friday, Saturday, and Sunday mornings. Back to business on Monday.

Tink comes in and out, with offers and admonishments and an eagle eye that spots the hot sauce splattered on the lowest part of the wall in the formal dining room.

Scooter gets a brand endorsement from a company that makes skate shoes. He shoots a video at the Pier 62 Skatepark, and at least a hundred people gather to watch. It all goes viral: not just the video but the videos of the video, and probably the videos of the videos of the video. Cece signs on with an eyelash conditioner brand, even though her lashes are naturally perfect. Nathan: an organic flour company. His scones go viral.

They are, as a group, attractive and fun-loving; they look good in their going-out-clubbing clothes, yes, but they also look good in the slouchy Morning After sweats they wear to breakfast or sitting around the living room on the gigantic throw pillows and artfully placed beanbag chairs, discussing the adventures and misadventures of the previous night.

What a relief it is to Sam to just be! After years of schools and bells and classes, after the unconventional but nevertheless tightly scheduled Broadway months, then the shooting of My Three Daughters, *then back home for more school and bells and schedules. Now all Sam has to do is have fun. Or look like she is having fun. Which is mostly the same thing. (Isn't it? Is it?)*

THE DAY AFTER July Fourth it all begins with a meet and greet in the rehearsal barn. The barn is on the market, but Amy has convinced the Realtor that the monthly rent the production can pay, plus the fact of Gertie Sanger's presence, will add to its cachet. By August, the production will move into the theater, and the for sale sign can go back up. All of this was reported to Sam by Uncle Timmy, who told Sam that hiring his sister was the best idea he's had in ages.

Gertie cleared her throat when he said that, and Uncle Timmy said, "Sorry. My mistake. The best idea that *Gertie* has had in ages."

"Nice job, Mom," Sam tells her mother, after she looks around the barn, admiring the taped-off stage area, the industrial-size fans in the corners. She means it, but she also thinks that the more praised and appreciated Amy is feeling, the less likely she is to pull out the college catalogs again.

Her mother grins. "Thank you!" she says, squeezing Sam's arm.

The meet and greet starts at ten o'clock sharp, with breakfast: bagels from Old Post Office Bagel Shop and coffee from Joy Bombs, both collected by Amy. Then comes the first read-through around the long rectangular table. The table was also procured by

Amy, delivered that morning by two guys in a big white truck that said ISLAND CATERING on the side.

After the meet and greet, the equity members of the production vote on the rehearsal schedule; Amy collects the ballots and opens them, marking each result on a sheet of paper. At eleven, the read-through begins. Sam plops down in one of the extra folding chairs, away from the table, next to her mother. Amy has her reading glasses on, and she's making notes in a notebook. The notebook, Sam notices, is wide-ruled, bright pink, spiral-bound—and slightly familiar.

"Mom?" she whispers. "Did you take that from my room?"

Amy looks at her and smiles, matching the level of Sam's voice with her own so that they don't disturb the actors. "I did! It was hardly used. Seemed silly to buy something new."

Sam rolls her eyes. "A notebook would have cost like a dollar fifty from CVS, Mom."

"But I like this one." Amy flips pages in reverse until she gets to the front. "Look. Here's a paragraph you wrote on *Because of Winn-Dixie* in third grade."

"*Mom!* Tear that *out* and throw it away." Sam shakes her head. "Please! Third grade."

"I couldn't bear to tear it out! You should read it. You have some really cogent things to say about the use of the grocery store as a plot device. You'd be a killer English major, Sam."

Sam rolls her eyes again. (She loved that book, though. Opal and her preacher father, the plucky dog, and, yes, the grocery store.) "What are you writing?" she asks, to change the subject.

"A to-do list longer than my arm."

"Let me see." Amy slides the notebook over to Sam and Sam reads: CURTAIN. *Plumber to review bathrooms in theater. Meet with publicist re: early buzz. Online ticketing system. Advertising in Block Island paper? Social media.*

Social media. Sam shudders. She keeps reading. *Bananas, broccoli, chicken.* "Bananas?"

"Yeah. I was making a grocery list at the same time." Amy shrugs. "I should probably start another page for that. Look at Timmy. He looks happy, doesn't he?"

Sam looks at her uncle. He's sitting at the head of the rectangular table, a script in front of him. He's following along with the actors; when the person speaking comes to the end of a page, they all flip the pages in unison, and an audible rustle goes through the barn. From where they sit Amy and Sam can't hear all of the actual words, sometimes just the cadence, but they can read the body language. Gertie, who is sitting to Uncle Timmy's right, is already getting laughs.

"Laughs at the table read!" whispers Sam. "That's how you know you're in the presence of a badass."

"Agreed," Amy whispers back.

Sam moves her chair a little closer so she can hear more clearly. She had thought she might take the jeep out after the breakfast part, and come back for Uncle Timmy later, but now that she's here she's sort of entranced. A cramped rehearsal space in Midtown Manhattan where sometimes you could hear music and tap dancing and singing from adjoining rooms, and an oversize barn on Block Island: these two places are not the same. And yet, and yet. Sam feels a pull of something, and she's transported back to the table read from *Mockingbird*—her uncle at the head of the table, Sam to his left. She'd always been able to memorize things quickly, and she'd committed nearly all of her lines to memory before the table read, but everyone else was holding their scripts so she pretended to need hers as well. Plus holding the script gave her hands something to do, so they wouldn't shake. She remembers how nervous she was—really terrified. Uncle Timmy took her aside before they began and said, *Sammy. You got this part for a reason. Because you're the right person for it. The only person doubting that right now is you.*

After that, she could do it.

"What are you thinking about?" her mom whispers. "You have a funny look on your face."

Sam bristles. "Nothing," she says.

"Oh. I thought maybe you were thinking about *Mockingbird*."

Is nothing private? thinks Sam. Are my thoughts not even my own?

The table read goes on, all five acts, faster than you would think, and at the end Benedick delivers the final lines: "Think not on him till tomorrow: I'll devise thee brave punishments for him. Strike up, pipers!"

Everyone claps.

There's something about the actor who plays Benedick that reminds Sam of Tucker. It's not specifically his looks, the way it was with the guy outside the coffee shop, but rather something in the way he tilts his head when he smiles. It's annoyingly charming. Ugh, thinks Sam. Am I going to see an echo of Tucker everywhere I go?

"Well done, everyone," says Uncle Timmy. "I think we're off to a fantastic start."

Sam's ready to go, but her uncle is deep in conversation with Gertie now, and the stage manager is hovering, clearly waiting her turn to talk to him. Sam finds her mom and asks, "Can I get a ride back to the house?"

"Hmm . . . ?" says Amy distractedly, looking up from Sam's third-grade notebook. "Sorry, sweetie, I'm heading to the theater. I've got to stop in with a question for the set builders, and I may be a while. But I can get you that far? And you could walk the rest."

"Walk?" Sam is aghast. "That's like five miles, Mom. I'm wearing platforms." She indicates her Havaianas.

"Oh, Sam. There's no way it's five miles. This whole island has a circumference of seven miles. It's probably two at the most."

Sam thinks about it. "It's got to be closer to four." She waits, but her mother has gone back to her writing. After a time she says, "I feel abandoned."

Amy peers at Sam over her readers. "Sorry, honey. Tell your therapist about it one day."

"*Mom!* You can't poke fun at mental illness! You'll get canceled."

"I'm not saying you have to be mentally ill to see a therapist. Everyone could benefit from a therapist."

"Now you're definitely going to get canceled. You're talking like it's okay to need therapy as long as you're not actually mentally ill."

"Sam. I'm not saying that." (She knows that of course her mother isn't saying that, but she wants to keep her mother's attention on her. She wants to say, *See how easily things get twisted around? Don't you see?*) "Besides," continues Amy, "I think I'm too old to get canceled."

Sam chews on a fingernail. "News flash, Mom. You're never too old to get canceled. Uncle Timmy could get canceled if he did the wrong thing, and he's like a hundred."

Amy is no longer even half listening. She's already on to the next thing on her list, her readers now pushed up on top of her head. The two guys from Island Catering have returned, and just like that the table is gone. The stage manager has given up waiting for Timothy and is making adjustments to the tape on the floor. Timothy is saying something to Gertie that she's scribbling in the margins of her script.

"You'll have to wait for your uncle," Amy says finally, glancing quickly at Sam. "I've got six hundred things on my list."

"Okay," Sam says. "I'll wait in the jeep." She sighs, feeling forsaken as she leaves the barn and slides into the jeep's passenger seat.

Once when she was living in Xanadu she'd walked, by herself, the thirty blocks and two avenues to the theater where *Mockingbird* had played. There was something else playing, obviously, a new play by a playwright she didn't know. It was just the time when the matinees were letting out, and there was a small hopeful clump of people by the stage door, waiting for it to open. She'd almost pushed herself right into the center of the clump and asked, *Who are you waiting for? What did you love about them?*

Tell me, she'd wanted to say to these people. *Tell me—tell everything.*

But her phone was buzzing, and Tink had called a house meeting she had to get back for, and there was content, content, content. She never found out who they were waiting for, or why.

Sam slips off her flip-flops and puts her feet on the jeep's dash, examining a freckle on her left knee. If it's not regret, what is she feeling after the read-through? Amelia Rees is going to make a fabulous Hero—better than Sam would have been. She doesn't regret not reading for the part. She didn't want the part! She pokes around at the sensation to see if she can identify it; she hadn't quite been able to earlier. She watches the actors filter out of the barn, blinking into the sun. The last person to emerge is her uncle, who waves and smiles at her as he starts toward the driver's seat, looking genuinely happy to see his niece.

She's got it—yes. She's identified the feeling. It's a tug of nostalgia, like a tiny pain.

Amy

THE FRIDAY OF the first week of rehearsals, Amy stands at the back of the rehearsal barn, watching the actors do their thing. They are rehearsing act 2, scene 2, where Don John and Borachio hatch their villainous plot. Timothy is sitting in a folding chair in front of the makeshift stage, reading glasses on, pen in hand, notebook on lap. Amy can tell from the particular angle of his chin that he's concentrating very hard. She rarely (never) gets to see Timothy like this—immersed in his work, no pretense or preening or pride, no audience. He's just a guy doing something he's good at, sitting among a bunch of people who are also good at what they do, and they're saying the words of a long-dead man that are somehow mostly still timeless and meaningful.

Next to Amy appears Marta, the once-a-week intern. Amy jumps. Marta is stealthy. She's holding a stack of envelopes, and she fans them toward Amy. Amy is grateful for the little bit of breeze the envelopes provide; it's hot in the barn; the giant fans are working as hard as they can but they simply can't keep up. (Jane, the stage manager, was right: they could have done with one more. Amy isn't going to come right out and admit it, not out loud, but she has an additional fan on order.)

"Paychecks," says Marta. Marta is one of Amy's former students at the high school, recently graduated, off to Trinity College in Hartford in the fall to study anthropology with a minor in theater.

"Ooooh. You got one in there for me?" Timothy had given Amy her first paycheck because rehearsals hadn't yet started. Amy and Jane have been on payroll longer than the actors, since their jobs began in June.

"Let me look, Ms. Trevino."

"You can call me Amy, Marta. You graduated! You're not my student any longer."

Marta looks at her severely. "I could never do that," she says. "You'll always be Ms. Trevino to me." She flips through the envelopes, frowning, then flips through again. "Hmm," she says. "I don't see one for you. That's funny. Do you want me to check with someone?"

"I'll do it," Amy says. "I'll check with Timothy. Probably an oversight."

"How's Sam doing?" asks Marta. "I heard she's back from New York, but I haven't seen her."

"Fine," says Amy. "Good! She's good." She looks carefully at Marta. What does Marta know?

"Huh," says Marta. "Okay. That's great to hear."

Amy thinks about probing a little, but she doesn't want Marta to know she doesn't know what Marta clearly does. She waits until Timothy finishes talking to Don John and Borachio, then stands next to him until he notices her.

"Hello!" Timothy removes his reading glasses, folds the arms, and slips the glasses inside his shirt pocket. Without them he looks younger and hipper, more celebrity than professor, although truthfully he's at the stage of life when he could easily go either way. "Need me for something?"

"I didn't get a check," she says. "Marta's passing them out now."

"I see," says Timothy. He looks startled, like Amy has caught him with his hand in the cookie jar, his shot glass near the rum bottle. "I'll have to check with Alexa."

That doesn't make sense. "Why would you check with Alexa? She's in L.A., right?"

"Amy," Timothy begins.

"Yeeeeees?" She draws the word out, because Timothy's expression is grave, like he's a doctor about to deliver a diagnosis, and, honestly, she's a little nervous.

"Never mind."

"Never mind what? Why are you acting like a weirdo?"

"I'm just going to come right out with it." But then he doesn't.

"*What?*" She's starting to get irritated.

"I'm paying you, Amy. The production isn't. Your paycheck is late because Alexa needs to send it from my account in California, and there was a delay with the processing. I wasn't going to tell you, I swore to myself many times that I wouldn't, but I changed my mind. I don't want it to become a thing."

It takes Amy a few seconds to catch up. This is the terminal diagnosis? "*You're* paying me? For this job? Out of your own pocket?"

"Well, out of my own bank account, I guess it's not technically a pock—"

She cuts him off. "But *why?*"

"Because Blake budgeted a specific amount of money for the production, and there was no salary for a production manager, only a stage manager. Gertie determined pretty quickly that we needed a PM, and I agreed. So, here you are."

She squints at him. "Why did you think I'd care if *you* were paying me, versus Blake?"

Timothy knits his eyebrows together. "Because I thought if you knew you would think it was a charity job."

"Hmm." She considers this. "Well, *is* it a charity job?"

"No! Of course not. But I'm paying you more than this job would normally pay—"

Aha! She'd thought the salary was generous, but she'd never worked for a summer theater, so she didn't know for sure. "So it *is* a charity job."

"*No!* Of course not. It's a job. That I happen to be paying you for. Paying you well."

She tries to take all of this in. When she really thinks about it, when she spells it out in her mind, should she be bothered, or should she be grateful? Their collective relationship with money— hers and Timothy's—and their relationship to each other's money, or lack of, has always been complicated. When their mother was sick and Amy took on the lion's share of the care, Timothy offered to compensate her. She refused—it felt weird, and wrong, to profit from their mother's suffering—but to be honest, it *was* a lot of work, and she and Greg could have used the money, and there were times when Amy was mad at herself for refusing.

Then there were the Christmas gifts he used to send: lavish to the point of being ridiculous. Once, a three-thousand-dollar set of kitchen knives. They had a perfectly good set of mid-range Wüsthofs they'd gotten when they were married! Another time, an Hermès blanket. She'd made the mistake of telling Greg she'd googled the blanket: it was $700. Greg, who was low-key about so many things, was livid about the blanket.

"Timothy," Amy said when they spoke after the holiday. "What in the world do you think I'm going to do with a seven-hundred-dollar blanket?"

"Sleep under it?" he suggested.

She snorted. "No. I'm going to fold it up and be too scared to touch it, that's what I'm going to do with it. Why'd you give me this?"

He admitted that his assistant had picked it out, and he didn't know the price—he didn't, in fact, know if $700 was a lot for a blanket.

"Seriously?" Amy had been incredulous. "Did we not grow up

in the same household? Do you actually not know that seven hundred dollars is a lot for a blanket?"

They'd agreed, after that, not to exchange gifts. He could give something to the kids, if he wanted, but that was it.

"Oh, *phew.*" Now, in the barn, Timothy actually wipes his brow. "I was so worried about this. I'm glad it's out in the open. Are we good?"

Still, something is gnawing at her. "Logically, we should be good. It shouldn't upset me, like I said. But on the other hand, it feels a little smarmy."

"So we're *not* good?"

"Well. What upsets me is that you lied about it."

Timothy frowns. "I didn't lie about it."

"But you did. You didn't tell me when you hired me. It was a lie of omission. And now that I think about it, I feel sort of dumb, like I wasn't really qualified for the job. Like you're just funneling money to me because you feel bad for us." Embarrassingly, her voice cracks at the end of this unanticipated monologue. *Is* she qualified for the job? Maybe not! Maybe once Timothy realized how close he'd be living this summer to Amy, he figured out a way to assuage his guilt for everything that had happened with Rose, and that's the only reason she's here.

"Oh, geez, Amy. If I was looking to funnel money to you I'd, I don't know, pay Henry's Middlebury tuition! If Greg would ever allow it. Which he wouldn't."

Amy concedes that Timothy is right there. Greg is way too proud to accept something like that, although, truth be told, tuition for private four-year colleges is practically criminal, and paying it probably wouldn't make even a tiny dent in Timothy's financial situation.

"Amy." Timothy stands and puts a hand on her shoulder, and she thinks about shrugging it off, but in the end she lets it stay. "I hired you because I need you, and because you're qualified, and because you are kicking ass at this job. Okay? Don't think about the money."

"Okay," she says. "It's all good." (Amy *hates* when people say something is "all good." Why did she just do it?) "I mean, thank you. Thank you for hiring me." Now she feels like she's groveling. Is she groveling?

"You're welcome. I'm happy to have you. I need you. I think this is nothing we need to speak of again. Your paycheck will be here Monday, and we'll be back on track after that."

"Thank you," she says again, more formally this time. It's fine, but it's also not fine. She's all mixed up inside. TGIF, she thinks. She needs to hop that ferry and get off this island, away from her brother for a few days, and back home to Greg, where she belongs.

Timothy

AT FLOYD'S HOUSE Timothy sleeps with the bedroom windows open, allowing in the sea breeze and the gentle hooting of a barn owl that seems to live nearby.

Today, when he wakes, he stretches and cracks his neck, once on each side. And if he doesn't exactly spring out of bed, at least he puts his feet down rather lightly on the area rug. He bends forward at the waist to come as close to touching his toes as is possible, then stretches his arms above his head in what he learned is part of a "sun salutation" sequence. He learned that in his first and last yoga class, lured there by a woman he'd dated the previous fall. He hated most of it—pigeon pose, cow face pose, even warrior were all beyond his interest or capabilities (and *everyone* can do warrior, the woman he was dating told him)—but the beginning of sun salutation has become part of his daily routine, even if he does it out of order and not very well. He likes the name.

The doors to both Sam's and Gertie's bedrooms are closed. Not a surprise. Sam sleeps like a teenager, Gertie like a nighthawk. Timothy's propensity for the early morning hours had often been a bone of contention between him and Gertie when they were married: he was always yawning by 10 P.M., right when Gertie was getting her second wind. He'd had to adjust for the theater world—secretly he loved Mondays, when the theaters were dark and he could slip into bed early—but since he's been back in Hollywood and on his own he's returned to his natural rhythms. Who cares if people notice his early departures from parties and premieres? He's a single man now, beholden to no one. He can sleep and wake as he pleases.

When he went to bed last night Gertie and Sam were hanging out in the living room, so he stuck in his earplugs. It wasn't any noise, however, but the memory of the conversation with Amy that kept him awake; his mind insisted on turning it over and over, looking for the holes or the weak spots. Finally he fell into a deep slumber—Amy said everything was fine, and he needed to trust her. When he slept, he slept like a baby, like a rock—like a baby rock!

Now he considers his morning. Coffee on the deck, overlooking the water: yes, please. If anyone had ever suggested in high school that Floyd Barringer would own a *high-quality espresso machine* they'd have been laughed right off the island. Of course hardly anyone at all drank espresso in the late 1970s. What a long way civilization has come—and at the same time, he supposes, what a long way it's fallen. (Just look, he thinks, at TikTok.)

Timothy feels so good that maybe he'll even take the steps down to the beach and put his toes in the sand or in the water. Maybe he'll dunk his whole body in the ocean! He dresses in swim trunks, just in case. Supposedly there are health benefits to a cold-water dunk once a day. Friends in Los Angeles have begun adding cold-plunge tubs to the ever-growing list of improvements for body, mind, and soul that money can buy. Infrared saunas. Powdered collagen. Heavy weights lifted and lowered for a mere three seconds every day. Kimchi.

After he's dunked, or not dunked, he'll look over his rehearsal notes, read through act 2 once again, and touch base with Alexa to see if there's anything going on in L.A. He'd like an update on the koi, for one thing, maybe even a short video of them.

He has a full day ahead of him, a productive day, just the way he likes it. He can't believe how *alive* he feels, with a good night of sleep and a robust to-do list. He practically jogs up the stairs to the main level of the house to warm up the espresso machine. Like a sleepy teen, the machine requires some time to prepare for the day.

At the top of the steps he pauses.

Things up here look a little—*different* from how they looked when he repaired to his room the night before. The neatly folded blankets on the couch are strewn about the room. One has a half-full teacup resting on it. Spilling hazard! Two of Gertie's scarves—no, wait, *three* of them—are hanging from the lamp-shade. (Fire hazard.) The television sound is off, but the picture is on. (Environmental hazard.) A bottle of rum and two shot glasses sit on the coffee table—*directly* on the coffee table, no coasters. (The rum is not, Timothy is relieved to see, the thousand-dollar-plus bottle from Blake, but it is a Black Tot Master Blender's Reserve—not exactly Captain Morgan.) In the kitchen he finds a hairbrush, two hair clips, another of Gertie's scarves, a cell phone charger plugged in but with the cord dangling onto the floor (tripping haz-ard), an uncapped Sharpie, a piece of celery with a bite taken out (*what?*), and two bowls with something (olive oil? butter?) pooling in the bottom. The garbage, which Timothy emptied three days ago, is overflowing. Four beer cans are sitting on the counter, as though they are expected to saunter into the recycling bin of their own free will.

Timothy begins to fume. He takes a break to make his coffee, foaming the milk perfectly and topping it with a shake of cin-namon. Then he sits on the deck, watching the day breaking all around him—the owls have been replaced with chirping sparrows, the moon with a vigorously rising sun. When Gertie emerges ninety minutes later, he's back in the kitchen, fuming resumed.

"I can't wake up today," says Gertie, yawning. She opens the refrigerator and stares into its depths for an inordinate amount of time (he has forgotten this habit of hers—a food spoiling hazard!) before turning and seeing Timothy's expression. "What's going on? Is something the matter?"

Opening his mouth just enough to let the word out, Timothy says, "Yes."

"Well, what? For heaven's sake, it's a beautiful morning in a beautiful place. What could possibly be the matter?"

Timothy emits a puff of air. "You two are the matter!"

"What two?"

"You and Sam! Your stuff is everywhere. You know I can't live with clutter!"

Gertie glances around. "Timothy. This isn't clutter. If you want to see clutter, look in Sam's bedroom. No, on second thought, *don't* look in Sam's bedroom. Definitely do not."

The last shred of peace from his wake-up, from his coffee, from his time on the deck dissolves. Timothy makes a noise between argh and pfffft. "I've been living like a bachelor for years."

"Trust me, I know," says Gertie.

"And suddenly I'm surrounded by females! With your—scarves, and your perfumes and your hair accessories—"

Gertie rolls her eyes. "You're hardly *surrounded,* darling. It's only two of us."

"I feel surrounded. How many scarves did you bring?"

"I don't know! Some of them? Most of them?" She shrugs. "You know I like to throw a scarf on over most outfits. It's my thing. I like to have one at the ready."

Just then Sam comes up, also yawning prettily. She's wearing a pajama set made up of shorts and a buttoned-up short-sleeve top, and her hair is artfully mussed. Without makeup she looks five years younger than she typically looks. She looks, in fact, like an advertisement for wholesome young adulthood, a look that belies the shot glasses and the bottle of Black Tot. "Morning, everyone. What's going on?"

"Morning, sweetie," says Gertie. "Your uncle was just lecturing me on the evils of my scarf habit."

"I wasn't—" says Timothy, and at the same time Sam says, "I *love* your scarves, Gertie. They're your thing!"

Timothy grabs a beach towel from the stack in the basket by the deck. He takes the outdoor steps down to the ground level fast, and he imagines that Gertie and Sam are watching his retreating back make its irritated way across the wide swath of emerald grass. He marches past the vegetation—scrub brush, arrowwood, goldenrod, and multiflora rose—that separates the yard from the steps that lead to the water, and he marches down the stairs. He peels off the T-shirt he slept in, drops it in a small mound near his towel, and wades into the water, which, even in July, on this side of the island, is bracing.

No matter. Better, even.

There's a rock a good distance out and he points his body toward it and swims. As he swims he becomes not Timothy Fleming of Benedict Canyon, of Hollywood and Broadway, but Timmy Fleming of a small ranch house in the center of Block Island, fifteen again, sixteen, everything ahead of him, nothing behind, swimming for the pure joy of it, in a body that never seems to tire.

Out to the rock, then back again, and by now his chest is heaving; his arms and legs are quivering; his core, that forgotten, crucial component, softened by middle age, has awoken in a new and vital way. He lies on his towel for a good long time, letting the air dry him, the emerging sun warm him, letting his memories and his imagination feed him—remembering, even, the first girl he kissed, on a floating dock in the middle of Great Salt Pond, a girl named Gwen, with strawberry lip gloss and ocean-blue eyes.

There is something after all, he decides, to that cold-water-plunge idea.

The house is quiet when he returns: not a footstep, not a giggle, not a word. Not a scarf, he realizes, stepping stealthily into the kitchen on cat burglar feet. The scarves are gone. The shot glasses are gone. The bottle of Black Tot is closed and has been returned to the liquor cart, taking its place next to Blake's exorbitant offering, which really, Timothy thinks, should have a sign on it that reads DO NOT TOUCH or POISON or even DO YOU HAVE ANY IDEA HOW MUCH EVEN A SIP OF THIS COSTS. The kitchen wastebasket is empty, with a fresh, still-pleated bag inside of it. And in the middle of the kitchen table (which is now wiped clean, as is the espresso machine, as is the farmhouse sink) sits a small rectangular box tied with a chocolate-brown bow, and the words *JOY BOMBS* stamped across it in gold script. He unties the bow and lifts the cover of the box and there he sees a line of the miniature whoopie pies, six of them, each with a different-colored filling. Under the box, a note, written in Sam's sloppy script (she, unlike Gertie, came of age when handwriting mandates had basically disappeared from school curricula):

Sorry about the mess. We will do better.
Love from your two girls.

Women, he thinks, selecting a whoopie pie with vibrant pink frosting (raspberry, if he were to place a wager). First Amy, now these two. They will be the death of me, he thinks. And the life of me too.

Amy

On Monday, refreshed from a weekend at home—on Saturday they'd had their neighbors, Cathy and Bob, over for drinks by the firepit, and on Sunday they'd eaten breakfast at Amy's favorite place, T's—Amy spends her morning on the island but not at the rehearsal barn. Even though, as she said, she's fine, she's *mostly* fine, about the paycheck, she found over the weekend that it irked her more than she'd realized. She doesn't want to deal with an overly solicitous Timothy, or a walking-on-eggshells Timothy, or, really, any Timothy at all. She has plenty of tasks to work on elsewhere.

In the early afternoon, while Amy is using the Wi-Fi at the library on Dodge Street to test the online ticketing system, she gets a call from the set builders. She steps outside to take it. There is a clog in one of the toilets in the men's room, and no plunger to be found. That's not even the worst of it. One of the guys thinks there might be a deeper problem in the pipes that will need to be fixed before the cast moves over to the theater for rehearsals in the beginning of August. *A deeper problem in the pipes* sounds ominous.

"I'll be over in a bit," she tells the set builder.

"Also? One more thing. We've been seeing some mouse droppings backstage. And one of the guys said he thought he heard scampering."

"Scampering?"

"Yeah. Like—mouse scampering."

Deep breath. This is what she's getting (over)paid for.

"Okay," she says. "I've got some things to finish up here, but I'll get over there by the late afternoon."

You are kicking ass at this job, Amy, she tells herself later, as she drives to Island Hardware to buy a plunger and mousetraps, as she pushes open the door to the bathroom, as she holds her breath and approaches the toilet. You are kicking ass.

Twenty minutes later Amy marches out of the theater's bathroom, carrying, in a plastic bag that she also bought at the hardware store, the plunger. There's nowhere to store it in the bathroom so she'll have to find another place. The set builders have left for the day, and the theater is quiet.

She doesn't have any bait for the mousetraps, so she's thinking of driving over to the grocery store or calling Sam to see what they might have in the kitchen on Mohegan Trail. Maybe, if she asks nicely, Sam will bring her some little bits of cheese or smears of peanut butter for the traps. Amy thinks of the poor little mice, intrepidly setting out for new territories, maybe to gather food for the young ones, and—

She can't do it, not yet.

She sits in a second-row seat and looks at the stage, imagining opening night. The set builders have been hard at work, and Leonato's villa is beginning to rise from the floor. Even though Amy knows that outside the theater's door Block Island is bustling with the heat and brio of a summer afternoon, in here it really could be sixteenth-century Messina.

Sometimes, when Sam was in *Mockingbird,* Amy sat in the back of the theater and listened to the director give notes. She'd loved the theater at those times, before the actors went back to their dressing rooms for costumes and makeup and the audience filed in, the building in one way stripped of its magic but in another way even more magical. She'd loved *Sam* extra at those times too, the way she was so riveted by the director, so respectful of the actors and the production.

A shadow falls over her, breaking her out of her trance. It's Timothy.

"Hey," he says. "I wondered if you needed help with that toilet. Jane told me about it."

"How did Jane know?"

"Set builders, I guess."

Amy rolls her eyes, figuring it's probably dim enough in the theater that he won't see that far. "I got it," she said, indicating the plunger. "It was just a clog. I'm sure the great and good Timothy Fleming doesn't really know his way around a toilet plunger. I have to get a plumber in, though. There might be a deeper problem in the pipes."

He winces. "Yeah, I don't really know my way around toilet plungers or pipes."

"I'm guessing at home you have people for this sort of thing."

He lowers himself into the seat next to her. "Well, sure. But you have people too."

She stares at him. "*I* have people?"

"You're married to a plumber!"

"I'm married," Amy says, "to an *HVAC guy*. Not the same." If Timothy feels chastened after this correction, he doesn't show it. He glances at her, then bumps her lightly with his elbow, playfully, the way he used to to get her out of a bad mood when she was, what? Seven, eight. A kid.

She pulls her elbow away.

"Geez, Amy. I thought we were okay about the paycheck thing."

"We are *fine* about the paycheck thing," she says untruthfully.

"So why are you so prickly with me? I'm sorry I got here too late. I would have plunged the toilet. I'm sure I could have figured it out."

The words bubble up inside her, and she thinks, If I say these next words, I can't take them back. "It's fine. It's not like I'm not used to doing the dirty work for both of us."

"Oh, come on. *What* are you talking about, Amy?"

Isn't this, after all, the place she was trying to get to? Well, she's here now: she may as well stay for a while. "Really, Timothy? Think back to the last time you were in this state, and why, and for how long."

He's silent for a moment, and then he says, "Mom?"

"Of course, Mom. What else?"

Timothy sighs, a long, possibly irritated sigh. "Fine," he says. "Is that what this is about? Okay, fine. Let's do this. But I'm not doing it without a drink."

"Fine," she says, like it's a threat.

"Let's go to Ballard's. It's probably happy hour," Timothy says. He rises from his seat and starts up the aisle.

Unhappy hour, thinks Amy. She finds a safe place for the plunger backstage, locks the theater, and follows Timothy out into the late afternoon. She stands for a few seconds, blinking, getting herself accustomed to the sunlight, and when her eyes are adjusted she sees that Timothy has gone on ahead of her. "Typical," she mutters. She crosses the street and heads east on Water Street, walk-jogging until she catches up with him. "Hey," she says. "Wait up." He wears his Red Sox cap pulled low over his eyes, and he slouches a little when he walks. He pauses, and they walk together.

"Outside or in?" he asks her when they get to Ballard's, and she says, "Outside, but only if there's an umbrella." Though it's four-thirty, the sun is still strong, and Amy's skin is fairer than Timothy's.

They take a seat at one of the outdoor tables.

"I'll order at the bar," says Timothy. "You feeling gin-ish, or rum-ish?"

"Neither," says Amy, then, after a moment, "Both or either."

Her heart is beating fast and her fingers feel warm. She's not used to arguing: the prospect of it is making her physically and emotionally uncomfortable. While Timothy is gone she looks around, trying to put her feelings in order, getting the lay of the land. So many bikinis. So many cocktails. So much volleyball. Amy has never been on a Caribbean vacation, but she imagines the vibe is not too far off from this: cabanas in the sand, a tiki bar, a band setting up for live music. Are they really in Rhode Island?

Timothy returns empty-handed and says, "I think we have waitress service here."

"*Server* service," she corrects. "I don't think we say *waitress* anymore."

He rolls his eyes and picks up the menu. "They have lobster thirteen ways! I think they only had one when we were growing up." He turns in his chair and cranes his neck. "Is that a *sushi* bar?"

Clearly Timothy is deflecting the real conversation. Okay. Amy will play along with that for a minute. "Geez. Sushi at Ballard's. Mom would roll over in her grave."

"And then she'd order a California roll." They are both quiet, neither of them mentioning that their mother's body was cremated, so the joke doesn't land. (Amy had arranged for the cremation. Of course. As well as the service and the luncheon after the service.)

Just then a lovely suntanned young woman with an Eastern European accent comes to take their order.

"Two Rum Runners, please," says Timothy. He looks at Amy for approval and she nods. Why the hell not? She has the whole ferry ride to sober up. "With a rum floater," Timothy adds. "What's your best rum?"

"I'm not sure," says the server.

"What's your most expensive rum?"

"I'll have to check. This is only my second day—"

Timothy holds up his hand. "Don't worry about it. Just tell the bartender a floater of the best rum." Amy tries not to let this irritate her, but she can't help it: It does. *Excuse me,* Timothy seems to be saying, *where do I put all of this money I have? Give it to the bartender. Give it to my sister. Give it to the rum lords. Just put it somewhere, because I can't hold it all.*

The drinks arrive quickly, and Amy, searching for a misdirect, nods toward the volleyball courts and says, "I have never understood how people play volleyball in a bikini."

"It is one of the mysteries of the universe," Timothy agrees. "But I don't think that's what you want to talk about."

She flexes her hand, then makes a fist, then releases it. "No, you're right," she says. "It's not."

"So what is it? Like I said, I thought we were okay about the paycheck thing on Friday."

"We were. We are okay about the paycheck thing. But when I was home over the weekend, I don't know, the paycheck thing spurred all these other thoughts that I've been trying to keep down this summer. And they just . . . well, excuse the plumbing imagery, but they bubbled up."

He purses his lips; he doesn't even smile at the plumbing joke. "What kind of thoughts?"

She takes a deep breath. "When Mom had only a month to live, and it was her eightieth birthday, you had Hugh Jackman call her and sing to her. Do you remember that?"

Amy can see by the way he tilts his head, by the way he looks away and blinks rapidly before meeting her eyes, that he's known all along that the Hugh Jackman thing bothered her. "Of course I remember that. This is what's on your mind four years later? Hugh Jackman?"

"What's bothering me," says Amy, "is your not being present at the end of Mom's life. What's bothering me is your leaving it all to me. And, yeah, when I learned you lied to me about the paycheck—"

"I didn't lie!"

"When I learned you *omitted the truth,* and when you show up *after* the toilet is unclogged, offering to help, and when you lure Sam away with a beautiful house, yeah, I guess I'm feeling some resentment."

Timothy takes a long sip of his drink and says, "I was as present for Mom as I was able to be, Amy."

"Getting Hugh Jackman to sing to her *does not count as being present,* Timmy! That's *giving* a present. *Being* present is driving to the appointments and getting the ice chips and changing the sheets when she sweated through them and asking the nurse for more fucking morphine because she couldn't stand the pain. That's being present."

"I lived across the country. I was working!"

"I was working too, Timmy. I've gone to work every single day of every single school year for the past twenty-five years. I think I've missed something like eleven days total over all those years, one of them being Mom's funeral. And don't you dare point out I've had summers off because most of the summers I've worked too."

He takes a long sip of his drink. "You could have hired someone for all of that care for Mom. I would have paid. I told you that at least seventy times. I offered to pay *you,* Amy. I knew how much time that was taking. But you refused!"

"That's not the point! The point wasn't to outsource. The point was to be there, in the flesh. To be there for her."

"I couldn't be there. I was on set."

"You could have left the set."

"Fine," he says. "I'm sorry I asked Hugh Jackman to sing to Mom on her birthday. Is that what you want?"

"*Timmy.* That's not what I'm asking you to apologize for, and you know it."

She watches him take a beat. "Okay. *Okay.* I'm sorry if you had to take on more than your share. But I was *working,* Amy. When I work, an entire film production works with me. Not just actors, but craft services, and set dressers, and wardrobe people and production assistants and a lot of other people too. I'm part of a giant machine. I'm a cog in a wheel, and I have responsibilities to the rest of the wheel. I can't just leave."

The rum is hitting her hard, but his words are hitting her too. "You're doing what you always do. You can't give an honest apology without this context that your shit is more important than everyone else's."

Timothy blinks and raises his eyebrows. "I don't think that's what I do."

"Of course you don't think it. You don't see it. It's your blind spot."

The server comes back, and Timothy says, "Another round, please." When they're alone again he swirls his straw around in what remains of his drink. "Mom *loved* Hugh Jackman. You know she did. It was a big deal for me to ask that, a favor like that, and a big deal for him to do it. I didn't take that lightly."

(Hugh Jackman had sung a part of "I Still Call Australia Home" from *The Boy from Oz*—a cappella—and Rose, who had never set foot in Australia, but who had seen the show on Broadway, had cried like a newborn.)

The server drops off the fresh drinks and asks about food.

"Maybe later," they say together.

"I didn't know how much the Hugh Jackman thing bothered you."

"You probably also don't know that after this I have to vacuum up mouse turds. I went to the hardware store and bought a dozen traps."

"Well, no. How would I know that if you didn't tell me? Call an exterminator. Or ask *me* to call an exterminator. Nobody asked you to buy mousetraps. Your martyr complex is really out of control."

She snaps back immediately, "No more out of control than your savior complex."

Timothy sits back and sips his drink. Amy turns away from her brother, points her face toward the water. He says, "There's no way Hugh Jackman is the biggest thing on your mind."

She folds her arms. "Okay." There's a long pause. "You're right. There's more. You took Sam away from me."

"*I* took her away?" Timothy's eyebrows shoot up toward the underside of the blue umbrella. "She practically showed up on my doorstep, looking for a place to stay! She asked to live on the island for the summer!" He's almost sputtering. "Amy! You know that's how it went down, right? She came home from New York, and she wanted a change. That's why college was invented, so young people and their parents could have a sanctioned break from each other. You didn't want to live at home when you were nineteen either."

She feels her lip tremble. "I'm not talking about only now. I'm talking about way back when. The L.A. year, when she was on *My Three Daughters*. After *Mockingbird*. You took her from me. Greg and I did all the hard stuff, all the early stuff, every diaper change and skinned knee and strep throat test and tear over a mean girl in middle school, but you bring the glamor. So you're the one Sam wants to spend the summer with. I guess it does feel a lot like what happened with Mom."

"Oh, come on now." But maybe he sees something in Amy's face that sends him a signal, because his face softens, and he takes a beat before he goes on. "Ame. Come on. She came back to you when the show ended, just like you asked. I did what you wanted me to. She was only gone a year!"

"She did." Amy tips her head an inch. "But I'll never have that exact year back. That crucial year, when she was becoming a teenager. She's my only daughter, and that was the only year she was exactly that age, and I missed all of it, and I'll never ever get that time back. And, yeah, Timmy, sometimes I blame you for that. I do." Amy shrugs.

"But *she* wanted to come to L.A. She asked to audition for the show. Remember? She begged. You could have said no if you didn't want her to go, you and Greg. Parents' prerogative. You signed all the papers. You booked the flight."

"You lured her there," says Amy. She will not give in on this, because she knows she's right. "With your agent, and your industry insider knowledge, and your . . . your Gertie. Your fancy house. We could have said no, sure. But she would have resented us forever."

"*I* didn't lure her. Maybe Hollywood lured her, but I just gave her a place to stay while she tried to figure out if it was what she wanted. I gave her back to you when you asked. I stuck to the script, just like you wanted me to. Going on location, blah blah, etc. I said everything you wanted me to say!"

"I know you did. But when she came back, she wasn't my little girl any longer." Her voice breaks at the end and she tries to hold it steady.

"Oh, Amy." Now there is real pity in Timothy's eyes, and Amy can't tell if that makes things worse or better. Worse, she decides. "I'm not a parent," he goes on. "But I would guess that every girl changes a lot at that age. She would have changed whether she was with you or not."

Amy shakes her head. "But the change would have been incremental." Sam had gotten her period for the first time that year when she was in Los Angeles, and Amy wasn't there with her. It was Gertie who bought her supplies, Gertie who gave her a heating pad to put on her stomach to vanquish those early cramps. Nobody even told Amy until two days later! "And then I got her back, but I lost her to that bizarre TikTok house, and now I've lost her again, to you and Gertie, *again*, and your nicer house, and the beaches, and—" She gestures to the private beach in front of Ballard's, the chair rentals, the cabanas. "And to all of this. Of course she'd rather be here, with your big life, instead of my small one."

"Your life isn't small."

"Well, *I* know that." (Does she?) "But I don't always think you know that. I don't think Sam knows that."

"'Those that do teach young babes/Do it with gentle means and easy tasks,'" says Timothy. "*Othello.*"

"'It is a wise father that knows his own child,'" retorts Amy. "*Merchant of Venice.*"

"Touché. All I'm saying, Amy, is that everything goes fast. The older you get, the faster it goes. Don't let this summer go to waste. Don't wish Sam back home, don't wish her off to college, don't wish her anywhere but where she is, close enough that you can see her every day if you want to."

"Thank you, Mr. Wisdom," says Amy, but she concedes that he makes a good point, so she smiles when she says it, and she kicks his foot under the table. They're still not finished, though, and she can see Timothy searching for the right thing to say.

"I just don't understand one part of all of this. What do you want from me, Amy? What are you looking for? Do you want me to be *less* generous with my money? I already don't send you Christmas presents, as per your request." (Just *per*, Amy wants to say. Not *as per*. But she doesn't.) "Less generous with my time? Or more generous? Do you want me to be closer to you, or do you want me to leave you alone? What do you want?"

What *does* she want? It's a fair question, and the answer comes to her in a rush, and yes, it might sound corny, and she cringes a little when she says it, but it's also very true, and she wants to say it out loud. "I want you to see me, Timothy!"

"I see you. I'm looking at you right now."

"I mean really see me. I want you to acknowledge everything I did, everything I do, without just offering money for it. I want you to take my life and my choices as seriously as you take your own, or Gertie's, or even Sam's." Amy turns her head and looks out at the beach, where there's a tongue of sand that turns into a breakwater stretching out into the ocean. On the stage, a band is beginning to set up. "Because they're good choices, Timothy. I made good choices."

A beat goes by, and then Timothy says, "I know you did. Your kids are amazing. And look at me. I haven't raised so much as a cat."

She thinks there might be a sadness around the edges of his eyes, but it vanishes so quickly she couldn't have said for sure that it was ever really there.

"Cats are overrated," says Amy. "If anything, you should get a rescue dog."

"Maybe," says Timothy. "Then again, maybe not. I've got koi."

The band starts to make warming-up noises, and some of the bikini-clad young women leave the volleyball court to run over to the live music pavilion. Running, thinks Amy, seems almost as fraught in a bikini as playing volleyball. But they appear not to mind. There is squealing. A young man with dreads taps the microphone and starts to sing.

"There's my cue," says Amy. In her days at NYU she was no stranger to live music: the Aztec Lounge, Alcatraz, the Pyramid Club—she and her friends were all over the East Village in their vintage clothes, curated from a dozen amazing thrift shops. (This was before the word *curated* became overused, affiliated mainly with social media posts.) "I'm probably going to skip the dancing today," she says. Timothy snorts. "And if you'll excuse me I have some mousetraps to deal with before I go home." She tries to say this with dignity, but admittedly she's not sure she lands the line.

Very formally he says, "Would you like help with those mouse traps?" and very formally she says, "I think I've got it. But thank you so much for offering."

Before she departs, Timothy takes her hand, and he squeezes it, and when he lets go he says, "I see you, Amy. I do. I always have, even if it didn't seem like it. And I think the choices you made are not only valid, but your choices led to the creation of my very favorite humans in the whole world."

She takes a deep breath and says—what? What should she say? That this is what she asked for, but it somehow still feels inadequate, because she couldn't articulate everything she was trying to get at? Should she say that she's worried he's just saying the lines, acting, but he doesn't really mean it? Or should she say that they're both still grieving the loss of their mother, and they both deserve to find their own way through it, even if the other person might not agree with how they choose to do that?

In the end she opts for this: "Okay, Timmy. I appreciate that." Then, because even at fifty-three she's still a little sister, and the job of the little sister is sometimes to inject levity when things get too heavy, she says, "Do you also see the check? Because I'm leaving you with it. You're older, but you're also rich AF."

Timothy looks bewildered. "What does *AF* mean?"

She shrugs. "I really don't know, but I hear the kids at school say it all the time, and this seemed like the right context."

He smiles. "I am more than happy to be left with the check."

"Thank you," she says.

"You're very welcome," he says.

She leaves Timothy at the table, remembering, as she walks back to the theater, when he was her sun and moon, her North Star. Sometimes he'd pop her in the front seat of their mother's station wagon and drive her around the perimeter of the island in the dark. There's a spot on Mohegan Trail, past Painted Rock, where he'd cut the headlights completely and take the turns a little too fast. Ever since, no coaster ride, no anything, has ever matched the terror and thrill of those ten seconds.

Timothy

AFTER THE DRINKS with Amy, Timothy can't settle down. He doesn't want to go back to Floyd's house. Either nobody will be there, and he'll be lonely, or Sam and Gertie will be there, and he'll feel the obligation to make pleasant conversation when he's not feeling pleasant at all, and that will make him feel even lonelier. He doesn't want to risk the rehearsal barn in case the stage manager is there, nor the theater, because perhaps Amy hasn't left yet.

So he does something he hasn't done since arriving on the island: he drives Floyd's jeep out to the house where he and Amy grew up, in the center of the island, not far from the airport, on a road that Timothy has had no reason to be on so far this summer. It is a small house, all one level, with three bedrooms and one and a half bathrooms, the whole thing under one thousand square feet, but sitting on a big piece of land. This is the house Timothy and his mother lived in alone for part of Timothy's childhood. At that time, with just the two of them, it had seemed roomy. They were renters for a year, and when Rose met her second husband, David, Rose and David bought the house together and David moved into the house with them, and then Amy was born, and after that it no longer seemed roomy, but Timothy doesn't remember it ever seeming especially cramped.

(His pool house in Benedict Canyon is a full fifteen hundred square feet all by itself, so it's hard to believe the Block Island house didn't feel cramped. But that's what his memory tells him.)

Timothy remembers now, driving by the airport, that sometimes, especially in summer months, when air traffic was busy, they could hear the sounds of the small planes taking off and landing. He remembers also that you could be in the house, or outside in the yard, and not even realize you were on an island, because you couldn't see the water without traveling at least a mile north or a couple of miles west. You couldn't always smell it either. He remembers the days before stern-loading ferries were introduced, which made it possible to get many more building materials to the island, thereby increasing the cottage boom. He remembers when one of the top jobs on the island was bellhop at the Narragansett Inn. He remembers when there was only one boat per day, arriving on the island at 11:00 and departing at 3:45. He remembers when a night out was an ice cream cone and a movie at the Empire Theatre.

All these memories, he knows, are popping up because of the fight with Amy, the inequalities in their lives, her worries about her life being perceived as smaller than his. When he gets to the house and pulls off onto the shoulder of the road, not audacious enough to brave the driveway, he sees that something isn't right.

The house isn't there.

He gets out. Has Timothy gotten confused, somehow turned around on the roads that bisect the island? He double-checks the address on his phone. He has the address correct.

The house is gone. All nine-hundred-plus square feet of it. In its place is a gorgeous home at least four times the size, all light wood, with an enormous, sloping roof, a three-car garage, an elaborate garden, a shed that is a miniature version of the house. A deck, a bird feeder, a mailbox, set on a stone pillar, that looks roomy enough to hold a golden retriever. All of this in place of Timothy's old bedroom, his Van Halen posters, the shelf that used to hold his *tape deck*, the closet that sheltered his basketball shoes, the galley kitchen with the Formica and the mustard-yellow four-burner stove. Gone, all gone.

"What the hell," he says. "What the actual hell."

Rose sold the house a few years before she died and made a handsome profit, because by then Block Island had become much more desirable. But he didn't know (had Rose known?) that she was selling their home to be demolished.

More memories come, fast and furious. His mother standing waist-deep in the water at Scotch Beach, shielding her eyes from the sun with one hand. He remembers her laugh, which was bright and merry, and remained so all the way until just before she died. He remembers the banana muffins she used to make. Amy liked them with chocolate chips and Timothy did not, and his mother, God bless her, took the time and the effort to carefully place the chocolate chips by hand inside six of the muffins for Amy. He remembers that she would come home after a long shift on the mainland, where she worked as a nurse, and that sometimes she would take off her work shoes and lay her feet in David's lap and he would massage them through her socks. She would tip her head back and moan, "That feels so good!" And, "What a *day* I had!"

You really can't go home again, thinks Timothy. Never mind the title of that movie: it's incorrect. You especially can't go home again if your home is gone. He backs up farther from the enormous, beautiful house, to get a better look at it, and he thinks of taking a photo for Amy, but things still feel uncertain with Amy so he doesn't. Let her come look at it herself if she wants to see it. Then he hears a honk, and a car moves around the bend in the road behind him, so close that he can almost feel the wind from it, and he jumps forward, heart pounding. He climbs back into the safety of the jeep.

Now he's melancholy *and* suffering from an adrenaline rush, which is a bewildering combination, and one, he eventually decides, that can be soothed only by bourbon. He parks Floyd's jeep behind Poor People's Pub, and, inside, sets himself up on a barstool. The bartender is young with enviable biceps, probably mid-twenties, well outside the demographic of most of Timothy's fans. He doesn't even gratify Timothy with a second glance. Which is fine.

Mostly.

"What'll it be?"

"Bourbon," Timothy says. "Let's make it a good one." He scans the shelves. "Basil Hayden's." After a beat he adds, "Please." It's not *this* guy's fault he got in a fight with his sister and that his trip up, down, and around Memory Lane has worked him into a funk.

"You got it." The bartender pours; he serves; Timothy drinks. "Anything to eat?"

Timothy scans the menu and orders truffle fries. Above the beer bottles behind the bar someone has hung a dozen or so confiscated fake IDs, and on the far end is a vintage PBR sign with a mustached surfer, a beer in his hand. The background music might have been chosen by Timothy himself, back in his high school days: classic Journey. Two of the tables are occupied, and there's a guy in a gray T-shirt at the opposite end of the bar, head down, scribbling on a yellow legal pad, a big glass of something beside him. Every now and then he takes a sip from the glass but for the most part his concentration on his notepad is total, and as enviable as the bartender's biceps.

Timothy nods toward him. "What's that guy doing, writing the Great American Novel?"

"I guess." The bartender shrugs. "He comes in most afternoons, sits right there, drinks two soda waters with lime, sometimes stays a few hours. Apparently he's some big-shot author, and he works better when he's not home."

Timothy looks over, mildly interested. "Yeah? So he actually *is* writing the Great American Novel?"

The bartender shrugs again. "I guess. I don't know, man. I studied business at URI and I'm doing this until I can go back for my MBA. Honestly, I don't read many novels."

"Me either," admits Timothy.

"Never really understood the point of fiction, you know?"

"Right," says Timothy. "Sure. I hear that." He's not going to go as far as agreeing wholeheartedly with that statement—Amy, for one, would metaphorically tan his hide—but he'll do his best to be friendly.

Timothy sips his bourbon and looks out at the summer traffic going by on Ocean Ave. Cars, mopeds, people on bike and on foot. A woman who looks a heck of a lot like Gertie passes by on a moped: long, strawberry-blond hair streaming behind her from underneath the helmet. And then he does a double take, and he realizes it *is* Gertie. Gertie is on a moped! Where on earth did Gertie get a moped? He whips out his phone.

That you? he types.

More bourbon. A painful amount of time goes by. Then, many, many minutes later, the reply comes. That me what?

You going by poor people's pub.

Three dots appear, then disappear, then return. Timothy finds it so disconcerting when this happens, those moving dots. Then this: Who wants to know. Timothy waits it out. Gertie can sometimes have a strange sense of humor. Next: Ha! Just kidding. yup, it was me. I'm home now. Just bought this, wanted to try it out. Was wondering where everyone is.

(Gertie Sanger bought a moped? This, Timothy could not, would not have predicted.)

Timothy sips some more, sips, in fact, until the glass is empty, and then—it takes him a couple tries to do this, the bourbon is hitting him—he writes seven words. If texts could have a tone he would have tried to make the tone of this one nonchalant, but texts don't have tones so he has to let the words land however they land on Gertie's phone screen.

Come back, he texts. I'm sitting at the bar.

This time there are no dots, no answer whatsoever, and Timothy's fingers are beginning to sweat, but fifteen minutes later Gertie walks through the door, and Timothy's heartbeat picks up more than he would like.

The bartender may not have recognized Timothy but he *does* know Gertie: he doesn't say so, not out loud, but his very biceps seem to stand at attention when she comes in, and he tries not to look too closely at her while also looking very, very closely. How can Gertie span the fan demographics in a way Timothy does not? Inwardly, he sighs. She is younger than he is, sure, but she's not the same age as Mr. Biceps! She has at least fifteen years on him. The Great American Novelist looks up from his yellow legal pad too, but his face yields nothing, no surprise or recognition, and then he looks back down and keeps writing. Probably a poker face. He is probably, in fact, writing about sitting down the bar from the famous Gertie Sanger.

"What's good here?" Gertie fixes Biceps with her best smile.

"Everything's good. What do you like?"

"I like cocktails, and I like tequila. Can I leave it with you?"

He gives her a half smile. "How do you feel about spice?" (Is he flirting?)

Gertie arches an eyebrow and says, "Not afraid of it." (Is Gertie flirting *back*?)

Biceps grins. "Then yeah, leave it with me. One more bourbon, sir?"

"At least one more," Timothy says, resenting the heck out of the *sir*.

While Biceps goes about his work, Timothy gives Gertie a

brief sketch of his talk with Amy. By the time he's done, she has a drink in front of her, and he has a refill.

"So," says Gertie. "What's bothering you the most about everything Amy said? That you think she's wrong and you want her to know it, or that you fear she's right?"

Timothy thinks about this. It's an uncomfortable question—it wedges itself underneath his collarbone. More bourbon. He sips; he feels the warmth spread through him.

"A little bit of both," he says finally. He wants Amy to be wrong. But he fears she may be right. "My mother cried when Hugh Jackman sang to her . . . happy-sad tears, you know? But overall good tears. So I assumed I'd done something meaningful for her."

"You did."

"But now I'm wondering." He pauses, and Gertie lets the pause play out. When they were married, she would have tried to fill it: she would have told Timothy what she thought he meant. "Now I'm wondering if I didn't kind of steal those tears from Amy, you know? If she didn't earn them more than I did, and I swooped in, and I took them." Gertie still says nothing, so he sips more bourbon. "Do you think I did?"

Gertie tents her fingers on top of the bar and chews her bottom lip. "I mean, when you put it that way . . ."

Her reaction makes him uncomfortable; he shifts. "So you think I did. I stole them."

"Not on purpose, Timmy. Of course your intentions were good. But maybe your ego stole from Amy just a little bit."

"You think I have an ego?"

"Of course you have an ego!"

More bourbon down the hatch, and there's Biceps again, looking at him questioningly. Timothy nods: *one more, yes, please.* He's not driving home, that's for sure.

"There's no such thing as an actor without an ego," Gertie goes on. "I mean, look at us! Always getting up in front of people, asking for their time and attention and their praise. Who do we think we are? We're looking for people to applaud us, Timmy, over and over and over again. That's what we all want, whether we admit it or not, every single person who's ever stepped on a stage or in front of a camera. Watch me, look at me, see what I can do. We're like seventy-five percent ego, on an average day. And with you, sometimes, darling, your ego takes over when it would be more appropriate for another part of you, like your compassion or your generosity or your love for your sister, which I know is real and true, to drive the bus."

Timothy considers this. "Really?"

"Sure."

"Does that happen a lot? With me? More than with other people?"

She sips her drink and considers him. "It happens," she says. "*A lot* is a strong phrase. Let's just say it happens."

"Why didn't you tell me any of that when we were married?"

Biceps is looking at his phone at the far end of the bar; Great American Novelist is scribbling away; the customers at one of the tables have left. He and Gertie are practically alone.

"Ha! Is this a conversation you would have wanted to have when we were married?"

"No."

"Exactly. But I can tell you now. We don't have to be quite as careful with each other now as we once were." She places her hand on top of his. He looks at her long fingers—Gertie has such beautiful hands. He remembers so much about those hands, and what they used to feel like on his stomach, in his hair, on the back of his neck. Everywhere else. Before he messed it all up.

"I'm afraid," he tells Gertie. "I'm afraid I've left too many mistakes in my wake."

"We're all afraid."

"Not you."

"Of course I am," says Gertie, and then she repeats it: "Of *course* I am. I'm as afraid as anyone."

"Another drink?" Biceps is in front of them again. Did he teleport from the other end of the bar?

"I think I should get this one home." Gertie still has her hand on Timothy's and he senses, or maybe he sees out of the corner of his eye, somebody take a photo of them with a phone: one of the two remaining customers. Had he not felt foggy from the bourbon he might have moved his head back and forth at just the right time to cause the photo to come out blurry, but he's too comfortable, Gertie's hand feels too good. "You're not driving, by the way," Gertie adds. "And I'm not leaving my new moped here. So you can get on the back. We'll squeeze."

"But Floyd's jeep . . ."

"We'll come back for Floyd's jeep later, when you're sobered up. Or tomorrow. The last thing we need is a DUI on the record of the great Timothy Fleming."

"I won't fit," he grumbles.

"Oh, you'll fit. I'll see to it."

Gertie is surprisingly adept on the moped, steering them through the dicey intersection with Corn Neck Road, along Ocean Ave, around the circle with the statue of Rebecca, which was named for the Bible's Rebecca at the Well and installed in 1896 by the Women's Christian Temperance Union.

"Sorry, Rebecca," Timothy whispers to her. He imagines he can see disappointment in her stone eyes, the stern set of her stone lips. Drink more water, she'd say if she could talk. He thinks about his ego. By the time they are heading up the hill on Spring Street and on toward Mohegan Trail, those thoughts have vanished, and he's very aware of his hands on Gertie's waist, ostensibly for balance.

Inside the house, Timothy is suddenly shy. Or maybe he just needs another drink. The worst part about day drinking is the headache that hits you immediately upon stopping; the only way to do day drinking correctly is to keep drinking until it is no longer day. Which, of course, it no longer is—but there is still a good deal of the night to contend with.

In the kitchen he stands for a moment at the window, pretending to take in the view, but in reality gearing himself up for a proposition. "Should we open the rum?" he asks, presenting the idea as though it has only just occurred to him, although in fact he's been thinking about it since Rebecca stared him down. "The fancy rum, from Blake?"

She's on him so quickly he scarcely knows what happened. "I don't think we need the rum," she says. She kisses him long and hard, and he puts his hands on her waist, and then he lets them fall lower, and she allows this too—even encourages it, he thinks— and then they are stumbling down the stairs, horny as a couple of teenagers, into Timothy's bedroom, and when they are in the bed, under the sheets, and he's inside her it's like something entirely new and entirely familiar at exactly the same time. It's amazing.

"Well!" says Gertie, after it's done. "That was unexpected."

"But nice?" He's nervous, asking this. He's starting to sober up a tiny bit.

"Oh, really nice!" she says. She lays a hand on his cheek. "Beyond nice. I'm just not sure what got into me. That was not what I anticipated three hours ago when I was buying a moped. It must have been the tequila."

"It could be good publicity for the play," he ventures. "Us, back together."

"We're not back together," says Gertie. "We just had sex one time."

"Well, sure," says Timothy. "Of course. Not *together* together. But maybe if we just let it slip out—"

"Nope," says Gertie, and she's out of bed, searching for her dress and her bra and her panties, then putting everything on quickly, then pulling her hair into a bun on the top of her head and wrapping it with an elastic band that seems to have appeared out of the very air. "I'm adamant about this. Absolutely adamant. If you say anything I'll deny the whole thing and that will make you look desperate, Timothy Fleming."

"Oh," he says, deflating. "Okay. I get it." Even though the sheet is covering him he feels dramatically, unfairly exposed. "So we'll never do that again, not ever ever ever?"

"I didn't say *that*." And then she leans over the bed and she kisses him again. "Thanks."

"The pleasure was all mine," he murmurs.

"Not all of it," she says. "Trust me." And when he opens his eyes to see if she's winking when she says that, he finds she's gone.

Amy

IT'S GREG WHO has the idea, the same week as her fight with Timothy. That Thursday, Greg and his crew are waiting for something or other to come in for their current job so everything is on hold until Monday. (Amy should know what the something or other is, but she was thinking about the disappointingly low advance ticket sales and wasn't listening carefully when he told her.) Greg has smaller jobs to tend to—he's got a list of customers a quarter mile long, and people who are waiting for estimates for new systems—but the next day is supposed to be A-plus weather. What if he takes the day off, catches the ferry over with Amy in the morning, and they take Sam out to breakfast or lunch?

"I can't ask her that," says Amy immediately. They're doing the dishes together after dinner. Amy keeps stepping over the place in the kitchen where Kona used to like to lie, even though Kona has been gone for weeks now. Amy sees it as a sign of respect. She's asked Bianca a couple of times how Kona is doing in her new home—secretly she's hoping Bianca will pass on the phone number or email for the new owners so Amy can ask herself—but Kona's adoption was "closed," Bianca told her, and there will be no further contact.

Greg pushes his hands into the soapy water; they emerge with a clean saucepan, which he rinses and hands to Amy for drying. He looks perplexed. "Why can't you ask her to go out to lunch?"

"I'm giving her space."

"Um. She has space. If I'm not mistaken she's not living here, is she?" He dries his hands on the checkered towel on the counter and looks dramatically in the corners of the kitchen, as if he might find Sam crouching in one of them.

"No," says Amy. "Of course not. But even so. I have these rules with myself. Lines I don't want to cross. I'm trying to be really careful, so I don't push her away."

"Well, I've hardly seen her since she came back from New York. I've been busy at work. I'd like to do it."

"You ask her," says Amy. "I feel too shy, like I'm asking a cute boy on a date. What if she rejects us?"

"I can handle rejection," says Greg. He's washed the last dish, so he removes the plug from the sink, and the water makes a squelching sound going down. "I had to ask you out three times before you finally said yes."

"You did *not*." Amy swats him with her dish towel. Actually, he's almost right, but it was four times, and she decides to keep the correction to herself.

"Do you get a lunch break?"

"I get a break anytime I want," says Amy. "I'm the boss."

"Fancy!"

"Not really. It's just that I'm not involved in day-to-day rehearsals, so my schedule is flexible." In fact, since the trip to Ballard's with Timothy, she's been spending more time tending to tasks outside the theater. Amy is wary of sticking her emotions too close to the flame and reigniting them. This week, a little distance has been good.

Greg kisses her neck and says, "Okay, boss. Leave it with me."

After the dishes she's sitting outside on the front steps, watching the sky pinken before the navy blue sets in, when Greg comes out and sits beside her. "We're on," he says. "I just talked to Sam. Lunch tomorrow. You pick a place."

"Really? That's great!" Amy feels unreasonably excited. Lunch with Greg and Sam! It will be like those halcyon days when Henry had gone off to college and it was the three of them at home. (The days were actually not all that halcyon, not all the time, and in fact Sam was almost never home, out with her friends nearly all the time, but Amy allows herself to paint the memory with the brush of nostalgia.) She stands to go inside.

"Something I said?" asks Greg.

"Something the mosquito said. He said, *I just bit your arm*." She holds out her hand to Greg and helps him up and together they go into the house.

On the ferry over in the morning they decide that Greg will take the Wagoneer, drop Amy at the barn, pick Sam up at the house on Mohegan Trail, and then swing back by for Amy at lunchtime. Amy chooses McAloon's, because it's close to the barn and not far from the theater, and when they've finished lunch Greg can drop her in town and take the Wagoneer for the rest of the day. Greg is wearing shorts that double as swim trunks, a T-shirt from PJ's Pub in Narragansett, sunglasses, flip-flops. He has a backpack with a towel and a bottle of water and sunscreen.

"You look like a kid about to hop on a bike for a summer adventure with your posse, not a man in your fifties responsible for a small business," says Amy, as they're waiting to board the ferry, looking at the fishing boats docked in the port at Galilee, watching the squawking gulls. "It's cute." Greg grins at her and says, "I wish I was a kid with a posse. Those were the days."

"I could do with a posse too," agrees Amy. "Where have all the posses gone?"

Greg wants to sit on the top deck, in the sun, and he stretches out with his head back and his face to the warmth. Amy typically chooses to ride inside or at least in the shade, but she sits next to Greg. He never takes time off during the week. He deserves the perfect summer day.

She lets Greg enjoy his perfect summer day for almost the whole ferry ride, and then, when she can see the line of hotels on Water Street coming into view, she taps him on the shoulder.

He lifts his sunglasses, opens one eye, and says, "May I help you?"

"Actually, you may. When you have time today do you think you could get Sam to tell you what exactly happened in New York? I know we're not googling. But we're halfway through July. I thought she might have said something by now."

He opens the other eye. "You haven't asked her?"

"Of course I've asked her! But she hasn't told me. She clams up whenever I bring it up." Amy presses her lips together in case Greg has any doubt about what clamming up looks like.

"Maybe it's because she doesn't want us to know."

"Stop being so reasonable! I know she doesn't want us to know. But don't you think we *should* know?"

"Why?"

"Because she's our daughter. So we can support her. Or—protect her. Or do whatever she needs."

"Maybe what she needs is not to think about it. Do you want to break the google pact?"

"No. I don't want to break the pact." She waits a moment and says, "Did *you* google her?"

"Nope. We have a deal."

"Exactly."

The ferry pulls in, and even though Amy makes this trip several times a week now she still gets caught up in the excitement that permeates the upper deck as people gather their things and get ready to disembark. This excitement is especially palpable on a Friday.

"If she doesn't want us to know, I say let's be respectful," says

Greg. He shrugs, as though it's just that easy. He stands so they can join the line of people heading down the stairs. Greg may look good in sunglasses, but sometimes the man is downright infuriating.

AMY HAS TO admit, albeit reluctantly, that Jane Wyndham is a good stage manager. In a concession to summer on an island, she has exchanged her long-sleeved black tops for black tank tops, which show off great arm muscles. The muscles aren't what make her a good stage manager though. She's got a good rapport with the actors, she's always at the right part in the script, she's always right next to Timothy when he needs her. This morning they're rehearsing act 3, scene 1, in Leonato's garden, when Hero, Margaret, and Ursula plot to convince Beatrice of Benedick's love for her.

At one point Amy finds herself getting distracted by what's happening on the stage, so she puts in the AirPods Henry gave her for Mother's Day—she thought she'd feel silly with them, but in fact she loves them—and plays music on her phone while she works. When she removes the AirPods she hears a familiar voice. She cocks her head toward the stage. It's Sam! She's deep in conversation with Timothy. When they're done talking, and Timothy calls for a break and picks up his phone, Amy moves closer to the stage, taps Sam on the shoulder, and says, "Hi! I thought Dad was picking you up."

To Amy's surprise and very great delight, Sam hugs her, and Amy breathes in the smell of her shampoo, and the scent of the perfume that Amy has noticed is new since New York—something darker and more mysterious than the one she used to wear.

"I got a ride in with Gertie. On her new moped! She's not called today but she said she wanted to go zipping around. I asked Dad to get you and me at the same time. I wanted to watch part of the rehearsal."

Timothy looks up from his phone and says, "She had a note!"

"For you?" Amy asks.

"No, silly. Of course not. For Amelia. Sam was spot-on. Something wasn't flowing in the beginning of the scene."

"What was the note?"

"Oh, nothing," says Sam, looking modestly at her flip-flops.

"The lady doth protest too much!" says Timothy (Amy rolls her eyes and is gratified that Sam rolls hers back). "It wasn't nothing! It definitely wasn't nothing. It was the line 'Make proud by princes, that advance their pride/Against the power that bred it.'"

Sam shrugs. "I just said I thought she was pausing too long between *pride* and *against*. You know, because there's a line break in the script, but there shouldn't be one when she says it. Which obviously happens all the time in Shakespeare. But something about that one line, she's not turning the corner the way she should."

"Turning the corner!" says Amy admiringly. "You're making your English teacher mother very proud. How'd you know that term?"

Sam ducks her head. "I know things."

"She sure does," says Timothy. "The other day she pointed out that Don John was dropping the ball in his scene with Borachio. She's got a knack for the theater, this one. Although it's not like we didn't know that already." He smiles proudly at Sam like she's just invented the ice cream cone.

"Well okay, then, Ms. Assistant Director," says Amy. "Ready to eat? Your dad will be waiting." To Timothy she says, "Greg is on the island. Do you want to join us for lunch?" She's hoping he'll say no; she really wants it to be just her, Greg, and Sam, but she's trying to be solicitous toward Timothy, in light of their sort-of truce.

"Gosh, I'd love to," says Timothy regretfully (or at least *acting* regretful; who's to say what's real?). "But I already have lunch plans."

"Oh, too bad," says Amy, taking a stab at regretful herself. "Next time!"

Gertie appears and says, "Ready."

"Ready," says Timothy.

"Gertie is your plans?"

"Yup. Gertie is my plans."

"For old times' sake?" Amy would have thought ex-spouses living in the same house would see enough of each other as it was, never mind adding in meals during the workday.

"Something like that," says Gertie, and Amy almost thinks she sees a bit of color creep its way into Gertie's cheeks.

At McAloon's they sit outside at one of the tables overlooking Corn Neck Road, watching the beach traffic wind around the curve in the road. They share an order of clam cakes, then Sam orders the burrata salad, Amy the seared tuna salad. Greg gets a burger, well done, because he claims to be allergic to salad, which of course is not true. Greg is in a top-notch mood, having spent the morning at Mansion Beach, which he reports was crowded but not overwhelmingly so. The water was the perfect temperature: cool enough to be refreshing, warm enough to allow for swift entry. After lunch he wants to drive Sam to Floyd's house and then check out Vaill Beach. The tip of his nose is sunburned, and there's a stripe of salt from the ocean dried on his cheek.

"I can't believe we don't come here all the time," he tells Amy. "This place is paradise! I can't believe *I* didn't come here more often, growing up. In fact I can't believe you don't want to walk down Memory Lane a couple times a summer."

Looking around the restaurant at other patrons, some drunk on Irish pints, some drunk on summer sunshine, Amy is tempted to agree. There's a good lunch crowd across the street on the deck of Yellow Kittens tavern too, and a constant stream of bikes and mopeds rounding the curve toward the north beaches. But it wasn't always this way. "Maybe in summer this is paradise," she says. "Believe me, the middle of January is a whole different story. Timmy got out of here the minute he turned eighteen, and after that, well—it was lonely. The wind can really whip around this place in the winter, and there's not much to do. There was no Internet in the olden days."

Sam nods like she understands a world without the Internet, but of course she doesn't.

When the clam cakes are gone and the plate has been cleared away, Sam says, "So . . . I'm glad you're both here. There's something I've been wanting to talk to you about."

She's going to tell us! thinks Amy. She's going to tell us what happened in New York! She hits her knee against Greg's under the table as if to say, *Here we go.* She wipes her mouth, folds her hands on the table, and looks at her daughter.

But before Sam can get to it, their entrées arrive, so they have to take a few minutes accepting, arranging, prepping their food. Greg squirts ketchup on his burger, and Amy steals a fry from his plate and pops it in her mouth.

"Shoot," says Greg, holding his burger with both hands and pointing it at Sam. "What did you want to talk to us about?"

Sam chews a bite of her salad, really taking her time with it, looking down. When she looks up, she meets their gazes squarely and says, "Money."

"Money?" Amy stops mid-chew.

"Specifically, my money. The money that's in my account from *Mockingbird* and *Daughters.*"

"Your college money," Amy clarifies.

"My *money* money," says Sam.

"Is there any brown mustard over there?" asks Greg. Greg likes lots of things—local IPAs, nine holes of golf on a Sunday, John Wick movies—but one thing he does not like is confrontation.

When Sam worked on Broadway, and then in Hollywood, Amy and Greg opened an account to deposit into any money earned, minus expenses for travel and living away from home. The law mandated only 15 percent be set aside for Sam, as a minor, but they put more in, every penny they could after expenses, with an eye always toward her college tuition. By the time Sam left L.A., after twenty-six episodes as a series regular, she had a nice chunk in there—enough to pay tuition and room and board at any college of her choosing.

Sam finds the brown mustard in the caddy and passes it to her father, maneuvering around his attempt at distraction. "Mom. I don't know if you've noticed, but I'm not in college."

"Well, not at the moment, no. I did happen to notice that," concedes Amy. "But it's not too late. There are schools with rolling admissions . . . or you could apply for the semester that begins in January. There are so many options. I'm available—we're both available—to help you figure it out. Aren't we, Greg?"

Greg is super focused on his burger, but he does make a sound that Amy takes to be affirmation.

"Whether or not I go to college," says Sam, "I earned that money, and I'd like to have the account only in my name now."

"That's fine, of course. But what are you going to do with it?" Truly, Amy is perplexed. She's not trying to steal Sam's money. She and Greg have touched nary a dime, even when it meant they had to take out loans to pay Henry's Middlebury tuition, even when it meant that the year their hot water heater and their roof both went they didn't take their usual trip to Cape Cod for a long weekend in July. It simply wasn't a consideration to use the money, because it wasn't theirs. But hadn't they all agreed it would be for college? They didn't have that in writing, but certainly they'd had at least a verbal agreement.

"I'm not sure yet. But I want a safety net. I want to be able to take my next steps, once I figure out what they are."

"*College* can be your safety net, Sammy. Education is the best safety net there is. Henry—"

Sam cuts her off. "Mom. I'm not Henry. I will never be Henry. I love him, and I'm happy that he's doing what he wants to do, whatever that is, because seriously, I don't understand it, but it's so far from what I want to do." She turns to Greg. "Dad?"

Greg clears his throat and lays his burger on his plate, patting the bun, as if the burger needs to go down for a nap. "She did earn the money," he says, almost apologetically, not looking at Amy.

"I *know* she earned it! I'm not trying to keep it from her. I'm not Jamie Spears."

Sam nearly chokes on a piece of lettuce. "Mom. I can't believe you know who Jamie Spears is."

"Everybody knows who Jamie Spears is."

"I don't know who Jamie Spears is," says Greg.

"Really? He's Britney—"

"Not now," says Sam. "It doesn't matter now. Can we stay on topic, please? I really want to talk about this while I have you both here."

"What if you take the money and move really far away?" says Amy. "To Hawaii or Hong Kong?"

"Why would I move to Hawaii or Hong Kong?"

"People do. Or . . . California. What if you move back to California?"

"I mean, I could." Sam shrugs. "I might. I could do anything. I'm just not sure what I want, so I'd like to keep my options open."

Amy misses the days when she and Greg were the supreme rulers of the household, when they could declare any topic something they needed to discuss alone, without children, before they'd deliver a verdict. Could Sam have a friend spend the night on Saturday? Was Henry allowed to go to the movies without a parent? *Dad and I will talk about it and let you know,* Amy would say. Or, *Let me discuss it with your mother,* from Greg. Now, just as Sam says, she's an adult, and the matter at hand is her very own money, which she earned, and Amy knows that the only correct answer is, *Yes, of course you can have your own money. No discussion necessary.*

"Yes, of course you can have your own money," says Amy.

"Right," says Greg. "It's yours."

"After all, just as you say, you earned it," continues Amy. "But if you do decide to go to college—"

"*Mom*," says Sam warningly, and Amy holds up her hands, as though her seared tuna might jump up and bite her.

"I know. I know. But I have to say it. Humor me, okay? If you do decide to go to college, and I'll indulge myself one more time by noting that I hope you will eventually decide to do that, you'll need this money. So make sure you remember that."

"Okay." Tiny eye roll, barely perceptible. But definitely there. Amy can see Sam biding her time; she's gotten what she wants out of the conversation, and now she just needs to ride it out to the end. "I'll remember that," she says.

"Good." Amy wipes her mouth with her napkin. "Let's pick a day soon when you can take the ferry over with me, and we'll go to BankNewport and get everything transferred over to your name. *Just* your name, with our names off the account. Okay?"

"Okay," says Sam. She smiles at Amy, and then at Greg, and her smile is so bright, and so hopeful, and so loving, that for a moment Amy forgets to worry that she might move to Hawaii or Hong Kong or California and remembers to be happy that right here, right now, she is with them.

And then, of course, unable to let well enough alone, Amy messes it up.

"Are you ready to talk about it now, sweetheart?"

Greg shoots Amy a warning look, which she does her very best to ignore, but which she cannot help but see out of the corner of her eye.

"Talk about what?" Sam looks from her father to her mother.

"About what happened in New York."

"*Mom!* No. I'm not ready. I may never be ready. Please. Stop. Asking." And then the clamshell, which hadn't really opened very far, snaps closed.

Timothy

TIMOTHY CATCHES GERTIE after rehearsal the Friday of the next week, when they are the only two left in the barn. It always takes Gertie a ridiculous amount of time to gather her things after rehearsal. Scarves, bottles of Evian. *Bits and bobs,* they'd call it in England. Gertie has lot of bits, and so many bobs.

Rehearsal had gone well—they worked on act 2, scene 1, when Beatrice mocks Benedick and Don John, and Timothy got that excited feeling in his stomach that he recognizes as a sign that this play is going to be really, really good. In general he tries to keep feelings like that to himself, so as not to jinx things. Earlier that day, when they broke for lunch, he called the restaurant at the Spring House Hotel and reserved a table for two at seven o'clock. He wants to take Gertie. It won't be a *date,* of course. Whatever they're doing in the bedroom is just old-fashioned, grown-up fun. They're not dating. But two exes can go out to dinner if they want, can't they, to talk about old times, or to studiously avoid talking about old times? Yes. They can.

"Oh, sweetheart," says Gertie, looking up from her massive handbag after he asks her. *Whole-body bag* is more like it, thinks Timothy. "That sounds lovely. But I have plans tonight."

"Plans?" Timothy stares at her blankly.

"Yes. Plans. You know when you decide to spend time with a

person or people and you all do the same thing at the same time? That's what plans are."

Instantly, Timothy feels both aggrieved and embarrassed. "With whom? With a person, or with people?"

She stops digging—she has either found what she was looking for or given up on it altogether—slings the strap of the bag over her shoulder, and looks at him. "Timothy, Timothy," she says. "We talked about this. We're not together! You don't need to take me to dinner."

"I know I don't need to. But I want to."

Gertie lays a hand alongside his cheek, holds it for a second, then pats it twice, the way one would a child's, and says, "I think that's lovely of you. But I have plans. What about tomorrow night?"

"Tomorrow night I'm going to Newport. Dinner with Barry. He's in town. Remember? I told you and Sam yesterday." For some reason he takes it personally that she didn't remember. Sometimes he gets the feeling that Gertie and Sam are only pretending to listen to him. "Do you want to come with me to Newport?"

"Don't we rehearse on Sunday?"

"We do. But we don't start until noon. We'll take the early ferry back."

She smiles at him. "You know what? I'd love to. Let's go to Newport! But for tonight—why don't you take Sam to dinner?"

Timothy starts to reply sulkily that he doesn't want to dine with *Sam*, he wants to dine with *Gertie*, but then he thinks about it and realizes that he does in fact want to dine with Sam. Even though they're living in the same house, they don't spend much time together. They pass in the downstairs hallway, outside the bedrooms, and sometimes they happen to be at the espresso machine at the same moment, but that isn't quality time. It isn't real conversation. He'd love to gather Sam's thoughts on Leonato's performance, maybe pick her brain a bit about Amy's mood.

Gertie leaves the barn, and Timothy texts Sam, and he's surprised and delighted to receive a reply almost immediately: Yesssss. Love 2. Meet u there? Plan B4.

Timothy sighs. How is it that everyone's life but his seems to be so full of plans? Ah, well. He'll take what he can get. Meet you there, he replies. He can't bear to try for the U.

Timothy arrives at the Spring House before Sam. He's a little nervous, as though he's meeting a blind date. In L.A., of course, he would have asked Alexa to make the reservation, but here, on his home turf, he'd called himself, requesting an outside table, private if possible. He's pleased when the hostess—streaks of pink in her hair, rows of piercings in her ears—leads him around the corner of the porch, where there are only two tables, both unoccupied.

"This other table is reserved for eight o' clock," the hostess tells him. "So you'll have plenty of privacy until then."

Does the hostess recognize him? Timothy has gotten pretty good at reading expressions over the years, and looking at this girl, he has to admit . . . no. No, she does not recognize him. Shhhh, he tells his ego. Don't worry about it. This girl is, what? Fifteen? Sixteen? Obviously not his demographic. And, anyway, how tiresome it would be to get accosted when he wants only to have a quiet dinner with his niece. Yes, that's exactly what it would be. Tiresome. It's so much better this way!

While he waits for Sam he orders a martini, dirty, double olives, and casts his eyes upon the glorious, glorious view: the sweep of winding road leading to Mohegan Bluffs; the majestic ocean beyond that; the ferry, in the distance, making its slow and deliberate way. Closer to him is the wide semicircle of Adirondack chairs, their substantial arms populated with cocktails, the chairs themselves with people. Then there is the vast green lawn, sloping toward the street, a single, shrieking child rolling down it, ba-dump, ba-dump, ba-dump. Doesn't look like a bit of fun, to Timothy. But there you are.

The martini arrives—icy, briny, perfect—and soon after the drink, here comes Sam. She's in a short sundress with spaghetti straps, hair in a bun, suntanned, and she looks both glamorous and grown-up and also exactly like the little girl who played Scout to his Atticus all those years ago. She's smiling. Timothy stands when she gets to the table, and he takes both of her hands, and she kisses him on the cheek.

"Hey, Uncle Timmy! This was such a nice idea, to have dinner together. Sorry I'm late. Am I late?"

"I believe I was early," Timothy says graciously, even though, yes, Sam is nine minutes late. The hill-rolling child has reached the bottom and sits for a moment (stunned? Delirious with joy? Possibly concussed?) before beginning the trudge back up.

"Nothing looks less fun to me than that," observes Sam. "Even when I was a kid I didn't like rolling down hills."

"I was just thinking the same thing! Must be a genetic disinclination." Timothy beams. Sam is here; the night is beautiful; all, for now, is right with the world.

When the server comes to take Sam's drink order Sam smiles at him and says, "Vodka and Red Bull, please. Tito's." The server is Sam's age or a little older, and he stares at Sam, maybe starstruck, maybe smitten, maybe trying to decide if he should ask her for ID. Maybe all three. A lot of people watched the Disney Channel when they were young, and those people have aged into young adults who are not immune to nostalgia.

Sam turns back to Timothy and smiles so widely and innocently that he doesn't have the heart or the courage to point out that she is not, in fact, of legal drinking age. He knows from reading the *Block Island Times* that underage drinking is becoming more and more of a problem on the island. Instead he says, "Won't the Red Bull keep you up?" and Sam chortles and says, "That's the point."

"I see." Timothy is officially old, as it turns out: few things sound more unsettling to him than caffeine past noon.

The server returns with the drink; they order. They decide to share two appetizers, the clams casino and the Point Judith calamari, and, for entrées, Timothy chooses the cod bianco and Sam the pappardelle Bolognese. They clink their glasses.

"This became my drink in New York," Sam tells him. "Scooter? One of the guys at Xanadu? He got me into it. I thought it sounded gross at first, but you know what? It's an acquired taste, and I totally acquired it. Like your bourbon, maybe!"

"Xanadu?" Timothy is genuinely confused. He spends some time choosing a clam and moving it onto his plate. A squeeze of lemon, the tiny fork. It's all sublime.

"The house. The apartment. The TikTok house, where I lived all of last year?" She pauses. "Wait, did you literally not know that's what I was doing last year?"

"Of course I knew." I literally knew, he thinks. I literally knew, but I hated to think about it, so I tried not to, and also I didn't know the house had a name. Sam meets his gaze over her own clam. Timothy isn't sure if she can read the disdain inside of his and, if she can, if he wants her to or not.

He doesn't *not* want her to.

But he also doesn't want to destroy the evening. Moving swiftly, he changes the subject. How does Sam think Amelia is doing as Hero? What about the scene in act 3 where Hero begins her plan to trick Beatrice into falling in love with Benedick? Does Sam think Amelia is laying it on too thick, or not thickly enough? Sam thinks it's just about right; she might lean just a *little* bit heavier on the line "Some cupids kill with arrows, some with traps." They both agree that Gertie is slaying (Sam's phrase) as Beatrice. Sarah Trail as Margaret has promise, but is struggling with the language.

When they are each halfway through their entrées Sam finishes her drink, and the server comes out of the shadows to ask if she'd like another. Should Timothy stop Sam from ordering another? Should he stop himself? Oh, why the hell press *pause* on the fun? The night is gorgeous; his companion is engaging; the food is a dream. He's eating well, and he's drinking slowly, so certainly he can make the short drive home after a second martini.

"I'll have one more as well," he says. He tilts his glass toward the server. "*Double* double olives this time, please." He thinks about that and says, "I suppose that'd be quadruple." The server laughs, and Timothy congratulates himself. He's still got it, the ol' charm.

It's not until the eight o'clock reservation arrives that things start to move southward. It's a family of five: three teenage daughters, ranging in age maybe from thirteen to seventeen, plus a father and a mother. As they sit and open their menus they all glance in Timothy's direction—getting the lay of the land, the way you do when you've just entered a new place. The whispering commences, and, Well, here we go, thinks Timothy. He may even say it aloud. Yes, he is saying it aloud, albeit quietly, to Sam—"Here we go, Sammy"—to prepare her, because there's no question now (the repeated glances, quick and jerky as a squirrel's over an acorn) that the family has recognized him. He clears his throat, straightens his spine, casual, playing it cool. He takes a small sip of martini number two, for fortification.

"Don't turn around," he tells Sam in a low voice. "One of them is approaching." Surprisingly, it's the middle girl. He had been expecting one of the parents. Maybe they've sent the girl as an emissary. Or maybe not. He's been told his early work remains quite accessible. Perhaps this girl is, as they say, a "film geek." Truth be told, though, she doesn't look like a geek of any kind. She looks—well, she looks like Sam. Similar dress, similar hair, similar confidence. She's holding not a cocktail napkin and a pen for an autograph, as Timothy had expected, but a bejeweled phone. On her face is not trepidation, but what Timothy could only describe as familiarity, perhaps even excitement.

"Excuse me?" she says. "Can we get a selfie with you?"

It takes Timothy a few seconds to absorb and translate the word *selfie*, converting it from the word *autograph* he was expecting, and thank goodness for those snippets of time, because they save him the humiliation of saying yes to the girl, who, it turns out, is looking at Sam, talking to Sam. Wanting a selfie *with Sam*.

"I can't do that, I'm sort of taking a break from social media," says Sam kindly. "I'm so sorry."

"Please? *Please* please? It's my sister's birthday." The girl points to her family, and the youngest sister waves and giggles. "We won't post it, if that's what matters. We just want to have it for ourselves."

Sam peers at her, maybe deciding whether or not to believe her. Finally Sam sighs. "Okay," she says. "Okay, I guess so. Because it's your sister's birthday. But really, I'm trusting you. Please don't post it. Can I trust you?"

"Definitely. You can definitely, one hundred percent trust us."

The girl motions to her sisters, and they get up and join, and they crouch around Sam's chair, and Middle lifts her phone high above all of them, and as if given a cue they make identical pout-smiles and hold them, and click. Well, there's no click, obviously, phones are silent, but there is the feeling of a click.

"Ohmygod, thank you," says Youngest. Middle nods. Eldest seems too overcome to do anything. She might, Timothy realizes, be crying.

"I can't believe it," stammers Eldest.

"You made our night," agrees Middle.

"You made our whole vacation." (This is Youngest.)

"I can't believe what she did to you," says Middle. "Evil Alice. She is the worst, the total and absolute worst."

(Who is Alice? wonders Timothy. And why is she evil?)

"Literally the worst," concurs Eldest, who has regained her composure enough to join in the conversation.

"Oh, well," says Sam with demureness and elegance. "It's okay. It's all behind me now. But thank you for saying that. I'm taking a break, and it's been really good for me."

(What's all behind Sam? Timothy doesn't know, but he sees something in Sam's look, a flash of vulnerability, an arrow in her armor.)

Eldest nods some more, until Middle says, "Come *on*, Olivia," and tugs at the sleeve of Eldest's denim jacket and they all bid Sam goodbye and thank her numerous times. As they repair to their table they give the impression of commoners backing away from royalty.

Timothy hears one of the girls say, "Katie, will you send that to me?" and he hears Katie reply, "Okay, I'm AirDropping it now." (What, Timothy wonders, is AirDropping? Sounds dangerous.)

"Well!" says Sam. She looks faintly flushed, somewhat exhilarated. She smiles at him. "Should we get dessert?" Timothy wonders if she's thinking of the cheesecake they used to share at Junior's after Wednesday evening performances of *Mockingbird*. That was one of his favorite parts of that Broadway run.

But the evening has changed. It has. Where once it was smooth, now it's rough; where flat and open, now dotted with potholes and land mines. Everything feels different after the interaction with the sisters from the other table.

"I don't think I have room for dessert," he says, more shortly than he means to, and then, because Sam looks disappointed, he adds, "But you can, if you want. You definitely can. You should get something." He calls over the server, requests the dessert menu.

"It's verbal," says the server, his eyes on Sam. "Let's see. Crème brûlée. And three flavors of gelat—"

"That's okay," says Sam. She smiles. "Thank you, but you don't have to go through the list. Now that I think about it I'm too full too. Let's call it a night."

Check, credit card, signature: Timothy busies himself with all of this, and Sam offers to pay her share, and he tells her not to be silly, and then they thread their way through the other porch tables, past the bar and the hostess stand and the seating area, where two couples are enjoying pre- or post-dinner drinks, until at last they are standing at the top of the hill, looking over the Adirondack chairs and the visible slice of the island. The sun hasn't yet set, but it's on its way, and there are streaks of pink and orange reaching across the sky.

They stand for a moment, admiring, and Timothy tries to regain his grasp on the evening, and then Sam says, "Okay, Mother Nature, we get it. You're flexing." She takes out her phone from her small cross-body bag and snaps a picture of the sky.

(What does it mean for Mother Nature to be flexing? Timothy's hold slips. He grunts. He hates phrases he doesn't understand.)

"You got grumpy." Sam's elbow reaches out and taps his playfully.

"I'm not grumpy," he says grumpily.

"Is it because of those girls? It seems like your mood turned after that."

"No. Of course not." He shakes his head irritably, trying, perhaps, to dislodge the nugget of truth from what Sam is saying. He's ashamed that she's seen through him so easily. "You didn't drive here, did you?"

Sam shakes her head. "I don't have a car, remember? Gertie dropped me off on the way to her plans."

"I'll get you home, if you're going home. I'm parked over here." He points toward the parking lot behind the hotel. He still sounds more truculent than he wants to.

"I'm going home," she says. "I think. At least for now. If I go out, it'll be later." Timothy supposes that her Red Bulls will allow for that. Ah, indefatigable youth. "But I can walk, if you're mad or whatever. You don't have to drive me."

Timothy is thrown. What has happened to their night? "I'm

not mad or whatever! I'm not mad. I'm not whatever," he says, willing it to be true. But indeed, he's starting to feel both mad *and* whatever. "It's going to get dark soon. You're not walking up the hill and all the way home. There's no shoulder on that road! You'll get flattened by a moped."

She nods. "Yeah. I probably would get flattened by a moped." A pause, and then, "Sorry they interrupted us." And then, more quietly, "I mean, sorry not sorry." (What does *that* mean? wonders Timothy. Who made up all these new terms, and who sanctioned them?) "Price of fame, I guess." Sam says this self-deprecatingly, with a little shrug of the shoulders, and something about that incenses Timothy.

"Okay, you know what, Sam?" he says, unable to hold his thoughts inside any longer, knowing that if he says any more after this he's rending the fabric of the evening, perhaps beyond repair. But he can't help himself. "I admit it. I do find myself in a bad mood all of a sudden."

Sam draws her eyebrows together and purses her lips. She looks so much like Amy when she does this! "But *why?*" she asks.

"It's your idea of fame. You, and everyone else your age. Those girls who came up to you, they should know you from your work in *Mockingbird,* your role in *My Three Daughters!* Not for what you did in some group home."

"Xanadu? You're talking about *Xanadu?*"

"Yes. I'm talking about Xanadu." He has trouble saying the word without derision or irony, but mostly he manages.

"It wasn't a *group home!* It was a collab house!" Sam sighs and folds her arms.

"I don't know what that is."

"It's a house for artistic collaboration. A house that makes it easy to produce and distribute content, because you're living with like-minded individuals who share the same goals. It's not, like, a halfway house."

Timothy can feel his left eyebrow rise dramatically, as though a director has just asked him to look skeptically at the other actor in the scene. (This is one of his *things,* that he can raise one eyebrow while leaving the other one where it sits. Some have said that his left eyebrow was the real star of *The Devil in Here.*) "What kind of content? Plays? Movies? Television scripts?"

Sam hesitates, then he sees her gather herself, take control. "Well, no. Videos. TikToks."

He rolls his eyes so far back he fears he might have sprained one of them. "For what reason?"

"For a lot of different reasons. Sometimes for entertainment, sometimes for companies."

"Commercials?" He tries to keep the disdain out of his voice—commercials have kept many an actor very well afloat in the lean times, himself included—but it creeps in anyway.

"Well, yeah. Sort of. But not like TV commercials. Product endorsements."

Timothy shakes his head. He casts a glance across the sweep of lawn, and back toward the bar, from which the sounds of lively, happy, Friday-night people reach them, and then Sam says, "You know what? I think I will walk. Thank you very much for dinner, it was delicious, but I need to clear my head."

He doesn't actually think she'll walk away, but there she goes, starting down the long driveway, partially lit, that slopes down from the parking lot. Amy would string him like a side of beef if he let Sam walk home from here in the dark.

"Sam!" He follows her. Normally she'd be quicker, having youth and fitness and self-righteousness on her side, but her platform sandals slow her progress, and he catches up to her about halfway down the driveway. "Sam! Stop. Let's finish this conversation. I think this is important."

She turns and unleashes on him what can only be properly described as a sneer. (Is this what it's like to father a teenager? Good

Lord, he is not equipped.) "Great," she says. "I'd love to. I'd love for you to throw shade on my work *some more*."

(What it *throwing shade*? He supposes he can figure this one out from context clues.)

Sam is looking away from him, toward the ocean, and even in the waning light he can pick up on the stubborn set of her shoulders, and, because of the bun in her hair, the tension in the back of her neck. God! Again she reminds him so much of her mother, and he feels the same twin sensations he feels with Amy: the desire to shake her out of her stubbornness while at the same time standing in admiration of it. Say what you want about the Trevino women, they do not back down.

"I'll go back for the car. You stay right here. But please stay off the road."

She has more to say though. "How would you know about any of it? I'm sure you've never watched any of my TikToks. You have no idea what they're like, or what I've been doing, or what kind of influence I have, or anything. You're stuck in the past, in something I did when I was twelve."

"You're right," he says unapologetically. "You're right, Sam. I've never watched a TikTok, yours or anyone else's, and I don't plan to."

"So you don't know what you're talking about. Admit it."

Suddenly it all bubbles up inside him—his frustration with Sam, his sadness about Gertie not wanting to dine with him, the proximity to his childhood home, and the inevitable, irrefutable fact of his own aging—and yes, probably, the two martinis. It bubbles up, and then it comes out, in these words, and in a tone and at a level that maybe later he'll regret but that right now he simply can't control:

"Here's what I know, Sam! Here's what I know. I know that you have a gigantic—what have I heard you call it?—a *platform*, with thousands of people who are interested in what you have to say—"

"Hundreds of thousands," corrects Sam.

"Okay, hundreds of thousands. Even better. Worse. Whatever. So you've got all these people, multiply those girls at the restaurant by however many girls there are like that in the country—"

"The world," she says. "My followers are international."

"Fine. The world. You've got this massive following, and you've got all of this talent, and you're not using it. *That's* why those girls bothered me, Sam. It's this crazy notion of fame that your generation buys into and feeds into and perpetuates, and it's all based on nothing. It's doing nothing."

"What do you want me to do with my platform? Huh?" She turns on him, eyes blazing. "*What?* With so many stupid—with all of the—after what . . . *God!*" She's breathing hard now. "Do you have some bright idea about what I should be doing?"

Timothy feels himself sputtering—if he were a cartoon character right now, there would be smoke spilling out of his ears. "Something! Anything. Something useful, instead of makeup tips and the like."

"I have never posted makeup tips!" screams Sam. She takes a deep breath, appears to try to regain her composure. More softly she says, "I don't do makeup. I don't even wear a lot of makeup, unless someone puts it on me. That was Cece's arena. Sometimes Evil Alice. I was more—lifestyle and fashion. A little bit of dancing sometimes. Some hairstyles. Not cooking. Cooking was Tucker." She looks momentarily pensive. "He made the best Bolognese."

"Lifestyle and fashion," he says. "Okay. But you could be getting people's attention about something important! You could be fixing climate change!"

She points to herself, incredulous. "Me? You want me to fix climate change?"

"Why not?" he bellows. "Why the hell not? You and your hundreds of thousands of fans."

"Followers," she says.

"Followers!" By now the people remaining in the Adirondack

chairs are turning around, craning to see what the ruckus is coming from the shadows. Timothy doesn't care though. The conversation feels momentous and important and all-consuming, and he's in it now, so in it he'll stay.

"Why don't *you* fix climate change, Uncle Timmy? Instead of trying to figure out what's wrong with my generation. It's you guys that wrecked the planet! Why's it our job to fix it? What are *you* doing with *your platform?*"

Damn it. Much as he doesn't want to admit it, Sam's absolutely right. His generation did wreck the planet. And what is he doing with his platform? Does he *have* a platform? Did he ever?

"Okay, fine, maybe not climate change. But why aren't you using your platform and your talent to expose people to something valuable . . . to art?"

"To *art?*"

He can still see the little girl in Sam, the twelve-year-old with the gap between her teeth, before the braces closed it. He remembers the way she delivered one particular line in the play: *Well, it'd be sort of like shootin' a mockingbird, wouldn't it?* Every single time she said it her voice cracked in the exact same way, Timothy's heart swelled, and the audience held their collective breath, stunned into silence.

"Sam," he says. "You know how much I think of your talent. You were brilliant in *My Three Daughters.* Your comic timing was spot-on. You stole that show from the older two girls. You know you did. You have that rare thing, where you can do light or you can do dark, but either way you get at just the perfect emotion. You *just get it.* There are people all over Hollywood who would sell their souls to be able to do that!" Then, almost to himself, musingly, he says, "If you had just stayed in L.A. . . . ." The words are out before he can take them back.

Sam pounces on this: "*If I had just stayed in L.A.?* How could I have stayed? You sent me away!"

Timothy's fight with his sister is still with him, still fresh. Sure, they papered over the holes, and they've been interacting reasonably, even amiably, but Timothy continues to smart from some of the things Amy said. His *savior complex*? He *took Amy's daughter away*? No. Nope. He'd only tried to do his best for everyone: for his mother, for Sam, for Amy herself. He's tired of absorbing blame. He's tired of being on his back foot. But mostly he's just very, very tired.

"I didn't send you away." That's it, five simple words, but with them comes an irrevocable shift.

Sam crosses her arms. "What are you talking about? Yes, you did. Remember? You had to go on location, and you didn't want to leave me with Gertie because she was up for that part in *Dark and Light*."

"I have to set the record straight on that, Sam. I wanted you to stay. Barry could have sent you out on auditions the day after the show got canceled. Your parents wanted you back. They made me say I was going on location, so that you'd go home."

She's confused. "But my mom said . . ."

He clears his throat; the olives from the martini threaten to repeat on him. "You'll have to talk to your mom about that, Sam."

"Okay. Fine. I will." She sets her lips together and nods briskly. "I definitely will."

"Wonderful. Good. So—can we have a truce?"

"I don't know. Are you sorry about what you said about my work in New York?"

Timothy considers this. He can't! He can't be sorry. He can't call it *work*. It isn't work. It's a bunch of silly videos. He opens his mouth, but no apology comes out, because there isn't one in there.

Sam narrows her eyes at him. She knows he isn't sorry. "*I just figured it out!*" she says. "I got it. I figured out what got you in a bad mood."

Timothy folds his arms. He's not a father, but he feels like this is a fatherly stance, wise and unyielding. "By all means, Sam, tell me," he says. "Please."

"It's not the platform, or climate change, or my acting career. It's not that those girls know who I am. It's that they *didn't* know who you are." Sam is nodding now, assessing him; in fact, she reminds him of a therapist in L.A. he saw long ago, in his thirties, who knew more about Timothy than he knew himself. "That's it. You're acting disdainful and judgmental, but really what you are is jealous. You're *jealous*."

A long, silent collection of seconds passes. They stare at each other, uncle and niece, as the summer night settles around them. A peal of laughter moves over from the Adirondack chairs, but here, at the moment, in this particular place, in their version of Mudville, there is no joy.

Timothy can see the regret on Sam's face immediately, but that knowledge is secondary to the actual, physical pain he feels in his gut, in his heart, all the way down to the soles of his feet. Is Sam right? *Is* he jealous of his niece? Yes. No. He doesn't know.

"You think I'm jealous of you? Standing around taking pictures of yourself, expecting to get famous for it? That's not art, Sammy. That's self-indulgence. That's a waste. A waste of you."

Even though the sky is now the dusky blue-black that comes just before nightfall, with the barest filament of color left, more floss than ribbon, he imagines he can see her winding up like a pitcher about to deliver a fastball, and here it comes. Wham. Bam. Over the plate, a perfect strike. "I'm not *expecting* to get famous," Sam says. "I'm *already* famous. And I'm so done with this conversation."

Sam

AFTER THE FIRST three months Tink pronounces Xanadu a success. The numbers look good: really good. "There's a lot of eyeballs on you guys," she says. "A lot of eyeballs." There's just one thing, Tink adds. Their neighbor, a tiny, wealthy octogenarian with jet-black hair, filed a noise complaint with the co-op board. Tink took care of it, but they need to be a little more careful. Tink adds a rule to the whiteboard: *Keep the noise at a seven out of ten.*

Xanadu spawns two sets of couples: Scooter and Kylie, Nathan and Alice.

Over Christmas, Sam expects that they will all scatter back to their homes of origin, but nobody leaves. Boom Boom and Kylie are Jewish. Scooter is from the Bronx, so he goes for part of the day to bring presents to his siblings and his mom, but he's back at Xanadu before dark. So Sam doesn't leave either. It's the first Christmas she's ever spent away from home. She misses her mom's special peppermint hot chocolate. She misses Christmas Eve Mass at St. Thomas More, when the children's choir sings "O Come, All Ye Faithful." She even misses Henry, who is bringing his girlfriend, Ava, home with him. Ava's parents are in Europe for the holiday.

But! Tink comes by in the morning with a gift for each of them: perfume for the girls, Xbox games for the boys. The eight of them make a Christmas video together. The weather outside is frightful, so they start drinking at 3 p.m.

Every so often over the past months, Sam's mother has called to check in, and Sam has told her small, tame stories about the camaraderie and hijinks in the house. She figured her mom would want to hear about the hijinks. Now she tells her about the time Kylie tried to make pesto but didn't screw the top to the food processor on correctly. You can imagine how that turned out: not well.

"What'd you do about the pesto?" her mom asks.

"Kylie used it for content."

"The pesto?"

"The video."

"So you guys are paid to . . . make food incorrectly? And make a mess, and take videos of the mess?" Amy says wonderingly.

"Not exactly."

"I've made dinner almost every night for the past twenty-two years and nobody's ever paid me to make a mess." Amy laughs, possibly mirthlessly.

"We're paid to produce content, Mom," says Sam. "A lot of different things can be content."

"Are you sure you don't want to come home, honey? Maybe for New Year's Eve, since you didn't make it for Christmas?" Sam's mother had been absolutely heartbroken that Sam hadn't come home for Christmas. How'd Sam know? Amy told her: I'm absolutely heartbroken, Sam.

On New Year's Eve they are all going to Tao Downtown. It's orchestrated, but it's supposed to look accidental. They have a table. She can't miss New Year's Eve.

"Mom. I'm sure." Then, as an afterthought: "But thank you." As a thought after the afterthought: "Really. Thank you." Her parents will probably play board games and drink prosecco. "Poor man's champagne," Alice calls prosecco.

The gang from Xanadu stays out until 4 A.M. *on New Year's Day. They dance and dance and dance. There are celebrities at Tao Downtown, real celebrities, like (minor) movie stars, but it turns out that to a lot of people the Xanadu crew are now celebrities too. It is on the dance floor at Tao Downtown on New Year's Eve that something starts between Tucker and Sam. When they're waiting for another round his hand finds hers under the table; when they're dancing, she can't stop staring at his neck, and imagining her lips on it. Does he feel it too? She's not sure, so she sets the thoughts aside and keeps dancing. The night is young. Not really, actually, but they are young, so it doesn't matter that the night is growing old.*

Tink comes by the next day after noon and discovers that one of the one-of-a-kind lights hanging over the kitchen island is broken. ("How can it be one of a kind?" whispers Tucker to Sam. "There are six of them.") He snakes his hand across Sam's back and she leans into him. She didn't make it up, the chemistry from the night before. Her knees are weak.

"Who's responsible?" Tink asks. "I need to know, now. I'm not fucking around, you guys." Her lip curls up in an unattractive way.

Nobody owns up. Nobody, in fact, remembers.

Tink has a video camera installed. "Sorry, gang," she says. "It's just that it's my reputation on the line here."

In January, Sam sleeps with Tucker for the first time. They try to keep it secret, sort of, at first . . . but not really, because people (followers) love collab house relationships.

"Own it," says Tink, when she learns that there is now a third couple in Xanadu. "Monetize it."

The thought of a bunch of middle schoolers sitting in their bedrooms like a collective third wheel in their relationship makes Sam a little uncomfortable. She's had one serious boyfriend before, junior year in high school, for eight months, but she's still pretty new at all of this, and she's not sure she wants everything to be content.

And yet the numbers and views and followers keep growing and growing. Coupled-Up Sam, it turns out, is far more valuable than Solo Sam. Who is she, really, to complain about who's watching? After all, this is what she came for. (Is it? Isn't it?)

Now Tucker and Sam, yes, it's official: they are a thing. They make a video to "Love You Like a Love Song" by Selena Gomez. Retro. Their followers go crazy. The song goes to the top of the Spotify downloads for that week; Selena Gomez thanks them on Twitter and calls them the "Golden Couple."

After a couple of weeks, Sam senses an evil stare from Alice anytime her hand brushes against Tucker's, or if he pulls her close to him when they're waiting in the kitchen for the top-of-the-line Jura GIGA 6 machine to dispense their espressos. Sam's not totally into public displays of affection, but sure, a certain amount can't be helped. They're all living in such close proximity. And she's so, so attracted to Tucker.

"Does Alice have a thing for you?" she asks Tucker. "I could have sworn she pushed the bathroom door into me when I was coming out."

"I don't think so." Tucker looks adorably perplexed. "Alice is with Nathan. And I'm with you. You're the one I want to be with."

She kisses him.

From around the corner, Alice clears her throat. Sam didn't know Alice was there and she jumps back from Tucker, her heart beating fast.

Her mistake, she thinks later, was falling in love. Was she in love? She doesn't know. What is love, anyway? What does it look like?

In April, Tink brings Sam and Tucker an endorsement offer for a new brand of chocolate peanut butter energy bars. "It's a no-brainer," she tells them. All they have to do is bump into each other on the subway, letting Sam's chocolate bar fall into Tucker's open jar of peanut butter. It's a callback to an old Reese's commercial, someone tells Sam. Their eyes meet over the jar, and the chemistry is almost palpable. Tucker earns $10,000; Sam earns $15,000, because she has more followers. After the video circulates, the bar sells like crazy. Every twelve-through-fourteen-year-old in the universe wants one.

That's an exaggeration, of course, but maybe not by much.

"I saw your video," Alice says one afternoon in the kitchen, when Sam is looking for spinach to put in her smoothie and Alice is looking for champagne to put in her pomegranate seeds.

"Okay," says Sam uncertainly. Is Alice going to offer a compliment?

"*That could have been me.*" The implication is clear: Alice feels that Sam has robbed her of something.

"*But you're with Nathan . . . ?*" says Sam. She turns on the Vitamix and lets it run for two full minutes. It's too loud, while the blender is running, for either of them to say anything to the other.

When the blender stops Alice says, "Nathan," like she's saying, "diaper rash," and stomps out of the kitchen, sloshing a pomegranate seed over the side of the champagne glass. Later, Boom Boom explains the situation to Sam; he's close with Nathan, and Nathan has shared some numbers with him. Endorsement offers for Nathan and Alice are down overall since Sam and Tucker became the newest Xanadu couple, and the offers they are getting are smaller than they used to be. "Sloppy seconds," Alice calls their offers. Alice is moody and unpredictable more than she is the "super-fun girl" Nathan fell for, Nathan tells Boom Boom, who tells Sam.

Nathan, Boom Boom tells Sam in strictest confidence, is thinking of breaking up with Alice. Nathan is wondering if Solo Nathan might do better out there than Coupled-Up Nathan. He hasn't made a decision yet; it's just a possibility he's keeping in mind.

In May, maybe inevitably, maybe not, come the photos.

SAM HEARS HER uncle call her name, but she doesn't answer, and she doesn't turn around. She seethes and simmers down the steep driveway, across the street, and onto the shoulder of Spring Street. The moon has risen, and it's almost full, so it's not dark, but it's certainly not light either. She's regretting the choice of her platform sandals. She's regretting what she said to her uncle. But she's mad at him too, for what he said to her. There's a knot of rage and humiliation lodged inside her rib cage, and she can't figure out how to get it loose.

It *is* a long walk home, and it *has* gotten dark, and it's true that the shoulder on this road is narrow, and not built for a casual nighttime stroll, or really any kind of stroll at all.

You know what? So what. She doesn't care. Uncle Timmy basically just judged everything she's ever done—he *belittled* her work at the collab house, which was actual, legitimate work. (Just ask her bank account, if you're not sure.) As though every single thing he'd worked on was worthy of an Oscar. Please! That movie on the navy submarine?

She calls Henry. He answers on the first ring, chipper and energetic as ever.

"Henry," she says. "Did *you* know I could have stayed in California after *My Three Daughters*? To pursue other acting opportunities? But Mom and Dad made me come back. Only they pretended it wasn't them."

"Hello to you too, Sam."

"Yeah," she says. "This whole time I thought I had to come home because Uncle Timmy had to go on location and I didn't have anywhere else to live, but as it turns out, that was just a *lie* Mom made him say so that I'd have to leave California. Can you believe it? Uncle Timmy just told me."

Henry says, "Hmm." Then he says, "He told you?"

She pauses and considers this. "Yeah," she said. "Accidentally, sort of, but yeah. Mom and Dad totally lied to me! Can you believe it?"

"I mean, kind of," says Henry. "You'd been gone for a while when your show ended. I was privy to a lot of conversations. I guess I'm not shocked they thought it was time for you to come home."

"But it's so unfair. They weren't even honest with me. I could be in a whole different place right now!"

There is a pause, and then Henry says, "You know what, Sam? I know you're going through some things. But maybe expand your tunnel vision."

"My *what*?" Sam spits this out, because she can't believe it: first Uncle Timmy, and now Henry. Is everyone against her? What did she ever do to any of them? "What are you talking about? What tunnel vision?"

"For starters," says Henry, "you haven't asked me a thing about myself or my summer. You haven't asked about the program I'm doing, or about Ava. You call me when you want something from me—comfort, or reassurance, or company. Other than that, I don't hear from you."

"That's not *true*, Henry."

"No? You sure? Think about it, Sam." She thinks about it. Henry might have a very small point. Very small indeed, but still a point. "'We are what we repeatedly do,'" says Henry.

"Huh?" says Sam.

"Aristotle. And the rest of the quote goes, 'Excellence, therefore, is not an act—'"

"Henry!"

"'But a habit,'" he finishes.

"That isn't helping."

"Have a good night, Sam," says Henry. "Be careful out there, okay?"

"Out where?"

But there's no answer: Henry is gone.

A car passes her on the other side of the road, going in the same direction she's going. Deep breath. Get ready. This is probably Uncle Timmy. The driver lowers the window and whistles and says, "Hey, baby girl. Need a ride?"

"No," Sam says.

"I'll give you a ride you won't forget!"

"Fuck off," says Sam, and the passenger says, "Oooh, looks like she's a spicy one!" And thankfully the window goes up and the car continues on and out of view.

"*Ugh!*" says Sam to the car. She is so. Over. Everything.

Uncle Timmy is just going to leave her to die on this road? Okay. Fine. Won't he feel bad about what he said to her when she turns up kidnapped, possibly murdered? Won't her parents feel bad too, when Timmy tells them he told her the truth about L.A.? She runs through her mental contact list and wonders who she can call, where she can go to avoid Uncle Timmy tonight. Tomorrow, he's already told her he's going to Newport to have dinner with Barry Goldman. But what will she do when (if) she ever makes it back to the house on Mohegan Trail? Sit in her room?

Sam hasn't tried her fake ID anywhere on the island, though she knows it's a good one because she used it in New York. She had enough of going out in New York to last a while, and most nights she's happy to lie on the couch in Floyd's living room, avoiding social media and enjoying some of the shows on the many streaming services Floyd has. (Floyd subscribes to everything; she's halfway through season two of *Ozark*.) She's purchased a couple of "beach reads" from the front table at Island Bound Bookstore, and she might even read one soon. (Whatever a beach read is!)

But tonight? Tonight, no *Ozark*. No beach read. Tonight, she's not going home. She doesn't want to talk to her uncle, and she doesn't want to go through the work of avoiding him either. Tonight, she's going out. She turns around, crosses the street, points herself toward downtown.

She knows that some of the cast members have become regulars at McAloon's, where she had lunch with her parents just a week ago. What the hell, she'll give it a try. Actors know how to make a night of it. She remembers that from her Broadway days. When she was in *Mockingbird* she was far too young to do anything after the shows but go home with her mother and go to bed, except for Wednesday nights, when she and her uncle went for a slice of cheesecake at Junior's, but she heard plenty of chatter about the shenanigans the rest of the cast got up to. They used to go out with the cast of *Hamilton*, the cast of *Fiddler*. Sam was witness to the hangover talk and the drunken-hookup talk.

She opens her Uber app and inputs McAloon's as her destination. Are there even Ubers on Block Island? She peers at her phone, walks into the yard at the 1661 Inn.

There seem to be only three Ubers available on the whole island. Eventually, after a couple of tries, she secures one of them, a Nissan Sentra driven by a Dan. She watches Dan's Nissan crawl toward her on the screen. Deep breath. Okay. She'll be fine. Where there's an Uber, there's a way.

Once Dan drops her outside the bar, under the sign with the two shamrocks, Sam pauses, momentarily paralyzed. What if nobody she knows is in there? Will she go home, or sidle up to the bar all by herself? Will she make friends, or be shunned? Will anyone in the bar who's not part of the cast recognize her (this could be bad) or not (this could be worse)? If she changes her mind and decides to spend her evening with Jason Bateman after all, will she be able to get that Uber back? Dan mentioned that he was headed out to a house party near Grace Point, all the way on the other side of the island. How long will it take him to return?

She's contemplating these questions when someone opens the bar's door and exits. It's a couple of guys, maybe forty or so, and they hold the door open for her. It's practically an invitation: she feels that she has no choice but to enter. Almost immediately she hears her name and sees a hand waving from the back of the room. The hand, it turns out, belongs to Jack Marshall, who plays Leonato. Next to him are Sarah Trail (she plays Margaret) and Charlie Andrake (a local kid, nonbinary, who plays the Messenger). Charlie looks sixteen, so either Sam has underestimated their age by a lot or they also have a very good fake ID. At the other end of the bar are a few more cast members: Don Pedro, Borachio, Claudio. They're talking to three girls in identical white shorts with identical, purposeful rips and frays. She recognizes a couple of the set guys too. Okay. *Okay.* She knows enough people here. She should stay. One drink! Then she'll Uber home, and by then her uncle might be in bed, and they can avoid each other.

Leonato and the Messenger move apart to make room for Sam, and she slides in and waits for the bartender to turn his attention to her. When asked, she shows her ID and holds her breath. The bartender doesn't question it. It's a really good fake ID. She buys a round for all of them, plops down her credit card, and the night, like a baby bird in a nest, starts to look up.

The third Red Bull and vodka of the night goes down easy—even easier than the first two, and she didn't exactly have to choke those into submission. The mood in the bar is upbeat, and soon enough all of the *Much Ado* people are clumped together in the small bar. Little snippets of conversation reach Sam:

". . . not even sure that the props department can . . ."

"You can't tell me that I wouldn't—"

"So I told him that I felt triggered but *then*—"

"*Three cats* and an iguana all in one—"

This last conversation is the one Sam thinks she might want to get in on, but when she looks around for its source she can't find it. Next thing she knows Borachio has his face really close to hers and he's asking what it's like to have *Timothy Fleming* as an uncle.

"I mean, he's so famous!" says Borachio. "It's like—it's like having Tom Cruise as an uncle or something."

"I guess so," says Sam. "Yeah, sort of. I mean, to me he's just an uncle." Just an uncle who wants me to use my platform to fix climate change, she thinks. Just an uncle who belittled my work and basically my whole generation. *That's not art, Sammy,* he'd said to her. *That's self-indulgence.*

"He scared me so much during the first rehearsal," Borachio confides. "I mean, I was *terrified*. I was like a kindergartener learning to read. I literally had to *sound out* the words. Then as we went on, I discovered he's just a guy. A person. Like the rest of us. Pretty easygoing, as it turns out."

Ha! Thinks Sam. *Easygoing.* As long as you don't attract more attention than he does, then he's perfectly easygoing!

"Actually," she tells Borachio. The next words are out before she can really consider them, because she's still frazzled from the fight, and underneath the frazzling, she's genuinely hurt. "Actually, he may seem easygoing on the outside, but you know what? Not on the inside. You cross him, you're going to pay for it."

"Wow," says Borachio. His eyes grow wide. "Really? Tell me more."

It is then that Sam sees a phone pointed at her; the phone, it turns out, is held by one of the white-shorts girls. "Getting it," she calls to another white-short girl. "Getting the whole conversation. This is going to go so viral!"

No no no no, thinks Sam. To the person with the phone she says, "Excuse me? Were you *recording me*?"

"Maybe," says the girl.

"You can't do that!"

The girl shrugs. "It's a free country."

Sam looks around wildly. What exactly did she just say? What did the girl record? She's been off social media all summer, and the first person to record her without her permission caught her saying something about her uncle. She feels her cheeks grow hot; she feels a liquid shame pour through her, pool at her feet.

"No," she says. "Delete it."

"Make me."

Borachio says, "Not cool," to the girl, and just then a woman swoops in. She's tall and pretty; she has long brown hair with a blue streak, a perfectly made-up face, and an air of purpose and authority. She holds her hand out to White Shorts.

"Phone," she says.

"WTF?" says White Shorts. "Who are you?"

"Shelly Salazar. Hollywood publicist. *Phone*." Miraculously, the girl hands it over. Shelly keeps a grip on the phone and points it toward the girl.

"What are you *doing*? Are you insane, lady?" says White Shorts.

"Face ID," says Shelly.

Smart! thinks Sam. Shelly swipes and presses expertly though the phone, opening the camera app, swiping and pressing some more. She hands the phone back to the girl. "I deleted the video, then deleted it from the deleted files. It's gone. I also sent your contact info to myself, while I was at it."

"You can't do that!" The girl looks to her companion, who shrugs. "You can't just—do that. That's my *phone*, my *private property*."

"Free country," says Shelly, and Sam smiles. Shelly goes on: "That video shows up anywhere, and I mean *anywhere*, and I will absolutely track you down. I know a lot of people who can really mess with you. Any questions?"

White Shorts shakes her head, and she and her two friends and *their* white shorts turn toward the exit, muttering to each other.

"Just so you know," one of them spits at Sam on the way out, "we think it's awful, what you did to Alice."

"*What?*" says Sam. These girls are Team Alice! Figures. "But I didn't—"

It's too late though; the girls have disappeared through the bar's doors and into the night.

"Doesn't matter," says Shelly, turning to Sam. "Doesn't matter what you say, they're going to think what they think."

"Thank you for saving me," whispers Sam to Shelly. "Are you really a Hollywood publicist? I thought my mom said you were in books and theater."

Shelly shrugs and says, "Eh. Close enough." Then she fixes Sam with a look that manages to be both supportive and disapproving at the same time. "You need to be careful with yourself, sweetie." Had the *sweetie* come from someone else it might have seemed demeaning or inappropriate; from Shelly, somehow, it feels just right. "You, of all people, should know that."

Sam takes a deep breath. Shelly must know her story. "I know," she says. "I should, I know." She turns back to Borachio and smiles her biggest smile. "I was totally kidding," she says. "Pulling your leg! Uncle Timmy is great. You're exactly right. He's just a person, like you or me!"

For some reason Borachio thinks this is the funniest thing he's heard all night, or possibly ever. "Uncle Timmy!" he cries. "Uncle Timmy." He can't stop laughing. He just *can't stop laughing,* and Sam almost laughs too, but actually she's still very shaken by what just happened with the girls and the phone, and what happened earlier with her uncle after dinner. It's been a shaky night. "Hey!" says Borachio. "We should have a party."

"Yes!" Charlie the Messenger is all for this. They pump their fist in the air. "Like a cast party, but a month before the show." They grab Sarah Trail by the elbow. "Sarah! We're having a cast party!"

Sarah turns to Sam, delighted. "We are? I love parties!" She points to Charlie. "You're local. You must know enough people to make a party."

"Oh, I know people," Charlie confirms. "I know pretty much everyone on this island. I know the bartender here—he lets me hang out sometimes, but he doesn't let me drink. Anyway. I could have a really good party."

"Perfect!" cries Sarah. "Your house?"

"Maybe," says Charlie. "Maybe. Let me check with my parents."

Charlie leaves and comes back a few minutes later, looking downtrodden. "We can't do it at my house. My parents said absolutely not, no way, no how." Charlie sighs. "This is all because of my sister."

"What about your sister?" asks Sarah.

"Oh, her high school graduation party three years ago got— well, let's just say it got a little bit out of control. I thought that was all in the past now but apparently it's still really very much in the present."

"Too bad!" says Sarah. "I don't even have a house—just a room in someone else's house." She turns to Sam. "I'm guessing you're not an option, right? Since you live with the director."

"Right," confirms Sam. Then she thinks about it. Didn't Uncle Timmy just tell her that he and Gertie were going to Newport tomorrow night to see Barry? "But maybe—"

"Maybe what?" says Charlie eagerly.

No. She can't offer up her uncle's house, which isn't even his house—it's Floyd's house. She could, of course, but she shouldn't— she wouldn't.

Would she?

She stands there for a moment, looking up at the whiskey bottles lined up on top of the bar, considering the Tale of Two Sams. On one side is the good Sam, respectful, grateful to her uncle, grateful to Shelly for bailing her out of a potentially danger- ous situation just now, grateful that what happened in New York wasn't worse.

On the other side is a different Sam. The second Sam's judg- ment is compromised by three drinks; the second Sam is still smarting from her conversation with her uncle. *Taking pictures of yourself, expecting to get famous for it.*

"Maybe *what?*" echoes Sarah.

"We can't have a *party*," the second Sam tells Sarah and Char- lie once she's sure Shelly is out of earshot (surely Shelly wouldn't approve). "But we can have a get-together, at my place. My uncle will be out of town tomorrow night."

Sarah perks right up at this and says, "Cast party!"

"Cast *get-together*," clarifies Sam. "Something small. We have to keep it super under control. Just a few people, the cast and maybe a couple of others. I'm serious." Sam points at Charlie. "Don't tell a lot of people," she says. "Even though you know everyone in this town, and even though you're a messenger."

Maggie

MAGGIE HEARS ABOUT the party from Marta, the summer intern, when she comes in for a coffee and a scone the next day before rehearsal. Marta, who likes to chat, who likes, as she admits herself, to be "in the know," mentions to Maggie that she heard from Charlie, who plays the Messenger, that Sam Trevino is hosting a party at her uncle's house that very evening. She leans over the counter, practically caressing the register, and whispers, "Her uncle will be out of town!"

Forty-five minutes later Sam herself comes in and orders a cappuccino with four shots of espresso.

"A quadruple?" asks Maggie. "You sure you want that?"

"Positive," Sam says. Her voice is scratchy. "I was out last night. Like, *out* out." She shakes her head. "It was a whole thing."

"Is that why you're not at rehearsal?" Sam has told Maggie that though she's not in the play she attends many of the rehearsals and helps her uncle out, sort of like an assistant director.

"No rehearsal today," says Sam. "Also, my uncle and I . . ." She pauses and looks pensively at the napkin holder on the counter. "Never mind. It's not important." She takes a sip of the drink. "This is perfect," she says. She sticks a five in the tip jar—it's almost a 100 percent tip!

"I heard your uncle is out of town," Maggie says before she can stop herself. Once the words are out, she can't take them back. Sam looks at her sharply.

"Where'd you hear that?"

Maggie hesitates. She doesn't want to get Marta in trouble. "Nowhere," she says. "I can't remember." Then, because she feels guilty and doesn't want to lie to Sam, she says, "Marta mentioned something about a party."

Sam sighs and says, *"Marta!* She was a year behind me in school. She was a nosy parker then, and she's a nosy parker now." She claps a hand over her mouth and says, "I can't believe I just said *nosy parker.* That's something my grandmother used to say. Anyway. It's not a party. It's a get-together. It's really just cast."

"Sure, yeah, of course," says Maggie, as nonchalant as you please. "I get it." In a smaller voice she says, "I did sign up to be an usher. I know that's not cast, but."

Sam hesitates. "You know what? It's fine. Come. You should come."

"Okay," says Maggie, trying so hard to act like this is no big deal she's afraid she might burst a vein. "Sure. I think I'm free." (She is so *definitely absolutely* free.) Riley is going to *freak out.* "Can I bring my friend Riley?" she asks. "And I'm sure Riley will want to bring her boyfriend, Jacob." She rolls her eyes to show that this is Riley's preference, not hers. "But that's it, I promise."

"Um," says Sam. "Well, but are you all fifteen?"

"Almost sixteen," clarifies Maggie. "Jacob's already sixteen."

Sam hesitates. "I just don't want to be responsible for like corrupting the youth of the island."

"Oh, you won't," says Maggie. "We go to summer parties all the time." She hopes Sam doesn't notice her tell, a bright red earlobe. "It's no big deal."

WHEN SHE WAS thirteen, two years ago, Maggie wore only T-shirts with slogans on them—*I don't want to taco 'bout it, it's nacho prob-*

lem, with a picture of a taco, was her favorite—but once she gave those up and discovered she actually had decent abs her wardrobe got *a lot* more interesting. Tonight she's wearing her high-waisted denim shorts and a V-neck cropped tank top in a deep rose that makes her tan glow. She's in Riley's bedroom, examining herself in Riley's full-length mirror. Despite her freckles, she's finally managed to get a decent tan. Riley has the boobs though, and the boyfriend. Even if it's only Jacob.

"I can't *believe* you got us invited to a party at Sam Trevino's house," says Riley. She stands back from the mirror to assess her mascara application. "Nice job by our little Maggie!"

Maggie rolls her eyes. "It's a get-together," she clarifies. "Small. Not a party." *Our little Maggie.* Yes, she's shorter than Riley, but in fact she's two months older. Ever since acquiring a boyfriend over the winter Riley has begun to treat Maggie like Maggie is Riley's hapless, naive younger sister. And it's not like Riley's boyfriend is any great catch. Not even close. Jacob is part of their eight-member class at Block Island's single, tiny school, and they've all known each other basically since time began. Personally Maggie thinks dating Jacob would be like dating your own brother. (Maggie doesn't have a brother—the closest approximation is Max, the son of Maggie's mom's live-in boyfriend, Anthony. Max is six.)

"I'm going to pee," announces Riley, and she disappears into the bathroom attached to her bedroom. Riley, like Maggie, is an only child, but unlike Maggie she doesn't have to share her bathroom with every member of the household; she has it all to herself.

Riley's phone, faceup on the bed, buzzes, and Maggie glances at it. Jacob. Ugh. Even when he's not here he has to intrude. Riley is not a believer in face ID or passwords or really privacy of any kind. She'd let anyone in the world into her phone. For some reason Maggie can't help herself: she picks up the phone and taps on the message. Ur so hot bae.

Ugh, again. Is this how Jacob and Riley text on a regular basis? She taps the message again, opening the text history between them, and she sees . . . wait, what? It's a photo taken in Riley's full-length mirror, the one Maggie was just using to adjust the straps of her tank top. And the person, whose face is not shown, is full-on naked. Well, not "the person"—it's Riley. Maggie recognizes the mole on Riley's stomach (noncancerous; she had it checked in the spring); she recognizes the boobs; she recognizes even the landing strip of pubic hair. She and Riley have been undressing in front of each other for ages. She knows what her friend looks like naked.

"So listen, I think if we tell my mom—" Riley is saying when she opens the bathroom door and sees Maggie holding the phone. Maggie drops it back on the bed, hot-potato-style, and Riley stares at her, then picks up the phone herself and looks at it. "Oh!" she says. "Did you see my latest photo shoot? *I* don't care. Go ahead and look."

Go ahead and look? Maggie is stymied. "Riley!" she says. "What do you mean, latest?"

"Latest and greatest," says Riley. "I think I finally got the lighting right. I look good, right?" She smiles. "See my tan line? It's super faint, not like yours, but I'll take what I can get."

"*Riley!*"

Now it's Riley's turn to roll her eyes. "Oh, come on, Mags. You aren't going to give me some mom-style lecture, are you?"

"But why?"

"Why what?"

"Why do you take those photos of yourself?"

"Sometimes Jacob asks me to, so I do."

"Does he do it back?"

"Sometimes. Sure."

Maggie shudders. "Riley! What if your mom sees?"

"She won't. I always have my phone with me."

"Still . . ."

"*What?* What's wrong with it? If I don't have a problem with it, why should you?"

"Because . . ." Maggie hesitates. "Because bad things could happen."

Riley scoffs. "What bad things?"

"You could get sex-trafficked!" Maggie sits on Riley's bed and pulls one of her oversize pillows to her chest. She rests her chin on the edge of the pillow. Riley's unconcern is baffling to her. Hasn't she heard the same horror stories as Maggie? Didn't their ninth-grade health teacher warn them against the dangers of this very activity?

Riley sighs. "How exactly would that work, Maggie? My own boyfriend is going to sex-traffic me?"

"Well no, but . . . you don't know, honestly. Let's say Jacob gets mad at you for something, like, I don't know, you hook up with a summer boy, and then he sends that photo to someone to get back at you, and that person sends it to someone else, and all of a sudden *your* photo is on some creepy website where pervy guys pay money to look at it . . ."

Her mother had made her read an article in the *New York Times* about a girl whose life was basically ruined after she sent nude photos to someone she trusted. Before this girl knew it she was a drug addict living out of her car. "You could be a drug addict living out of your car before you know it."

"You can't even see my face!" protests Riley.

"Even so. Things can get out of your control." She thinks about Sam Trevino.

"Jacob's not going to do anything like that. I trust him, okay?" Riley sits down next to Maggie on the bed. Maggie can smell her Ariana Grande perfume and her mint gum. "I know you don't understand because you haven't been in a relationship yet—"

"That's not what this is about," Maggie tells the pillow. Riley's superior tone is really getting under her skin. She doesn't even know if she wants a boyfriend! Why does Riley have to make her feel bad for not having one?

"Maybe it is, maybe it isn't. I don't know. But listen, you're not going to find a guy who doesn't want this. This is just how it is. This is how we have to be."

"What if it isn't how I want to be?"

Riley shrugs. "I don't know, Mags. I didn't create the world. I just live here. And I'm being careful. You don't need to worry about me, okay?"

"Okay." She can't help it though. She's a worrier.

"Let's go to the party."

"*Get-together*," says Maggie. She tries to summon the excitement she'd felt when Sam came into the café earlier; the excitement, even, that she'd felt ten minutes ago, before she'd first looked at the phone. But she can't find it.

When she and Riley dismount their bikes on Mohegan Trail after a long, hilly ride during which Riley worries aloud that she's sweating off her perfume and Maggie worries internally that she's sweating *on* some reprehensible body odor, Maggie feels like she's finally about to experience a real-life Taylor Swift Fourth of July party circa 2013–2016. The house is lit up like a Christmas tree. There are cars parked up and down the long driveway and, in one instance, on the wide green lawn. Music is coming from the open windows; people are spilling out of the double front doors. More people are on the grass, sitting on the steps leading into the house, on the second-floor wraparound deck.

"Holy shit," breathes Riley.

"Holy shit," agrees Maggie. This is definitely not the small get-together Sam had described.

"Do you think these are all people from the play?" asks Riley.

"I don't know," says Maggie. "I guess? Probably? Or maybe they're summer people. I don't recognize anyone."

"Do you think we're the only people from school here?"

"Maybe?"

"God, that would be amazing," says Riley. "If we were the only ones? Can you even. We could be entirely different people. We could reinvent ourselves!"

Maggie feels a tap on her shoulder and turns around. It's Sam! "Hey, girl," says Sam. "Welcome! Um, so, it's a *little* bigger than I was planning, I think things sort of snowballed." She takes a deep breath and says, as if to herself, "But it's going to be okay. I know it's going to be okay." She glances back and forth between Riley and Maggie. "I'm so glad you guys are here," says Sam. "But. I don't want to be, like, an enabler of underage drinking. You guys didn't drive here, did you?" Maggie doesn't want to remind Sam that she and Riley aren't old enough for driver's licenses, so she just shakes her head. "Okay, good. In that case. You didn't hear this from me. But there are hard seltzers in the kitchen. I think there's a keg somewhere over there . . ." She gestures vaguely behind her. "Whatever you do, take it slow. And definitely, definitely stay away from the rum. The rum is not for amateurs. Oh! And the most important thing. Do you see that big blue bucket over there?" The girls nod. "I need you to put your phones in there until you're ready to leave. House rules, okay?" Without waiting for an answer, Sam whirls away, into the crowd.

"I can't believe that just happened," says Riley. "Sam Trevino. I just can't believe it."

"I know, right?" Maggie starts to feel the power shift slightly back in her direction. Maybe she doesn't have a boyfriend, maybe she doesn't know how to light a nude selfie correctly, but *she* is the reason they are here.

Riley purses her lips and looks around at the clumps of people everywhere. She marches over to the blue bucket, and Maggie follows her, and they both drop their phones in.

"How will we find them later?" Maggie worries.

"We'll figure it out. Jacob will be here in fifteen minutes. Let's go get a drink." Neither one of them has been drunk before. Once in the late spring they were planning to share a vodka and lemonade when Riley's parents were out to dinner at Kimberly's, but Riley's mother had a bad reaction to an oyster and her parents came home ninety minutes earlier than they were supposed to. Riley and Maggie had to sacrifice their carefully crafted cocktail to the kitchen-drain gods.

Maggie follows Riley across the lawn, down the walkway, into the house, and up a set of stairs that leads to the main floor. She's taking in the scene. A couple is making out in a corner. A group of five is playing some indiscernible drinking game at the low living room table. A woman in her twenties is crying softly into a red Solo cup. Riley, whose absence Maggie hadn't even noticed, returns with two cans of Truly in her hands.

"Black cherry or raspberry lime?" Riley asks. "There was also grapefruit, but *blech*."

"Black cherry, please," Maggie says. She feels like she's a kindergartener at a restaurant and Riley is her sophisticated server. Maggie has to hand it to her though: Riley is acting cool as a cucumber, like the two of them actually have experience going to parties.

The first few sips of Truly go down with some effort—Maggie has never loved carbonated beverages, and the aftertaste of the alcohol introduces an uncomfortable little zing into the back of her throat. But she perseveres, a good little soldier, and before she knows it the can is three-quarters of the way gone, then completely empty. By the time she's done Jacob has arrived, and he and Riley kiss as though one of them has been on a desert island for forty-two days, and then they disappear, presumably to make out somewhere more private.

Maggie helps herself to another Truly, raspberry lime this time, then carries it outside and to the far edge of the lawn and gets to work on it. There's a stone wall parting this yard from the land next to it, and she lowers herself to a seated position on the ground with her back against the wall.

She belches softly, then looks around to see if anyone heard her. Nobody is paying her any mind at all. She doesn't know where Sam went. She can still hear the music from here. The Weeknd, of course. Obvious choice, but still fun. Nobody is officially dancing; however, some of the shadowy bodies are swaying. Maggie is within a few arms' lengths of dozens of people, but she may as well be alone. She supposes she could find her bike and cycle home, but she doesn't feel like putting up with questions from her mom or from Anthony or, worse, from Max, who is visiting them and whose incessant questions put Maggie's teeth on edge. Does Maggie know that there are only five thousand Chilean dolphins left in the wild? Does she know that there will be a total solar eclipse on April 8, 2024? Has she seen the video with the dog riding on a turtle? (Yes, Max, literally everybody has seen that video. Maggie begins to wonder about the wisdom of giving a six-year-old access to the Internet.) Sometimes the questions are of a more personal nature. Where is Maggie going? Why? Can he come? Why not?

She concentrates again on Truly Number Two. This one is going down *much* easier than Truly Number One had. Her thoughts unbutton themselves and go free, and all she can think about is the photo on Riley's phone, and the conversation that they had after.

This is just how it is. This is how we have to be. The hooded look, the careless shrug.

A few more sips.

The edges of the night begin to blur. She looks skyward, at the nearly full moon. The moon is blurry. Is it blurry for everyone?

"Is the moon blurry?" she asks the person closest to her, a girl with long dark hair and a pierced nose with a glinting gem in it.

The girl looks up at the moon, then looks back at Maggie and smiles. "Not to me. But also I'm sober. I'm in rehearsals, and I don't drink when I'm in rehearsals."

"Oh," says Maggie. (Isn't everyone here in rehearsals?) "Right. Of course. That's how you know Sam."

"Yup." She holds out a hand for Maggie to shake. "My name's Amelia."

"Maggie."

"Come sit," Amelia says, pointing to the wall she's sitting on. It's the same wall Maggie was leaning her back against, but it follows the grade of the lawn and is shorter where Amelia is. Why not? Maggie sits. "Did you come here alone?" Amelia asks.

"No." Maggie waves a hand in the general direction of the house, of the moon. "I came with my friend Riley. But she's . . ." Her voice trails off, and she's suddenly filled with an unnameable sadness. "It doesn't matter," she says finally.

Amelia moves closer to her on the wall. She's wearing perfume. Maggie doesn't know enough about perfume to know what it is, she's only familiar with Riley's Ariana Grande perfume, but it smells nice. "Friend troubles?" she says. "You can tell me about it, if you want. Believe me, I've been there. God, I'm happy to be out of high school. Graduating was the best thing that ever happened to me. How old are you?"

"Sixteen," says Maggie, because that feels more dignified than her actual age. She'll be sixteen in the fall, so it's not too far off.

Amelia pulls a vape pen from the pocket of her shorts and inhales. "I'm sorry!" she says. "How rude of me. I didn't even offer." She holds it out to Maggie. "It's weed."

"I thought you had to stay sober for rehearsal."

"Yeah, I can't do alcohol. That messes with me. This just calms me down." Amelia shrugs.

"No, thank you," says Maggie. She cringes a little; to her own ears she sounds formal and polite and very much not yet sixteen. She and Riley went through a vaping phase a couple of summers ago, the same summer Maggie had a tremendous crush on a French boy named Hugo whose father owned a food truck that gave Maggie's mother a lot of grief. Their vape pens took flavored cartridges, not weed. It was a brief phase and ultimately not worth the wrath of Maggie's mother when she found the equipment in Maggie's backpack.

"So tell me what's going on. With your friend or whatever. I'm a neutral party."

"Oh, that's okay. Thanks. It's stupid."

"My mom always says, if it's bothering you, it's not stupid. And then I'd tell her whatever was bothering me, and she was totally right. It didn't feel stupid anymore."

Maggie thinks about this. Her mother used to be someone she could talk to, but since Anthony moved in her attention has been so . . . *claimed*. Joy Sousa is a pie, and that pie used to be divided exactly in two: half for Joy Bombs, and half for Maggie. Then Anthony moved in, so the pie got divided into three pieces. Sometimes more! Max, for example, doesn't share Anthony's piece. He gets his very own. Maybe a smaller piece, but still a piece.

"What's your part in the play?" she asks Amelia. "Is it a good part?"

"Sure. I'm Hero. It's a big part. And. To be in a play with Gertie Sanger? When I haven't even started college? The kids in my program are going to freak out. That's, like, a *dream*. But TBH there are some cringey things about the character that I wish I could change."

"Like what?" They read *Romeo and Juliet* in school last year but otherwise Maggie has managed to evade Shakespeare.

"Well, like. Here's the big one. Hero gets totally set up by these jerks who tell this guy she's about to marry that they saw her with someone else so she's not the virtuous woman he thought he was marrying." Amelia inhales from her vape again. "This was in the way olden days, of course, so virginity was a big deal, you know.

Not like it is today. So this asshole believes the lie and humiliates my character in front of basically the whole town at the wedding, and refuses to marry her."

"That sucks," says Maggie.

"*Sucks*," confirms Amelia. "Then, when it's proven that it was all a lie and that Hero's precious virtue *is* intact, he takes her back. And she's like, Yay! Which is kind of gross. And then they live happily ever after. So to answer your original question, yes, it's a good part, the second female lead in the play, and I'm lucky to have it, but I'd be lying if I said I agreed with our girl Hero's choices. You know?"

"Right," says Maggie. "I know." Amelia is so much more interesting than anyone she knows on Block Island. She's doing things that are interesting, and she's having important, interesting thoughts about them, and she pulls off a nose ring so well.

"Anyway," says Amelia. "Enough about Shakespeare! Tell me about your friend. Randy?"

"Riley."

"Riley. Tell me about Riley."

Maggie drains Truly Number Two and sets the can down on the wall next to her. The party is still raging, but they're in the suburbs of it. Amelia is looking at Maggie like she really cares about what she has to say, and it feels so good to have someone listen to her that even though it is *extremely* off-brand for Maggie to spill a private story to someone she's just met, here she is, telling Amelia about picking up Riley's phone and seeing the photos and also about the conversation they had after. "So it's just . . ." she finishes. "It just bummed me out. Like really? Is that actually how everyone has to be? I mean, is that what *you* do for boys?"

"Never," says Amelia. "I can say with absolute honesty that I have never sent a nude selfie to a boy."

"You haven't?"

"I haven't."

"Okay." Relief floods over Maggie. "I don't want that to be true. I mean, I haven't even had my first kiss yet. I'm so behind."

There's a pause, and then Amelia says, "I could kiss you."

Maggie looks up quickly. Amelia is studying her with a face that's friendly and open. "You?"

"Sure. Why not? You'd have the first one over with, and you could move on."

Maggie considers this. "Are you . . . I mean, I don't even know if I am—"

Amelia takes her hand and winds their fingers together. "You're adorable," she says. "Sweet Maggie. You don't have to decide your whole life right now, what you are or aren't. It's a beautiful night. You're at a party. Just . . ."

Just what? thinks Maggie. But Amelia doesn't finish the sentence. Instead she leans toward Maggie, and Maggie doesn't lean away. Amelia's lips are slightly salty, and a little bit sweet too. At first Maggie is too stunned to kiss back. Then something inside her wakes up, and she's moving her lips too, and then Amelia parts Maggie's lips with her tongue, ever so lightly, and this goes on for—how long? Minutes? Hours? Days? Long enough for Maggie to feel something inside her start to open—until Amelia's phone rings, and she pulls away from Maggie.

Don't stop, thinks Maggie. But also, Do stop.

"I'm sorry," Amelia whispers. "I'm so sorry. I've been waiting for this call from my agent, that's why I didn't put my phone in the bucket. Don't tell anyone."

"That's okay," says Maggie, but she's not sure if Amelia heard her, because she's already talking on the phone. Amelia walks a little bit away from Maggie but Maggie can still hear her give a yelp of joy and say, "I got it? Are you serious? Please tell me you're not fucking around with me—yes. Yes! Absolutely. Tell them yes yes yes. I'll call Northwestern on Monday."

When she comes back to Maggie her eyes are blazing and she

says, "I can't believe it. I can't *believe* it. I just got the phone call of a lifetime. Holy shit. Pinch me. I'm so glad I didn't put my phone in the bucket." She holds out her bare arm, but Maggie doesn't think she *actually* means for Maggie to pinch her, so she just sort of pats it.

Then there is a roar, and for a moment all of the sound from the party stops, and a man strides up the walk bellowing, "*Samantha!*" and that's when Maggie gets on her bike and gets the heck out of there, because the great Timothy Fleming is home, and he's not happy.

Timothy

TIMOTHY IS IN the rehearsal barn, puttering around and seething. He'd left the house as soon as he'd awoken—he didn't want to see Sam, he didn't want to see Gertie, he didn't want to see anyone!—so instead of making coffee at home he'd gone straight to Joy Bombs for a triple latte with an extra shot. And he feels— nothing. Still tired. Well, tired and jittery. Is that worse than tired and not jittery? He doesn't know. He's just happy to be alone. He's *so angry* with Sam. On the way to Newport he couldn't stop replaying their fight in his mind. She'd called him jealous; he'd called her self-indulgent. Then, instead of talking it out a day or two later, as he'd hoped they might do, she'd thrown a party at Timothy's house, which isn't even Timothy's house! It's Floyd's house! He's incensed. She'd apologized, over and over again, but still. He's seething.

His sister comes into the barn. She's holding her own cup of Joy Bombs coffee, and she's smiling. "Morning, sunshine!" she says. Her skin looks fresh, her eyes look bright, her voice sounds chipper. This is the last thing he needs.

"What are you doing here?" Amy doesn't typically come to the island on Sundays even if they have rehearsal. Sunday is her day at home with Greg.

"I'm meeting the curtain person at eleven," she says, "and I left my notebook here on Friday." She peers at him. "What are *you* doing here? And why do you look so awful?"

"Because I didn't sleep!" he roars. "Because I got home from Newport at midnight."

His phone buzzes. It's Alexa. He ignores the call.

Amy looks confused. "There's a ferry that gets in at midnight?"

"Of course not. No. Barry's friend brought us over in his boat."

Amy busies herself looking through a pile of papers on a small table near the stage. When she finds her notebook she holds it up triumphantly, but Timothy is too cranky even to acknowledge it. "I thought you two were staying in Newport," says Amy.

"We were. But Gertie ate something from the charcuterie board and got one of her migraines, and her medicine was at the house, so the friend offered to bring us home." He sighs and adds, "I don't know if it was the salami or the blue cheese. She should have known to stay away from both of them."

"Triggers," agrees Amy. "Is she okay?"

"She's sleeping in. I've told Jane to call off rehearsal for the day."

"Why didn't you sleep in?"

"I was too angry to sleep."

"What were you angry at? The charcuterie?"

"No. Not the charcuterie. When I got home at midnight, the house was lit up like Gatsby's. And *your daughter* was throwing one hell of a party."

Amy gasps. "*No!*" she says. "Sam?"

"Yes," says Timothy. His voice crackles. "That daughter, yes."

"A *party?*"

"One hell of a party," Timothy repeats.

"Oh, geez. I'm sorry, Timmy! Where is she now?"

"Probably sleeping."

"I'll go talk to her. I'll go talk to her right away." She glances at her watch. "I'll push back the curtain person if I have to."

"I don't know what good talking to her *now* will do," grumbles Timothy, but Amy is already out the door.

Once Amy has gone Timothy's phone buzzes again with Alexa's number.

He scratches his chin. If Alexa hasn't left a voice mail the first time, and if she is calling again so soon, she must have a good reason. He takes a deep, deep breath. He really doesn't want to think about L.A. right now. He hopes this isn't a bad wildfire report. He hopes his koi are okay.

His voice ekes out its best possible greeting. "Alexa!"

"Timothy, hey!" (For the first two months she worked for him Alexa refused to call him anything but Mr. Fleming. Timothy took this as proof that she'd been raised up right, with good, solid New England manners. Finally, after enough prodding, she relented from the formality.) Alexa sounds breathless—has she already completed a CrossFit class or a run on the beach even at such an early hour? How he envies Alexa the energy of her youth! He tries to set back his sagging shoulders, lift his sagging chin. "Listen, I'm sorry to bother you on a Sunday morning," she says. "But there's something I thought you should know."

Timothy raises the hand not holding the phone and gently massages his temples. Another deep breath, filling up the lung cavity, releasing. "Go ahead . . . ?"

"Okay. So. Last night I was out with a bunch of the assistants. Casual, you know, just a couple of drinks and we were all going to have an early night—"

"An early night. Sounds great," says Timothy, trying not to come across as bitter.

"Yeah. It actually was. So anyway, this guy was there, I forget his name, I think I'd met him once before because he was talking to me like we knew each other. Jeff something? He works for Simon Richdale, who works for Mabel Shanahan—"

"Sure." Mabel Shanahan Casting: one of the best.

"And he was telling me that they just cast this new Hulu show, because they're going to start shooting right away, like next week, they're in a real hurry for this one, you know how Hulu gets when they want something."

"Yup." Timothy does know how Hulu gets when they want something.

"And he starts naming the cast, right? And one name in particular sounded familiar."

"Okay," says Timothy. The cobwebs in his head are making it hard to follow this conversation, but he's trying. Mabel Shanahan, Hulu, casting, familiar name. He takes another sip of the coffee. Finally can feel his brain cells yawning open.

"And I was racking my brain to see why it sounded so familiar, you know, and all of a sudden it hit me. Timothy, Amelia Rees got cast in this Hulu show."

Everything around Timothy goes blurry. He clutches the corner of the table. "*My* Amelia Rees? *This* Amelia Rees? My Hero?"

"Your Hero. Yes. Exactly. I was going to call you last night, but I couldn't get a signal in there, and then even though it was a *super*-early night, by the time I got home I thought maybe you'd gone to bed, because it was like midnight back east, so I didn't want to bother you."

"Ha," says Timothy. "I was *not* in bed by midnight."

"Oh! So I could have called. Maybe I should have called. I'm sorry to be the bearer of bad news."

Timothy coughs and tries to find a modicum of good cheer. It's hard to come by. "It's good news for Amelia," he says. "A Hulu show can make a career."

"Yes. Yes, of course, great for Amelia. But not so good for you."

"It's terrible news for me," admits Timothy.

Long silence, then Alexa says, "Is there anything I can do to help you?"

"Not unless you can find me another Hero on this island."

"I wish I could. I really do." Alexa clears her throat. "Timothy?"

"Yup?" His mind is already wading through the possibilities. It doesn't take long, because there aren't many: It's a quick wade. More like a dip.

"While I have you. Just one more question. So sorry. I know your mind is on other things. Understandably. Would you mind if I take Monday and Tuesday off next week? My mom and her husband and my little sister are coming for a visit."

Timothy doesn't know that much about Alexa's life: she's fairly private. Honestly, he appreciates the restraint. Too many young people hang it all out online these days. (Exhibit A: his very own niece.) Once, when he was going to the funeral of a director he knew, Alexa mentioned that she had a boyfriend who died shortly before she moved to L.A. Sad. But since then she has never mentioned him, and she's only talked about her family a few times. He knows that her father is somewhere in L.A., but that Alexa doesn't live with him, and he knows that her mother is newly married and that there's a little sister, much younger than Alexa. Timothy recognizes that her family coming to visit is a big deal, and he tries for a moment to put the news about Amelia Rees aside.

"Of course. Of course you can have a couple of days off. Take more if you need them. There's not much to do right now, while I'm out here. Where are they staying?"

Alexa makes a little pffft noise and says, "I'm trying to figure that out. I want to find a hotel that says, *Look, we're in L.A.* but not, *We're going to have a stroke when we see the bill.* You know? And that's harder than it sounds. Like, obviously they're not going to stay at the Chateau Marmont!"

"Sure," says Timothy. "That classic New England frugality." Goes along with the manners, he thinks. "Why don't you have them stay there?"

"Where?"

"There. At my place."

"At *your* place? Absolutely not."

"Why not?"

"Because they'd freak out. The excitement might actually kill them, and then I wouldn't have my family."

"It's there. It's available. It's empty. Talk to Marnie, make sure the cleaners come in before and after. Stay there with them, if you want."

A pause on the line. He can hear Alexa breathing. Finally she says, "Wait, seriously? Do you mean it? Honestly I think that would make my mother's *whole life.*"

"I mean it," says Timothy. "I definitely mean it. Now, if you'll excuse me, I've got to go figure out this Hero situation."

Amy

AMY DRIVES THE rolling hills of Spring Street and Mohegan Trail faster than she should; not a good idea, considering how many bikes and mopeds traverse those roads on a summer's day. She makes herself slow down around the curves. She pulls down the long driveway leading to Floyd Barringer's house, parks, rings the doorbell. No answer. She raps on the door with her knuckles, rap rap rap, and still no answer. She rings again. Sam must be in here—right? Where else would she be?

She checks her phone. They have a family location sharing app, but she tries not to stalk her children very often, so she rarely uses it. Now she opens it. Greg is fishing with his buddy Pete at Black Point, Henry is on the campus of Middlebury—philosophizing, she supposes, even on a Sunday—and Amy and Sam are right here, just off Mohegan Trail on Block Island. The screen shows hers and Sam's little avatars practically on top of one another.

Amy rings again. Sam must be *sleeping off* the *party that she had*. But Amy will wait all day if she has to, to talk to her. She'll push the curtain person even later. While she waits she surveys the front of the house. She squints at something in the boxwood next to the front door, then bends and looks closer. A Truly can! Flavor: black cherry. She picks it up. Status: empty, slightly dented. She sighs.

Amy is about to ring the doorbell again when she hears footsteps approaching from inside the house. She'd know those footsteps anywhere; Sam has a very distinctive gait. She lands on her heels and rolls through to the balls of her feet. When she was a kid she wore out her sneakers in such a funny way, grinding the edges down. Does she still do that? Amy hasn't looked at the bottoms of Sam's sneakers in some time.

The door swings open, and there's Sam. "Hey," says Sam. She looks terrible, even worse than Timothy. Dark circles under her eyes, messy hair. She sounds bad too; there's a crack in her voice.

"Can I come in?"

Sam shrugs again and stands aside for Amy to enter, keeping her back angled away.

"Sam. I just came from seeing Uncle Timmy." Sam's shoulders tense. Amy tries to keep her voice calm and measured but she isn't *feeling* calm and measured. "If Gertie is sleeping, let's go upstairs." Sam waits for Amy to go up the stairs, then she follows her. When they reach the main floor Sam flops on the couch and Amy, remaining standing, says, "I can't believe you had a party! Sam! What were you thinking?"

Sam closes her eyes, and rests her head on the back of the couch. When she opens her eyes she sighs and says, "It wasn't supposed to be a party. It was supposed to be a get-together, just the cast and a couple others. It got a little out of control."

"Whoever it was supposed to be! That's incredibly disrespectful to your uncle. It would have been disrespectful even it was his house, but this is *someone else's house* that you're lucky enough to be living in. That's extra disrespectful."

"I thought he wasn't coming home. I would have had it all cleaned up."

"That doesn't matter. That's not the point."

Sam snorts.

"Did you just *snort*?"

"Maybe."

"Why?"

"I just think it's pretty funny that you, of all people, are worried about honesty."

Amy does a quick mental rundown of her last several interactions with her daughter. All very normal, everything on the up-and-up. She can't come up with anything untoward. "What in the world are you talking about?"

Sam gets up and walks to the table in the breakfast nook; she sits, so Amy sits too. Sam says, "When my Disney show was canceled." Amy's stomach drops. "Uncle Timmy told me that it wasn't up to him, whether or not I stayed out there. He told me it was up to you. You lied to me and told me Uncle Timmy had to go on location. You had *him* lie to me. He never went away on location that year! Check his IMDb. I did. He didn't shoot anything outside of L.A. until I was a sophomore in high school."

Amy's heart is beating faster and her palms are starting to sweat. "When did he tell you this? And *why?*"

"It doesn't matter." It does matter though. Did Timothy tell Sam this because he was still mad about *their* fight? Here she'd thought they were doing well—that they'd made some real progress!

"Whatever Timmy told you—it's not exactly the whole story, Sam."

Sam rises from the table and stomps down the stairs, and Amy, stonewalled, bewildered, doesn't follow her.

Time passes. How many minutes? Amy doesn't look at her watch. She waits for a while to see if Sam will emerge from her bedroom and come back upstairs, so they can talk. When she doesn't, she takes an exploratory trip around the main floor of Floyd Barringer's house. Amy had been so young when Timmy was in high school—she was just the pesky little sister, not really even old enough to tag along, not threatening enough to be an actual bother. But she remembered Floyd because he was always nice to her, and she had a little bit of a crush on him. Not a real one, of course: when the boys were seniors in high school she was just a little peanut of a thing, nine or so. Sometimes Floyd and Timothy would drop her off or pick her up at a friend's house, and they always smelled like forbidden things: cigarette smoke and leather motorcycle jackets and something else, earthier, that she now realizes was probably weed.

She studies the photo of Floyd and his adult children—one boy, one girl—that sits on the mantel in the open-concept living room. Floyd has the puffy face that signifies wealth and success across a certain swath of America, and that part isn't familiar, because he used to be thin as a reed, but his smile is recognizable, and she likes the way he has an arm around each of his kids. He looks loving and proud and supportive without being possessive. Go Floyd, she thinks. You seem to have it figured out. A house like this, a family like that.

She steps out on the deck and looks at the slice of Vaill Beach visible from here. To the left is the looming, forbidding beauty of Mohegan Bluffs. She thinks about the Niantic and Mohegan people, who battled for supremacy of the island, until the Niantic forced the Mohegans to their deaths over the cliffs. Why must humans always be fighting one another, each side armed with a stalwart belief in its own agenda? Look at her and Sam, look at her and Timothy!

Eventually she goes back inside, descends the stairs to the bedroom level, and knocks on Sam's door. The door to the room where Gertie sleeps is still closed, so she keeps her knocking soft.

"I'm not here," says Sam, but Amy keeps at it, and finally Sam releases an audible sigh and says, "Come in, I *guess.*"

Sam is lying on her bed, arms folded, staring at the ceiling. It takes a moment for Amy to figure out what's different about her and then she realizes she rarely sees her daughter not in motion, not on a screen or in conversation, not laughing or talking or moving. She's completely, utterly still.

"May I sit?" Amy tips her head toward the bed. Sam grants her a grudging nod before moving over about an eighth of an inch. Well, that's something. Amy sits. "Timmy's right," she says. "All that time in New York, for *Mockingbird*. Then another year away from home for *My Three Daughters*. Your dad and I talked about it, and we didn't want you to grow up in Timmy's world. We wanted you to grow up in the world that we made for you and Henry. We figured that if acting was something you really wanted to do you'd find your way back to it. We figured you didn't need to be a child actor to be an actor."

"I don't know," says Sam. "I don't know what I needed to be. I don't know what I should have been." Her face crumples and she looks like a little girl once again, like the girl who used to write letters to the Elf on the Shelf in the off-season because she was worried he'd think nobody loved him for who he really was outside of Christmas.

"It was the right thing for you to come home then, and if we had to . . . massage things a little to get you there, and if that upsets you, well, I'm sorry. I am sorry."

"Lie," said Sam. "Not massage."

"Fine. Yes, okay. Lie." Amy's hand hovers over Sam's leg. She wants to put a hand on her calf, to reassure her, but she can sense that Sam doesn't want to be touched right then. So she tries to reassure her with her voice instead. "Sam, honey. You've got so much ahead of you. We didn't want you to rush that. We wanted you to be able to make those decisions later, with the grounding of a solid home behind you. You're just getting to the good part right now."

Sam's voice cracks as she pushes herself up onto her elbows, swings her legs around, and says, "This is the good part? Are you kidding me? Holy shit, Mom. If this is the good part, then what is the bad part going to be like?"

Amy considers this. "Okay, fair," she says. "Very fair. It might look like the good part to me right now because I'm like a hundred, and you have so much collagen that I forget that it's hard to be nineteen sometimes—but I guess what I'm saying is, these are the times when you can take risks, and do things without the consequences being enormous, and figure things out. That's why we wanted you to go to a regular high school first. That's one of the reasons I think college would be good for you."

"*Risks?*" says Sam.

"Sure. Risks."

"Look who's talking," says Sam quietly.

"*Excuse* me?" says Amy.

"I said, Look who's talking." Sam's voice is louder this time, and clearer. "The person with the least risky life I know."

Amy's skin is stinging, as though Sam has actually slapped her. Softly she says, "*What?*"

"I mean, you're not exactly an expert on taking chances, Mom. Uncle Timmy has told me how much promise you had as a playwright. You left New York and stopped writing before you even got started. Safer. You wanted me home from L.A. because it was safer. You teach high school because it's safer. You're not really an advertisement for risk-taking yourself."

Sam may as well have kicked Amy in the ribs. She can hardly breathe.

"Mom—" says Sam, and it's clear by her face she realizes she's gone too far. Amy holds up her hand as if to keep any other words from coming out of Sam's mouth. If she were to defend herself she'd say she teaches high school because she loves teaching high school. She'd say young teenagers who are lucky enough to have loving parents belong at home with them. She'd say she never wanted to be a playwright all that badly anyway, which isn't true, and she'd say that she's confident in the life that she and Greg built for their family, which *is* true. But she's hurt and she's angry, and she's not going to defend herself.

Amy closes the bedroom door softly behind her as she leaves. She thinks about checking in with Gertie to see if she needs anything, but she decides it's better to let her sleep. She walks up the stairs to collect her keys and her phone. Out the front door to the Wagoneer, where she sits for a moment, engine and air-conditioning both on, to collect her thoughts and examine her feelings.

Her phone rings: Timothy.

"If you're calling to yell at me too, please don't," she says. "Please just—don't."

"I'm not calling to yell at you. I'm calling to tell you about Amelia Rees."

After Amy left the barn, Timothy tells her, he got a call from Alexa with some unsettling news. Then he checked his email and found a long, apologetic message from Amelia. She'd just gotten the call about the Hulu show, and she had to get out to L.A. immediately. She was taking the early ferry so she could get to Logan for a flight. She was so sorry not to have this conversation in person. She was sorry to let him down. She was sorry about everything. She was grateful for the chance to be in the play, but she couldn't imagine turning down an opportunity like this and then looking back on it with regret, and she was . . . well, she was gone.

"*No!*" says Amy. For a moment she forgets that she's mad at Timothy for telling Sam the L.A. thing. "No no no. What are we going to do?"

"There's only one thing I think we can do."

"What's that?"

"Ask Sam to take on the role. Can you do that for me, Amy? I think she'd take it better coming from you."

The unfairness of this request coming from Timothy *now* chafes Amy immediately. "No. Definitely not, Timothy. No, I can't. As a matter of fact, I'm not exactly on good terms with my daughter right now."

"Because of the party?"

"Well. That's how the conversation started, me getting mad at her about the party. But we got off the subject pretty quickly because she told me that *you* told her about our agreement to get her to come home from L.A."

"She didn't! Amy."

"Why'd you do that, Timothy? Why, after all this time? Were you trying to get back at me for something? It wasn't that long ago that we talked about you respecting my choices, and now this?"

"Oh, shit. *Shit,* Amy. I'm sorry. There's a backstory to it. Let me explain."

"Nope. No." Amy holds up the hand not gripping the phone, although there is nobody in the car to see. "I don't want to hear any backstory right now. I don't have time for it, and I don't have energy for it. I'm going to the theater to meet the curtain person, and if you have something you want to ask Sam, you're going to have to ask her yourself."

Timothy

"You look like you're headed for the gallows," Timothy says to Sam fifteen minutes later. After talking to Amy he'd texted Sam and told her he was going to pick her up and that she should be ready. He figured, after the night before, that he wouldn't get any pushback, and he was right: he didn't.

"I feel like I'm headed for the gallows," Sam admits. "Am I?"

Timothy glances over at her. She's wearing a hat Timothy hasn't seen before—navy blue, with an outline of the island in white, and she pulls the brim down and slouches in the passenger seat. "Nah," he says. "You're headed for Joy Bombs. Am I right in guessing you could use a coffee, and maybe some sugar and some fat?"

"All of the above," says Sam.

"How's Gertie?" he asks. "Any proof of life from her?"

Sam shakes her head. "Not a peep. I think she's still sleeping."

"Okay, good. She needs to sleep at least fourteen hours after taking that medicine, and then she should be her lovely self once again."

"I remember," says Sam softly. Of course, thinks Timothy. Sam lived with them for a year. She's experienced Gertie's migraines.

"Anyway, besides getting you some sugar and some fat, there's something I want to talk to you about."

A sigh escapes from Sam; Timothy gives her credit for the fact that it's barely audible, but she loses points for sighing in the first place. "Is it the party?" she says. "I really am sorry. I messed up. It got out of control, but I never should have okayed it in the first place. I don't know how to make it up to you—but I'm sorry."

"It's not about the party. The party's over. I got mad; you apologized. There's not much else we can do about something that's in the past. Do I wish you hadn't done it? Of course I do. Am I glad nothing happened that I would have been liable for, or, worse, that *Floyd* would have been liable for? Yes. I am immeasurably glad about that. So let's move on, shall we?"

"We shall," says Sam. "We most definitely shall."

Timothy parks the jeep near Joy Bombs and says, "Good."

"So . . ." she says a few minutes later, when they have their coffees and whoopie pies and their seats too. "If we're not here to talk about the party, what are we here for?"

He clears his throat. He's so nervous! "Amelia Rees has left the production," he says.

"*What?*"

"She got a Hulu show. She's gone. She's off the island already, on her way to California." He takes a sip of his coffee—his second cup of the day. He's almost starting to feel normal. Well, *normal* is a strong word. He's starting to feel better. "And I want you to consider taking over her role."

"No, thank you," says Sam immediately, almost primly.

Timothy takes a beat and tells himself not to react too quickly. "No *thank you*? I'm not offering you a scone, Sam. I'm giving you an opportunity, and I'm asking you to help out." He's trying not to let all of his feelings jump out at once—but this is important. If Sam doesn't say yes, he doesn't have a backup plan.

"I'm not the right person. You should get someone who auditioned and didn't get the part. I didn't even try out."

"The thing is, Sam." He tries to keep his voice steady. "The thing is, you're exactly the right person. I can't get someone else. Opening night is just over two weeks away, Sam. Nobody else knows the part."

"Someone can learn a part in two weeks. It just takes concentration." Sam is suddenly very busy with her napkin. She folds it into little squares, then unfolds it, and considers it. She starts to fold it again.

Timothy puts his hand over Sam's, partly to quiet the movement and partly to get her attention. Sam looks at him, startled. "There's nobody else on this island right now who could do it, so even if we found someone elsewhere we'd have to get them over here, find a place to put them up, and get them to learn a boatload of Shakespeare before beginning rehearsals. You're here already. You know the part. You offered Amelia some very cogent notes."

Sam makes a face. "It's just because I'm a quick study. I memorize things automatically. I didn't do it on purpose."

"Sam. You have a real feel for the part. You know the lines, yes, but you also know the emotion behind the lines."

Sam looks at him levelly. "I have a feel for Hero when I'm offering notes. When there's no risk involved. Trust me, I'm not the right person to do it."

"But you are! You are exactly the right person."

Sam sighs, irritated, crosses her arms and says, "Are you making me do it?"

"Jesus. Of course not, Sam. I would never *make* you do something like this. I couldn't even if I wanted to. You're an adult. I'm simply asking. That's all I'm doing. You know how talented I think you are. When we had our . . . conversation Friday night . . ."

"Argument," she says.

He tips his head toward her. "Fine. Argument. I was starting to tell you that, but we got onto the subject of why and when you left L.A. When you're dealing with real material, real art, you've got such a knack—"

He can tell instantly by her expression that he's said the wrong thing, again.

"Who are *you* to say what's art and what's not? You're—what? The great art judge? The art *arbiter*?"

"Well, no," he hedges. "But some things are basic knowledge. Agreed upon."

"By *who*?"

He falters. He knows he's right, but he doesn't have the answer to prove it. "By—people."

She shakes her head. "Thank you for the offer," she says. "And for the coffee. But I don't think I can do anything public right now."

She gets up, and she walks out of the café, and Timothy doesn't think it's exaggerating to say that a little piece of his heart walks out with her. (How, he wonders, will Sam get home?) When Gertie is awake he's going to have to tell her about Amelia, and they'll need to make haste contacting casting in New York to see who they can find on no notice.

He sits there for several minutes, paralyzed by the task ahead. Then, as he's rising from the table, pushing in his chair, Sam comes back in. There's a slight sheen to her skin. Maybe she's been searching her soul, or maybe she's simply been sweating.

"Sam," he begins. "I didn't mean to make you think—"

"I'll do it," she says. "I'll do the role."

"You will?"

"I will.

"What changed?"

"I called my mom."

"And—?"

Sam shrugs. "It's a whole thing I don't need to get into, about taking risks . . . and . . ." She looks like she has more to say but she lets her words trail off and says simply, "Moms."

"Oh, *Sam,*" says Timothy. He feels a catch at the back of his throat. "I'm so happy. I'm just so—happy."

Sam rolls her eyes. "Don't freak out too hard, Uncle Timmy. It's really not that big of a deal."

"Of course not," says Timothy, playing it so very, very cool. "It's a small deal. What do you say we get on home and check on Gertie, tell her all about this development."

"Uncle Timmy?" she says, on the way home, as they wind up Spring Street. "I know I said it already, but I really am sorry about the party."

He clears his throat and says, "Okay. But let's not have anything like that happen again."

"Definitely not," says Sam. After a beat she says, "You sounded like a dad when you said that. Stern and a little bit scary."

He laughs. "I doubt that." Then he adds, "I am not cut out to be a father, Sam." Spring Street turns to Mohegan Trail, and the brush becomes thicker, the houses more obscured.

"Why do you say that?"

"I don't think I have the instincts. For one thing, this party situation. I can't tell if I'm forgiving you too easily or not easily enough."

Sam thinks about this. "I think you're forgiving me just the right amount," she says. She taps her fingers on the side of the jeep. "And I think you'd make a great father. But maybe uncle is the role you were really born to play."

He pulls into Floyd's driveway. He nods slowly and feels a squeezing sensation on his heart. "Maybe it is, Sammy. Maybe it just is."

Sam

THE PRODUCTION HAS moved from the barn on Corn Neck Road to the stage of the Empire Theatre, where they've begun rehearsing scenes as the technicians test the lights and the actors work with their blocking in the new space. Tuesday they'll begin to run through the whole show, with the actors trying out little bits of their costumes—shoes, swords—that might give them trouble.

As such a late arrival, Sam is permitted to be on book as long as she needs to—her uncle told her this, and Jane, the stage manager, confirmed it—but she feels a strong compulsion to know as many of her lines as possible. So on the last Saturday of July she carries an iced latte (oat milk), her script, her phone, and a towel out onto the deck of the house on Mohegan Trail. It was nuts in town when she got the coffee from Joy Bombs (on days when her mother is not required to be on the island, Sam is allowed to drive the Wagoneer) and, like a proper local, she's decided that on a weekend at the height of summer, staying at home is the right play.

She moves a lounger into the shade: the cast has been heavily warned against getting any sun in the days leading up to the show—nothing looks worse under stage makeup, says Jane, than a tan or a burn.

She has the house to herself. She doesn't know where her uncle and Gertie are. Timothy might have gone to the theater; Gertie might be off on her moped.

She's looking through scene 4 of act 3, when Hero, in the company of Margaret and Beatrice, is dressing for her wedding. Sam has already memorized most of Hero's longer lines in other scenes, and many of the lines in this scene belong to Beatrice and Margaret, with Hero offering only interjections here and there, but she knows that sometimes these are the easiest lines to trip over: the small ones, when an actor can get caught up watching the other actors in the scene and forget to speak. She wonders if Gertie might be back soon. Maybe they can run through the scene together so Sam can check this one off her list and move on.

She texts Gertie to see when she might be home and to ask her if she's interested in running lines. No answer. Sam sighs and flips her phone facedown on her towel. The sun has shifted direction and no matter how she holds the script or adjusts the angle of her head or her sunglasses she can't seem to escape it.

When a rivulet of sweat begins to make its way down the side of her body she declares to no one, "That's it!" She stands and collects her things, opens the slider, shuffles her way into the living room—the shuffling is necessary because of the awkward way she's got everything balanced against her body—and dumps towel, water bottle, et al. onto a kitchen stool.

Now what? She digs her phone out of the pile. No answer from Gertie. She opens the refrigerator. She's not really hungry, she's just bored, and it's a good thing too, because nobody in the house has done a real grocery shop in quite some time. There's a block of cheddar, and a bottle of white wine, and a pint of blueberries that look as though their heyday was so far in the past as to be no longer visible in the rearview. It's drearier even than the kitchen at Xanadu used to get—and that could get dreary indeed—because at least in New York they could order delivery of virtually anything anytime, day or night.

"We need a mother in this house," she says out loud and then, almost as if in answer, a peal of female laughter floats up the stairs from the bedroom level. Is Gertie home, and ignoring her text? Or is Uncle Timmy . . . not at the theater after all, but *entertaining*? She shudders at the thought. Before she has time to take any preventative action, such as vacating the living room, or hiding in the empty refrigerator, she hears one of the bedroom doors open, and the laugh travels up the stairs, followed by an unmistakable male tread.

"Oh!" says Sam. "*Oh.*" Suddenly understanding. Because the laugh belongs to Gertie, who's walking up the stairs in a robe, which she is hastily tying, and the male tread belongs to Uncle Timmy, who is—thank *God*—fully dressed, in shorts and a T-shirt, yet somehow still conveying an air of having recently been engaged in behavior that is, if not precisely illicit, then at the very least scandalous and surprising. "*Oh,*" says Sam again. "I didn't know you were home. I didn't see the jeep."

"Had to lend it to Jane to pick up a few things with the props department," says Timothy.

"Sam!" says Gertie. She arranges her face in an expression of innocence that, despite Gertie's acting pedigree, Sam can see right through. "We were just . . ."

"Please don't say *running lines*," says Sam, rolling her eyes. "I'm an adult. I know better."

"Who wants a glass of lemonade?" Uncle Timmy asks, as if there's nothing at all to explain.

"I'd love one!" says Gertie, too quickly. She sits down on the couch and tucks her legs up elegantly underneath her.

"I don't think we have lemonade," says Sam. "Just wine."

"Well, then. I'll go get us some. Mind if I take the Wagoneer?"

"Of course I don't mind. Keys are in it."

"BRB, as the kids say."

"I don't think the kids say that," says Sam. But it's too late; her uncle is gone, leaving Sam to turn her attention to Gertie. "Are you two back together?"

A faint blush creeps across Gertie's ivory cheeks. "I'm sorry I missed your text. I'd love to run lines with you. And no, we're not back together. We're just . . . having a little bit of fun. You know."

Sam feels her eyes go wide. "*Having*? As in present tense?"

Gertie clears her throat. "As opposed to future?"

"As opposed to *past*! Has this been going on for a while?"

"Oh, I don't know." Gertie loosens her famous hair from her casual bun, and it cascades around her shoulders (the shorter layers) and down her back (the longer). "Since, maybe, early July?"

"Early July? It's almost August! That's practically a month."

Gertie puts a hand on Sam's forearm. "Does it bother you? I'm sorry, Sammy. We should have been more discreet. I thought we *were* being discreet. I don't want to make you uncomfortable, send you running back to Narragansett."

"I'm not uncomfortable. And I'm *definitely* not running back to Narragansett. I'm just—it's just—maybe you *are* getting back together. That would be great."

"Oh, Sam. Don't look so hopeful, darling. This isn't *The Parent Trap*. This is just life."

"But I wish you guys were still together." She feels a tug of nostalgia for her time in L.A.

Gertie nods. "Sometimes I do too. But I can't hold down someone who doesn't want to be held down. That wasn't healthy for either of us, when I tried it before."

"I think he's changed."

Gertie seems to really consider this before she answers. "I spent a long time trying to make your uncle change, and, failing that, waiting to see if he might change on his own. But the truth is, Sam, people don't change. We are who we are."

Sam's eyes begin unexpectedly to fill. She blinks a few times fast, hoping Gertie doesn't notice. "So . . . so you're not getting back together?"

Gertie's smile is small and wistful. "No," she says. "No, we're not getting back together. And I think that's the right thing for both of us. Not *think*, I *know* it is."

People *don't* change, thinks Sam. It's such a basic statement, but it's also true, as true and right as anything Henry has quoted from his philosophers. So why do we all spend so much of our time trying to change everyone around us? Sam has accused her mother of wanting her to be someone she's not, but hasn't Sam been doing the same to Amy?

"I'm going to go downstairs and throw on something more appropriate, okay, Sammy?" says Gertie. "What are you going to do?"

Sam shrugs. "I guess I'm going to sit here and wait for Uncle Timmy to come back with that lemonade. But I have a feeling he's not going to rush back. So maybe while we're waiting, we can run those lines?"

August

Timothy

SAM HAS HERO's lines down cold.

"I'll still hold the script," she tells Timothy. "Just in case. But I don't technically need it. I think I've got it."

"You're a *marvel*, Sammy. You are simply a marvel. You memorized Shakespeare in the time it takes most people to memorize Shel Silverstein."

"'I cannot go to school today,'" quotes Sam. "'Said little Peggy Ann McKay.' I've got my Silverstein down too, see?" She smiles wickedly. It's so good, thinks Timothy, to have what he thinks of as the Real Sam back. He's really happy they've put the fight behind them, and they've put the party behind them, and they're getting down to actual work. "Seriously though. I'm not as fast as you're giving me credit for. It's just because I sat through a bunch of rehearsals and picked up lines that way. I could probably do Claudio too."

"Absolu*tely* not," says Claudio. "My granny has tickets to the third night. Do you want to crush her soul?"

It's the first of August, there are eight days to go until opening. Neither Timothy nor Amy can afford to spend time fighting with the other; he apologized one more time about telling Sam the L.A. thing, and then they both had to let it go.

Today, while some members of the cast are rehearsing, others have final costume fittings. The set builders are in the final stages of their work, hammering away at an errant nail, glue-gunning a stray piece of ivy to the villa's facade. Truly, truly, truly, knows Timothy, there isn't a moment to lose. His adrenaline is high; his sleep is low. He loves every single minute of this part of the process.

Knowing all of her lines doesn't make Sam not nervous; Timothy understands that. Of course she's nervous! Timothy has to remember that she has every right to be. She hasn't acted on a stage in seven years; she's only been Hero for a little over a week.

"Butterflies," she reports, pointing to her stomach, the first time she gets on the stage to learn the blocking. "So. Many. Butterflies." She's holding her body very carefully, like she's made of glass and might break if moved the wrong way.

Timothy watches Gertie cross the stage to Sam. She wraps her arm around her, and she puts her head very close to Sam's, and she whispers something to her. Timothy can't hear the words, but he can see Sam's rigid back soften under Gertie's touch, and then he sees her smile, and then he hears her laugh, and that's how he knows it's going to be all right.

Today they started early: nine o'clock. They will run through the whole show twice.

Shakespeare's plays were originally performed without intermissions, so their inclusion in modern-day performances is at the discretion of the director. Timothy has chosen to break between acts 3 and 4—more than halfway through the run time, but logical, from a dramatic perspective. Today the actors will get a short break at the intermission point in each run-through. This will give Timothy some time to confer with the stage manager, to see if there's anything going on he needs to be aware of.

By the middle of next week, they'll be opening!

The cast has taken to the stage like they've been there all summer; the blocking translates easily from barn to theater, which,

Timothy knows from experience, isn't always the way. Borachio's long, logistically heavy speech, during which he outlines the plan for tricking Claudio into believing in Hero's infidelity, has always been a challenge, with Borachio dropping lines like they're hot potatoes—but today the speech goes off without a hitch.

Drunken Borachio brags about his deception; Margaret dresses Hero for the wedding; Beatrice professes to have a cold when in fact she's lovesick. And on they sail to the beginning of act 4, just before Claudio and Hero's wedding, the dramatic center of the entire play. Claudio, instead of taking Hero's hand in marriage, shuns her, accusing her of infidelity because of the false story Borachio cooked up.

As these lines approach, Sam's aspect changes completely. She starts fumbling with her script and messing up the blocking. She almost knocks down her own father, Leonato, as he stands next to her in the outdoor church that the carpenters have constructed with an archway of flowers. This is the place where Hero is supposed to show her emotions—emotions Timothy knows Sam is more than capable of displaying, every bit as capable as Amelia Rees was. But she can barely get her lines out. What is going on?

Timothy makes a note for Sam.

"She knows the heat of a luxurious bed," accuses Claudio. "Her blush is guiltiness, not modesty."

Sam: "I talk'd with no man at that hour, my lord!" She's supposed to sound plaintive here, disconsolate. Instead she sounds wooden. *What is going on?*

Timothy makes another note.

Leonato, wretched: "Hath no man's dagger here a point for me?"

Here, Hero is supposed to swoon, and Timothy knows Sam knows how to swoon. He knows it, because it was *Sam* who helped *Amelia* learn to swoon in early barn rehearsals. Sam can swoon like she's getting paid to do it, her rent is due, and her bank account is empty! But her swoon looks like a swoon you'd see in a third-grade production of . . . well, he can't think of a third-grade production that would require swooning. But that's the level of swoon he's seeing here.

"Hold!" he calls. Sam rises. She drops her script, picks it back up.

"Break!" calls Timothy.

"Again?" says Claudio. "Shouldn't we run the rest of it straight through . . . ?"

"*Break!*" repeats Timothy, in his don't-cross-me voice, which he doesn't use often. "Actually, you know what? Let's break for lunch now. Then we'll pick up here."

"It's only eleven-fifteen . . ." Claudio persists. Gah, Claudio is a talented actor, but as a person sometimes he really gets on Timothy's nerves.

"We'll break for lunch now," says Timothy firmly. "I'll see everybody back here in an hour, and we'll do acts four and five, break for fifteen, and run the whole thing through without stopping. Got it?"

"Got it," says everyone, except Sam, who nods, and Claudio, who rolls his eyes.

Sam

SAM KNOWS HE's calling this break because of her. She slinks to the edge of the stage, wondering if she can also slink down the steps and out the door without being noticed. But no. Gertie, bless her soul, blocks her, turning her body carefully so that nobody else can see that the two of them are talking.

"What's wrong?" asks Gertie. "Sammy, what is it?"

Sam can feel that her cheeks are warm. Her elbows itch the way they do when she's anxious. Once she told Tucker about that and he knelt down and *kissed* each of her elbows. It was a very corny thing to do, but it was also very sweet. Sometimes she really, really misses Tucker.

"I don't know," she tells Gertie. "I think I'm just tired?" She looks around for her water bottle. She's so thirsty! Her elbows itch some more. She's not sure she could eat.

Gertie holds Sam's eyes. "Something is going on," she says. Gertie is not a mother, but she's looking at Sam with a mother's piercing gaze. "Come. Sit in the back row with me for a minute. Tell me what it is." From somewhere—thin air? A bag that Sam can't see?—she produces two icy cold plastic water bottles. She hands one to Sam, and leads her to two seats in the back row. All of the seats are now in perfect working order, thanks to Amy. The curtain will be hung the following day, also thanks to Amy. Gertie holds down one of the seats for Sam, like Sam is either Gertie's date or a toddler who doesn't know how seats work, and Sam sits. She opens the water bottle and drinks. The water might be the best thing she's ever tasted.

"It's this play," Sam says finally, almost spitting the words. "This *story*. I think we should change it. Do you think Uncle Timmy would be into considering an alternate ending?"

Gertie laughs, then sees that Sam is serious, then stops laughing. "Are you asking me if your uncle would be interested in changing the ending of a Shakespeare play?"

"Yes."

"Eight days out from opening night?"

"Yes. Well, not the whole ending. The Benedick and Beatrice parts can stay."

"Excellent. I'm not as quick at learning lines as you are, so I'm happy to hear that."

Sam half smiles. "But the Hero part? *Ugh*."

"Tell me more," says Gertie. "I think I know what you're getting at, but why don't you spell it out for me like I don't."

Sam sighs and fiddles with the label on the water bottle. "I just can't believe Hero goes through what she goes through, and then she decides to stay with this guy! I mean, what the hell? He accuses her of sleeping with someone else. Which she didn't even do. And instead of confronting her about it in private, like a reasonable person who heard some gossip, he humiliates her on her wedding day in front of the whole town. And *then*, he's going to marry some other girl, because, what, he just can't conceive of living without a wife? Pathetic."

"Pathetic," agrees Gertie.

"So he'll take some random other girl in her place? Okay, that's weird. And the only reason he marries Hero after all is because he doesn't know it's Hero. And then Hero's like, oh, never mind that you made me pass out from stress and humiliation in front of all of my *wedding guests* and then I had to *pretend to be dead* to survive it all, I still think it's a great idea if we get married. I would love to be your woman, and, like, bear your children and sweep your floors and make you breakfast every morning." She notices that Gertie is smiling and she says, "I'm serious. When you look at it that way, it's a terrible story. Isn't it?"

Gertie drinks from her own water bottle, and then sits for almost a full minute, like she's really, truly considering what Sam said. The theater is quiet now; everybody else, even the hammering and glueing set builders, even Jane, the stage manager, who takes only short breaks, has gone to find lunch. But the thought of leaving the dark theater and joining the heat and the crowds on Water Street appeals to Sam about as much as dating the actor who plays Claudio appeals to her.

"Isn't it?" repeats Sam when Gertie doesn't answer.

"In some ways."

"In *some* ways?"

"Sam. Honey. Yes, in all the ways that you just outlined, it's a terrible story. But it's not real."

"It feels real to me!" Sam feels like she wants to cry. "It feels real to me."

"It's a story, Sam," says Gertie. "It's make-believe. And it takes place in fifteen eighty-something. Women didn't have a lot of choices back then. Our job is to act it out—we're not here to judge or condone it by today's standards. We're just telling the story."

"But what if we gave ourselves a different job?"

Again, Gertie seems to consider this. After a good long time and a few more sips of water she says, "If we were to change every play from a different era to fit modern sensibilities, we'd lose a lot more than we'd gain. We'd lose the preservation of works of art. We'd lose moments in history that, like it or not, did exist. That's what revivals are all about. That's why they're called revivals—not rewritings. If you were to ask the dramaturg about changing the ending, I'm pretty sure that's what he'd say. Your uncle would say, I think I'm having a heart attack."

"I get that." Sam swipes at her eyes. Her nose is starting to run. Gertie reaches into her bag (now Sam sees the bag—it was there all along!) and pulls out a tissue and offers it to Sam. Sam takes it and dabs at her eyes, blows her nose. "But—"

"But what?" Gertie prompts.

Deep inhale, settle the breath. "It's just. Modern sensibilities or not, has *nothing* changed in all of these hundreds of years?"

"Sure. Of course. A lot has changed in all of these hundreds of years."

"Not necessarily. Hero might have different choices for the ending if she were here today, but, *fuck*, Gertie, the beginning is still exactly the same now as it was then." Gertie starts to shake her head; Sam watches her think about it some more and then, slowly, she nods. "Right? You know I'm right! People are like, Embrace your sexuality! Be proud of your body! *Own it, girl!* And then in the next breath, Well, not like *that*. Not with that person. Not this way, not that way. God, not *that* body. Not where I can see it!" She has to pause for a deep inhale, a long exhale. "And sometimes it's really hard to know what to do, or how to do it. How to behave. How to *be*. I'm just not really sure how to *be* anymore, Gertie." It's the longest monologue she's spoken all day, and when she's done Gertie turns toward her and opens her arms, and Sam leans over the seat and goes into them, and Gertie gives her the biggest, warmest hug. "I'm not sure how to be, or what to do."

"Sam," says Gertie, into Sam's hair.

"What?" Sam is muffled against Gertie's shirt, but she likes it here and she doesn't want to move. Everyone else on the island smells like a combination of body odor, sunscreen, and fried clams by this point in the summer, but not Gertie. Gertie smells like an expensive private spa.

"Do you know what I think you should do really soon?"

"What?"

"Doesn't have to be today, but soon. I think you should talk to your mother."

So the next day this is exactly what Sam does. After rehearsal she pulls her mother aside and says, "Mom. What do you say we go out for a drink?"

"A drink? Sam, you're nineteen."

Sam tips her head at Amy. "I don't want to shock you, Mom. But some kids my age have *fake IDs* that *get them into bars* even though they aren't twenty-one."

Amy looks flustered and says, "*I'm* not risking that, Sam. Can you imagine if you got busted for underage drinking and Timmy lost his second Hero in a week? Don't you read the *Block Island Times*?"

"Um. *No.*"

"Well, if you did you'd know that underage drinking is no joke here. This island takes its reputation seriously. As it should!"

"Okay," says Sam. "It's just that—I think I'm ready to talk about what happened in New York."

Amy's eyes grow wide. She thinks for a minute, then snaps her fingers. "You know what? How about a compromise. I'll pick up a bottle of wine, and we'll go to the remote part of the beach by the Mohegan Bluffs steps and we'll each have a glass."

"Yeah?"

"*One* glass. I have to meet Shelly Salazar to talk about publicity before I go home tonight."

"One and a half," says Sam. "Compromise."

One morning in the middle of May, when the flowers and the tourists and the morally questionable horses and buggies are out in full force in Central Park, Sam comes back from a jog to find that her phone is blowing up. Before she has a chance to see why, Tucker meets her at the door and pulls her into his bedroom.

"Don't freak out," he says, handing her a glass of water. (Very thoughtful, she thinks later, when the dust has settled, and what a lot of dust it is. What a long time it takes to settle.) "Whatever you do, promise me you won't freak out."

"I can't promise that. I don't know what you're talking about."

"Here, sit down." He points to the corner of the room, where there is, yes, another beanbag chair. Sam's heart pitter-patters. She lowers herself into the beanbag chair as gracefully as is possible to do such a thing, which is to say, not all that gracefully.

"There are some photos online," he says. He clears his throat. "Um. Nude photos."

"Of us?" Sam's stomach drops to the floor. This is literally the thing her mother has been warning her about since she was knee-high to a grasshopper. Don't ever ever ever trust anyone with private photos of yourself. Don't even take them! So she hasn't. She has never taken them.

"Well. Sort of. Except I'm not in them."

"Of me? Just me?" He nods. "Let me see." She holds out her hand for Tucker's phone. "Did you pull them up? Pull them up."

"I don't know if you really need to—"

"Let. Me. See." She doesn't recognize the sound she makes as one that could have come from her; it's a low warning growl like a grizzly bear might make when a hiker has gotten too close. "Give. Me. The. Phone."

Tucker gives her the phone. Sam looks at the photos only once, for fewer than ten seconds, and then she has to look away. No. No. But— maybe? When next she speaks, her voice is shaking. "Tucker? Did you take photos of me? Did someone get hold of your phone, or—" She gasps, horrified at the thought she's just had. "Did you put these out there?" The photos are slightly blurry, like maybe they're screenshots from a video. "Did you video us?"

He shakes his head, takes the phone back from her. "Of course not.

I wouldn't do that without your knowledge. You know that, right?" She shakes her head slowly. "Sam? You know that. Why would I do this, and then bring it to your attention?"

"But there's no other explanation. I'm not naked in front of anyone else. I don't even sleep naked." She sleeps in a tank and Aerie short shorts in brushed cotton. She has them in four different colors.

"Sam. You know me. I wouldn't do that. Are you sure there are no older photos of you out there?"

"What the hell, Tucker?" Did he really just ask her that? "Yes, I'm sure. I'm positive."

"Okay," he says. "I'm sorry."

"Can I see again?"

Tucker brings the photos back up and together they peer at the phone, and after she gives them a much longer look, she says, "That's not me."

"You sure?" says Tucker. "It looks like you."

"I think I know what my own breasts look like! And if this is me, where's the turtle tattoo on my ankle?" She lifts up the hem of her leggings and points at the turtle, then enlarges the right ankle in one of the photos. Nothing.

"Right," agrees Tucker slowly. "The turtle." He narrows his eyes. "But if this isn't you, it's somebody pretending to be you who looks a lot like you."

They look at each other and say the same name at the same time, in a shared breath. "Alice."

TikTok explodes with the news of Sam's nude photos. "The Queen of TikTok Without Her Crown." "Tarnished Golden Girl." (Gold can't tarnish, thinks Sam, so it doesn't make any sense, but whoever said the Internet makes sense?) People say all kinds of things. Flattering things about her body (Alice's body), unflattering things about Sam herself. She's a slut; she's a whore; she's a goddess; a feminist; a victim; a perpetrator. Terrible, good, terrible, good: the pendulum swings back and forth, for three full days: the longest three days of Sam's life.

"But it's not even me!" Sam protests to anyone who will listen. She wants to make a statement, but Tink says no, a statement will only make things worse. Tink cautions her against throwing another house member under the bus. "But Alice threw me under the bus!" says Sam.

Nobody seems to be listening. Nobody seems to care. It doesn't matter what the truth is; it matters only what the Internet says.

Sam confronts Alice. Alice denies. What would Alice have to gain from faking nude photos of Sam? Alice asks. Alice has nothing against Sam! She smiles sweetly and asks Sam if she can get her something. A cup of lavender tea, maybe? To calm her down? Many people find lavender tea very soothing.

"You're trying to drive me out," suggests Sam. "So you can go after Tucker."

"Go after Tucker?" Alice rolls her eyes. "I'm with Nathan. You know that."

What is Sam supposed to do, ask Alice to remove her clothes so Sam can inspect her breasts and compare them with the photos?

"Please," she whispers to Alice.

"Please what?"

"Please undo what you did."

Alice folds her arms and says, "I didn't do anything."

Sam makes a video telling her fans and followers exactly what happened. She shows her ankle, with the turtle tattoo. She gets a lot of comments of support. Thousands. More. She also gets a lot of terrible comments. She only reads a few of them, but they sear themselves into her brain. Someone in the supportive comments calls Alice "Evil Alice" and the name sticks among Sam's followers and fans.

It doesn't much matter what the comments from the not-fans say: comments about her (not-her) body, about her morals, about her judgment or her skin-care routine or her diet. Sam can't put the genie back in the bottle. Everywhere she goes now she imagines people not seeing her fully clothed, authentic self, but imagining her naked. Plus, for every three or four Sam fans there's a fan for Evil Alice. That's the way the world works.

Evil Alice's fans turn on Sam with a vengeance. She is trying to "force Alice out." She is "too embarrassed to admit the truth so settled on blaming Alice." She is "a vengefull bitch" [sic]; people in the comments often don't know how to spell. Sam's mother, besides being horrified by the comments for obvious reasons, if she'd seen them, would have been horrified by the spelling too.

Tweet upon tweet, post upon post upon post, comment upon comment upon comment. People in Sam's camp; people in Evil Alice's camp. People in neither camp who just want to hear themselves talk, who want to "be part of the conversation." Not that it's a conversation. It's more like a shouting match. Everyone's yelling, but nobody can hear anyone else.

Suddenly, they are a house divided. Nathan takes Alice's side, of course. Boom Boom too, which smarts. Tucker takes Sam's, and Cece does too. Kylie is hard to read. Scooter tries to toe the middle line but Sam can sense that he is distancing himself from the whole mess, even though he must know—he must!—that Alice is in the wrong. When she approaches Scooter to talk about it he raises both his hands and says, "I can't, sweet girl. I can't help."

Scooter grew up in a poor neighborhood in the Bronx. He wants to make money so his mom, raising four kids on her own, can afford an apartment in a better building. Sam can't really blame him for protecting his online image, but still. It hurts. It hurts a lot.

Maybe, thinks Sam, Tink will help, if Sam tries again with her. She always tells them she's there if they need her.

Sam asks Tink to meet her somewhere away from the house, away from the cameras. They meet at a Starbucks on Seventy-fifth and Amsterdam and they sit at a tiny table in the corner. Sam faces the wall, because she wants to, and Tink faces out into the Starbucks, because Sam sat first and she doesn't have another option. Sam tells Tink the whole story and then sits back expectantly, waiting to see what Tink will say or do. Tink is incredibly powerful. She must know a way to fix this. Tink is looking down at her straw wrapper, making tiny knots in it. After a time (a long time), she looks at Sam, but not actually meeting her eyes; she seems to be looking at a commotion near the barista. Two customers have reached for the same triple foam latte.

Finally Tink says: "I'm not sure how I can help you with this, Sam. I mean, it's not the best look for you, obviously. But everyone's follower counts are way up. Way, way up."

"Well, I know it's not the best look for me, Tink! It's not a look I was going for! I didn't do it. The photos aren't me. I'm asking for your help to make it go away. You always said you were in it for the long-term for us. So I need you to help fix this, for the long-term. I need you to do something about Alice. I need you to undo what she did."

Tink's phone buzzes and she draws it out of her shoulder bag and looks at her text. She begins typing a reply.

"Tink," says Sam. "We're in the middle of a conversation here." (This is something Sam's mother has said to Sam countless times. Now she gets it.)

"Sorry," says Tink, looking intently at the screen. "Just something I have to deal with here."

"But I'm something you have to deal with," says Sam. "And I'm right here, right now. Deal with me."

Tink looks up and says, "You know what though? I think I'll make another reservation for you all to go to Tao. Any place you and Alice go together now—people are going to go bananas. It'll be Content with a capital C." Tink rises. "I really have to go do this thing now."

At Tao, Sam hides in the bathroom most of the night. She's miserable. When she gets back to Xanadu, Sam posts once more, saying goodbye to her fans and followers. She's closing her TikTok account for now. She's leaving social media. She needs a giant reset.

She packs her bags and she makes her bed neatly for the very last time. She empties her little garbage can into the kitchen garbage—it's mostly full of tissues, from crying. She says goodbye to Tucker, who's sleeping. He wakes up and begs her not to go, but even Tucker looks a little worn out. Still hot, obviously, but a little worn out. Tucker, she decides, when

she closes the door to her bedroom, is already a part of her past, not her
future.

On her way out she steps over . . . ew, is that a taco shell? Next to
Murph's dog leash? She doesn't want to know. She just wants to get out.
She wants to go home.

"Oh, honey." Sam's mom looks like she's going to cry. She takes
a sip (more like a gulp) of her wine and says, "Why didn't you talk
to me about any of this? Why didn't you *tell* me?"

They're sitting on one of the wide flat rocks not far from the
bottom of Mohegan Bluffs. The walk down the steps was fine—all
141 of them—but the real challenge will be walking back up. Amy
bought a screw-top bottle of pinot grigio at the liquor store, and
two plastic cups, and, for good measure, a package of fancy crack-
ers, which they're eating with gusto. It's almost four o'clock, and
there are only a few people scattered across the rocky beach. One
brave soul is in the water. How that person maneuvered over the
rocks to get into the water is anybody's guess.

Sam shrugs. "Well, for one thing, it was embarrassing. I didn't
want to talk about it. I was humiliated."

"But it wasn't your fault! It was nothing you did."

"Still. *Humiliating.* Also, I didn't want you to feel bad for me. And
I didn't want you to say I told you so, that I shouldn't have gone
there in the first place. I didn't want you to say I would have been
better off in college."

"I wasn't going to say I told you so."

"I knew you just wanted me to be normal, a regular college
kid. I knew you wanted me to be . . . Henry."

Amy laughs. "Oh, Sammy. You think that. But I don't want you
to be Henry. And Henry isn't normal."

Sam sniffles and swipes her arm across her nose. Her mother,
ironically, does not seem to have a tissue to offer, even though
she's an actual mother. Fair enough, she supposes. Amy can't
think of everything. "He isn't?"

"Of course not. My dear child, he's studying *philosophy*. Do you think that's a 'normal'"—she makes air quotes with the index finger of each hand—"thing to do? Or do you think that's Henry's own way of trying to make sense out of his own chaotic inner world?"

Sam sips from her own wineglass. She'd rather, given the choice, be drinking a Red Bull and vodka, but she's trying to enjoy the wine: it's better than nothing, and this conversation would be way too awkward with nothing. "Henry has a chaotic inner world? I thought he was totally zen. I thought he was the Golden Child."

Amy laughs again. "No more than you."

"Oh, please," says Sam.

"I mean it. You're both the Golden Children. And of course Henry has a chaotic inner world. Everybody does. And nobody is normal. Normal doesn't exist."

"Come on. That's not true. You? Dad? You guys are *so* normal. You still give each other valentines. You have Friday-night date night. And look at your pants. The fact that you're wearing pants at the beach is not normal, but the pants themselves are *so normal*."

"I'm wearing pants because I'm working! And I'll have you know these pants came from an exclusive boutique!"

Sam rolls her eyes. "Does it rhyme with *Marget* and have a bull's-eye as its symbol?"

"No comment," says Amy.

"'No comment' is a comment in and of itself." Sam pauses. "But you're normal. Admit it."

"I think what you're talking about is being comfortable rather than normal."

"So you're comfortable," Sam concedes. "And normal."

Amy sighs. "Sure, yes. I guess I'm a little bit of both. And maybe I'm a little bit less than brave. I spend a lot of my time trying to get bored teenagers to care about other people's writing because I didn't keep up with my own, as you were so kind to point out to me not that long ago. And then when school's over each day I march down to the auditorium and direct slightly less bored— but still sometimes bored—teenagers in plays I wish I'd written myself." She takes a long sip of wine and says, "I get it, Sam. I get why you think my life is small. It makes me sad, because I stand behind all the reasons I chose this life, and I love being your mom, and Henry's mom—and I really don't think I'd trade it for what Timothy has. But I get it." She looks down the beach, where a young woman and a child are trying to walk on the slippery rocks close to the water. The child, a little girl, can't get purchase on the rocks, and finally the young woman (mother? nanny?) scoops her up and carries her.

"Mom. *I* don't think your life is small."

Her mom turns to her; in the changing light of an almost-late-summer afternoon, her eyes seem lit from within. "You don't?"

"No. Of course not. I worry that *you* think your life is small. I worry that you wanted something bigger, and didn't go after it. I know I hurt your feelings, at the house that day. I was mad, and maybe I was looking for a soft spot, but I didn't mean to be hurtful."

Amy smiles. "Don't look so worried. It's okay. I also *love* my job. I love the nutty hormonal teenagers and the makeshift sets and the makeup stains on my clothes and everything about the plays. I love watching a totally shy kid come alive onstage, even though I know and he knows that he'll probably never act again once this particular show is over."

"But do you ever worry? That you chose the wrong path?"

"There is no path, honey."

"There isn't? I thought there was a path. I was told there's a path!"

"Not really. There are just choices, and more choices, over and over again, all the way through to the end, like a big game of Choose Your Own Adventure."

"But what if you don't choose? What if things just . . . happen?"

"I suppose that even what looks like not choosing is a choice. Henry might wake up one day in ten years and wonder why he's living with someone who color-codes the pantry and vacuums invisible crumbs off the garage floor."

Sam gasps. "You don't like Ava? Mom! I thought you loved Ava!"

"Of course I love Ava."

"*Ish*," suggests Sam.

"Not *ish*. She's got her head on straight, and she loves the heck out of your brother, and there's a lot to be said for that. She was there for Christmas, unlike some people."

"Ouch," says Sam.

"I'm just saying what looks like a very tidy life right now can explode into something messy in the future. And what looks messy now can tidy itself up quite nicely one day. That's what I'm saying." They're both silent for a moment, watching the waves crash against the rocks. When Amy speaks next there's a little quaver in her voice. "When you were a little girl," she says, then pauses.

"Oh, boy," says Sam. Where is this story going?

"When you were very small, I had you with me at the grocery store. You were sitting in the seat in the front of the cart, I guess you were about three, and this tiny old lady in a giant wool coat came up to us, and she said you reminded her of Shirley Temple."

"Shirley Temple, like the drink that you add vodka to to make a cocktail?"

Amy rolls her eyes. "You're not supposed to add vodka to it. It's supposed to be a drink for children, Samantha. Shirley Temple the child star. After whom the drink was named. The one with all the blond ringlets? I thought this was a funny comparison, because obviously you aren't blond. But you were curly then."

"Now I'm just wavy." Sam sighs. "Unless I blow it out."

"*Anyway*, this adorable old lady said it was a 'twinkle in your eyes' that reminded her of Shirley. And you've always had that. You've had this light around you, this beautiful light."

Sam is quiet for a moment. She feels like she's lost the twinkle, she's lost the light. How can she get it back? She makes a little pile of sand, knocks it over with her foot.

"Mom?"

"Yes?"

"How'd Shirley Temple turn out?"

"You know what? Better than expected. She grew up and was no longer the little girl she was known for being. She gave up acting pretty early on, and later in her life she became a diplomat. Like an actual international diplomat, not someone who has a gentle way of telling a friend they've chosen the wrong lipstick color for their skin tone."

"Hmm," says Sam. "A diplomat."

"You see? There's always an opportunity for another act."

"There are some awful things about me online, Mom. I don't want you to see them. I'm so—I'm so ashamed."

"I won't see them."

"You might, accidentally."

"I'll never look for them, Sam. You know I know how to google, right?" She gives Sam a look and Sam concedes that, yes, her mother knows how to google. "If I'd wanted to find out anything about you I would have by now. If I wanted to know why you'd come home, I could have searched for the answer. But I figured you'd tell me when you wanted to tell me. So as far as I'm concerned, whatever anyone says about you or anyone else online doesn't exist to me." She snaps her fingers. "See? It's all gone, just like that."

Sam looks to the horizon. She imagines she can see the mainland, but of course all she can see is the endless, endless ocean, with the wind turbines rising out of the water. "It's not that easy, Mom."

"Isn't it, though? Maybe it can be, if you let it. You should read Joan Didion on being young in New York. 'Goodbye to All That.'"

"I've read it," says Sam morosely. "We read it for narrative non-fiction, junior year. Ms. Coolidge."

"Okay! So you know, then. Those early years, the age you are now, you can make mistakes and they don't count against you. You get a lot of clean slates in the beginning."

"Joan Didion didn't have the Internet!" cries Sam. "I can ignore it for a while, I can swear off of it, but it's all out there."

"But you don't have to look. You don't ever have to look. And there's so much noise online. Yours is already static in the background."

"I don't know," says Sam. "I just don't know about that." Then she says, "Mom?"

"Yes?"

"Do you promise Henry isn't normal?"

"I promise that there's no such thing as normal," says Amy. "Normal is a myth." She screws the top back on the bottle of wine, and she puts the bottle in her bag, and she stands and holds a hand out to Sam. "I'd much rather talk to you longer. But I'm meeting Shelly Salazar about publicity, so I think we'd better start up those steps."

"Ugh," says Sam. All of her problems still exist in the same way they did when she and her mother walked down the steps, and though nothing has changed in a concrete way, everything feels just a little bit like it has.

Amy

AFTER WHAT SAM told her, Amy wants to shake her fist at the world; she wants to scream with rage. She wants to track down Evil Alice and poke out her eyeballs, or at least give her a very stern talking-to, and maybe ask to speak with her mother.

Young people have so much more to deal with now! When she was nineteen, home on Block Island from NYU for the summer, her biggest worry was finding out where the bonfire was that night—not, for heaven's sake, wondering who'd captured any-one's embarrassing or private moments with a camera and then set the images loose for all the world to peruse. It's easy to forget sometimes, when you're admiring the shininess of teenage girls' hair, how effortlessly they wear crop tops, that their burdens, which may at first seem featherlight, can be heavy indeed.

But Amy doesn't have time to track down Evil Alice or her mother. There are seven days to go until they open, and she has to keep her eyes on the prize. Thank goodness she chose Joy Bombs, not Poor People's Pub, for the publicity update with Shelly. She needs to clear the wine from her brain and get some answers from Shelly, who's lately been slippery as a greased-up eel. Ticket sales still aren't anywhere close to where they should be, and it's time to panic.

After she drops Sam home and heads back into town Amy has

a few minutes to spare, so once she's parked she sits in the Wagoneer and calls Greg. He's still working. He answers, but in his
I'm in the middle of something voice. There's a certain breathlessness
to it.

"I know what happened in New York," she says.

"Hang on," he says. He says something unintelligible to someone in the background, something stern that sounds like a warning
or admonition, then he comes back. "I'm so glad you know," he says.
"I've been waiting."

"Waiting for what?"

"For you to google. So we could talk about it."

"*Gregory! What* did you just say?"

He takes a beat. She can imagine him chewing his thumbnail
the way he does when he's in an awkward situation. "Nothing," he
says. "I didn't say anything."

"You googled Sam? And didn't tell me?"

"Didn't you? You just said you know!"

"I never googled. Sam told me, just now."

He takes a longer beat. "I'm sorry," he says. "I just couldn't take
not knowing. I couldn't take it. And then once I knew, I couldn't
tell you. I knew it would kill you, to know what happened. Hang
on, sorry." He speaks again to someone on the site and then says,
"Okay, I'm back. Do you forgive me?"

"No," she says.

Greg laughs uncertainly. "So . . . should I call my lawyer to get
the divorce papers going?"

"Not yet. Maybe tomorrow."

"If it helps, I felt worse after knowing than I did before knowing."

"It helps a little," she says. "Only a very little. But I can't believe
you googled outside of the relationship."

"I know," he says. "I can't believe it either." He pauses. "Well,

I'm glad she told you. So now that we both know . . . do you want to talk about it? We're wrapping up here soon."

Does Amy want to talk about? She might not be ready yet. She might have to process, or let Sam process. It would be easy to tip over into being mad at Greg, but she's tired of being mad. She wants to be at peace. She wants to choose the graceful route. "Not now," she says. "And anyway, even if I wanted to talk more, I can't. I have a meeting."

After they hang up, and Shelly arrives, Shelly orders a dirty chai, and Amy a decaf cappuccino. They select a table near the door. Shelly's facing the door, and they haven't even begun their conversation when her face lights up and she springs from her chair and hugs a man who has just come in. He's good-looking in a rumpled way, with brown hair, a gray T-shirt, and jeans. He looks like a guy who would play a sexy professor in a limited series set on a college campus. Amy is fine with the fact that Shelly has run into a friend, but, Ticktock, she thinks. We've got to get going on this meeting.

When Shelly eventually releases the man, he makes his way to the counter and talks to Joy Bombs's owner, Joy Sousa. While they're talking he takes Joy's hand across the counter and squeezes it, and—oh! Amy sees now. *This* is Anthony Puckett, the writer, about whom Holly told Amy the day she first learned about Shelly. The one who lives with Joy Bombs Joy; the one who's been working on the same book since moving to the island.

"That guy right there is the reason I came to this island for the first time," says Shelly, when Anthony chooses a seat on the other side of the café, and Shelly returns to Amy.

"Yeah? That's the writer, right?"

"Yup. When I worked in book publicity, I was trying to set up this photo shoot with him and his dad, Leonard Puckett, and Annie Leibovitz . . . it was a whole thing. It was going to be this father-son reconciliation shoot." She waves a manicured hand; Amy wonders where on Block Island one can get a manicure like that. When she was growing up, fancy nail treatments, like espresso-based beverages, were things that one procured either off-island or not at all. "It never panned out. The photo shoot. Then the dad died so I guess it never will." Shelly sighs and stares wistfully into her dirty chai. "But I fell in love with this island on that original trip. In fact I thought for just a second there was a spark between me and Anthony, but looking back I think he was already dating Joy, so I guess that was my imagination."

"I guess so," says Amy. Then, encouragingly, "It happens."

"It sure does," Shelly says. "Seems to happen to me a lot."

Amy clears her throat and opens her trusty notebook. "Okay, let's see . . . there are a few things we need to go over, but two big things are ticket presales and reviews. I'm not loving these numbers. I mean, we've got Gertie Sanger onstage and Timothy Fleming directing. People should be drawing daggers over these tickets. Right?"

"Right," says Shelly. Now that she's done talking about Anthony Puckett she looks composed, nonchalant, and not at all like Amy's words have anything to do with her job. "They totally should. These tickets should be selling themselves!"

"So what's happening?"

"That's what I want to know," says Shelly. She looks at Amy expectantly. "I was just on Nantucket for three days, for a wedding, and I rolled back into town, and I said the same thing to myself when I checked the numbers. I was like, These tickets should be selling themselves!" (At least that's the manicure explained: a wedding on Nantucket.)

"Well . . ." Amy takes a small, bewildered sip of her decaf cappuccino. "Do you have any ideas about why they aren't?"

"Hmm. Do I have any ideas about why they aren't." Shelly taps her fingers on the table, ba-dum, ba-dum, ba-dum. "Let's see. We are on an island, without direct accessibility to many of the major news outlets. And the summer season is super crowded . . . I mean, you've got Williamstown. Shakespeare in the Park at the Delacorte. The Ogunquit Playhouse is killing it this season."

Amy arches an eyebrow at Shelly. This is her teacher face, the one she unleashes on students who have not finished the assigned pages of *The Odyssey*. (Who is she kidding? Nobody reads all of the assigned pages of *The Odyssey*. Her entire freshman lit class deserves this look.) "Well. I mean, in light of all of that, do you think we need to, I mean . . . *publicize* this more?"

"Definitely," says Shelly.

"Okay, so . . ." Amy is stymied. "We're sort of running out of time. You're in charge of publicity, so maybe just . . . work on that? Some more publicity?"

"Absolutely," says Shelly. "Of course."

Amy shakes her head and turns back to her notebook. "What about a reviewer from the *Times*, when we open? I know we discussed that a long time ago."

Shelly whistles. "I mean, yeah. That would be great. That would be ideal. But that's a big get."

"Right. So." Amy looks down at her notebook, then back up. "Aren't you the one who could be the getter?"

"Hmm." Shelly's gaze keeps sliding over to Anthony, who has a notebook out and is writing furiously.

"Shelly!" says Amy. She feels like snapping her fingers to bring Shelly's attention back to her.

"Sure, okay," says Shelly. She takes a long pull of her dirty chai. "I can try for the *Times*."

"Would you already have had to have done that? Don't they need to—plan to send someone?"

"I bet they do! It's a little bit of a process to get here. I'm telling you, this Nantucket wedding took it right out of me for a while. Three days to celebrate, at least four to recover."

Amy sighs. "Shelly. Don't take this the wrong way, but I thought you knew a little more about how publicity works than you seem to." Shelly looks instantly crestfallen, but Amy is not backing down. "There's a lot riding on this," she says. "All we can do is move forward from where we are. But I wish we were somewhere different." She glances at her watch. "I'm getting the ferry in fifteen minutes." She needs to call Henry on the way home; she's been so wrapped up in life on the island that's she's scarcely talked to him lately. "Why don't you make some calls, and report back to me tomorrow?"

"Yes, Captain," says Shelly. "Aye aye." She salutes Amy, who never thought she'd say that teenagers were easier to work with than thirty-year-old women.

Sam

WHEN SAM STEPS out of the theater and into the summer chaos three days later, she can't see anything for at least twenty seconds: the sun is so bright, and so audacious. After so many full run-throughs, she's exhausted.

Her vision comes back only partially at first, and when it does she's positive her eyes are playing tricks on her because she thinks the guy standing in front of the clothing store is Henry. First she's seeing Tucker everywhere on the island, and now her brother?

Then her vision clears, and it *is* Henry! He's walking toward her and smiling, and he wraps her in a big bear hug, squeezing her tight.

"Hey there, little sis," he says. Next to him is Ava, who's wearing cutoff shorts and a gray Middlebury T-shirt with navy-blue writing. Somehow she manages to make the outfit look elegant. But that's Ava for you.

"Hello, Ava!" says Sam. She hugs Ava. "What are you two *doing* here?"

"Mom summoned us. She said with the recent casting change this play is now officially a can't-miss theater experience. So we wanted to come for opening night. And we thought we'd have a few vacation days while we were at it."

"That's amazing! Are you staying with Mom and Dad? Or do

you want to stay at Uncle Timothy's? I could see what he says—he's still inside, wrapping up a couple of things. He's going to be so happy to see you!"

Henry holds up a hand and says, "We got a room at the 1661 Inn."

Sam whistles. "Wow, Henry," she says. "The pay for philosophers must really have gone up since I last checked."

"Ha ha," says Henry. He's one of the only people Sam knows who can get away with saying the words *ha ha* instead of actually laughing, and not looking ridiculous. "The pay for philosophers remains on the lower end of the scale. This is Ava's treat."

Ava smiles modestly and nods, making her long, shiny hair shimmer.

"We were lucky they had a cancellation," says Henry. "We called at just the right time."

"Maybe we should go check in?" Ava says to Henry. She puts her hand around Henry's waist in a way that feels so intimate Sam figures she may as well have said, *and test out the bed.*

"Sure," says Henry. "We can walk from here, right?"

"Absolutely," says Sam. "It's right up the hill there. I'd drop you off, but I rode my bike."

"Not a problem," says Henry. "We love to walk." Henry holds out his hand for the straps of Ava's overnight bag and shoulders it. Sam recognizes the bag as the three-pocket duffel by Away in blush color. Many men would have looked out of place carrying it, but Henry manages it; he just looks like a good boyfriend. Sam hopes Ava knows how lucky she is. "I just want to talk to Sam real quick about that thing . . ." he tells Ava.

"What thing?" Sam asks. Ava steps quietly away to look in a shop window; Classy move, thinks Sam.

"Mom's worried about ticket sales for the play."

"She is? She's worried about ticket sales? She hasn't told me that!" Sam feels childishly insulted. This was the way she felt in fifth grade when she realized Henry had let her go on believing in Santa Claus long after he'd stopped. She'd felt so excluded!

"I don't think she wanted to make *you* worry. That's why she told me. I'm a neutral party, that's all. Not involved in the endeavor."

Sam chews on her fingernail. "Is she like *really* worried?"

Henry laughs. "I don't know! How do you tell that, with Mom?"

"Good point." Sam sucks in her bottom lip and looks from Henry to Ava and back again. "Does Uncle Timmy know she's worried? Does *Gertie* know? God, I can't believe people aren't flocking here by the zillions to see Gertie. She's so famous. And she's so good in this part."

Ava, listening all along, pipes up. "I'm sure everybody would come, if they knew about it. Somehow not enough people know. That must be the problem."

"Right," says Henry. "Mom said something about putting all of her publicity eggs in a bad basket, or something."

"Huh," says Sam. "Huh. Okay."

An idea is blossoming.

After she points Henry and Ava up the hill, she unlocks her bike from the rack in the back of the theater. But she doesn't cycle home. The wheels are starting to turn, and not just on her bike. She remembers her dinner with Uncle Timmy. *You've got this massive following, and you're doing nothing with it.*

Sam can't fix the planet, but in this little corner of it she can make a difference. This she can do.

She heads the other way on Water Street, left on Dodge to the four-way stop, then turns right on Corn Neck Road. When she gets to the new beach pavilion at Fred Benson, she pulls her bike into the rack. The first thing she sees is the banner announcing the next movie night at the pavilion: *The Devil in Here.* She rolls her eyes. Of *course.*

It takes a little while for her apps to come in, because she has to download all of them and she has to think hard to remember her passwords. The apps start to filter in one by one, cautiously, like the first early guests at a party, and she logs in. TikTok. Twitter. VSCO. Snapchat. Even, in a nod to the olds, Facebook.

And then she finds the best lighting on the beach, and she begins her first video in a long, long time. Once she has the beach scene covered, she gets back on her bike. She takes a video of the Empire, with the poster for the play hanging outside. She happens by the dock just as the afternoon ferry is unloading, so she shoots that too. She gets a great shot of a girl on a moped. She gets a shot of the afternoon crowd at Ballard's, and Rebecca, the statue in the middle of the traffic circle, and the famous porch of the National Hotel. She stops at the exotic animal farm across from the 1661 Inn and she captures the zedonk, the kangaroos, the lemurs. She tries to imagine the logistics of getting kangaroos and a zedonk onto an island—ferry? Or private boat? On her way back to Floyd's house she stops and videos the outside of the Spring House Hotel, with the Adirondack chairs and the wide green lawn.

By the time she gets home she's absolutely wiped out. She's thirsty. Her legs are shaking from so much cycling. But she feels better than she's felt all summer as she pulls out a chair in the breakfast nook, plugs in her dying phone, and gets to work.

Sam. Trevino. Is. Back.

Timothy

"AREN'T YOU A sight for sore eyes," says Timothy when he meets his assistant, Alexa, at the ferry. Alexa is wearing a knee-length sundress, sandals, sunglasses. She looks so put-together—so capable! He feels like hugging her, in an appropriate, avuncular way, but he can't do that. He's witnessed enough Hollywood scandals. "Didn't you just get off a red-eye?"

"Yes." She glances at her phone. "Well, like three hours ago."

"You look fresh as a daisy! How is this possible?"

"You flew me first-class."

When Timothy gets off a red-eye in first-class he looks like a mushroom recently dug up from a faraway wood. "And . . . ?"

"A first-class seat on a red-eye is more comfortable than my apartment," explains Alexa. "I slept like a baby on a CBD tincture, then I napped again in the car from the airport. I'm ready to work! What do you need from me?"

What does Timothy need from Alexa? It's a reasonable question. Alexa is looking every which way, taking in the crush of people getting off the ferry, the bikes, the mopeds, the people drinking and relaxing on the porch of the National.

"Nothing right now," he says. "Let's go get a drink. Or a coffee. Which would you prefer?"

Alexa considers this. "Coffee, I think. Is there a good place?"

"Oh, believe me. There's a *very* good place. Alexa, have you ever had a mini whoopie pie?" Alexa shakes her head.

"I can't believe I've never been to Block Island before," says Alexa, once they're settled with their drinks in Joy Bombs. "Point Judith is only a couple of hours away from where I grew up, in Newburyport."

"Well, I grew up here," says Timothy. "And *I've* never been to Newburyport!"

"You should go. It's really beautiful. I was *so* ready to leave there when I moved out west. But now I think about it a lot." Her pretty face looks sad and wistful. "I even dream about it sometimes."

"A hometown can have a very powerful pull. Especially if it holds memories of people who are no longer with you." Timothy's thinking of his mother. Maybe Amy is right. Maybe he did leave all the dirty work to her. Maybe having Hugh Jackman sing to Rose didn't have the impact he'd imagined it would. Maybe he could have done more, while he had the chance.

The door swings open, and in comes Amy. This is a happy coincidence; they hadn't arranged to meet. Her face is shining and her eyes are bright, and she appears to be a little breathless. She goes right to the counter and orders, not even looking around, a woman on a mission. Once she has her drink, Timothy calls her over.

Before he can introduce Alexa, Amy says, "You're not going to believe this. You know how the ticket sales were a little . . . disappointing not so long ago?"

"No," said Timothy. "Nobody told me that."

Amy claps her hand over her mouth. When she drops it she says, "That's right. I was waiting to tell you, in case things turned around. Well, guess what? Things turned around. We've got the next eight shows completely sold out. Miriam at the theater said they couldn't keep up with all the calls they've been getting. From all over the country. And not just that. Somebody called from Wales. The country, not the marine mammals."

Alexa says, "I'm not at all surprised, because of what Sam did." She squints at Amy. "Are you Sam's mom? I see the resemblance."

Timothy says impatiently, "Yes, this is my sister, Amy Trevino, Sam's mom and intrepid production manager. Amy, this is my assistant, Alexa Thornhill. Alexa—what did Sam do?"

At the same time Amy asks, "You know Sam?"

Alexa, the traitor, answers Amy first. "I mean, I know her in the same way everyone else knows her. She was like so famous. I don't blame her for disappearing for a while, letting everything blow over. If it was me I probably would have done the same thing. The online world can be vicious."

"What did Sam *do*?" Timothy repeats.

"The TikTok. About the play. You haven't seen it? She posted yesterday. Here. I'll show you." Alexa takes out her phone, swipes, swipes, and points it at Timothy and Amy.

It's Sam! She's standing outside the Empire Theatre, in front of the poster.

"Hey, everyone," Sam says. "I know it's been a long time. I'm not back for good, but I'm back real quick to tell you something important." She goes on then for maybe a minute, maybe a little longer, talking about the play, about Block Island, about Timothy Fleming, about Gertie Sanger. At the end she says, "We'd love to see the *New York Times* theater critic here. Trust me. It's worth the trip. You'll be happy you came." After that comes a montage of different parts of the island: the beach, Ballard's, the Adirondack chairs on Spring Street. The zedonk at the exotic animal farm! The whole thing is set to a song that Amy doesn't know but that Alexa is singing softly along to.

"That's it?" says Timothy. "That's the whole thing?"

"That's the whole thing." Alexa points to the right of the screen, where there's a vertical row of symbols. "This heart shows us how many people liked it."

"One and a half people?" says Timothy.

"One and a half *million* people. Since yesterday."

"Hold on," says Timothy. "That many people saw this?"

"Yup," says Alexa. "But then, see this arrow here? That's how many people forwarded it to someone else. That's, let's see, another one hundred and seven thousand people. And these little dots here? Those are the comments. Twenty-one thousand so far. Timothy, it looks like your little island has gone viral."

His and Sam's roadside fight comes back to him. What he had said to her, when he got all over her about not doing something with her platform.

"Hol-ee shit," Timothy says. "Pardon my French. But I think I might owe someone an apology."

Sam

SAM'S ON THE back deck, sunglasses and hat, light long-sleeved button-up top over her bikini, when she hears the slider open. Uncle Timmy.

"I've come to ask a favor," he says. He clears his throat. "But first to offer an apology." Sam removes her glasses and looks at her uncle. "I saw the video you made." Sam can feel her expression changing, becoming warier. She holds her breath, and then Uncle Timmy says, "And I think it's amazing."

She exhales and grins. "Yeah? You think that was an okay use of my platform?"

"I think it was a *tremendous* use of your platform. And I'm sorry that I doubted you. I'm sorry I didn't take your work seriously. You have single-handedly sold out the run."

"Nice," she says, nodding, trying to play it cool, though her insides are doing a happy dance. "Apology accepted." She takes a beat, then says, "What's the favor?"

"My assistant, Alexa, has recently arrived on the island. I thought maybe you could show her around a bit. She's from Massachusetts, but this is her first time on Block Island. I think you two actually have a lot in common. Take her to lunch, maybe? She's staying at the Hotel Manisses. She's expecting you in an hour. My treat. Put it on my card." He holds out an American Express

Platinum card. "She'll be on the island for opening night, visit her family for a few days, and come back before the run ends."

Inwardly, Sam rolls her eyes. It's just like a grown-up to think that all young people in approximately the same age group have something in common and thereby will automatically get along. When you are three or four years old, this principle might hold. But it's not that way now. At the same time, she knows she still stands on shaky ground with Timothy. They've each apologized to each other now: she for the party, he for dismissing her platform. Deep down, though, maybe on the lower mantle level of their relationship, near the core, a rift is still possible.

"I can pay for lunch," she says. "But thank you."

"Thank *you*," says Uncle Timothy.

Timothy says she can take the jeep; he'll be home until that evening's rehearsal. He shows Sam a photo of Alexa on his phone so she'll recognize her. In the photo, one of those candids people sometimes take on a television or movie set, Alexa is holding out a clipboard toward Timothy. She's petite, with long, wavy brown hair, and she's wearing a printed, belted dress and platform sandals. She looks nice.

It's just lunch, Sam tells herself as she gets into the jeep and makes her way toward the Manisses. When Sam gets to the hotel Alexa is easy to recognize. She's alone, and she's waiting outside, wearing a sundress and flip-flops, and she's about three times prettier than anyone surrounding her. High bun. Fantastic bone structure. Really good eyebrows. Light makeup, slightly nervous smile. Sam pulls into the small parking area, Alexa waves, and Sam waves back.

Does this Alexa know (or care) anything about Sam? Has she seen the photos? Probably. What if she has seen the photos but not the defense of the photos? What if she thinks the photos are actually *Sam*? All of the feelings Sam has kept pushed so carefully down since Memorial Day come roiling to the surface. They spin around and around her insides, like damp clothes in the washing machine. Sam doesn't like the feeling. This is why she gave up social media. This is why she gave up new people.

"Hi," Alexa says, climbing into the passenger seat of the jeep. "I'm Alexa. Thank you for babysitting me."

Darn it. Sam likes her. This is exactly what she isn't looking for: a new friend. But she smiles and says, "Hi, Alexa. My uncle has told me a lot about you. All good, I promise."

For lunch, Alexa decides on The Oar, overlooking Great Salt Pond. Sam hasn't eaten here yet, but she's heard great things. Plus, there's parking, and they don't take reservations, so there's no shame in not having one. They luck out by getting a table after only ten minutes.

True to its name, oars of all shapes, sizes, and colors hang from the ceiling. Alexa and Sam spend some time commenting on the oars (*So many! Where do they all come from? How'd they get them up there?* Etc.). Then the server comes to take their drink order.

"I can't have a drink or anything," says Sam to Alexa, feeling slightly apologetic. "Rehearsal tonight." To the server she says, "Iced tea, please."

"I'm on the clock!" says Alexa. "Iced tea for me too."

"My uncle talks about you like you walk on water."

"Ha!" says Alexa. "I definitely do not walk on water. I barely swim! He's a good boss."

Sam coughs politely. When she lived with her uncle and Gertie for that year, he went through three assistants. She's glad to hear he's settled down.

Once they have their iced teas and order their food (lobster club for Alexa—Sam is happy to see that she's not one of those girls who doesn't eat!—and spicy tuna roll for Sam) they both start to say something at the same time.

"Go ahead," says Alexa.

"No, *you* go ahead." Sam feels like she's the official host of this outing, so she should let Alexa go first.

"I was just going to say, it's so funny to see you in person. I'm a fan!"

Sam's stomach lurches. "If it's okay with you," she says, "I don't want to talk about any of that Xanadu stuff. I'm really trying to put it behind me." She wants to be polite but firm—very firm. "It was pretty awful. I'm not even on social media right now, except for one thing I just did for the play. I'm pretty scarred from everything that happened."

"Not Xanadu!" Alexa chortles. "Ohmygosh, I wasn't going to bring that up. That's a bunch of bullshit."

"But you knew about it?" asks Sam. She doesn't want to know, but also she feels like she needs to know. "I mean, you've heard of Xanadu? Do you know the basics?"

It's at this moment that their food arrives, giving them each something to concentrate on. When the server departs Alexa says, "I mean, I guess? As much as anyone knows about anything. Sort of as background noise. But I don't go on TikTok much. I really didn't pay attention. Who can keep up with everything? It's exhausting."

"*Exhaus*ting," whispers Sam. *Exhausting* is exactly the right word for it.

"Believe me, I get it," says Alexa.

"You do?" asks Sam. "You get it?" The spicy tuna roll is fantastic, but Sam tries to take it slow; she doesn't want it to repeat on her later, in rehearsal. She's already learned a few things this summer that don't mix with the stage. Anything fried. Burgers. A three-egg omelet involving meat.

"Yeah, I do. It's a shitty world sometimes, and if you open yourself up to it . . . well, it can really suck. I used to do this YouTube channel . . . it was silly."

"What was it?"

Alexa shakes her head and laughs. "I get embarrassed saying it out loud."

Sam is intrigued. "Was it something *dirty*?"

"Oh, God no. *No*. It was called Silk Stockings. I sat in a chair and explained things about the stock market. It was very innocent, actually. And basic! So basic. I didn't even know that much about the stock market. I was just explaining little baby concepts, stuff that anyone could look up on their own. But you know what, people have made money from less online, so I figured, why not give it a shot?"

"Were you wearing like silk stockings?"

"No! Definitely not. I was wearing clothes like I'm wearing now. Nothing scandalous. It was just a play on words, you see, with the stock market? Stockings?"

"Ohhh," says Sam. "I get it. That's clever."

"Well. Not really. I told you! It was silly. But I made enough money to get started in L.A., so that's what mattered. Anyway, every now and then I would look at the comments, and, holy shit, people could be gross and mean for absolutely no reason."

"Yes!" says Sam. "Why are people like that?"

Alexa shakes her head. "I wish I knew. I'd read some of this stuff, and I'd be like, what did I ever do to *you*? Or, worse, I'd be like, You want to do *what* to me? If my mom ever read that stuff, she'd flip out. That's one reason I shut it down. Plus, once I had what I was trying to save for moving I didn't need it anymore. Anyway. When I said I recognized you, I was talking about *My Three Daughters*." Alexa ducks her head, looking suddenly shy. "I was a fan."

"You were?" Sam is surprised. Alexa must be, what? Twenty-one, twenty-two? So when *My Three Daughters* was on she was fifteen or sixteen. Not exactly the target audience for a Disney show.

Alexa smiles and take a sip of her iced tea. "My little sister,

Morgan, used to watch it. She was a big Disney Channel junkie. So I'd watch with her to 'keep her company' "—she puts air quotes around the last three words—"but really even though I was technically too old for it I loved it." She pauses, wipes her mouth, and says, "We went through a—through a family tragedy around then, and honestly a lot of the time all we wanted to do was watch TV and not talk to each other about how sad we were."

"I'm so sorry," says Sam. She wants to know what the family tragedy was, but she doesn't think Alexa is going to tell her.

"That's okay. It was a long time ago now."

Sam clears her throat; this is her cue, she figures, to change the subject. "So what are you going to do while you're here? Does my uncle have you working like crazy, or do you get to have some fun?"

"A little bit of both."

"Are you a beach person? I can tell you what's what. You've never been here, right? Tell me what you like. Rocky, with atmosphere and amazing sunsets? That's Vaill. Long and sandy and warmer water but maybe more crowded? Mansion or Scotch. Bathrooms and a pavilion? Fred Benson. Beach bar? Ballard's."

"Wow." Alexa blinks rapidly. "So many choices! I grew up near the beach but we didn't have this much variety."

"Right?" says Sam. "It's kind of ridiculous! I grew up in Narragansett and same for me. So what do you like? I'd take you myself, but I'm supposed to stay out of the sun, you know, this close to the show opening. But I can point you in the right direction."

Alexa hesitates. "Thank you. I might skip the beach. I love the beaches in California, but New England beaches . . ."

"Too cold? I get it. Sometimes you really have to brace yourself, right? Try Scotch, though. You'd be surprised how warm it is."

Alexa blinks rapidly again. Problem with her contact, maybe? Sam wonders.

"It's not that. I don't mind the cold. It's more that . . . it's more that the beach this time of year reminds me of something." She clears her throat. "Reminds me of an old boyfriend."

"Ohhhh," says Sam. "I get that too. I'll probably never be able to have a slice of Ray's Pizza without thinking about Tucker. We used to go there all the time. Did it end badly with this boyfriend?"

Alexa clears her throat, takes a long drink of her iced tea, clears her throat again. "He died."

He *died*? "*What?* Holy shit, Alexa! I'm so sorry I asked you. Geez. I'm sorry."

"It's okay." Alexa smiles. "Really, it's okay. It happened three years ago. And I'm the one who brought it up. It's not your fault."

"Can I—can I ask what happened?" First a family loss, and now this? Alexa is an actual tragic heroine, while Sam has spent all summer moaning about someone being mean to her on social media.

"Car accident. He was alone. A deer ran out in front of his car."

"I'm sorry," says Sam, for what feels like the hundredth time.

Alexa chews and swallows the last bite of her lobster club. She smiles a crooked, sad smile—the kind of smile you see on people who might start crying any minute. "It sounds silly, when I say it out loud. But I owe him a lot. Basically he made me nicer. I wasn't very nice before I met him."

"You weren't? You seem super nice to me."

"I'm nicer now. Back then I hated my friends, and I was tired of where I lived, and I wasn't as nice to my little sister as I could have been. I definitely wasn't as nice to my mom as I could have been. I was scared to be excited about anything, you know? Like I thought I was too cool for whatever." She dabs at invisible tears with a fresh napkin and says, "Shit, Sam, I'm sorry. You're nice enough to take me out to lunch and here I am treating you like a therapist."

"I don't mind," says Sam. "I like it! I'm sort of . . . light on friends right now." This is the first time she's said this out loud, or even really acknowledged it at all, but now she realizes how true it is. Without her high school friends around, without her Xanadu crew, she's been gravitating hard toward the over-forty crowd.

"I'm sorry!" says Alexa. "Is it because of—" She clears her throat dramatically. "You know, because of *the thing*? Sorry. I know you don't want to talk about it."

"Kind of. Sure, a little bit. A lot, I guess. You realize when you leave social media how much some of your 'friendships'"—she does air quotes—"were on the surface. But also, all my high school friends went to college, so they have like these totally different lives from mine. Roommates and sororities and midterms, you know? And it's hard for me to relate. Meanwhile I know my mom would love for me to go to college like yesterday." She rolls her eyes.

"*I* didn't go to college," says Alexa. "I'd be starting my last year if I'd gone when everyone else in my high school class did. I got accepted into my mother's alma mater, Colby, and my mom wanted me to go *so* badly. So I hear what you're saying. I could see it on my mom's face every time she looked at me, how much she wanted me to go. She was so excited for me to have the same experiences she did. *My best friends are my college friends,* she was always telling me. But at the end of the day I wanted different experiences. I wanted to move to California. I wanted to start working as soon as I could. Honestly I felt like I just wanted my life to begin."

"Have you regretted it?"

"Nope. Not once. Not a single time."

"Okay," says Sam. She breathes a sigh of relief both inwardly and outwardly. "Okay, that's really good to hear."

By now the server has cleared everything but their water glasses. The line of people waiting to get a table is starting to look legit—people crowded by the host stand, people clumped up on the green grass outside the restaurant—so, before an awkward silence has the chance to set in, Sam picks up the check.

"I'm getting that," says Alexa.

"Nope," says Sam. "Absolutely not. If you don't put that wallet away I'm going to throw it into Great Salt Pond, I swear to God."

"Well, okay, then!" says Alexa. "I need my wallet for the rest of the trip, so in that case I accept. Thank you."

They wind their way through the tables, taking a last look at the oars hung every which way from the ceiling, crisscrossing over each other, and walk outside to the parking lot.

"I'm going to go take a photo," says Alexa. "If that's okay. Do we have time?"

"We have time!" While Alexa is gone Sam breathes in the particular smell of Great Salt Pond and takes in the sounds of boats pulling in and departing. She's so focused on that that when Alexa lays a hand on her bare arm she jumps.

"Hey," says Alexa. "I didn't mean to scare you. I just wanted to thank you for letting me talk. I left home not too long after my boyfriend died—I was leaving anyway, like I said, but I left probably a little sooner than I would have. And nobody in my L.A. life knew him, or even knows about what happened, so I just don't ever talk about it."

"I'm glad to be talked to," says Sam. "I really am." She smiles.

Once they're back in the jeep she asks, "Do you want to see a little of the island? Or head right back to your hotel? I don't know if Uncle Timmy has plans for you, things he needs you to do." When she lived with Timothy and Gertie, the assistants were a rotating series of young women and sometimes young men around Alexa's age, and though Sam knew they had specific jobs and duties she never knew what those jobs were and which person performed which duties. Their work was a low hum in the background, like the buzzing of bees.

"He doesn't," says Alexa. "Really he hardly needs me here at all. I wanted to come, to see my family, and to see the play, and he was nice enough to call it work, and to let me come for a long stretch."

"That's great," says Sam. "We'll take the long way back, then. That way we can avoid the traffic on Ocean." She takes a right on West Side Road, past Ball O'Brien Park, past the Island Cemetery, then, when West Side splits, a left on Beacon Hill, bisecting the center of the island. She shows Alexa the small airport, with the restaurant inside that is supposed to be excellent, although Sam has never been, and she points out the Native American cemetery. When they get to the intersection of Lakeside Drive and Mohegan Trail she stops and shows Alexa Painted Rock, explaining it to Alexa the way Maggie explained it to her: it's a landmark that's been painted over hundreds of times with island messages, from wedding proposals to quotes from the Beatles and a bunch of stuff in between.

"I love it!" cries Alexa. "This place is a-mazing. I can't believe I lived a couple of hours away from the ferry my whole life."

"I lived right across the water!" says Sam. "And after my grandmother moved away we mostly stopped coming."

When she pulls up in front of Hotel Manisses she gives herself a mental pat on the back. Two months ago she was just getting to know the island herself; now she's giving tours like a semiprofessional guide.

"This was really nice. Thank you, Sam. I can't wait to see the play."

The play! Dress rehearsal tonight! Sam's stomach starts to flutter. She hopes it isn't the sushi. When she accepted the role she'd let herself think about lines, and rehearsals, and costume fittings, and working with her uncle, and being onstage with Gertie—but she'd sort of forgotten that at some point there would be a real, live audience, and she could flub a line or mess up her entrance.

"Thank you," she says to Alexa. She feels weak in the knees.

No, it isn't the sushi. The sushi was amazing. It's the foe of every actor who's trod the boards: it's good old-fashioned nerves.

The Island

ON ANY GIVEN night on Block Island there are dozens—nay, hundreds—of tiny dramas playing out. We should emphasize that by this we mean any *summer* night. In the off-season, with only one thousand year-round residents, the number falls proportionately, and you might get ten dramas, or fewer.

This particular night, there's a wedding party in town. Not a surprise! There's always a wedding party in town in August! The rehearsal dinner is at the Harbor Grill. Seafood risotto is the main course, preceded by crab cakes and pulled pork sliders, and followed by a scrumptious mango cheesecake. The best man gets too drunk, as best men sometimes do, and lets slip a story about the groom-to-be and a girl on the dance floor at the Omni Las Vegas during the bachelor party. "Nothing happened!" the groom-to-be tells the teary bride-to-be, protected by her cadre of bridesmaids, each with a set of daggers in her eyes. (Nothing did, in fact, happen on the dance floor that night in Vegas. Just dancing. But nevertheless, drama.)

On the far side of the island, in a little cottage on Dorry's Cove Road, a twenty-eight-year-old woman has just taken a third test to confirm her fourth pregnancy, which will result in, if she carries to term, her first child. She's waiting for her wife, a doctor at the Block Island Medical Center, to come home from her twelve-hour shift so she can tell her. It's a quiet drama, rooted in both loss and hope.

On Dodge Street a writer named Anthony Puckett writes THE END on the final page of a manuscript he's been working on for the better part of two years. He pours himself a scotch in honor of his late father, whom the book is about, and who always poured a scotch to celebrate writing THE END on any of his manuscripts. He calls his mother, Dorothy, to tell her he's finally done. Unbeknownst to Anthony, Dorothy has been working on her own version of the story, and unbeknownst to both, her manuscript will hit publishers' desks at the same time his does. Drama.

Some us have lived on this island for decades, and some of us are only here for the summer or the week or maybe even just the night. Our dramas are big and small, personal and public, instructive and destructive, like those of any community.

But the *real* drama, this night, is inside the Empire Theatre as the ticket holders take their seats. It's a sold-out show, and the diligent ushers, Maggie Sousa and her sort-of best friend, Riley, have all but a few straggling latecomers seated just before the curtain rises, revealing a vine-covered, balcony-studded villa of long-ago Messina.

Amy

AMY WATCHES OPENING night from the back of the theater. Henry, Greg, and Ava have seats in the fifth row, in the center, but she doesn't want to sit with them. She wants to watch alone. Timothy is watching from an undisclosed location so he can take notes to give for the following night.

In the few minutes before the curtains part, Amy scans the crowd. It's a full house. She sees friends and strangers and people who fall exactly in between: two teachers from her department at the high school (friends), a man in oversize black-framed glasses who she was told *may* be from the *New York Times* (stranger), her old babysitting charge Holly, sitting with Joy Sousa and Anthony Puckett (exactly in between). Maggie, Joy's daughter, is working as an usher. Maggie is flushed and busy, leading people to their seats. Every advance-sale ticket for the next eleven shows is sold, thanks to Sam.

The house manager makes the announcements about the fire exits and the prohibition of cameras and cell phones, and then a hush falls over the crowd. It's the same hush everywhere. Amy has heard this hush on Broadway, before every show of *To Kill a Mockingbird*, and at the off-off-off Broadway productions she attended during college, and in her own high school auditorium, before each and every production she's been a part of. She bets the hush is international, and it shows you that theatergoing remains a shared, universal experience.

The curtain opens, and instantly Amy is transported to sixteenth-century Messina, and the stone facade of Leonato's Italian villa, with the wrought iron balcony and the tangle of vines down the front. The set is spectacular. The lighting is spectacular. The costumes are spectacular. Little old Block Island, which Amy used to think of as poky and remote, is bringing it.

When Gertie enters, along with Leonato, Sam, and the Messenger, the applause is immediate and thunderous. There are a couple of whistles; there's a little bit of stomping. Everyone in the cast has been told to expect this. People go crazy when they see an actual movie star on the stage. They go *crazy*!

Leonato holds for the applause, then holds some more, then at last it dies down, and he speaks the first line of the play:

I learn in this letter that Don Peter of Arragon
Comes this night to Messina.

And they are off and running.

Somehow, even though she watched the costume fittings, and part of the dress rehearsal, and pored over the preproduction stills, Amy isn't prepared for seeing her daughter onstage, in Hero's costume: the Renaissance gown, square at the neck, cinched tight at the waist, with long, puffy sleeves. So accustomed is Amy to seeing her daughter attired in next to nothing—the shortest of shorts, the cropped-est of tops, her PJs, her bikini—that she almost doesn't recognize her, especially under the lights, with the makeup, saying the lines.

Amy never puts on Shakespeare plays at her high school. To be honest, she's not really sure why Shakespeare is still the go-to for high school nonmusical productions, with so many other wonderful playwrights to choose from. Why not Tracy Letts, Arthur

Miller? Where's Alice Childress, Lillian Hellman, Lisa Kron? Of course she's read plenty of Shakespeare; of course she's seen her share of the plays. But often she's wondered: Why this one guy? Why always *him*?

She starts to get it as she stands in the back of the theater and hears Gertie Sanger say:

It is so indeed; he is no less than a stuffed man:
But for the stuffing—well, we are all mortal.

We *are* all mortal, thinks Amy. We are! And isn't that just the crux of everything. And didn't Shakespeare just know it. Didn't he just know a lot back then that's still true today: the weight of societal expectations, the lightness of love.

The Messenger: I see, lady, the gentleman is not in your books.
Beatrice: No; an he were, I would burn my study.

When she delivers this line she tosses a sardonic look toward the audience.

Everybody laughs. It's funny! It's legitimately, even now, in the third decade of the twenty-first century, funny! *Much Ado* is a comic masterpiece for a reason. It's got everything. Witty language, a clever plot, the magic element of all romantic comedies, from Hughes to Ephron to Emily Henry, which is that everyone—except Beatrice and Benedick—including the audience, knows that Beatrice and Benedick are made for each other. Amy sees now too that Timothy's direction, his own comic sensibility, his care with which way Gertie turns her shoulders when she utters a particular line, the body language between the two leads that he's teased out, thread by thread, beat by beat, deserves its own attention and praise.

Then, of course, before the intermission the feeling turns more ominous, when Don John approaches Claudio with the lie about

Hero. Amy's stomach clenches. She remembers everything Sam told her about what happened in New York, and why she came home, and how badly she wanted to hide.

During intermission, Amy herself hides in the lighting booth. She doesn't want to see anyone. She's too nervous for the second act, for Sam, for Timothy. From up here all she can make out is an energetic murmur, a buzz and a hum as people head toward the concessions or maybe even outside for a sip of nighttime air before returning to their seats.

"How do you think it's going?" she asks Tommy, the lighting guy. Her feet are sweating: that's her tell, that's what happens when she gets nervous.

"Lights are working," he says.

"But the rest of it . . . ?"

Tommy shrugs and rubs his palms on his jeans. "My job is the lights," he says. A Shakespearian, Tommy is not.

Amy sighs and taps her fingers on the spotlight casing.

"I'm going to stretch my legs," says Tommy. "You're making me nervous."

"You're making *me* nervous," she says right back, but too late, Tommy is gone.

Finally Amy turns on her cell phone and texts Greg, Henry, and Ava: Are people liking it.

She waits, and waits some more. Finally the answer comes, from Greg.

Babe, says the text. People are loving it. Champagne Glass Emoji, Celebratory Heart Emoji. Amy's spirits lift.

Tommy returns. "People are loving it," Amy tells him. She holds up her phone as proof but Tommy is already dimming the lights so the audience knows to return to their seats; he doesn't answer.

Another text comes in from Greg: Met the producer. Amy draws in her breath. *Blake!* Said he's blown away. Amy exhales. Okay. Okay! Blake is happy. She can relax.

Amy retreats down to the back of the theater.

And now the second half, the scene in the outdoor church: Hero's wedding day, when she will be accused falsely of infidelity and watch her dreams of a happy married life dissolve before her eyes. The wedding dress is stunning, made in a similar style to the dress Sam wore in the first act, with intricate beading that catches the light when she turns, and a veil that flows from the crown of her head and down her back. Amy's heart hurts thinking about each age Sam has been. It feels like an actual pain, like somebody has driven something sharp into her chest cavity, and then twisted it, and she has to breathe deeply so that it can become bearable. She looks at this young woman onstage and thinks of Sam at age three, chubby legs running down the beach; six, seven, eight, missing teeth, Christmas mornings, birthday parties, science fair projects; Sam as Scout; as the little sister in *My Three Daughters;* as a desultory regular Rhode Island high school student, occasionally breaking curfew or sneering at something her parents said but just as often making them laugh until they cried; Sam as a Tik-Tok sensation, a member of a collab household (honestly, what *is* that? Amy is still trying to figure it out)—and now, Sam as Hero, resplendent, heartbroken, falling to the ground on her wedding day. Hero, who has done nothing wrong but to fall in love, and trust. Sam, the very same!

Thy slander hath gone through and through her heart.

Amy wants to tap the shoulder of the person in the last row and say, *You see Hero up there? She's mine. Greg and I made that kid. Isn't she lovely? She's holding her own with Gertie Sanger!*

The slanderous plot is revealed; the lovers are reunited; Beatrice and Benedick agree to marry. All's well that ends well, thinks Amy, though of course that's a different play.

The curtain lowers, and the lights come up, and then the curtain rises again for bows. Somebody has handed identical bouquets of flowers to Sam and Gertie. Standing ovation. Curtain calls, Gertie shining like a constellation, Sam smiling so hard her face must be hurting. Amy can see Timmy now, in the second row, on the aisle, standing, his hands clasped together. She sees Gertie catch his eye, and she watches Timmy do a little half bow toward her.

Hell, thinks Amy, no wonder we're still performing Shakespeare, still reading him and picking apart his dialogue and mining him for thoughts on societal expectations and gender roles. Because he still has relevance. Words can have relevance for a really long time, and it's the people who take the risk, who put their words down, who get to enjoy that relevance.

You're not exactly an expert on taking chances, Sam had told her. The words had stung because they were true. But did they have to be true forever?

The curtain lowers for the final time, and the audience begins to gather handbags and programs and cell phones and move toward the exit. Amy, swimming against the tide, goes to find her family. She's looking for Greg when she feels a tap on her shoulder and she turns around: Timothy.

"It was amazing," she says, and means it. "You did it."

"*We* did it," says Timothy. Are his eyes wet? His eyes are wet! "We did it." He opens his arms and Amy opens hers, and he doesn't have to say again that he sees her or appreciates her, and she doesn't have to say that she understands his choices too, because it's all right there.

"Much Ado" Is Everything

"MUCH ADO" IS EVERYTHING
Much Ado About Nothing, Empire Theatre, New Shoreham, RI
New York Times

By Charles C. Ritic

How much Shakespeare can we take in, at how many summer theaters? The answer, it seems, is as many productions as are offered, in as many guises.

Until last night, the most recent production of *Much Ado About Nothing* this reviewer took in was the Public Theater's delightful staging at the Delacorte on Central Park West in 2019—a pre-COVID summer that now, with the perspective that time's passing affords, seems in many ways innocent and quaint.

Pandemics eventually come under control; the phoenix rises from the ashes; Shakespeare endures. These are lessons for our time. And so on a sultry summer's night we ferried across Block Island Sound from Newport and settled into the well-air-conditioned Empire Theatre on Block Island, a tiny island off the coast of Rhode Island. Block Island is a New England oasis lacking both the provisions and the flashiness of a Nantucket or a Vineyard. I hadn't been there since I was a boy, and was happy to return to immerse myself in a production of one of Shakespeare's most popular comedies, with stage direction by Timothy Fleming, sets by Mason Miller, costumes by Shanita Grace, and starring the effervescent Gertie Sanger.

Much Ado remains popular for a reason. Like the best of Shakespeare, its themes are timeless—love and distrust, deception and cowardice and valor. The two couples at the center of the plot are Benedick and Beatrice and Claudio and Hero. The former couple profess not to love each other, until they do; the second profess only to love each other, until they don't, then do again. Eventually, everybody gets married.

Miller's sets transform this well-used stage (the theater has variously existed as an old-time roller rink, a movie theater, and a craft emporium) into the Messina of Shakespeare's day, replete with rose gardens, a vine-covered villa, and iron balconies.

Summer theater historically attracts a high caliber of performer, but for a theater so small, and an island so relatively unsung, to attract the likes of Gertie Sanger is a rarity indeed. Ms. Sanger's film roles have often depended on her ability to thrive in extreme close-ups—the batting of an eye, the slow release of a tear, the swinging of a lock of that famous strawberry-blond hair—but I'm happy to report that her talent holds up when the "camera" pulls back. Ms. Sanger, a classically trained actor, brings comedic grace and timing to the role of Beatrice, whose stage directions require her to be by turns impish and wisecracking, sharp-tongued, vulnerable: in short, to run the whole Shakespearian gamut.

Ms. Sanger's talent is apparent not just in what she does but also in what she doesn't do—she doesn't steal the show from the other actors. Neil Hannan as Benedick and Geoffrey Hare as Claudio, each coming to this performance with an impressive stage résumé, also give strong performances, and the chemistry between Sanger and Hannan gives their will-they-or-won't-they merriment (of *course* they will) a razor-sharp edge.

One cast member who deserves particular notice is Samantha Trevino, niece of the director, who stepped in to fill the role, reportedly at the last minute, when the actor originally cast left the production suddenly. Trevino enjoyed a much-lauded run of *To Kill a Mockingbird* some seven years ago, playing the part of Scout to her uncle's Atticus Finch, before a stint in the Disney Channel Multiverse, and, most recently, the world of TikTok fame. As Hero, Ms. Trevino positively shines, and it's almost impossible to believe the role wasn't hers all along, and that she wasn't born speaking Shakespeare. This is the sort of breakout performance the term "breakout performance" was created to describe.

One of the challenges in presenting a play like this in times like these is whether or how to reconcile the anachronisms of the era in which it was written with present-day norms and attitudes. How do we continue to enjoy plays penned more than 400 years ago when around us the world swirls, the planet melts, races and genders collide? Some directors decide to reinvent and reexamine. Mr. Fleming has chosen to give us the play as we imagine Shakespeare originally staged and wrote it, allowing the brilliance of the performances and sets, the preciseness of the stage direction, and the timelessness of the human condition to transport. My advice to you is to get thee to the island without delay to see this production.

When the show ended, theatergoers who failed to secure a room in one of the island's bustling, sold-out hotels (this critic included) made the short walk to the ferry, a spring in their step. The night was glorious, the infusion of top-notch theater in an unexpected place invigorating. Incongruously, contemporary music reached the ears from Block Island's National Hotel, its famous porch so full of revelers it seemed almost to sway of its own accord. And one cannot help but think that the Bard surely would have approved. Perhaps he even would have had a piece of advice to offer.

Strike up, pipers!

Timothy

THE SHOW GOES on like this for all twelve nights of the run. Because of the *Times* piece *Much Ado About Nothing* is suddenly the hottest ticket anywhere—hotter than anything in Connecticut, or Maine, or at Williamstown. Shelly Salazar reports that she has so many requests for house seats she can hardly answer them all, never mind fulfill the requests. (Finally, Shelly Salazar is doing her job!)

A reviewer from the *Washington Post* wants to come, a writer from *Variety*, from the *Hollywood Reporter,* from the *Boston Globe.* Shelly has to pick and choose among the requests—she has to prioritize. There simply aren't enough seats for everyone; there simply aren't enough nights.

Timothy wants to freeze time right where they are now, at the end of the eighth night, with three shows to go. Not the night of the last show—that's too sad. Not the night of the first show—things felt too wobbly and uncertain then, and nobody knew how the play would be received.

The next morning Timothy wakes with the idea of extending the run through Labor Day. It's not like the Empire Theatre has a whole summer season planned. All he has to do is ask Vinny St. James if he can pay more money for more time. He holds the idea to him like a promise, like a winning poker hand, and in the middle of the morning, when Gertie knocks on his bedroom door, fresh from the shower, wearing only a robe, he broaches it. She leans against the door, and he sits in the straight-backed chair in the corner, leaning forward. He's close enough that he could touch her (and lord knows he *wants* to touch her), but he doesn't. He just talks. She listens while he tells her what he's thinking, her bottom lip caught between her teeth. When he's finished he sits back expectantly, and she shakes her head.

"I can't do more nights, Timothy," she tells him.

"What? Why not?" He's legitimately surprised. "The tickets are selling themselves. The profit is there, for Blake. Why would anyone leave Block Island before Labor Day if they didn't have to? Late August is the best part of summer in New England!"

Gertie points at the bed, he nods, and she settles back on top of the comforter, her legs crossed demurely at the ankles—or anyway, as demurely as a person wearing nothing but a robe can do anything. "I told you at the beginning of all this, I'm expected in Portugal on the twenty-fifth to start shooting *Death by Proxy*."

"Push it," suggests Timothy. (She had told him, but he'd forgotten.)

"I can't push it. My start date is locked."

Timothy rises from the chair and lies down on the bed next to Gertie. He nuzzles his face into the side of Gertie's neck and says, "Maybe I'll go with you. I love Portugal. I can hang out in your trailer, bring you glasses of *vinho verde*. I could be your boy toy."

He feels a shift in the atmosphere. Gertie puts one of her hands on top of his. "No, thank you," she says politely—even primly. She sits up, her back against one of the two big square pillows, and tucks her legs under her, spreading the robe over her knees like a blanket.

"To which part? I was kidding about the boy toy thing. Mostly.

Although I'd be happy to oblige. Obviously." He considers winking, but that might be a bridge too far. Along with the robe, she's wearing a funny expression.

"No, thank you to all of it, is what I mean." She retightens the bathrobe belt where it's come loose.

"To *all of it*?"

"Timothy. This was fun between us this summer, but that's all it was. Fun. A summer romance."

He arches the famous eyebrow at her, but she's not meeting his gaze. "It doesn't have to be, Gertie. It could be bigger than that. It could be like it used to be."

She rises from the bed and stands beside it. "No," she says. "I can't do that, Timothy. I'm not interested in going back to where we once were. I'm going to Portugal on my own."

"But where we once were was amazing! You know it was."

"It was," she says. "At one time, it was amazing. And you took that away from us, when you started up with half of Hollywood."

Can a heart deflate? Timothy isn't sure, but if it's possible, his just did. "Give me another chance. Please, Gertie. We're so good together. I didn't appreciate it before, the way I should have. But I appreciate it now! I won't disappoint you."

Gertie considers him. "You know, Timothy. Sometimes I feel like I'm still that wide-eyed girl at Juilliard, scared out of my damn mind—"

Again with the Juilliard, Timothy thinks. But he says, "That bar with the sinks full of ice, right?"

"Right," says Gertie. "But the point is that sometimes I feel like *that* girl, and sometimes I feel one hundred years old and just sort of over the whole thing, you know? The whole fame thing, the whole acting thing. Sometimes I don't know how to keep finding the joy. But if there's anything I learned from us, or rather I guess I should say from the end of us, it's that I have to find that joy on my own. I can't depend on you for that. You broke my heart, Timothy. Really and truly, you broke it. And I've never recovered. Not all the way."

He feels a sharp pain behind his eyes, and in the center of his body, between his ribs. Is this where his soul lives? Does his *soul* hurt? "I'm sorry, Gertie. My darling. I know I did. I know how foolish I was. And I'm so sorry."

"I believe you," she says gently. "I do believe that. But that doesn't undo it, you see. I can't go back to a time before you hurt me. I have to live at a different angle from you than I did in the past. That was the cost of all of it."

The morning light filtering in through the window illuminates her face like the softest stage light. Gertie Sanger. The famous bone structure, the light green eyes, the alabaster skin. It's a face so familiar to so many people, but he always thought it was most familiar to him because he got to see it in every one of its guises: terror and ecstasy and melancholy and grief and joy and hope and fear. Now he understands that she's been holding a part of herself back from him all summer, and that what she's been showing him is the same thing she's been showing everyone else. Even in bed, even without clothes, she has kept a part of herself covered. To protect herself, so that he can't hurt her again.

"You're right," he says finally. "Gertie, you're right." There's something sad in Gertie's face—but there's something brave there too, and the brave part is what finally makes his heart crack.

"This show was everything I wanted it to be, Timothy. That *Times* review was more than I dreamed of."

"Thanks to Sam for getting the reviewer there."

"Thanks to Sam." She smiles. "I'm reading for two plays when I get back from Portugal."

"You're *reading*? Gertie Sanger is auditioning?"

She shrugs. "I told my agent I want to audition, to make sure whatever I take on is the right next step. You know we all get to a point where we could stop working. You've been there for years and years now. But we want to keep going anyway. I want to pick exactly the right project. So I'm taking my time, and auditioning, and really checking out who and what is involved in anything I'm considering."

"What are the plays?"

"One is a new one by Tracy Letts at Second Stage. I haven't read it yet. One is a Broadway revival of *The Cherry Orchard*."

"Ah," he says. "Good old Chekhov. Madame Ranevskaya?"

"Yes."

He nods slowly. "I can see it. I vote for the Chekhov." (Sam, he thinks, would make a perfect Anya. He wonders what kind of strings he'd have to pull to get her considered for that. Probably the strings he'd have to pull hardest, come to think of it, would be with Sam herself.) "Nothing against Letts, but I love *The Cherry Orchard*. And I'm always up for a revival."

"I know you are." She smiles, a wide, open, guileless smile, and this time it doesn't look like she's holding anything back. This time it looks like it's all there in front of him, every piece of her, vulnerable and exposed, like a dog offering its tender belly to the world. "I am too," she says. "I really am always up for a revival." She leans over and kisses him on the cheek, and he understands from the way her lips do not linger that this is where they will stop. They'll see each other, of course. Their circles will always overlap. But here, in a bedroom in a borrowed house: here's where their story ends.

"I think we should toast to new beginnings," she says. "Stay right here." She leaves the bedroom, and when she returns she's carrying the Rhum Clément 1952 and two glasses.

"Are we going to *open this*?" asks Timothy.

"We can't fly with it! We'll have a little taste now, just a tiny one, and we'll finish the rest when the show's run is over. We'll share it only with our favorite people. Sam can have a little."

"I suppose Amy can have a *small* glass," concedes Timothy. He's kidding, of course. Amy can have as much as she wants.

Gertie opens the bottle and pours them each a tiny bit. "Cheers," she says.

"'I do love nothing in the world so well as you: Is not that strange?'" he says. Benedick's line. He clinks his glass lightly against Gertie's. She clinks back.

"'As strange as the thing I know not,'" she says. Beatrice's.

Sam

THE PLAN IS that Alexa will drive Sam, Gertie, and Timothy, along with their luggage, to the ferry in Floyd's Wagoneer, then drive the car back, lock up the house, and take an Uber to the ferry herself. Sam knows she should have told them the night before, when they formulated the plan, to save Alexa the extra trip. But she couldn't bring herself to, not yet.

"Why don't we all just take an Uber?" she suggests now, on departure day, when Alexa arrives at the house after checking out of her room at the Hotel Manisses. "Then Alexa doesn't have to backtrack."

"The only Ubers I've found on this island are sedans," says Gertie. "I couldn't fit a third of my luggage in a sedan."

"I don't mind," says Alexa. "This is literally what I get paid for. Assisting."

"You're not *my* assistant," says Sam.

"True," says Alexa. "But I think you're grandfathered in."

"Wouldn't I be uncled in?" Sam asks before going into her bedroom and shutting the door. Humor can be an excellent tool for deflection. What she's deflecting from is the fact that her suitcase isn't packed, her bed isn't stripped, her sheets aren't piled up in the laundry room to make things easier for the housecleaner. In fact, Sam is going to clean the house herself, top to bottom, soup to nuts, head to tail. That's the arrangement she worked out with Floyd Barringer, in exchange for staying in the house through Labor Day. Riley's mom, Holly, helped her find an off-season rental that begins the Tuesday after the holiday, an adorable two-bedroom condo on Ocean Ave, in the same building as The Cracked Mug. When next summer comes Sam will have to find somewhere else to live, or she'll have to absorb a dramatic increase in rent, as the condo rents weekly in the season. But for this time of year, for this time in her life, it's perfect. When Holly first showed it to her, and when Sam peeked in the tiny second bedroom, she found it decorated nautically, with a navy-blue bedspread, brass knobs on the dresser, and a blue-and-gold decorative pillow with SEAS THE DAY embroidered in fancy script.

"I'll take it," she told Holly. "I'm ready to seas all of the days."

"Chop chop!" hollers Uncle Timmy now, in his loud director voice. He's in the kitchen, but Sam can hear him all the way downstairs, in the bedroom. "Gertie? You ready? Sam? Let's goooooo. Let's pack up the car. I don't want to miss that ferry."

Sam cannot, after all, stand the suspense of having a secret nobody else knows. When she hears Gertie making a commotion by the front door, readying her luggage, she emerges from her bedroom and announces, "I'm not going."

"What?" Gertie turns around, her eyes inscrutable behind big dark glasses, her hair suitably glamorous. "I'm sorry, what'd you say, Sammy?"

"I'm not going," says Sam. "I'm staying here."

Timothy, returning from bringing a load to the car, fills the doorway. He's squinting from the sun, and lines are radiating from the corners of his eyes. "What do you mean? In Floyd's house?"

"Just through Labor Day. I've got a rental after that."

She explains it all, as quickly as she can (they do have a ferry to catch).

Earlier that week Sam talked to Vinny St. James about the

possibility of developing a real season at the Empire the following summer. He was interested, but he has no connections beyond the island; he didn't really know what a summer season would entail. Sam does. She's been thinking about it. She'd made some calls. She's been figuring how to use her influence for good, the way Timothy had wanted her to.

They'll need financial backing, of course, but Sam has enough in her bank account to get started. They'll need access to playwrights and casting directors and people who understand the murky world of equity contracts. They'll need new plays! Sam told Vinny that she isn't interested in an entire summer of revivals. One revival is wonderful, even necessary; many theatergoers like to anchor themselves in the familiar, no maritime pun intended. But Sam wants emerging voices too, and underrepresented voices, and loud, angry voices. The more she talked about it, the more excited Vinny St. James became, and the more excited Vinny St. James became the more excited Sam became too.

Once she had approval from Vinny to use the theater she arranged a call with Blake Allard. He was in an excellent mood because *Much Ado* had been received so well, and because his rum business had enjoyed a particularly strong season. Rum was becoming the new bourbon, which was just what Blake had predicted. Sam explained to Blake what she and Vinny had talked about; she described her vision for the following summer. A mini Williamstown, an island-size Ogunquit.

"I don't have the capacity to make that happen," said Blake. "The mental capacity, the connections."

"But you have the money."

"Sure. I have money coming out of most of my orifices."

Gross, thought Sam. But she held her tongue, because she knew she had what Blake Allard didn't have: time, and energy, and youth, and enough connections to get started.

"That sounds exactly like something Blake Allard would say," says Gertie now, as Sam relays the conversation. "The thing with the orifices. But you know what? It's mostly true." She pushes her sunglasses to the top of her head, and her green eyes are shining. "I think it's *fabulous,* Sam. If you can arrange for two house seats for me on opening night of the first play of next summer's season, I'll be there, with bells on."

Uncle Timmy looks a little more skeptical. "You're going to stay here all year?"

"Yes," says Sam. "I'm going to use the second bedroom in the condo I'm renting as an office." She'll keep the SEAS THE DAY pillow, but she'll move in a desk and a chair. "When I need to, I'll go to New York. But I'm pretty sure I can do a lot from here."

"The winters on this island are *very* long," says Uncle Timmy. "Like, they can bring you to an Arctic Circle level of madness."

"I know," says Sam. "I mean, I don't know. But I can imagine. I'm prepared. If I get lonely, Narragansett is just a ferry ride away. I don't think my mom is going to let me descend to an Arctic Circle level of madness."

"That's true," says Timothy. "Have you told your mom yet?"

"Not yet," says Sam. "She's next, after you guys get on the ferry."

"She'll be over the moon, to have you so close. Both of your parents will. Although she might be infuriated that you're this close but not living at home."

"I think she'll be okay with it," says Sam. "And also, I can always go visit Henry and Ava in Middlebury."

From the driveway, two quick beeps of the car horn. It's Alexa, summoning them.

"We'd better go," says Gertie.

"*I'll* drop you off," says Sam. "Now that you know the plan. Then Alexa won't have to come back."

It's a tight fit, the four of them plus the luggage, but they make it work. Gertie takes the passenger seat, Sam drives, and Alexa and Timothy balance in the back with the bags.

"I'm going to miss it here," says Gertie. She gazes out the window as the car rises and falls along Mohegan Trail. Little glimpses of the ocean reach them as the road twists. Far offshore, the turning of the wind turbines looks lazy, lackadaisical, but Sam knows that the turbines are actually working very hard. "I really, really am."

"Oh, but the Algarve," says Timothy. "That's just gorgeous. *That*, you're really going to love." He sounds wistful as he says that, and Sam glances in the rearview mirror, but his expression is impossible to read, because he has put on his own sunglasses, maybe to hide the outside world from him, maybe to hide himself from the outside world. Probably a little bit of both.

They pass the Southeast Lighthouse, and then Mohegan Trail turns into Spring Street, and on the left they can see the Spring House Hotel, and then the 1611 Inn, then down the hill they go, and Sam maneuvers around the little traffic circle near the theater.

"Bye, theater," says Gertie.

"Bye, theater," echoes Timothy.

"I've been meaning to ask this all summer," says Gertie. "Who is that? The statue in the middle of the circle?"

"That's Rebecca," says Timothy. "She was put there by the Women's Christian Temperance Union in the late eighteen hundreds, to curb alcohol consumption on the island."

"Girl," says Sam. "I don't think you're really killing it."

From the back seat Alexa laughs.

The ferry parking lot is busy, as it always is, and Sam pulls as close as she can to the passenger drop-off point, then puts the Wagoneer in park and hops out so she can help unload the bags. Alexa disappears and comes back with a luggage cart, then disappears again. Gertie whips out a baseball cap, puts it on, and winds her hair into a low bun. With the addition of the hat and the subtraction of the hair she's transformed herself into an average person, just another vacationer whose time in the sun has come to an end.

"Sammy," says Gertie. She opens her arms and into them goes Sam. Despite the shimmering summer heat Gertie looks and smells as fresh as a mountain spring, and she feels as cool as one too. "Sammy, Sammy, Sammy. It was the summer of a lifetime. Truly it was, and I wouldn't have wanted to do it without you. I *couldn't* have done it without you."

Sam is suddenly too overcome to speak. She nods into Gertie's neck, and then she lets go of her, and then she hugs Uncle Timothy, and by this time Alexa is back, without the luggage, so—why not?—Sam hugs Alexa too.

Timothy places his hand lightly on Gertie's forearm, and she doesn't move away, but Sam notices she doesn't move closer either. "Shall we beat on?" Which Sam figures is some kind of actor-y code for *we really can't miss this ferry.*

"We shall," says Gertie. Her voice is throaty with some kind of emotion—regret? Love? A combination?

And then the three of them turn, and melt into the crowd, and Sam watches them until she can't make them out any longer.

Timothy

BACK IN BENEDICT Canyon, in front of his koi pond, Timothy feels pensive. It's good to be back in L.A., but it's also terrible to be back in L.A. He misses the house on Mohegan Trail, and the wraparound deck, and the steps leading down to the beach. He misses the frigid Atlantic water, and the rise and fall of the hills as he drove the jeep around the island. And he misses Sam, and Gertie. He misses the air and the light of New England. He misses the trees. Here the air feels thinner, the light a bit flatter. He's been invited for dinner at Magari, and for drinks at the Hollywood Roosevelt, and even to one of Jennifer Aniston's famously intimate dinner parties, and he's declined all of these, because what he really wants is to be with his family. He even misses Amy—he *especially* misses Amy. He's thinking of inviting everyone out to L.A. for Christmas.

What's the end of summer in L.A. anyway? Nothing. There are no seasons to L.A.; therefore, the end of one season and the beginning of another signifies very little. He closes his eyes, imagining what the ferries must look like now, the upper decks full, the Bloody Marys flowing. He imagines Ballard's: the volleyball court, the reggae band. He thinks about the lines at the ice cream shops. Poor People's Pub; McAloon's; the porch at the National. His heart hurts.

When he opens his eyes, Alexa is standing in front of him. "Sorry!" she says. "Sorry. I didn't know if you were asleep. I didn't want to wake you."

"I wasn't sleeping," he says. "I was . . . daydreaming."

"Barry's here for you. Should I show him back?"

Timothy sighs. Is he in a Barry mood? Not really, but it doesn't so much matter. He's not in any kind of mood. "Yes, please. Show him back."

"Hey, hey!" says Barry. He steps over the small wooden bridge that crosses the koi pond. He's carrying a bottle of kombucha. His sunglasses are pushed to the top of his head. Barry has been Timothy's agent for decades now, but somehow he still looks much the same as he did during their very first meeting.

"Barry," says Timothy. "To what do I owe the pleasure of a house call? Did somebody die?"

"Not that I know of," says Barry. "I come bearing news! May I?" He indicates the bench adjacent to Timothy's chair, and, when Timothy nods, he sits. He makes a big show of screwing the top off the kombucha and taking a long pull. Timothy shudders: How can people drink that stuff? When Barry lowers the bottle he says, "They want you in London!"

Timothy sits up a little straighter. "Who wants me in London?"

"Regent's Park needs an interim artistic director for their summer season. Someone just left abruptly. It could turn into a permanent position, or it could be for just one year. Apparently somebody associated with it saw your little play on Block Island and was mightily impressed."

"What's the pay?"

Barry looks at him. He might be raising his eyebrows at Timothy, but he appears to have recently refreshed his Botox so it's hard to say for sure. His tan is deep and even. His cologne is almost too much, but it might in fact be just enough. "The pay is terrible," he says. "Is that a deal breaker?"

"Nope."

"I didn't think so."

"What's the season? Have they planned it yet?"

"In process," says Barry. "You'd be part of that process. But you'd have to get some actual clothes on and get over there pretty quickly."

"I'm wearing clothes," Timothy says. He's wearing shorts, a navy T-shirt screen printed with an outline of Block Island and the word *home* written across it, and his Red Sox cap. Nobody in L.A. wears shorts. Definitely not men in L.A. But on the island this summer he'd come to appreciate them.

"Those aren't clothes," says Barry. "Those are *cloths*. What do you say? To London?"

"What are *those* pants?" he asks Barry, pointing.

"This?" Barry fingers the fabric above his knee. "This is a meta pant. See? Stretchy. They're a transition from the sweats we all got too used to during the pandemic."

"You never wore sweats during the pandemic."

"You're right," says Barry. "Not I. But many did."

"I'll think about it," Timothy says. "I don't know if I want to leave my koi for that long." Grumpy and Bashful seem to have struck up a friendship while he was back east, which was not a turn of events he had expected, but he's not mad at it.

"You're kidding, right?"

Instead of answering Timothy asks a question of his own. "Barry? Do you think the movies are done with me?"

Barry thinks about this. He really thinks, going through the whole kombucha-sipping process again, then staring for a while at the koi.

"I don't," Barry says at last. "I really don't think the movies will be done with Timothy Fleming for a long, long time. But is there any chance *you're* done with the *movies*?"

"I don't know," says Timothy. "I worry sometimes that I've stayed too long at the party."

Barry laughs, then, seeing that Timothy is serious, stops laughing. "You know what I always say? As long as the party is still going, there's no such thing as staying too long. And the party, my friend, is still going."

"Artistic director," muses Timothy. It might be exciting. Or it might be lonely. It might be challenging. It might be all three, plus some more things he hasn't even thought of yet.

Barry looks at his watch. He thinks he's being discreet, but he's not. He taps his fingers on his pants, carefully not saying anything.

Finally Timothy says, "You know what? I think I'd like to do it."

"I should tell them yes?"

"You should tell them yes. I'm not familiar with a season there. Do they do new works, or revivals?"

"Heck if I know," says Barry. "Probably both."

"Okay, good. Because I do love a revival, Barry. I really do."

"I've heard that about you, sweetie." Barry pats Timothy's hand and rises from the bench. On to the next client; on to the next deal. "I've heard that you love a revival."

Amy

AMY HAS JUST sat down at the desk in the corner of her bedroom, where typically she grades student papers. In front of her is a yellow legal pad, her good fountain pen with a box of refill cartridges, and her thoughts. It's been a long time since Amy has faced a blank pad of paper, one without even a to-do list, and she eyes it warily, like an arctic fox eyeing a vole.

Her phone, which is downstairs in the kitchen, the better to keep her attention where it belongs, rings. Ignore it, she tells herself. School starts in one week, and you have only this precious string of days in front of you. You cannot afford distractions.

The phone stops ringing. See? she tells herself. Nothing is that important. If it's really important, they'll call back.

The ringing starts again.

Aw, heck. She'll just run down and take a gander at who the caller is. Just to make sure it's not an emergency. What if Sam, all alone on Block Island, needs her? What if Henry and Ava, back in Vermont, need her? What if, God forbid, something happened to Greg at work? If the caller is none of these people, she won't answer. She's just going to take the *very quickest peek* at the caller ID.

"I'm just going to look!" she says aloud on her way down the stairs. "It's a perfectly reasonable thing to do."

It's not Henry and Ava, nor Sam, nor Greg. It's an unknown

local number. But what if Henry or Sam lost their phones, and they're calling from a different number? In May, when Sam really needed her, *she'd* called from an unknown number, at the rental place, and imagine if Amy had ignored that? Sam might still be at the Enterprise in North Kingston, all these months later!

Perhaps she should answer, just in case. And then she'll get immediately to work.

She answers.

"Amy! I'm so glad I caught you. It's Bianca, from Friends Forever! Did I catch you at a bad time? I'm in the office, not on my cell, so you probably didn't recognize the number. I usually call from my cell."

"Right," says Amy. "I actually am in the middle of someth—"

Bianca cuts her off; in the way of many true dog people, she reads canine context clues more easily than human ones. "I just wanted to see if you might be up for another houseguest sometime soon. Well, by *soon* I mean tomorrow. I've got this gorgeous boy looking for his furever home, and I thought of you right away. His name is Charlie. I'm sure he'll get snapped right up, he's mostly Lab, and you know how quickly the Labs go."

Amy hesitates. No, says her inner voice. Absolutely not. But she does know how quickly the Labs get snapped up, so her outer voice says, "How old?"

"Three. And I'll be honest with you. He's a *little* bit of a doozy."

"Bad attitude, or bad habits?"

"Little bit of both," admits Bianca. "Mostly I would classify him as high energy. But he's nothing you can't handle, Amy. You're one of our most reliable foster moms. As long as you don't take your eyes off him for more than ten seconds you should be fine. I'm joking! Sort of. You're one of our stars, so naturally I thought of you first."

Amy takes a deep breath and walks back up the stairs to her bedroom/office, holding the phone to her ear and thinking.

Bianca's flattery is almost working. She sits in the chair and leans back. She's not used to looking out for herself. She's used to looking out for her children, and her husband, and her students, and, this summer, for everyone involved in *Much Ado About Nothing*.

What would Shakespeare say? WWSS? *Let every man be a master of his time.* That's what he'd say, and he'd be right.

"I'm so sorry, Bianca," Amy says. "I would love to help out, I really would." Her instinct is to offer excuses. School is starting! (It is.) She's repapering the downstairs bath! (She's not.) She'll be out of town for two days! (She won't.) Bianca should definitely ask her next time! (Should she?) But she simply says, "This time I can't. The timing doesn't work for me." It might not sound like a big accomplishment to anyone else, putting her paw down in just this way, but to Amy it is. To Amy it's substantial.

She ends the call. The yellow legal pad is looking at her accusingly. "I said no!" she tells it. "You should be grateful. I don't want to hear any more lip out of you." She uncaps her fountain pen, presses the nib to the paper, and watches the ink flow as she writes.

Act 1, scene 1. Setting.

That was the easy part.

She doesn't want to count her chickens, but if she can get something on paper before next spring she may have an in with a hot new summer theater on Block Island she's heard is looking for emerging voices.

EPILOGUE: SEPTEMBER

Sam

THE ISLAND REALLY does clear out after Labor Day; Maggie wasn't kidding when she told Sam that! The weekends are still lively—there are weddings and bachelorette parties and older couples no longer tied to their children's school calendars. But the weekdays are very quiet. Maggie is in school. Some businesses have closed; others have reduced hours. The beaches have vast stretches of unoccupied sand.

Sam needs some rhythm to her days while she gets her new life off the ground, so she's offered to walk Maggie's dog, Pickles, each afternoon.

Maybe Uncle Timothy is right; maybe Sam will tire of the solitude out here when winter sets in and the wind starts whipping and the ferry service is sometimes interrupted for days at a time by inclement weather. But so far she thinks she's going to be okay. Every other Sunday she's going to take the ferry to Point Judith, where her mother or father will pick her up at the dock and drive her to Narragansett for dinner. She'll sleep in her childhood bed, and take the early ferry back on Monday morning. She promised her parents these biweekly visits in exchange for them not bringing up college for at least a year. In a year, she's told them, she'll be happy to reassess.

One Thursday in the middle of September she's walking Pickles near the ferry dock, having just come off Ballard's Beach. She glances toward the passengers filing across the parking lot, as she always does, just out of habit, then does a double take. One of the passengers looks a lot like someone she used to know. One of the passengers looks a lot like Tucker. But she's been seeing Tucker look-alikes all summer: What's one more, really, to add to the pile? He'll probably turn his head and she'll see a giant mole or a scar that distinguishes him from Tucker.

Then, as he draws closer, she realizes something. It's *Tucker.* It's Tucker! What is Tucker doing here? She's wary, given how they parted, but her heart is thrumming too.

"What are *you doing here?*" She's trying not to smile, not right away, not too easily, but she's smiling anyway.

"I'm looking for you. I tried to call you like every day after you left. I missed you like crazy. I thought you'd fallen off the earth."

"I got a new phone number," she says. "My old phone got wet, and I figured, why not start fresh with a different number?" She squints at him. "This is Pickles, by the way." Pickles regards Tucker, reserving judgment. "I guess you saw the TikTok about the play."

"Yeah. It was awesome. I sent you like a million more DMs after I saw it."

"I wasn't checking my DMs," she says. "I only went on to post the video—the rest of it I'm not ready for."

"Sure, yeah. I get that."

(Anyway, thinks Sam, the play opened a little over a month ago; why'd it take so long for him to come?)

As if he's reading her thoughts Tucker says, "I really wanted to see that play, you know. But Tink said I had 'obligations' during that time. She wouldn't sign off."

"Tink," says Sam. For an instant it all comes rushing back to her. The whiteboard, the rules, the content—and, yes, the camaraderie, the nightclubs, the fame, the fun. Then the humiliation, the loss of control over her own life and her own reputation. The anxiety and stress. "How'd you get out? Jailbreak?"

"Yeah. Something like that. I mean, no. Actually, I left Xanadu for good."

"You did?"

"Yup. I was done with the whole thing. Honestly, I should have left sooner, right after you did. It was so toxic, that place. But I needed the money." He puts his hand gently on the back of her neck, the way he used to, and he says, "I'm sorry I didn't find you sooner."

Sam's first instinct is to say, *That's okay.* Her first instinct is to try to keep Tucker from feeling bad about any of it, to protect him. "I didn't make it easy to get found," she says. But then she asks herself why she needs to protect someone else from pain that was hers. Shouldn't it be the other way around—shouldn't Tucker be more concerned about her than she is about Tucker?

"Right!" Tucker looks relieved. "You sure didn't."

"On the other hand," says Sam. "If you *really* wanted to find me, you probably could have tried a little harder." Tucker draws in his breath and doesn't say anything, so Sam decides to elaborate. "I was really hurting," she says. "I mean, *really* hurting. And I was all alone with it."

She watches Tucker take this in. His eyes flick back toward the ferry, then they roam the parking lot, then they eventually come to rest on her, and a little shiver goes through Sam's body. "You're right," he says. "I could have tried harder, and I didn't. I'm sorry, Sam. Will you give me another chance?"

Will she?

"I don't know," she says. "I have to think about it. I've got a big project I'm working on, and it's going to be a really busy year. I sort of have to wait and see where everything else in my life fits in around it."

Tucker smiles uncertainly. "Should I get on the next ferry back?"

"No! No. We should hang out for the day."

"Okay, good. We'll hang out for the day." He picks up her hand, the one not holding the leash, and threads his fingers through hers. "You know what I could use?"

"What?"

"A coffee." He smiles at her and her stomach does a triple flip. Darn it. "Know a good place to get one?"

"I know a really good place," she says. Pickles's ears stand at attention, and Sam senses a commotion behind them. She turns. Yup. A clot of teenage girls approaching. Cell phones up. (Why aren't these girls in school?)

"Uh-oh," she says. "You've been recognized." She picks up the leash, and she hands Tucker the hat she's wearing. Gertie sent it to her from the Algarve: a trucker-style hat with a generous brim. "Here," she says. "Wear this. Follow me. Tucker, have you ever had a mini whoopie pie?"

ACKNOWLEDGMENTS

THANK YOU TO everyone at William Morrow: Liate Stehlik, Jennifer Hart, Amelia Wood, Julie Paulauski, Molly Gendell, Ariana Sinclair, and the salespeople, copy editors, proofreaders, and production people who keep things moving and get the books where they need to go. My editor, Kate Nintzel, performed her editorial duties on this book with her usual patience and brilliance, and I have been honored to work with her on four books. It recently became time to rehome me, and she placed me into the welcoming arms of Liz Stein, with whom I am excited to move forward and continue in the Morrow family.

I owe Elisabeth Weed at The Book Group, a giant, permanent thank-you for all these years of everything. And DJ Kim answers every question promptly and knowledgeably—I'd be lost without her.

Jennifer Truelove was my expert on all things film in this book, and she always has a famous person at the ready for extra details. Margaret and Wally Dunn were my theater experts, and they helped from the first pages, walking me through every step of my fictional production from conception to opening night. Margaret gave an extra careful read at the end of the process. Thank you to Michael Urie for the Juilliard memories. Thank you also to Sarah McKaig and Keith Lang.

The community of wonderful book people on Instagram seems to multiply year after year, and so many of them have been great supporters of my work and have introduced me to books I might not have known about. I would like to thank each of them by name but I'd never get them all. Bookstagrammers, I'm in awe of your enthusiastic posts and your gorgeous photos and the strength of your voices. I believe you've changed the book landscape vastly and for the better.

Almost every establishment mentioned in this book actually exists on Block Island. Joy Bombs doesn't, so if you go looking for it you'll be disappointed. I created Joy Bombs for my novel *The Islanders* with the help of Chococoa Baking Co. in Newburyport, who first introduced me to the mini whoopie pie. Thank you to Block Island for being such a welcoming, friendly, beautiful place to set a book. In the years I have spent getting to know the island I have come to understand why its residents are proud of its unique character and keen to retain it. I tried to do right by you, even if here and there I had to add an Uber or a lighting booth or a curtain that may not exist in real life.

Independent booksellers are the lifeblood of the book world. The two I know the best are Jabberwocky and The Book Shop of Beverly Farms. There are so many throughout New England (I am grateful to NEIBA) and the country who have supported my books too, and no author would be anywhere without them. An extra-special thank-you to Island Bound Bookstore on Block Island.

My Newburyport Bad Intentions ladies, who are always #in for anything, thank you.

Thank you to my parents, John and Sara Mitchell, and my sister, Shannon Mitchell, for constant support along with really good book publication gifts. And last but not least, thank you to my home squad, Addie, Violet, and Josie, and my husband, Brian, all of whom keep me busy and laughing and feeling loved and lucky every single day.